John Lemley

Autobiography and Personal Recollections of John Lemley

Editor of the Golden Censer, with seven years experience as editor and public

speaker

John Lemley

Autobiography and Personal Recollections of John Lemley
Editor of the Golden Censer, with seven years experience as editor and public speaker

ISBN/EAN: 9783337015602

Printed in Europe, USA, Canada, Australia, Japan

Cover: Foto ©Raphael Reischuk / pixelio.de

More available books at **www.hansebooks.com**

AUTOBIOGRAPHY

AND

PERSONAL RECOLLECTIONS •

OF

JOHN LEMLEY,

EDITOR OF THE

GOLDEN CENSER,

WITH

SEVEN YEARS' EXPERIENCE

AS

EDITOR AND PUBLIC SPEAKER.

———

ROCKFORD, ILLINOIS.
———
1875.

Yours Respectfully
John Lemley

To My Friends, made so through contact as editor and reader, whose sympathy, confidence, and approval of the bold and fearless editorial labors, have encouraged, inspired, and cheered me through the vicissitudes and fortunes of an arduous task and strange experiences of seven eventful years; and to Mrs. L. H. Lansing, Mrs. Joseph Hayes, Rev. Isaiah B. Coleman, and to the young people who may appreciate a struggling life, I dedicate this Autobiography and Personal Recollections with gratitude and affection.

PREFACE

While the sacred Book everywhere presents life as short, as the flower of the field, it also informs us that it is full of sorrow, and, if by reason of strength, it should be prolonged to "threescore years and ten, yet is their strength labor and sorrow." It is also a fact that every human life is an event in itself. As no two leaves in the vast forest of leaves are alike, as no two blades of grass in the fields are an exact counterpart of each other, as no two faces precisely resemble each other, so every life differs from all other lives. It is in the recognition of these facts that the study of autobiographies becomes interesting to us. While every man builds his own character, yet, to some extent at least, we gather lessons and experiences from the lives of those who have gone before, and from each other. In the grand temple of existence, every human creature furnishes a lively stone.

That there should also be great diversities in the conditions of our lives, cannot be wondered at when we for a moment reflect and observe the almost endless capacities of individuals. Here is a Newton, there an idiot; here a Dives, there a Lazarus; here a Bismarck, with his "Blood and Iron Policy," there a humble, inoffensive peasant. Some men have wealth, affluence, position, honor, and distinction thrust upon them, while others have a life-long struggle with poverty, sickness, misfortune and calamities. Some men laugh at impossibilities, and with energies that make successes out of other men's failures, push over every obstacle. While we admire moral courage in our fellows, we should not forget to pity those who have the up-hill end of human life.

But to our purpose. The life about to be sketched has been a struggling óne. The boyhood of the subject has been spent in the school of adversity. Surrounded by all the comforts and luxuries of his childhood home upon the Rhine, he becomes, by a sudden stroke of adversity, the poor German boy in a strange land, surrounded by new circumstances and relations, and a new people, and is forced to go from door to door as a beggar-boy, driven thither by fate and intemperance. Then the bitter struggle through adverse fortunes and sickness for existence' sake—then the partially successful efforts in obtaining an education—and the final issue in the establishment of the GOLDEN CENSER.

The whole narrative enforces the thought that the young can make more of life than they in their impatience usually suppose, and that even afflictions and adversities may be turned to the Father's glory. It is very true that in the dark days, when there was no one to help—before he learned to trust in God — he now and then sat down in the way of life and wept as if his heart would break — yet he never gave up the struggle. Hope always triumphed.

From the present standpoint, as he looks over the history of the past, it seems almost like a dream. Fifteen years ago, he never expected to be able to even read the Bible, and declined to receive a copy of the same from the hand of a lady because of the then supposed impossibility. That he has since been able to read it, and appreciate its value, must be evident to every one who has marked the scholarly productions and editorials in the GOLDEN CENSER.

Finally, this preface would not be complete did we not state that the change in Mr. Lemley's surroundings does not make him proud or high-minded. He is the same humble-minded, plainly-clad, unassuming person he ever has been. He has neither taste for, nor is his sympathy with, the fashions and frivolities of the age.

CONTENTS.

Chapter VII

Chapter VIII.

Chapter IX.

Chapter X.

Chapter XI.

Chapter XII.

Chapter XIII.

CHAPTER XX.

INTRODUCTORY.

It is only by the urgent and oft-repeated requests, and earnest solicitations of many of the GOLDEN CENSER patrons and personal friends that I have at all been prevailed upon and persuaded to give to them and the public the imperfect narrative contained in the following pages. Concious of human weakness, and of my own imperfections, I shrink from the task imposed upon me. It is with no small degree of timidity that I unfold the history of my short, yet eventful life. All who know me best have often observed my retiring disposition and simplicity of manners—almost bordering an awkwardness—always seeking the companionship of the common people, and content with the humbler walks of life—earnest, uncompromising, fearless, and devoted to the peculiar work to which God has called me, and to which I have consecrated what little ability I may possess, with an earnest desire to glorify my Heavenly Father upon the earth, and to faithfully do the work he has given me to do.

A bird's-eye sketch of my life was first prepared for the initial number of the GOLDEN CENSER. It was necessarily brief and imperfect. Presenting only the darker side, the truthfulness of the sketch was very seriously questioned, and many persons called upon me to satisfy themselves of my honesty and sincerity. Two years later a pamphlet of sixty-four pages was prepared. In this I obviated some of the apparent incredibilities by giving more at length the circumstances which led to my misfortunes. Still, many people labored under the impression that the picture was overdrawn. But it seemed much more reasonable than the first effort, and was so favorably received that I was importuned to give a still fuller account in the GOLDEN CENSER. I carefully revised and gave a much more extended history. This met with such general approval, and seemed to speak to the hearts of so many people, that long before it was concluded, I was again urged to give it in a more connected and permanent shape. However, even now, I hear of expressions such as these! "It is a remarkable history, *if true*." To remove all doubts from the minds of the credulous, I cannot hope to do, but it shall be my purpose to so enlarge upon all these points which seemed to have called forth such expressions, as to make this narrative reasonable to a *reasonable mind*. The picture is a dark one in very many respects, and I shall faithfully give it just as it is.

It has ever been my aim and steadfast purpose to seek that wisdom which cometh down from heaven, and which raises the heart above the adulations of men or the applause of popular opinion, and which outweighs them all. It is one thing to write the biography of some great hero, philosopher or divine, and another to narrate the events of a struggling life, hence the more do I shrink from this task when I reflect that the narrative which I am about to write is that of a worse than orphan boy—poor—ignorant —in a strange country—discarded and buffeted. It is also an acknowledged fact, attested by all who have experienced the stern reality, that the majority of mankind do not sympathize with the unfortunate, the fallen, the suffering. Those who have all heart can wish are little prepared to enter into the feelings of the life struggles of a poor, homeless wanderer in a cold, selfish, sinful world.

In this, as indeed in all my efforts, I make no pretentions to literary merits, and humbly trust this candid avowal will, in a measure at least, disarm criticism. This indeed is only a

"Short and simple annal of the poor,"

and if the perusal of this narrative should cheer some fainting, aching, sorrowing heart on the world's thorny highway, and lead him to an acknowledgment of the God who has guided my footsteps, I shall feel more than repaid for my efforts. Truth, and nothing but the truth, must constitute the merit of this sketch, if indeed it possess any merit at all; and many who may read these lines know that real life often furnishes stranger stories than romance ever dreamed of; and that facts are frequently more startling than fiction.

I further state as I advance in the history under consideration, that I shall speak of things pleasant and painful. Also, whatever may be the criticism of the reader upon the actions of either my father or of strangers, it must be understood that at this remote period and in changed circumstances, I could have no motive to speak ill of any one. I shall simply enter into the feelings in which I suffered, and shall avoid comments—leaving the reader to draw his own conclusions. In the language of a greater than your editor, I write "with charity for all and malice toward none."

I must remove another objection, and that is, too many people look upon published lives of men as if they should be blameless, and perfect. This, indeed is often aimed at by the men who write them, but, as I write this in person, very modesty and a love of truth and candor compel me to adhere strictly to the events under consideration. I make no claim to perfection or infallibilty. There is but one man living who does, and he makes so many miserable blunders, that I would be ashamed to set up a like claim. Let the Pope enjoy his infallibility all by himself. If I were to live my life over again I should act very differently from what I have done, but, as I cannot do this, I shall write as I lived, not as I would have lived with the maturer experience of manhood. I hope the reader will bear this in mind, as it is important to a proper understanding of the sketch.

There is one perplexity I meet in the very outset of the narrative, and that is, the year in which I was born. My early disadvantages closed up all avenues of knowledge. But I have made faithful inquiry, and probably I was born in 1843. There cannot be more than one year either way, and hence, for the sake of establishing subsequent dates in the sketch, I shall, with this explanation, assume 1843 to be the correct year. Finally, it is my earnest desire that this history may not simply amuse and interest, but help and stimulate both old and young, the prosperous and the unfortunate, in the battle of life, encourage the despondent, and aid the struggling in their efforts to rise above adverse circumstances. If I were asked to whom I was most indebted for the molding influence that shaped my manhood, I would answer, to God, and a sacred memory of a good mother.

I most earnestly hope, with this introduction, if there be any one who must still criticise this simple narrative, they will exercise charity, constantly keeping before their mind, that through all the sufferings, sorrows, and vicissitudes of my early life, I had neither counsellor nor guide.

Respectfully,

The Author.

AUTOBIOGRAPHY.

CHAPTER I.

PARENTAGE—THE OLD HOMESTEAD—CHILDHOOD.

In these days of transatlantic visits, a traveler, in the outskirts of a lovely village, in the province of Hesse-Darmstadt, Germany, might have noticed a stone house standing back from the street, and half-concealed by the foliage of fruit trees, shrubs and flowers. This is the homestead where I was born. So far as memory serves me, my parents were in very comfortable circumstances. I have heard my mother say that they owned four acres of land—and land in Germany is valuable—and the house in which we lived. My father had been an officer in the German army, and at the time of which I write was a merchant in my native village. Ease and comfort, to say nothing of luxury and plenty, were manifest on every hand. Of course I cannot speak of society or the position my father's family occupied in the community, as all these things were beyond my years and understanding. But I do know that we had a large circle of relatives, living, not only in the immediate vicinity, but at a distance. And when these visited our house, then we children (there were three of us, viz., John, Peter and Mary, I name them in the order of their ages) had a right merry time. And, oh, such beautiful presents! They made our eyes snap and sparkle, and our hearts leap with joy. No childhood could have been more happy than was mine. I had a kind, indulgent father and a tender, loving mother.

Our home was very beautifully located in a quiet, secluded spot. Near by, a brooklet of crystal water wound its way through meadow and grove, now basking in the clear sunlight, now rippling half concealed by the overspreading foliage, now laughing as gentle zephyrs swept its glassy surface. In the plain before us three hamlets nestled, pointing their minarets heavenward. Near by was that ever-beautiful river, the Rhine, while in the distance Mintz lay in solemn grandeur with its domes and palaces shimmering in the sunlight. On either hand the undulation of the country, with its green fields and groves, its farm-houses and villas, formed a picture upon which the eye ever loves to gaze.

The seasons were ever delighful, the atmosphere being mild the year round, and springtime seemed heaven let down to earth. To breathe its balmy air; to listen to the music of the flowing rills, murmuring brooks, dashing cascades, songs of birds, play of zephyrs through the trees, and shrubs, and flowers; to behold the ever-changing variety of landscape, hill and valley, mound and dale, lawn and glen, to breathe the fragrance of flowers of every hue and color; to look upon the morning dews glistening like pearls in the clear sunlight, and to gaze upon the sunset's tinseling on the evening sky, colors far surpassing the skill of artists,—formed contrasts rare and beautiful.

Oh, with what joy I used to gather the flowers that bloomed in endless variety hard by where the crystal spray of that inland river dashes against the pebbly and ever-varied shore, and with childish skill weave them into a wreath—a happy surprise for mother!

The clear silvery chimes of the village bells sounding through the forest and along. the hillsides in tones so sweetly musical, announcing in accents both soft and mellow to the weary toilers of earth that another Sabbath of rest and meditation and spiritual refreshment had dawned over the world; the clear blue sky with its genial sun and bland atmosphere by day, and bright beaming stars by night; the rich and varied foliage of forests; the anthem which nature's minstrels poured forth from every branch and bower; the music of the rills singing so cheerily in their meanderings through meadows, glens and groves; the vine-clad hills, laden with the purple fruitage of the year; the innocent glee of my playmates; the golden hours when no sorrow enters the heart,—are as fresh in my memory as but of yesterday.

And often, in after years, when circumstances were changed, and sorrow and anguish had wrung the hot, scalding tears from my eyes, I have lived over and over again in memory those bright, happy, sunny hours of my childhood, and in them I have found great consolation. I thank God for a happy childhood.

My parents being Catholics, I of course was early instructed in the duties and usages of that church. The paraphernalia displayed on festal-days, and the processions in which the whole community participated when they marched from the church to the shrine of some dead saint, were quite pleasing to my curious mind. Indeed it was imposing to see the white flags and banners unfurled and waving in the morning breeze, and to listen to the chanting of some sacred hymn. Upon the whole, the altar glittering with imagery, the burning candles, the odor of the frankincense from swinging censers, the costly robes of the priests, were quite fascinating.

Though my parents were both Catholics, and all my early instruction was given by that church, yet, since I could think for myself, I could not accept of the unscriptural and half-heathenish mummeries of that great but apostate church. However, I am constrained to believe that many people dying in her communion will be saved. My own precious mother lived and died in the faith of that

2

church.   But because of this, it is no thanks to the priests
or Roman prelates who bind heavy burdens upon the people, and do not so much as touch them with their fingers.
Again, there is a great difference between the German
Catholic and the Irish.   The American sees Catholicism
through the Irish—the most devoted and most bigoted nation.   In saying this, I would not speak disrespectfully of
the Irish people.   No.   So far as they are under the yoke
of this unmerciful priesthood, I pity them, for a more generous and whole-souled people do not exist on the face of
the globe.   Irish genius is at once brilliant and sparkling.
My being saved from the molding influences of this church,
I can account for in no other way than that God held the
destiny of my life in his hand.

But to return.   At the lawful age I was sent to school.
Memory does not serve me to relate at what age I was sent,
or how long I attended school.   But I do remember the
first morning at school.   It was one of those lovely spring
days when the flowers breathed their fragrance into the air,
and the birds sang so sweetly, and all nature laughed for
very gladness.   I remember the first book given me.   Its
neat appearance—not its contents—as a matter of course
made it very attractive to me.   Politeness to our school-
fellows, deference to our teachers, and our best manners to
the priests were among the first things learned.   We were
never allowed to address a grown person without first removing our hats and making a bow.   I can truly say that
we were early trained at the school to respect grown people.   The story of the prophet and the disobedient children, and of the bears coming out of the woods to destroy
them, was often repeated as an example of disobedience.

It would be no particular interest to the reader for me to
relate what grand good times we had during the holidays.
It will be remembered that Christmas originated with the
German people, and they, more than any other nation,
celebrate during this festal week.

The groves and forests in Germany are kept very choice. By a law of the land the peasantry are permitted to go through these forests and pick up all sticks and branches that may lay on the ground. They can also remove any dead and dry limbs from the trees. To accomplish this, they have long slender poles with an iron hook fastened on one end, and with these they pull down the dry limbs. Thus the forests are kept very neat and clean by the peasantry.

Another curiosity in these forests is, here and there, usually in large trees are excavations in the trunks of the trees about four or five feet from the ground, and in these images are placed, such as the Virgin Mary, or some of the saints, and protected by glass being placed over them. Whenever any one happened to come upon one of these images, he had to fall upon his knees and pray to it. I remember at one time I accompanied my grandmother on a visit to a distant village, and she took a foot-path through a grove, and I could not help but notice how many times the good old lady stopped to render up devotions before these forest shrines.

The highways are constructed at a greater cost than some of the railways in this country. The roads are all macadamized, and ruts and mud are unknown. The wagons also, are different from those of this country. The wagon tires usually are from four to five inches wide.

Though the houses in this country are most all built of stone, yet straw is used for roofing. Thus a traveler may enter a German village, and the straw-thatched roofs will remind him of the Orient. These roofs in dry weather take fire very quickly, yet a conflagration is a thing seldom witnessed, so careful are the Germans of fire. Stoves are unknown, ovens being used altogether.

As before observed, we had a goodly number of relatives and friends; entertaining many guests, and, in turn, visiting them. These were happy occasions for me, for then I could see the country, pick such large plums, pears, apples, and receive so many good things.

One day I was permitted to accompany an aunt of mine to a city some miles distant. This was the first time I was ever in a large city, and my curiosity was raised to its highest pitch on beholding the large, massive blocks, the rumbling of carriages, wagons and carts, the crowded streets, shaded walks, beautiful parks with their rare shrubs and trees, palace residences half hidden by foliage, fountains jetting out cool and sparkling water; in short, I was wild with delight and excitement. After showing me the city, my aunt started to go up some stairs. She ascended four or five flights, and I followed as fast as my feet would let me, but I was quite tired, and failed to keep up, and she, not noticing but what I was close behind her, turned a corner, and I lost sight of her. After having gained the last flight of stairs, I wandered over the large building trying to find where she had gone to. Meeting with no success, I again returned to the street. Then, upon seeing strange faces going hither and thither, it occurred to me for the first time that I was in a large city, far away from home—and lost! Overcome by this thought, I sat down and wept as if my heart would break. Oh, I did feel so bad! At length my aunt came down stairs laughing at me because I was "boo-hooing." A lot of large red cherries, however, healed my wounded feelings. But I did feel ashamed of myself when aunt, upon our arrival at home, related how I had been a "cry-baby."

Boys will be boys, and are always in the way, so one day, while some masons were at work on our house, I was climbing up on a ladder after a workman who was carrying bricks, when one slipped out of his hand, and, coming down, struck me and brought me to the ground bruised and bleeding. At another time some of the neighboring boys were going to have a "huckleberry pick," and I wanted to go too, but they did not wish me to go, being too young, they alleged, and likely to tire out before their return. I could not think of giving up, so I followed after them. They repeatedly ordered me to return home, and seeing I was bent on following, rolled a stone down the hill which struck me and cut my head to a frightful extent.

Aside from these incidents, my childhood days were sunny, and I had all my heart could desire. My parents were very kind to us children. Well do I remember how my father used to take me upon his knee and tell me stories of America until I was carried away with delight. The glowing descriptions he gave of this country so impressed my imagination that I thought the United States to be the Eden of earth.

My father was also a great sportsman, and frequently he permitted me to accompany him to the groves. Oh, what happy hours those were to me! With what glee I climbed the sun-clad hills, or descended into the flower-covered valleys, or chased the butterflies through the shady glens, or listened to the hum of the bees as they passed from flower to flower, or the heart-thrilling songs of the birds resounding through the groves! O happy days of yore, come back to this aching heart of mine! Let me be a child again, if but for to-night! Ah, who does not love the remembrance of such happy days as these? Truly, their memory has been a solace — a healing balm to my poor, aching head and desolate heart while struggling in this sinful world.

CHAPTER II.

The Preparation—The Sale—The Departure—On the Rhine—Antwerp—On the Ocean.

All set times and seasons come full soon. Viewed in the future, the restless, impatient mind longs for the speedy arrival of the hour which may measure some great event in our lives. Thus did I long for the eventful hour. My parents talked much about our departure to America. and my youthful mind was filled with strange conceptions of the western world.

Like all good mothers, mine made garment after garment for herself and children. The needle was kept nimbly plying from morning until night. Grandma, aunts, servants, and all who could sew, bent their energies to the task, until trunk after trunk was filled.

At length the time when my father purposed removing to America had arrived, and the old homestead was sold for whatever it brought. Some time, however, was consumed in the usual preparation for such a long journey. The eventful day of our departure arrived full soon. The morning was calm, and the sun never lifted his golden brow over the eastern hills more lovely. At an early hour friends, neighbors — in fact, the whole village— assembled in front of our house to witness our departure.

There was a solemn, melancholy sound when father, for the last time, closed the door of the dear old home. Silently my mother entered the carriage with a heart almost crushed, for around that home were linked some of the dearest associations of her life. Down many a cheek rolled tears of sympathy for her efforts to give up all and seek a home beyond the swelling ocean, and in a foreign land. Indeed it was a solemn hour, and strong arms faltered as the hand of friendship was extended for the last time.

The carriage moved slowly away, while weeping friends and an aged grandmother, whose heart seemed almost broken beneath her load of grief, tried to persuade father to remain. As mother looked back for the last time upon her weeping brothers and sisters and aged mother, she wept like a child. Oh, it was hard to give up *all!*

It was all strange to me. I did not understand then why mother thus wept. This, doubtless, was the setting of her sun of happiness. Oh, the sorrows which some changes bring! How infinitely better, in many instances, would it be to let well-enough alone. But poor mother was never very anxious to leave her home in the father-land.

Why my father sold this home, I cannot tell, unless he was actuated by that restless spirit found in every breast which seeks to better its condition. Why my parents removed from the shores of the Rhine to try their fortunes in a new and strange country, is equally a mystery, for they might have lived happily and died contented, as did our ancestry before us, in the old homestead. But times change, and we change with them.

Of course I was too young to take in the magnitude of the change, or to realize the consequences which followed. I did not even fully understand why our friends wept so bitterly at our departure. The long preparation, the great supply of new garments, the purchase of many valuable articles, the frequent conversations of our prospective home over the ocean, served only to stimulate my fancy, and to make me restless for the departure. Not so with my poor mother. It must have been the greatest trial of her life. Indeed she cried so bitterly that the journey was almost given up. But this could not be done. The home was sold, our goods shipped, and go we must. However, as we passed along, mother became more composed, but I think she never saw a happy day afterward.

After a few hour's ride, we arrived at Mintz, where we took a steamer for Cologne. Scarcely had the steamer left the city where printing was invented, than the sceneries for which the river is noted presented themselves. Between Mintz and Cologne are great vineyards, and wine is extensively manufactured. On either side of the river the country is broken, and along the hill-sides the vines hang heavy with grapes, as far as the eye can see. I was carried away with delight and admiration as I beheld the multitude of objects that passed before my eyes. A short distance below Mintz, we passed the beautiful village of Bingen — celebrated in song as " Bingen on the Rhine." Ah, well might one be a soldier in Algiers, if the prayer of one — not a sister — followed from such a lovely spot as this. Basking in the sunlight, half concealed by the surrounding vineyards, its minarets reflecting in the river below, it was a gem rare and lovely. O land of the beautiful! How can I paint thy enchanting glories? I spent the whole day gazing upon the vine-clad hills, lowly cottages, towering castles, elegant palaces and curiously constructed villas peeping through leafy groves. Evening came, but I was still permitted, in company with my parents, to remain on deck and drink in the rich scenery. The bright orb of day sinking behind the distant hills, tinseled upon the western sky colors surpassing by far all works of art, the dews falling so gently, the herds ruminating in the lawns, the peasantry thronging their cottage doors, the children playing on the shore, their innocent glee ringing merrily upon the calm, twilight air, the birds hushed in their bowers, the hum of the distant village subdued, rendered the hour very impressive. The silvery rays of the rising moon at length shone through the rich foliage down upon the river; the stars one by one came out; not a zephyr ruffled the bosom of the stream, which reflected on its glassy surface a thousand glittering stars; the villas and castles, with their white colonnades, seen through the somber shade of the dense foliage, arose like colosseums; the lights streaming from palace windows fell upon the surface of the river like columns of gold; the parks and flower-gardens along the shore breathed their fragrance on the evening air; the everlasting hills, sleeping in grim repose, awakened a sublimity not to be equaled.

We arrived at Cologne about 10 o'clock in the evening. I slept soundly that night. The following morning father showed us the city. Cologne is a city of palaces and statuary; so it seemed to me as I beheld its crystal fountains, its colossal statues, its royal palaces, and its neatly paved avenues. From this city we took the cars for Antwerp. I was ever on the lookout for objects of interest, which seemed to abound on every hand. On, on the iron horse rushed through villages and towns, only a few of which I can here notice. Liege on the Muse is almost on the boundary line of Prussia and Belgium. Here I noticed a very large castle, the property, I presume, of some rich lord. Here, as well as at all other places, I saw soldiers dressed in the Belgium costume, the uniform being dark blue, with a red stripe down the seam of the pants, and they wore large black fur caps that I fail to describe, with white plumes in them. As we approached Louvan, I observed the peasantry standing in front of their cottages with their hands in their pants' pockets, pipes in their mouths, and red wooden shoes upon their feet, gazing at the train. They looked quite comical. Machlin on the Dyle is romantically situated on the river.

After a long ride we arrived at Antwerp. We remained

a week in this city. It seemed to me that the week was one continuous festal-day. For to military displays, the marching of troops, the sound of music, the floating of flags, the crash of musketry, and the roar of cannon there was no end. While here I had the pleasure of hearing the chiming of a bell from the highest spire in the world. The cathedral was a massive structure, and on a cloudy day its spire to my youthful eyes seemed lost among the clouds.

At last the morning arrived when the ship was to set sail for the "land of the free and the home of the brave." The vessel left her wharf about 10 o'clock, and passed down the Scheldt, and in a few hours a fair wind drove us far out into the North Sea. To the east lay the albin shores, to the west Holland, before us the boundless ocean, while in our rear the lofty domes and spires of Antwerp and Rotterdam were being lost in the distance. I must confess that I viewed the receding shores of my native land from the deck of the vessel with a shade of sadness. I gave a farewell sigh, and in that sigh expired the last happy hour of my childhood. I began to realize what it was to leave the sunny hills of my own native land, never more to be looked upon, to leave friends never to be seen by my mortal eye. But here we were at last, out upon the ocean, sailing over the watery paths to a home beyond the tide.

The next morning found us out of sight of land. All around us was the vast deep, bounded only by the lowering horizon. About noon of this day I went down into the cabin to "enjoy" an attack of sea-sickness, which lasted a couple of days.

For six long weeks the monotony of a treacherous voyage was only broken by the occasional passing of a vessel.

Great extremes are often witnessed in the passage over the Atlantic. While I have seen the ocean waves so high that, as their huge surges dashed against the sides of the ship, a vast volume of water would roll over the deck with such violence as seemed to sweep everything before it; I have also seen the bosom of the deep so calm that not a ripple or wavelet could be discovered. I have seen the sun sink into the ocean like a ball of fire. Oh, who can relate the beauties of sunrise or sunset at sea? I have seen the rainbow, after some tempest had shook the mighty deep, span its great arch over the angry waters in colors so beautiful as to make one forget the dread frowns of the storm-cloud which had just displayed the wrath and power of the Almighty. I remember at sunset one evening, a lot of passengers had gathered on the bow of the boat, and so calm was the water, that a little crust of dry bread cast into the sea by a passenger, showed that the vessel was making none or but little progress. While there were many lively incidents connected with our ocean voyage, yet I did not enjoy the passage.

Day after day, on over the great Atlantic, amid its fierce rolling waves we sailed, when, one evening, as the passengers were on deck watching the sun sink into his watery grave, and the sea-birds sporting over the water, the captain informed us that on the morrow we would see land! Upon the announcement of this there went up a shout of gladness from the entire company. And hope beamed from the merry countenance and sparkling eyes of many a youth and maiden, as they looked at each other and re-assured themselves of happy homes on the nearing shores — homes where sorrow could never enter. We all retired earlier than usual that night, in order that we might rise early to behold coming events.

The first rays of light on the following morning found a goodly number on deck looking, if haply land might be discovered. Peering through morn's early dusk, a dark outline loomed up in the distance. "I see land! I see land!" exclaimed a dozen voices. And a thrill of joy ran from heart to heart. All were wild with excitement.

In the meantime the sun made his appearance in the
east.   And before us the American continent presented its
rock-bound shores, its forests, its mountains and its hills
and dales.   Far inland I espied the spires and massive
brick walls of New York City.   As we neared the harbor,
vessels from every clime, and of every size—from a little
schooner up to the mighty steamship—thronged the waters,
some going, some coming—the large ocean steamships moving like floating palaces among the minor crafts.

CHAPTER III.

Landing—A Sudden Reverse—Starvation—The Weeping Mother—Befriended.

Upon landing, my father failed to find his baggage, and the whole of it, together with all the money, must have been stolen, either in Antwerp after he shipped it, or in New York by the "sharpers," who are the pest of the immigrant. This was a dark hour for father. Cast on a foreign shore without a dollar, with three children, and no home nor friends. All our clothing being in the lost chests, we had nothing but what was on our persons. He procured a place for us to stay while he tried to find work.

I can do no more than accept the oft-repeated statements from my parents in regard to the loss of their money and clothing. But it always seemed strange to me why my father should put his money into a chest—shrewd man that he was—and why he took no security from the ship-owners for the baggage.

It would seem that my father thought his goods aboard the ship all the while until he came to look for them in New York, when, though he repeatedly went to the ship-owner, he could learn nothing of what had become of them.

That he lost much in money, I have always believed, for mother over and over referred to the loss, and doubtless that, with other events which I will soon record, hastened her untimely death. Not only was all the money lost, but all our clothing, and we must have had enough to last us several years.

But the saddest spectacle of all was to see poor mother, for she seemed almost crushed under our misfortune.

Wearied by the long journey and no place to refresh our-selves, nor friends to sympathize with us, it was very dark.

During the day, mother worked hard over the wash-tub in washing such garments as she could. It is with pride I refer to this. She knew how to preside at the wash-tub as well as in refined society, and in the present case, in more respects than one, it was a necessity.

Alone among strangers and stopping at a house where we were not welcomed, because we had no money, knowing that poverty was now staring us in the face, she doubtless thought of her native land and of the happy home across the waters so recently and reluctantly left, for every now and then I noticed the silent tears stealing down her care-worn cheek. I felt so sad to see her weep, that I tried to comfort her all I could by putting my arms about her neck, and kissing away the falling tears. It was all I could do. Oh, what heart-aching reflections she must have had on that day, left as she was in a strange city, all alone with the care of three children.

Our circumstances were very distressing! We had not one cent. We did not even have a dinner to stay our hun-ger. In the evening, father returned, his efforts having been fruitless. All hope seemed now to be gone. Not a mouthful of food had we tasted since morning, and the land-lord refused us shelter for the night.

Truly it was a trying time. My father had wandered all over the great city in vain, looking for work, until, foot-sore, faint with hunger, and discouraged, he returned to his family.

Mother had worked hard in trying to cleanse our gar-ments and our persons, and all this without so much as a dry crust of bread, while the children were faint for very hunger. These things are beyond the power of pen to de-scribe. The ceaseless tread, the bustle of the scrambling crowd, the strange sounds of an unknown tongue, of which we could not understand a word, all seemed to mock us in our humiliation, and in our distressing proverty; for in New York City, as well as elsewhere, the poor immigrant and his family oftener meet with ridicule for their strange costume and inability to speak the language, than with sympathy and protection. What to do, or where to go, father did not know. He learned, however, that a steamer was about to start for Albany, N. Y., where the chances of obtaining work were much greater. We went aboard. How father obtained passage, I do not know. The night was a supperless one, and it was long and dismal. It was too cold to sleep, and we were so hungry that the minutes seemed hours to us.

The great steamer, like a thing of life, plowed the waters of the noble Hudson—Hudson so justly celebrated for its varied and enchanting sceneries, and, in these respects, not unlike the Rhine; but how changed our condition! The outline of the towering mountains now only seemed a dreary mocking mass, the lights streaming from the towns and villages as we passed along only mocked us by their seeming friendly rays, for there was no spread table to welcome us, and ever, whether weeping or pleading at my mother's knee for just a crust, this something gnawing within would not be satisfied. O merciful Father, send us a loaf of bread!

At length morning dawned, and the steamer landed us at Albany about four o'clock. Father at once found a place for us to stay in the ruins of a burnt building, while he again looked for work. Again we were left alone, and for an hour we shivered with the cold. After a while, however, the sun warmed our chilled bodies. This day was more dreary to mother than the day before, for we had not only to contend with the cravings of hunger, but had to endure the vulgar jests and unfeeling flings of idle gazers. Poor woman! she wept most of the entire day. Though hunger was gnawing at our vitals, yet we murmured as little as possible. Mary, our only sister, was then an infant in mother's arms, and sick. Notwithstanding the sorrow and grief, as well as hunger and the care of a sick baby, which, combined, were fast bending her down in anguish, we children, towards night, our reasons overcome by the no-longer-endurable cravings of hunger, huddled around her and entreated her with weeping eyes to give us something to eat.

There within the blackened and charred walls, windowless and doorless and roofless, exposed to the night air and falling dew, with stomachs so faint we could not stand or walk, with eyes red with weeping, mother patiently tried to quiet us, while waiting the return of father, assuring us that perhaps with his return relief might come.

Gladly would she have given us, for she was always so kind, but she had not wherewith to give. Poor woman, with her babe clasped to her bosom, fast folded in her arms, she herself seated upon a stone in the ruins of that burned building, and we boys clinging by her side moaning for a morsel to satisfy the cravings of hunger, was more than the stoutest heart could see unmoved. O God pity the helpless!

Father returned in the evening, tired and hungry, and tears stood in his eyes as he said, "I can find no work." Then and there father and mother sobbed aloud as if their hearts would break, while we children in mercy cried for something to eat. Already we had tasted no food for two days, and starvation was doing its work.

How changed all this from our happy home upon the Rhine! Truly the day-dreams of America had long ago fled. We were strangers in a strange land, helpless, and reduced to poverty — on the verge of starvation. Oh, is there none to help, none to pity? Must we lay down within these ruins, thousands of miles from our own dear land,

and die? Is there no heart of sympathy, no arm to deliver?
O great God, thou who feedest the ravens, and clothest
the flowers of the field, feed us and shelter us in this far-
away land.

But there was now no alternative for us except to pass
the night in the ruins of the old building. Mother was so
exhausted by this time that she was almost helpless. So
father tried to make the best bed he could. Upon taking
some clothing out of a large traveling bag, he found a piece
of dried beef which was there unknown to us. We offered
up thanks to heaven for its discovery. But it was only a
crumb for so many mouths. Yet it was the sweetest and
most-relished meal — if meal it can be called.— ever par-
taken of, and it was the first food since landing on the continent.

Oh, how changed the condition! There in the ruins with
nothing but heaven to shelter us, we huddled together to
repose in sleep. But it was so cold that we could neither
sleep nor remain quiet, so, as a last extremity, father gathered some sticks and built a fire in the ruins to aid us in
keeping warm. The light soon attracted some citizens to
the spot to learn as to its cause. To their inquiries, father
told them his condition, and how he had lost everything;
how he had looked for work without success, and that his
family was there helpless.

When father had related these events, a noble and kind-
hearted gentleman — may he reap his reward in heaven —
stepped forward and volunteered to take us to his house.
We gladly accepted the invitation, and bid farewell to the
old ruins. Taking us through several streets, we came to
his home. He invited us in, and soon had a bountiful supper
prepared for us. We ate until we were ashamed to eat
more, so hungry were we. After supper the evening was
spent in conversation—for he was a German. We children,
however, retired early, and so did mother. Oh, it seemed

3

so good to be in a quiet room once more, for the constant rocking and tossing of the vessel, the running to and fro on the deck at all hours of the night, the sounding of the waves against the sides of the ship, had broken us more or less of our rest. How sweet and refreshing sleep was to us that night—especially to poor mother!

However strange it may seem to the reader, yet during that night and for several days we experienced the peculiar motion of the vessel. It must be felt — it cannot be described.

With all my diligent inquiries in after years, I was never able to learn our benefactor's name, and I presume never will in this world, but verily he will never lose his reward. The act shall be cherished in my memory until the latest breath of time, and in heaven (for such a good man must go to heaven), I will thank him for the mighty deliverance. Such acts are the wayside angels that must make glad the very heart of God, and call forth the admiration of wandering angels, as it certainly called forth our unfeigned and everlasting gratitude.

CHAPTER IV.

Seeking a Home—Reduced to Beggary—The Effects of an Unaccustomed Climate—Embarrassment for the Want of Language—Being Fired Upon.

In the morning, after a bountiful breakfast, and many thanks to the very kind gentleman for his hospitality, and being much refreshed, we set out on foot to find a home. Crossing the Hudson, we traveled into the country.

About 10 o'clock, we children became so tired that we entreated the privilege of sitting down by the road-side to rest our weary feet and aching limbs.

At noon we took dinner with a German family, where we remained until two o'clock.

Towards evening, after a day of weary walking, father succeeded in finding work, and we moved into a small house on the farm.

I have no remembrance of dates of months as yet, and hence can only reckon time by the seasons. This must have been the last of May or the first of June, 1848, for corn was just coming up.. My father went to work, but he could draw no wages till he had earned some, so there seemed no alternative for us but to beg. This was very trying to mother. She grieved much over the thought that her children were now compelled to go from door to door and beg for a living.

Life, indeed, looked dark and wearisome to her.

I, being the only one of the children large enough, had to perform this task. Oh, how changed the condition of only a few months ago! How the memory of my home on the Rhine followed me wherever I went. What bitter pangs the humble, destitute and helpless condition brought to our aching hearts. Oh, how hard for one who had never known or felt a want, now to go among strangers, of whose language I knew not a word, to ask alms! Oh, it was so humiliating! All summer I had to do this. Oh, how tiresome to travel all day in the dust and under the burning rays of the sun in a climate much warmer than was ours! It had such a peculiar effect upon me. During the hot hours of noonday, my limbs would feel as if they would sink under me. I will not attempt to picture the misery and heart-achings endured this summer. Ah, how can I?

Father worked hard, early and late, for Mr. Vanalstine, in hopes of providing for his family, but was turned away in the fall without a cent of his wages.

We learned when it was too late, that this man, Vanalstine, made it a practice to procure foreign help who were ignorant of the laws and usages of this country, and have them work through the season, and then turn them away without their wages. This, it seems, was the unhappy luck of my poor discouraged father. Oh, it went so hard with him! Mr. Vanalstine was not only mean, but ugly, for, after the season of farm labor· had closed, and he had withheld my father's wages, he tried to get rid of us altogether. We were living in a small dwelling-house on his farm, and had to go to the stock-yard for the water we used. This, at the close of my father's services, he forbade us to do. We disregarded his unreasonable requests, and obtained water as before. Indeed it was the only place where we could obtain it. One Sabbath, at the request of mother, Peter and I went to the stock-yard pump for some water. Mr. Vanalstine saw us, and shouted to us to pour the water upon the ground. This we refused to do. Upon this, he fired a gun, the report of which frightened us, and we ran to the house. I do not suppose it was loaded, but was only intended to scare us, which it certainly did. But then we were poor and helpless aud we had to endure these insults without redress. Doubtless my father would have used the law in collecting his wages, but he was a stranger in a strange land, and knew nothing of its laws.

The place where my father worked was Blooming Grove—sometimes called Bath—and is about two miles east of Greenbush. The farm was about a mile south of the village. That the reader may not express surprise with the reflection that we had only traveled two miles from Albany, and hence could not have been very tired, I would explain that we wandered up one road and down another, looking for a home. We traveled far enough to have taken us to Sand Lake.

Coming to a new country and among a strange people, one is met with constant surprises, both in society and in nature. For example: I was excited beyond measure to hear the song of the mosquito in the twilight, or to see, when later and darker, the flashes of light from the lightning-bug, and I suppose I was about as green as the two Irishmen who came to this country and happened out in the country in the edge of the evening, and were being followed by the mosquito, when one proposed to the other that they lie down upon the ground and cover themselves up with their blankets until the mosquito had lost them. They did so. Laying some time, one thought he would peep out from under his covering, when, behold, he espied a lightning-bug. Upon this he turned to his companion, exclaiming, "It's of no use; they are out here (meaning the mosquitoes) with lanterns looking for us!" Well, many things struck me about as strangely.

Most of the people in this section were wealthy, and in many houses I saw colored girls as servants at the table, and these servants invariably wore a yellow dress, and the hair was done up in a pyramidal shape on the crown of the head.

This reminds me of an incident which took place in New York, and which I ought to have narrated elsewhere, for it had such an effect upon me at the time: While in New York city, I happened to be sitting on the steps of the hotel where we stopped, my attention all absorbed in investigating a peanut which I had found in the street, and something I had never seen, when all at once I felt a man's hand resting on my head. Upon looking up, I was terror-struck, for behold a huge black face, with jet black eyes, clear white teeth, and with a mouth stretched from ear to ear, was grinning at me. I was so frightened that I gasped for breath. I thought it was the devil himself, let loose from hell, who had surely come after me. I shrieked for mercy, and begged him to spare me a little while longer, and, amid despairing sobs, cried out for mother to rescue me. It was fun for him, but terror to me. This, of course, was the first negro I had ever seen—as the negro is unknown in Germany—at least so far as I know. The peanut is also unknown. Thus many things were both new and strange to me.

CHAPTER V.

REMOVAL—FATHER IN JAIL.—DISTRESS AT HOME.

From Blooming Grove we moved some three miles south-east where father had taken nine acres of potatoes to dig on shares. Here a new field of labor presented itself. From morning till night I had to pull potato tops, and carry the potatoes into piles. It was hard, tiresome work, yet much easier than begging. The autumn passed quickly away.

Only a few incidents, and I pass. As before observed, we used no stoves in Germany, hence my mother was entirely ignorant as to their use. In baking bread, she would either burn it half up, or it would be heavy and of a lead color. She had quite a time in learning to cook on a stove.

One Sabbath afternoon we children wandered into the beautiful grove near by, noting the different plants and shrubs, until we came to a stream of water. Here we found some pieces of planks near a place were the flood-wood choked up the water. We crossed and re-crossed upon a raft made of these planks, and were having a fine time, when the raft in mid-stream came to pieces and we were let into the water, which was over our heads. We worked hard, and at last I succeeded in reaching the shore; but Peter was yet floundering in deep water, and apparently drowning. I set up a cry for help, but we were away from the hearing of any one, and he was going down for the third time. Terror-stricken, I leaped into the water, and caught hold of the middle of a plank, and, as he came up, gasping for breath, I grabbed him by the hair of the head, and held his head upon the plank. With one hand and arm across the plank, with a firm grasp in the hair of Peter's head, and with the other stroking in the water, and shouting at the top of my voice for help, I succeeded at last in reaching the shore. The reader may rest assured that we did not go near that brook again.

One Sabbath afternoon an old decrepit man came to our house. He was very strange acting. After gibbering to us children a while, and frightening us very much, he went out into the potato-patch, picked up a handful of tops and wiped his mouth with them, saying, as he did so, that it was a testimony against us for refusing him bread. I could not comprehend this, as mother had just given him something to eat.

Winter drew on apace. The falling leaves, the ripening nuts, the cold frosty mornings, chilling northern blasts, all proclaimed that soon we would experience our first American winter. .

We were poor, and had no money, hence we obtained permission of the proprietor of the grove above referred to, to pick up such limbs as might be on the ground rotting. Hence, our fuel was gathered by picking up such limbs in the woods as lay on the ground decaying. A Yankee neighbor, who evidently was too sensitive to have a quiet, peaceable German family live within half a mile of him, represented to the owner of the forest, who lived in the city, that we were cutting down the most promising trees in his woods.

As a result, father was arrested and lodged in jail in Troy, being forced to leave his family in mid-winter without the necessaries of life.

I do not know whether he was lawfully imprisoned or not. I can only give the event as it occurred. Mother was now left in the dead of winter with a family of children, in a small open house, surrounded on three sides by woods, and over half a mile from any human being. We got along the first week of my father's imprisonment quite comfortably so far as food was concerned. Though I remember mother often sat down and wept bitter tears. Poor woman! pen refuses to write down her sufferings.

During this time, our drum-oven stove refused to bake, so mother took the sheet-iron drum apart, and cleaned out the ashes. It was in the morning she commenced her work. The taking apart was only a task of a few minutes, but when she came to put it together again, she was not equal to the task.

For ten mortal hours she worked over that drum-oven in the cold of winter, without success. I tried to help her all I could, but I was not large enough to be of much service. Faithfully had she worked until about noon, when she became discouraged. She left it, sat down and wept. But this would not do, so she went at it again. Three times she gave it up, and then would make another attempt. We suffered with the cold, and her fingers were so stiff with the cold that she could hardly use them. But, about dark, she succeeded in getting it in its place, and a united prayer went up to heaven for the deliverance.

But father was still kept in prison ten miles away. We had no food, and as a necessity, I was again forced to beg. Oh, how I suffered as I had to weather the piercing storms of winter! Being poorly clad, I froze my hands, my feet, nose and ears. Oh, the sufferings endured while wading through the drifting snows!

At length father returned to us, being released from prison. Oh, what an object of pity! He was covered from head to foot with vermin. He said he could not help it. His quarters in the jail were filthy and repulsive. He seemed to be a broken-down and discouraged man. From that day he wore a sad, dejected look.

CHAPTER VI.

Removal—The Old Steam Sawmill—More Sorrows—
Forced to Beg—Frozen Feet—Climbing the Moun-
tains — A Whipping — Run away — Return — Given
Away.

In the spring father moved to East Sand Lake. Here
the real sorrow of my life began. One would think that
the summer and winter just past were enough, but they
were only a forerunner of what was in the near future.
Up to this time our struggles and sorrows were in common, and our mutual sympathy soothed many a weary
hour.

But there was another enemy at our door—it was a hell-
born enemy—than whom there is not another in the land
more heartless and home-destroying. It is rum. It pains
me to record it here, but as truthfulness constitutes the
merit of this narrative, I must write down these events
however heart-rending. Father took to drinking, and in
writing this I pity the man; his troubles were great and
his discouragements more. The accursed demon alcohol
stole away his affections for his wife and children, and it
made him recreant and a burden to us. Added to this, we
had no means of support. Oh, what a trial it was to my
poor mother! Her tears and her sighs left a lasting impression upon me.

I think there is something radically the cause of the
false and rash act in the man who will go to drinking simply because troubles crowd upon him. It ever a man wants
to keep a pure heart, a clear conscience, and a balanced
head, it is when in trouble. God will help those who will

put their trust in him. In the day of your adversity, oh, young man, stand in the dignity of your manhood, with brow toward heaven, and back to every snare of hell. All heaven is pledged to help you, if you will but perform your part. Oh, that we had the moral heroes that would dare to do right at any cost!

But what a slimy monster intemperance is. What ruin has it not wrought? For seven years I have denounced this vice, presented it in all its naked deformity, and faithfully warned the young to touch not, taste not, handle not, for in it is the deadly sting of the poisoned adder. Without speaking disrespectfully of my father, I do claim that had liquor been let alone, he could have struggled over all obstacles (and we would have gladly helped him in the effort), and in this country of opportunities have rendered his family happy in an unbroken home circle, had that home been ever so humble.

Yes, it is this demon of hell which wrought our ruin, and hence it is that the GOLDEN CENSER wages eternal war against the rum power. I have often been blamed by people —yes, Christian people—for my earnestness in warning the public of this enemy. But despite their chidings and discouragements, I have continued to hold up this evil in all its naked deformity. There is no compromise with me in this matter. No one need be in doubt long on this issue as to where I stand.

> " I here declare eternal strife,
> Ay, battle to the hilt, with those
> Who traffic in the nation's woes,
> And live upon the nation's life."

Had I the power, I would go up and down this broad land, enter every city and every street, and write in letters of living fire over the door of every saloon, with the blood of sixty thousand yearly victims to this fell destroyer,

"This is the gateway to hell: as you value your immortal souls, enter not."

O young reader, be warned; be warned in time! All along the pathway of your mortal life are reared the scarlet altars of intemperance. Two hundred thousand! Pause a moment and read these figures again; two hundred thousand yearly worship at these altars of hell; and sixty thousand are offered as victims on these altars of intemperance. And have you ever thought of the terrible effects of this rank poison, its terrible workings upon the brain? In short, have you ever seen the poor drunkard in delirium tremens? If not, come and see, as I have seen him. There he lies upon his bed, at once the terror and the pity of his friends, in the same breath weeping and laughing, grinning and sighing, cursing and praying. Ever and anon the room rings with shouts and shrieks, so terrible as to attract large crowds around him. Would you look upon a fellow being wrecked in body and soul? Draw near and mark those frightful eyeballs, those distended nostrils, those cadaverous cheeks, that brow, covered with drops of cold and clammy perspiration. See how he starts and shudders, and shrieks for help, while his blue, emaciated hands grasp for a hold as if his soul were drowning. Now his delirious fancy peoples the apartment with stalking specters and menacing fiends, and he points to them with trembling finger, and asks you if you do not see their ghostly forms and hear their clanking chains, and as they glide about the room, he gazes after them until his strained eyes seem starting from their sockets, and speaks to them in awful language. Then he thinks his bed a nest of slimy snakes and loathsome vermin, and he covers his head in speechless terror, as if he would sink into the earth under the eye of a basilisk, or utters a feeble, choking cry, and beseeches you to tear the terrible serpents from his neck. With one hand he plucks the spiders from his ears, and with the other wrenches from his back the fangs of scorpions. This moment he sighs as if his heart were breaking; the next he shrieks as if all hell were broken loose upon him. Anon he buries his head beneath the bed-clothes as if to hide him from the gaze of some infernal visitant, and the quick, convulsive tremor shoots to the extremities of his frame.

His physical energies at length exhausted, he lies gasping and quivering upon his couch, and his eyes, having lost all voluntary motion, roll like meteors, and his tongue, bitten and bleeding, hangs from his foaming mouth like that of a wild horse on the burning prairies. His hands are clenched so tightly that the very blood is forced beneath the nails, Go and gaze upon such a scene as this, if you have the nerve to endure it, and as you gaze let me whisper a word in your ear: This is the work of alcohol. And some men drink it to get rid of trouble! My poor father thought he could thus drown all his sorrows.

But do you know how the drunkard dies? Come and see. There he lies, helpless as a babe, and turning violently from side to side like a fierce tiger brought to bay by the hunter. There he lies, consumed within by slow and lingering tortures, or holding long communion with foul, unsheeted ghosts, or dark spirits of hell. There he lies, eyes bloodshot, cheeks haggard, lips shriveled, teeth blackened, hair matted, until the poor wretch looks as if perdition had already devoured him. Thus he dies, unlamented. None weep at his funeral, and none have a tear to shed for his memory save the beggared orphan that wanders in his loneliness, the heart-broken widow that mourns the wreck of her earthly hopes, and the pious parent that bends over the dust of her son, and cries in agony: "O my son, would to God I had died for thee, my son, my son!"

And who has wrought this mighty ruin? Alcohol, that prime minister of death and hell. Common murderers destroy only the body; but he, like the destroying angel in Egypt, goes up into the inner chamber of that godly palace, the soul, and smites the firstborn of intellect. He seizes conscience, that faithful sentinel, and gags him to prevent his giving an alarm. He seizes memory, that faithful secretary, and sends him away into relentless exile; puts out the eye of understanding and leaves that Samson of the soul to grope about in blindness; dethrones reason, paralyzes genius, binds volition in a dungeon, and assassinates every intellectual and moral faculty in God's temple. Nor is this all. Alcohol murders the immortal in man, and makes it as motionless as a rock. He renders his victims insensible alike to the meltings of Calvary and the thunders of Sinai. As one has said, " He gives them serpents and scorpions for bread, and they go hissing and darting through the whole man, stinging to madness body and soul, turning husbands into furies, and fathers into fiends, till they seem born of hell and prepared for damnation; and then hurries them to the brink of the burning lake and plunges them in."

Thus alcohol is man's mightiest foe, hostile to his highest and holiest interest, to health, fortune and intellect, to moral principle, social happiness, and hope for both worlds.

It is this enemy of our common humanity, the GOLDEN CENSER has battled, often under discouragements, but God being my helper, I will battle unto the end. Oh, how it makes my heart ache when I see the people so slow to wipe out this curse of humanity. Why, in the face of the praying women, have Christian voters licensed the rum traffic, thereby saying in the ear of the community, " We will grant these saloons the instruments of death, we will dare them to ruin our sons"? For, be it known that every Christian who votes the continuance of this monster vice, in fact says: " I do hereby grant the right, licensed, lawful right, backed by the strong arm of the law, to every saloon in my community, to entice, tempt, entrap and ruin my

son, and to destroy the happiness and peace of my family."
And these Christian fathers wonder why their sons are not
converted. Oh, be not deceived! God is not mocked; a
curse is in the land and a blight is upon that soul which
trifles with the Almighty. O God, who is sufficient for
these things? Help, oh, help the brave souls who nobly dare
to cry aloud, and spare not against this monster evil!

But what could we do? In the face of these events and
surroundings, I was again forced to go from door to door,
and, by asking alms, provide for the family. I found the
people disposed to give, but my oft-repeated visits soon
wearied them, and many withheld their charities, scolding
me for coming so often. Upon entering a house, a smiling
face of a beautiful woman would turn to a frowning one, as
she shut the door in my face. I would be so tired that I
often sank down in my steps. Nights I would pass in barns,
under straw-stacks or by the road-side — for who would
keep a beggar? I could endure all this during the warm
season, but the cold winter weather tried me. I had to go
from fifteen to twenty miles in my trips, and be gone two
days. Of course I had only such clothes upon my person
as I could beg, which often were insufficient to keep me
from the pinching cold. I was often questioned to see if
I would not cross myself in my statements, until, shivering
with cold, and tears in my eyes, I would leave of my own
accord, and when I would patiently answer all their questions, they would bluff me off, by saying they had nothing
to give. School-houses used to be dreaded by me, for the
boys would insult me in various ways, often throwing stones
at me. It was sport for them, but I had feelings which I
could vent only in tears. But there were some kind people, thank God, who pitied me. Whenever I did meet
with success, and I was loaded down with provisions, the
task of carrying it fifteen miles on my shoulders often so
exhausted me that sharp knives dissecting every joint in

me could have been no more painful. If it was a stormy day, my garments would be wet through, and often frozen on my person. Moreover, if I failed to bring home as much as I could possibly carry — which I was only too willing to do provided the people gave it to me—my father would whip me and send me to bed hungry, even denying me a morsel of the bread which I had begged.

It may be suggested here by the reader, that I ought to have eaten before arriving at home. To which I can only reply: My anxiety to please my father often caused me to forego the cravings of hunger. Besides, after being out in the cold all day with thin clothing, I would be so chilled, that it was easier to endure hunger than to eat frozen bread while climbing the mountain, faint under a heavy load, amid ice and snow, on a cold winter night.

One day, wearing an old pair of boots which were all open at the toes, and filled with snow and ice, a kind boy, whose heart was much larger than his boots, gave me a pair which were a little too small. I put them on, but they were so hard that they soon hurt my feet. Toward night they became almost unendurable. I was yet ten miles from home, and it was bitter cold. There was no alternative but to brave the pain. I did so, arriving late in the evening. Upon examination, my feet were frozen in my boots, which were so tight that in pulling them off, both of my great toe nails pulled out by the roots — my toes being so badly frozen. Oh! oh! the misery.

In this condition I had to brave the remaining winter. Oh, weary life with all its bitter pangs. How often I sighed to be at rest in the eternal sleep of death.

Upon another occasion, stopping at a house, a crazy man with a large butcher-knife in his hand came at me, swearing he would kill me if he caught me. I ran for life. How far he chased me I know not, but toward the last I was so near overcome with exhaustion, that upon looking around, my face burned with heat, and I could actually hear my heart beat. I never was so overcome with terror in my life.

Thus, if the reader can conceive of the sufferings in enduring whippings at home, the heartless abuse from selfish, unthinking people abroad, long, dreary journeys, frozen feet, hands, and face, weariness of body and grief of heart, the taunts, sneers, and vulgar jests from those who love mirth at the expense of others, you have the picture of three long, long years of suffering.

It is but just to add here that my mother was an industrious, hard-working woman, and that she did all she could not only to relieve me, but to cheer and encourage me in my weary toils. But father, under the influence of rum, ruled with a rod of iron, and we were helpless and at his mercy.

I will here relate an incident, and then hastily pass over this dark picture of my suffering. One hot day in the month of August, I was set to work by my father to trim a large, fallen hemlock with a dull axe. The day was exceedingly warm, and the sun shone upon me oppressively. There was not the least rustle of wind through the forest leaves. Not making quite as rapid progress as he desired, he threatened me with a whipping. I did the very best I could, and the sweat rolled off me in great drops. Notwithstanding my exertions, about four o'clock I received the promised punishment. Cutting a green birch rod, he plied it upon my person with such vigor and violence that the blood flowed from every gash which the unrelenting rod was making. From head to feet I was covered with ghastly wounds and bruises. Having satiated his rage upon me, he ordered me to start for home, but in my attempt to do so, he brought me to the ground again with a severe blow. Faint, I was prostrated at his feet, bleeding from many wounds. In despair I entreated, " O father, have

4

mercy! *have mercy!*" But it was to no purpose. At length he abandoned me. Covered with frightful wounds, and faint, I gathered up strength, arose from the ground, smarting under pain, and went home. On my way I wept bitter tears from a deeply wounded heart. I thought that I was outraged without just cause, and that too by a parent who ought to have loved and protected me, for I tried to be a good boy — a dutiful son, performing patiently every duty required of me. Arriving at home, I told mother what had befallen me, and entreated her to protect me. But she could only sympathize with me.

Truly life was brimful of suffering and relentless toil. Oh, would there not dawn a brighter day over my miserable life? Oh, how I sighed over my deplorable condition! How happy I thought those boys who had kind, doting parents, comfortable clothes, enough to shield them from the ills of a life like mine, who never knew what it was to weep. Indeed, as I listened to their innocent laugh, and witnessed their merry glee, making the morning air vocal, and the privilege of going to school, it brought to remembrance other days, when I too was happy, and in childhood's glee was permitted to pluck the blooming flowers of the valley, and to ramble beside the murmuring streamlet. Alas! when I think how changed, it only adds misery to my suffering. Now despair broods in midnight darkness over my inmost soul, and only finds relief through tears which unbidden flow. O world, what have I done, that thou art so cruel to a defenseless, forsaken, uncared-for child of thine?

All these things took place at the old sawmill, which, by the way, at that time consisted of only a huge pile of sawdust, some old machinery, and a pond filled with fallen trees, and of four log houses. It was located about four miles up the mountains, east from East Sand Lake, and, in my begging tours, I had to descend these mountains before reaching people who were able to give.

We lived in this place about a year and a half. And it was emphatically a mountain life, for the rugged crags towered high in air, and the dense forests of hemlock, pine, beech, and other large trees, were imposing and wild in their appearance. The only thing very attractive to me in this wild home of the forest, was its water, which, pure, sweet, and sparkling, bubbled out of the ground in many places. The birds, too, in summer time, made the solitude vocal with their sweet songs. In winter I could go out to some sunny southern spot and pick the wintergreen, fresh and beautiful, when all around was deep snow. These were some of the things that cheered my poor aching heart, for I loved nature in all its aspects and under its varied forms. The blessed Savior loved the solitudes of the mountains; he told of the birds, and called our attention to the "lilies of the valley." declaring that "Solomon in all his glory was not arrayed like one of these." There often is a solace in the wayside flower, if we will but stop and gather it.

From this place my father again moved about three miles southeast, into a small log-house near Green's sawmill, and about four miles east of the village of Alps.

As before observed, my time was mostly occupied in supporting the family by begging. It was very disagreeable and discouraging work, for, while people were kind at first and disposed to give liberally, yet, by my oft-repeated visits, they became tired of me. This made it all the harder for me, for I was forced to do this unwelcome task. Aside from the long mountain journeys, and the frowns of a father whom liquor had ruined, upon entering a house I would be so tired that while the good lady was preparing me something, I would lean against the door-casing and stand first on one foot and then on the other. Oh, how they would ache. But then there was no rest for me. Every bone, in my body ached, for my flesh was bruised and pounded at home, and made raw and sore by the pressure of my burdens, and the long walks and the facing of all kinds of weather. Added to this, I was frequently abused by merciless teamsters, who would often lay the lash of their whip over my head and shoulders for no other reason than that I was a poor, miserable beggar, and " it was good enough for me," for who was there to redress my grievances? I could only weep, and the hot, scalding tears flowed when only God beheld the suffering boy.

One evening, returning from one of my tours a little earlier than usual, mother spread the table and we sat down to eat. Scarcely had we done so when father entered the house, having just returned from Alps, and, without note or comment, told Peter to get him the rope which mother used for a clothes-line. Mother asked him what he was going to do with it. He made no reply. She, fearing that all was not right, opened wide the door and screamed to us children to flee for life. Being frightened at this alarm we all rushed out of the room, some going one way and some another, and father, as oftentimes before, was the sole occupant of the house, while mother and children spent a supperless night crouching under the bushes, wherever they happened to light in their terror to escape.

At another time, while Peter and I were engaged in bringing firewood, being a considerable distance from the house, we unexpectedly met father in the way. Without ever saying a word or giving a reason, he grasped Peter by the collar and with a club pounded him over the head and shoulders until I thought the child was dead, for he had ceased to scream. I entreated father to let him go, but all to no purpose. Such treatment made us very much afraid of father.

About New Years of this same year I was told by my father to go to Alps for a jug of molasses, he charging me that I should not fall down and break the jug, for if I did he would shoot me. Of course I promised not to fall.

There had been a heavy fall of snow, and for a day or two it had rained and then suddenly frozen, so that the whole mountain-side was a field of ice. I started down the steep hill, picking my way very carefully lest I should fall. But I had scarcely passed out of sight of the house when I slipped, came down upon the back of my head with violence enough to see stars, and, oh, the poor jug! the whole bottom was broken out. Hurt as I was, yet I was more frightened. I could hear my heart beat for terror. What could I do? If I went back I feared father would execute his threat. The jug was broken, and there was no way for me to replace it with another. In my tremor of fear I resolved to flee for my life. I did so. I pressed on in the cold of winter to find me a home among strangers for the first time. I continued my journey for several days, when I commenced asking for a home. For eight days I looked in vain. It was in the dead of winter and no one wanted a boy. Becoming discouraged and depressed in mind by my fruitless efforts, I turned back, and after a two weeks' absence, arrived at my father's house with drooping head and weeping eyes, for I feared some terrible punishment awaited me. I poured forth the bitterness of my heart by telling the events just as they took place, and the reason why I ran away. To my great astonishment I did not even receive a whipping for this attempt at running away. I think father feared if he punished me for this, I might at some future day make another and a more successful attempt, and thus deprive him of my valuable services as a beggar.

The last year at home brought no relief. My mother by dint of hard labor had earned the money and purchased a cow, and cut grass enough with a hand-sickle in the glens of the mountain, and carried it home on her head—a German mode of carrying—to keep the cow through the winter. But here another misfortune set in. The cow had

hurt herself in some way, she grew worse, and finally died.
This was a terrible stroke to my heart-broken mother, for
the cow had been a great support. Mother and I set out
on foot to represent our loss, and if possible, raise money
enough to purchase another cow. We traveled, I know
not how many miles, but little help did we get. About 10
o'clock of the fourth day, near the margin of a beautiful
lake, and within full sight of the village of Nassau, weary
and discouraged, she sat down by the roadside and relieved
her aching heart in a flood of tears. Oh, I did feel so sorry
for her! I tried to encourage her all I could, and pointed
toward the village, and told her I would enter every house
alone while she sat quietly under a shade tree to rest.
These words seemed to cheer her, and, foot-sore as we were,
we entered Nassau, and I canvassed the village while she
rested. But we became discouraged, having raised only
about six dollars.

At another time, failing to find lodging in a barn, and,
as the weather was quite cold, I asked at the houses for
permission to stay all night. But no one would keep "the
beggar boy." As a last resort, I lay down by the side of a
straw stack. The evening was far spent, and folks were
retiring. Sleep, I could not for the cold. I pulled straw
and tried to cover myself up, but the cold crept through.
All night I suffered. I would get up and run, then I would
rub my limbs, then lay down as securely as possible. Yet
it would seem that I could not survive. What a fearful
night this was. The slowly moving hours at length crept
on, and morning appeared. I started to climb over the
fence. To my surprise, I could not get my feet upon the
boards without great exertion, and when I had reached
the top, I fell down upon the hard, frozen ground. I lay
for some minutes in a stupor, and at length, hearing a man
in a barn near by, I shouted. He came and took me up
and carried me to his house. I could not tell what was the

matter with me. They built a hot fire and I sat up so close to the stove that I burned my clothes, yet I shook like a leaf in the wind, and it was 8 o'clock before I became composed. Such is the life of a drunkard's child.

But here a change took place. Industry was the characteristic trait in me which attracted the attention of the community, and quite a number of times father was waited upon by various persons for the purpose of having me bound out to them. At length, some other influence than right reason prevailed on him to *give* me away, which he did to a man by the name of Richmond Merry.

Before I step from the parental roof, it is not improper for me to add that two brothers had been born to me. The family now consisted of five children, namely, Peter, Mary, Joseph, Jacob, and the writer. Joseph was born at the old steam sawmill, and Jacob in the house near Green's sawmill.

CHAPTER VII.

THE OLD FOLKS—AN EVENTFUL SABBATH—AUTUMN DAYS
—GOING WEST—A TERRIBLE WINTER—FLEEING FOR
LIFE.

Accordingly, one spring morning in April, 1852, I bade
good-by to kindred, and set out for my new home. On
my way a thousand hopes and fears flitted through my
mind. As I passed along, my soul was refreshed in listening to the carols of returning birds. Breathing the mild
atmosphere coming from the sunny southern climes, basking in the clear morning sunlight, admiring the wintergreen along the mountain foot-path, beholding the evergreen
glades on either side, the sparkling lakelet smiling with the
flush of spring, were objects that beguiled my pensive
mind. The home to which I was going was humble, located at the foot of Sugar. Hill, West Steventown, N. Y.
The people with whom I was going to live were aged, poor,
ignorant and irreligious—both using profane language, and
the man drank to excess. My industry and good conduct,
together with an inborn disposition toward honesty, did
not fail to attract the attention of the old folks, who had a
peculiar way of telling everybody what a good boy they
had. Soon the odium of the "beggar boy" passed away.
As the old lady wore the crown and swayed the scepter, I
was only responsible to her for my conduct, though she, I
confess, was not always easy to please, for she often indulged in violent spells of anger.

Sabbaths were little regarded, I frequently having to
work on that day.

Being deprived of school privileges, I learned my lessons by experience, as the following will illustrate: One snapping cold day in winter, while harnessing our old horse, following my instructions, I breathed on the bit to draw out the frost. Curious to know how I had succeeded, I touched my tongue to it. No sooner done than it stuck to the bit. There was no time to ask what must be done. I gave it a jerk, and out came the bit all covered with my tongue. My mouth was sore for many days. But then I had no disposition to try the bit that way again.

The seasons of the swiftly passing years came and went. I never wearied in beholding the springing grass, bursting buds, unfolding flowers, and singing birds. How delicious to breathe the pure mountain air! With what delight I climbed the rugged hills from whose summits I beheld the Hudson on whose bosom the rays of the sun sparkled like orient gems. I could see Albany with its palace walls setting against the western sky. On the east rose the lofty peaks of the Green Mountains; toward the north lay spread out dense forests, covering thousands of acres with their lofty hemlocks and pines. To the southwest the valley of the Hudson with its fertile fields, lovely hamlets, half-secluded farm-houses and picturesque scenery, presented a picture rare and beautiful. In short, from these heights I beheld, in miniature, the lovely realms and exalted kingdoms of the world.

Living with such people, it must not be thought strange if I appropriated all Sabbaths, on which I did not have to work, in seeking such diversions as best suited my mind. If springtime, I rambled through the glens and mountain paths in pursuit of flowers, or, reclining under some shade tree, the caroling of birds beguiled the sunny hours away. If summer, then picking berries, which everywhere grew in abundance, was the all-absorbing pastime. If autumn, then the gathering of nuts was the climax of all.

Very frequently I had to go to Alps, the nearest village, after liquor for the old man. One Sabbath a neighbor wanted me to go after some for him. Now he was a very doubtful paymaster, and I did not like to trust him. However, I went, thinking on the way how I should manage to get my pay. Returning, I concluded to hide the jug under some bushes near the house. He looked surprised at seeing me without the jug and asked what had become of it. I told him I had hid it near by, and would go after it upon receiving my pay. He was nonplused, and, I suppose, pretty "dry," and he came down with the money.

But the autumn was the most pleasing of all the year, for then the groves were filled with nuts, and such pastime as I enjoyed in gathering them for winter.

While living with these aged people, I formed the acquaintance of Warren and Addie Wait, whose mother, Mrs. L. H. Wait (now Mrs. L. H. Lansing), I found to be a most excellent woman. Quite a number of Sabbaths I enticed them to go with me and gather flowers in the glens. It did not please Mrs. Wait. So the next Sunday she asked me if I did not know it was wrong to break the Sabbath. I told her I did not know it was. She said she wished I would go to Sabbath-school with Warren and Addie, instead of going off into the woods. "Sabbath-school," I repeated, wondering what that could be, for I had never heard of such a thing. She then explained it to me. Still, being somewhat doubtful, I asked her if she thought they would take me, for I had in mind the fact that everybody knew me as the beggar boy, and it was impressed upon my mind that everybody despised me. She assured me that they would be glad to have me come. "*Glad* to have *me* come," I repeated in great wonder, and at once promised her I would go.

Upon this I hastened home in high glee, conjecturing as to what a Sabbath-school could be. At the appointed hour the following Sabbath I was at the church. I stood on the steps, for that was as far as I dared go, waiting for Mrs. Wait. It required some nerve to stand there as the people passed in. The thought that all knew me as the little beggar cut my feelings to the quick. It was only my promise that held me there to the gaze of the multitude. For, should I go away, the good lady, who had not yet arrived, would think that I had not been there, and my promise would be broken. At length she came, complimented me for my promptness, and passed in.

Hope again gave place to fear. I thought that I was not worthy to be a member of the school, perhaps I was too wicked, and was just in the act of turning away, when I felt a gentle touch on my shoulders. Upon looking around, I saw the superintendent, who, with a pleasing smile, invited me in. With downcast eyes I followed the man up the aisle to a teacher, who received me kindly. The teacher gave me a book. I opened it, when, to my astonishment, I saw some beautiful pictures! He tried to have me say the letters after him. But it was of no use as long as there remained a picture unseen. Nor was I satisfied with a hasty look, but I examined them minutely. The teacher seeing how absorbed I was, let me satisfy my curiosity, and finally told me he would give me the book on condition that I learned the letters which he showed me. What a gift! A man elected to the presidency of the United States could have felt no deeper satisfaction over his success than I did over the anticipated possession of that book. After school I went home in company with Mrs. Wait and her children, Addie and Warren. Of course I was proud to show her my book, and to relate what the teacher had said to me. She smiled at my artless and childish simplicity, and encouraged my efforts. As I lived about a mile farther toward the mountains than Mrs. Wait, and as the summer's sun was already going toward the

West, I hastened home in high glee, resolved to learn the letters and obtain the book.

But then, when I arrived there, and the book was shown, there was an unlooked-for obstacle in the way. The old lady did not like the idea of seeing books in my hands, and frowned on me, remarking that "larnin' alwus spil'd pe'ple," and if I was "goin' to larn" I would be good for nothing. I felt disappointed, for I knew if she opposed me I might as well give up, as she was very set in her ways. I wanted to keep the book so much that I entreated her to put me on trial for one week. She reluctantly consented.

Knowing her changeableness, I did not dare to study in her presence, so I went away by myself, and after another good look at the pictures, studied the shape of every letter so thoroughly that their forms were stamped on my mind. During the week while at work with the old man, I would describe their shape to him, who then would tell me their names. Thus I learned all the letters before the week was up, and did as much work as usual, for I wanted to convince the old lady that "larnin' " did not spoil me; indeed she did not even know that I had studied at all.

The following Sabbath was one of those bright June mornings when all nature stands dressed in its most lovely garments, and the birds in the calmness of the morning sing as if their little throats would burst, and the chime of the church bell, wafted along the hillsides and through the valleys, produced a holy and heavenly influence on my mind. While wrapt in my thoughts amid these surroundings, I passed the first neighbor's, Mr. Weatherby's. Mrs. Weatherby, who has now gone to her reward, stood in the doorway and asked me about those letters. I told her they were all learned. She thought it was impossible, for she knew I had to work hard, early and late. To relieve her mind, I repeated them to her satisfaction and approval. She bade me become a man. At such good words I felt manly and passed on. I stopped at Mrs. Wait's, where the same questions were asked and the same answers given. In company we went to church and the Sabbath-school. The alphabet was promptly recited, to the approval and satisfaction of the teacher. It is unnecessary to add that I won and obtained the book. Thus, dear reader, your humble editor learned his letters at the age of twelve.

To the Sabbath-school is he indebted for his first steps in learning. But even here I had obstacles to overcome. Some Sabbaths I had to stay at home and work. To overcome this difficulty, I asked the old people to give me a stint for seven days. When this could be done, they gave it me, and then I would work with added energy to accomplish in six days what was given me for seven. But they could not always give me a task, hence the old folks would make me work so late on the Sabbath that I had to run most of the three miles to get to school in time. The session was in the afternoon at two o'clock. Under these difficulties I attended Sabbath-school for about three months. And they were the happiest three months of my mountain life. During this time I became known throughout the whole parish for my eagerness to learn, and many sympathized with me, and one man even offered to take me and send me to school, if I would come and live with him. But this offer I did not dare to accept for fear my father would take me home, and I preferred living with the old people to returning to a life of suffering; though candor compels me to confess that my apprenticed home was little better than the parental roof. At the Sabbath-school a good lady presented me with a beautiful copy of the Bible. At first I declined to take it, assuring her I never would be able to read it. I did not think that I would ever be able to read like the educated people. But she prevailed upon me to take it, assuring me that I would live to see the time when I would be able to read from that Bible. I was astonished at her remark, wondering if it were possible for me to ever acquire so much knowledge, and, kindly thanking her, I accepted the book.

This put a new idea into my mind and I resolved to keep the Bible and learn to read it. I treasured these two books as the most sacred gifts of my life, but, I am sorry to add, they were both stolen from me some years later.

I became very much attached to the Sabbath-school, and during my stay in it, learned to read a little in the book given me by my teacher. All these things took place at the white meeting-house in West Steventown, N. Y. The Rev. Isaiah B. Coleman was pastor of the church, and, I will here add, is pastor yet, and doubtless, as his eyes fall on this narrative, will remember the little Sabbath-school boy of long ago. Oh! how I prized this opportunity to learn, but even this privilege was of short duration, for in the autumn, the old folks moved to Albany, Green county, Wisconsin.

Perhaps it may be interesting to the reader to know what occupation I followed while living with the old folks in the mountains. Well, during the early part of the season, I helped the old lady 'gather herbs, which she took to the New Lebanon Shakers and sold. The autumns were spent in burning coal, and the winters in making shingles. But of all dreads, was the coal-burning season, for it became my duty to act as watch part of the night. The old gentleman would usually stay the fore part. Upon his arrival at home he would call me up about midnight, and with lantern in hand, I would start off over the lonely mountain path to the coal-pit. I confess I dreaded to go out at that hour of the night, when ghosts in their frightful forms walked the earth, and every bush and stump appeared one to me. For so many ghost stories had been related in my hearing, that I really believed in their existence.

Besides, I had to pass through a forest of dense saplings—the abode of snakes, frogs and toads, and not unfrequently was frightened out of my wits by stepping on their cold, slimy backs with my bare feet. And to pass the after part of the night in the mountain all alone, I confess took considerable nerve. But all this was a thousand times better than to beg from door to door. For the benefit of the young reader I would here say, in regard to ghosts, that, having carefully investigated the subject, I am prepared to affirm that no such thing as a ghost exists. Most, if not all, fancied ghosts, are optical delusions. If any one is curious to trace this subject still farther, I would refer him to Dick, who explains and illustrates it to the satisfaction of every mind.

All of this summer the old people had been receiving frequent letters from a married daughter in the West, and they were making preparations to move West. I had heard them say so much about it, that I had painted in my mind a country second to the Eden of old. I wanted to see such a country—a country in such contrast with my mountain home, that not even a stone could be obtained to throw at the birds ! For the benefit of my eastern readers, I will add that this is literally true of many sections of Illinois, Wisconsin and Iowa. Revolving these things in my mind, I asked the old gentleman one day, if he would let me go with him. To my surprise he readily consented. The next thing in the way was to get the consent of my father. So I went to see him about it. After a long conversation, he asked me if I wanted to go so far from home. I answered in the affirmative. He was silent for some minutes, doubtless revolving in his mind whether it was best to let me go, but he gave his permission. The appointed day was approaching. Upon the morning of our departure, I made mother a visit. She felt very sad. I told her I would be a good boy. And then all her acts of kindness flashed into my mind. How loving she had been, how often she had shielded me. When I came home from my long trips in begging, half frozen, tired and hungry, how she used to cheer my aching heart by kind words. Oh, she was such a good mother! and now, I am leaving her to go far away. These thoughts caused me to almost repent of my purpose. Yet the memory of the past was bitter. With this before my mind, and yet with many regrets, I left the family group standing in the door-way of our humble mountain home weeping. For a moment I faltered. But it seemed best I should go. The past was a sad reality, the present rife with anxiety, with hopes and fears, the future shrouded with a vail impenetrable. I tried to reconcile myself as best I could. Though I regretted to give up my mother, sister and brothers, yet the thought of being placed beyond the reach of father, whom I had learned to fear, was a great consolation. With hopes for better days, I turned my face westward, in fond expectation that upon the fertile plains beyond the mountains, industry would soon secure me a happy home.

I should here add that Peter had been given away in the same manner that I had been, and hence he was not at home at the time I took my departure, but I went to his home to bid him good-by. There were mutual regrets and sadness between us at the thought of having me go so far away where we could not see each other, for we loved each other as a common sorrow only could unite two hearts. But I told him that father's cruelty was the only reason why I took this step. He sighed and said: "Oh, could I only go with you!" I spent a number of hours with him, then we parted, both weeping.

I hastened forward to the village of Alps, where I joined the old people, for I had come another road. Here we spent the first night on our journey. As the twilight shut out the light of day, and the towering mountain over against the village cast a somber shade upon the opposite hillside, it was a fit emblem of my own sad heart, for, in more respects than one, it had been a remarkable day. I had left all that was dear to my own heart weeping for me, and I wept for them. But such are some of the pangs of sorrow in a home made desolate by alcohol.

The following morning we started about four o'clock for Troy. As we were passing along the dusky way—for it was in the month of October—the grey light of early morning faded out, and the full flush of the crimsoned eastern sky lighted up the face of nature, and as we passed over a hill, the sun, full orbed, flashed and sparkled his golden beams over the mountain summit, and then, as I looked toward the glories of approaching day, I thought of the dear ones at home, and as the mountain faded from my view, I wept, and longed to turn back. But this could not be.

While thus pensive and absorbed with my thoughts, we had, unheeded by me, passed through Sand Lake, and were now nearing Alba, and shortly arrived in Troy.

Here new sights and scenes diverted my thoughts. I looked upon the beauties of this city with admiration. At the depot all was excitement. Bells were ringing, whistles were blowing, engines moving, trains coming and going, baggage and express wagons rolling over the pavements. All these things to a green mountain boy, whose eyes and ears, and perhaps mouth, were wide open, were strange and surprising.

At length we took our seats in the cars. I sat by a window looking out upon another train which happened to move out of the depot first. I surely thought it was our train that moved. But then I was green, for I did not understand the philosophy of it. After bustling about of

5

porters, checking of baggage, ringing of engine bell, escaping of steam, a general scramble of passengers, the train moved out of the depot, slowly winding its serpentine way through the city, over bridges, under streets and over crossings, increasing in speed as it went, until at length it rushed with reckless force through cuts, over embankments, and past farm-houses, as if anxious to carry me forever beyond the reach of a tyrant hand.

As the iron horse was careering over the track of steel, my mind prognosticated of the future. In the far West I was going to enjoy a happy home, be a good boy who might honor my mother; would never, no *never* touch a drop of liquor, but on the other hand, would be industrious, grow up a thrifty man, earn the means with which to purchase a farm, and in the strength of early manhood return to make glad a mother's heart as she looked upon the noble form of her firstborn. These were some of the thoughts that passed through my mind.

Buffalo was reached at length, where we took a steamer for Monroe City. "The Western World" was the name of the boat upon which we took passage, and its name was very suggestive to me, for was I not going to that new, strange and wonderful world?

At eight o'clock in the evening the rattle of trucks ceased, the ceaseless tread upon the wharf became subdued, the bell rang, orders were given from the deck of the pilot-house, the flag which had floated in the breeze was hauled in, and the ponderous wheels struggled with the elements, and away over the lake moved the great boat.

At Monroe City we took the cars for Chicago. At a little station beyond Cold Water the engine broke down, and we were detained for some time. But another took the place of the disabled one, and we arrived in Chicago without further trouble. Here we took another steamer for Milwaukee, where we again took the cars for Janesville, and from thence, twenty-two miles by team, to Albany, Green Co., Wis., the end of our journey. After leaving Janesville, I for the first time saw prairies, and I can only describe them as an ocean of land bounded on all sides by the horizon, and dotted here and there by dwelling-houses. The whole was a sight beautiful to behold, as these prairies stretched away in every direction as far as the eye could see. Here, too, I saw vast fields of corn, and while trying to take in the vastness of one of these fields, a farmer passed us loaded with golden ears of corn. One ear happened to drop from his wagon. I jumped out and picked it up. Oh! what a large ear. Twenty-two rows upon it, and oh, what kernels! a quarter of an inch in depth. Down East eight rows was the average; but here was one of twenty-two, whose cob was larger than the whole ear down in New York State. This must be a wonderful country, I thought.

Stopping for the night at Magnolia, we arrived next day about noon in the beautiful village of Albany. Mr. Preston's residence was about one and a half miles southwest of the village. He lived on the Campbell farm. The road, part of the way lay through a "bur-oak opening," skirted on the west by a prairie. It was one of those October days when all nature glows in the mellow sunlight, the fields look as if taking on their garments for winter, and the groves are dressed in crimson foliage. It was such a day as this upon which we arrived at Mr. Preston's.

We were very kindly received. A sumptuous feast had been prepared against our coming, and the tables groaned under their loads of the best eatables the West could give. With such a reception, and with the material evidences of affluence on every hand, I surely thought I would be very happy.

Mr. Preston's family consisted of himself, his wife, one daughter, and three hired men. The house was located upon the bank of a small stream which emptied into Sugar river; the farm was large, the yard filled with cattle, the barn with three spans of horses, and in the pasture were over a thousand sheep. Surely, I thought, in such a home as this, the old people would pass down the valley of old age in peace and happiness, and I should have such a home as I had not enjoyed since I left the Rhine.

Nancy—for that was the name of the daughter—took pleasure in showing me around. We went out into the fields, rambled through the groves, beside the river, and over the prairies. She also knew the names of most of the wild birds, among which were prairie chickens, quails, wild geese, cranes, snipes, ducks, and many smaller ones, and there were such hosts of them in the fields and on the river.

Just-as I began to get fairly acquainted with my new home, there came an unanticipated and unexpected change, for it turned out that the old folks gave what little of this world's goods they had—counting me in as one of the articles—to Mr. Preston, his son-in-law. It was now late in the autumn, and the leaves, yellow and sere, lay strewn over the ground, while the northern blasts sighed through the barren branches a sad, mournful requiem. For a few months I was kindly treated, but soon the cords of cruelty were fastened about me, and my items of work each day, were these: I had to take care of 1000 sheep, 12 head of cattle, and to cut wood enough to supply two stoves. Mornings I had to be out before daylight, and as I mounted the hay-stacks, and the keen prairie winds would go through my thin clothes, I often thought I should perish before accomplishing my task. Moreover, the old lady had such a mean disposition that no one could live in peace with her, and the old man disagreeing with the son-in-law, the son-in-law quarreling with the old folks, anarchy and contention filled up the unhappy hours. They being so hateful to each other, it was not strange that I should be abused. Through exposure to wind and rain I was taken sick, which produced still more ill-will, for Preston whined and swore that he did not thank the old folks for bringing a boy to be sick at his expense, and to mitigate his wrath, I was neglected on a bed of suffering.

Scarcely was I able to leave the sick-room before I had to resume my work again. Mornings, long before daylight, I had to climb the hay-stacks, and as the northern winds swept over the wild prairies, they would almost lift me from the stacks. Had they given me comfortable clothing, my task would have been much easier, but with thin clothing and no mittens—for they were too cruel to provide me with any—my hands would get so cold that I could scarcely hold the fork, and several times I froze my hands, feet, and other parts of my body. Aside from all this, the man Preston was very fractious, and his treatment most heartless. If I did anything wrong, he abused me; if I did well, he abused me, so there was no encouragement to please him. Oh, how my heart would ache and sigh for relief! But I was a poor child, over a thousand miles from home and friends, alone in the world and given over to the caprice of heartless and godless men. Thus I toiled and suffered all winter, with no one to help or pity. But the seasons do not last always.

Rosy-footed spring, with its brightly-beaming smiles and soft, balmy air, at length drove the stern monarch Winter to the North. And I earnestly hoped my tasks would become more endurable. But in this I was disappointed, for they increased my burdens.

One day I was sent to find the sheep. I had failed in finding them, though I had faithfully and diligently looked for them, and it was quite late in the evening when I returned and reported myself. Preston was so vexed at this, that he said he would whip me "within an inch of my life," if I did not go and find them before I went to

bed.   I was frightened.   I was confident he would redeem
such promises.   I could not go out upon the prairies and
find in the darkness what I had failed to find in the light
of day.   But go I must, and go I did, not after the sheep,
however, but sought refuge in flight.   I wandered over the
prairies, and, late in the night, sought shelter in an old log
hut, which stood deserted and unoccupied.   In the morning I continued my journey over Mt. Pleasant, wandered,
I do not know where, but arrived about four o'clock in the
afternoon at a village called Monticello.   Here I stopped
in a store to get something to eat.   While eating a few
dry crackers, the man asked me who I was and where I
came from.   I told him I was from Albany, Wis., and was
seeking a home.   I also told him my parents were dead
and that I was left alone in the world.

Right here let me pause and remind the reader of my
promise in the introduction.   I then stated that truth shall
constitute the merit of this narrative.   I could not for a
moment uphold falsehood as something for the young to
follow, nor do I introduce this for any such purpose.   As
I advance, there will events be related which, if I had to
live my life over again, with the experience I now have,
I could not be persuaded to commit.   If the reader will
bear in mind the motive of my presenting events just as
they took place, I will not in the future of this narrative
occupy your time in explanations.   In the incident above
related, looking at it from the stand-point of a mature
judgment, I am positive if I had told the plain truth, I
would have been more successful.   But I was only a poor,
homeless boy and acted on the impulse of the moment.

While being thus questioned by the store-keeper, his
wife came in.   She was rather pleased with my appearance, and asked me if I would not live with them.   I
replied in the affirmative, and gladly accepted the invitation.

CHAPTER VIII.

BITTEN BY A RATTLESNAKE—AT THE GATE OF DEATH—
DRIVEN INTO THE HARVEST-FIELD—FAINTING—TURNED
OUT UPON THE WORLD—A DROVER—TAKEN WITH FEVER
AND AGUE—LEFT IN A STRANGE CITY ALONE.

I found them to be most excellent people. And the new home was such a contrast to the one I had left. Here I had only one horse to take care of, and a small garden to attend, and to run errands—all of which I was ready and glad to do. The good people commenced making me clothes suitable to wear to church. They had also expressed their intention to send me to school for the summer as soon as the term opened. To this end—the good lady was a real mother to me—she even had me study and recite to her, for, she said, her boy must be as smart as the other school-boys. All this seemed like a dream. Could it be possible. there were such whole-souled, such noble-hearted people? But it was a fact. And it would seem that better days were in the future.

But, alas! all these hopes were suddenly turned to ashes and I grew sick at heart when one day, after I had been there about three weeks, a man came into the store who knew all about me—knew of my running away, and of Preston's fruitless efforts to find me. I overheard him tell the good people that I was a runaway. Confounded, covered with shame, and conscience lashing me for the lie I had told, and the fearful anticipations of being delivered up, I went out of the back door, stole over the garden fence, and ran away from this place. Though scalding tears ran down my cheeks, and I bitterly repented the falsehood, yet this, it seems, was the only way I could atone for the sin. Oh, how I regretted to leave this place. But it could not be helped.

I continued my flight, passed through Monroe, from there southward, and vainly sought another home. I wandered about over the prairies for over a week in a fruitless search of a place. At length, failing in my efforts, and my conscience lashing me for the falsehood told to such good people, I returned and surrendered myself to Preston. As might be anticipated, I received the merited punishment. I did not complain of this, for I thought it was because I had told that awful falsehood.

Having met the ends of justice, I now hoped for better days, but it would seem that what I had experienced was only a prelude to what was to follow, and that my life had been prolonged to meet a most horrible death under the following circumstances:

I was at work on some low lands near Sugar River, spreading grass after three men. I used a long pole, spreading two swaths at a time. As I was intent on my work, I tossed a huge rattlesnake into the air which appeared to have been concealed under the swath. As soon as I saw it, it so frightened me that I knew not which way I jumped. In its descent it came very near falling on my head, but by a dodge on my part, it buried its poisonous fangs in one of my ankles. Coiling up and raising its cerulean neck high in the air, with the rapid vibration of its forked tongue, it was in the act of striking another blow, when I barely escaped.

The deed was done! I was bitten by a rattlesnake! They told me the wound was fatal, and death would soon follow: that in a few hours I would be in eternity, and the pain I was suffering confirmed what they said. The feeling I experienced partook of the nature of a bee sting, but the pain was a hundred-fold more intense. One could almost see the flesh puff up, so rapid was the swelling. One of the men ran for the doctor, another bound tobacco over the bite, while a third told me to run to the house, which was · half a mile distant.

The advice of the ·last was ill-timed, for by running I heated my blood, and consequently carried the poison with greater rapidity through my system.

When I arrived at the house they applied a fresh quantity of tobacco, and gave me a pint of whisky to drink, but the latter I could not retain on my stomach. As soon as the physician came, he ordered two sacks to be filled with ashes. These he placed one on each side of my ankle, with the instruction that they be saturated with warm water every fifteen minutes. He also gave me some medicine, the name of which I do not remember. This was to be the remedy. It was to kill me or the poison, and it came very near doing the former. Water was strictly forbidden me. My lips were parched, my tongue swollen, and my throat and stomach seemed on fire. I was undergoing all the sufferings that a mortal could. In vain I cried and begged for "a drop of water to cool my parched tongue." The only way they could keep me within bounds, was by threatening to apply more warm water to the sacks of ashes.

It now seemed to me that I was but one remove from the gates of death, and it mattered but little; there would not one tear fall for me—none would weep over my lonely grave—no loving mother repair to the silent spot at eventide, just as the sun is sinking down the West, to plant the flowers I loved best upon the rude mound above me. Yes, my dear mother was ignorant of the pain I was suffering; of the fact that her absent boy was on the verge of eternity.

Time passed away. Oh, how long the minutes! Being wild for the want of water, the old man thought I would die if it was longer withheld, and I could but die if he gave me some. So he took a tin pail to get some fresh.

No sooner had he gone, than off the bed I plunged for the
water-pail which contained but a little. By sundown the
lye had eaten all of the flesh away, leaving the joints and
bones naked. But I had not yet suffered enough, for they
filled all the cavities which the lye had made with saleratus. Oh, horrors! They were murdering me by inches!
The saleratus seemed like the application of burning fire.
The piercing pain of the snake's bite, the raging of a fever,
the thirst so intense that my tongue was swollen beyond
speech, made night fearful, and minutes seemed years. I
could literally feel the saleratus eating away my flesh and
bones. In the morning they removed the bandages, when
the frightful appearance of my leg made it manifest that
something else must speedily be done. Upon the removal
of the bandages, the looks of the work which the saleratus had done clearly suggested that if it was applied much
longer it would eat my foot away. I told them that I was
willing to die; I did not wish to be tormented in that way
any longer. In spite of their efforts to eat the poison out,
it was rapidly working its way to the seat of life. Already the swelling was above my knee, and I could live .
but a few hours at the longest. Indeed death would have
been an angel of mercy in that hour of agony.

What transpired after this I know not, for the sufferings
I underwent made me delirious.

Since this part of the sketch has been in print 1 have
had several call on me at my office who told me they saw
me at the time above referred to, and their account of my
appearance was startling. The above is given only up to
the time when reason was overcome by the tortures of the
body. Hon. J. H. Venton, of Broadhead, Wis., who saw
me at the time, said he had no reasonable expectation that
I would ever recover.

When I began to return to consciousness everything
seemed so strange. The voices, the looks, the actions, all

appeared changed. People from far and near gathered to see the boy bitten by a snake. Indeed, it is not possible for me to depict my sufferings. I have since learned that I was so reduced, and my moans were so plaintive and sad, my leg was so frightful to behold that many who had come to see me, turned away without the sight. I was a helpless sufferer for about six weeks. Food had a very noxious taste, and water gruel eaten hot was the only thing I could eat or retain on my stomach.

As soon as I sufficiently recovered, Mr. Preston told me I had been for over six weeks at his expense, and I must pay for it by my industry. I have always been willing to work, and loved to work, but, notwithstanding my readiness to obey, for me to enter a harvest-field under a burning August sun, reduced in strength as I was, and the swelling not being sufficiently subsided to wear a boot—besides my ankle was all raw, the flesh having been eaten away to the very bone, so that I could hardly endure the pressure of the cotton bandages, let alone wearing a boot or shoe—to go into a harvest-field under such bodily suffering, was simply going to my grave; yet, in this condition, I was told to go and work in the field. The command was imperative, and to disobey it was death. I obeyed and made the attempt.

Upon entering the field the sharp stubbles pierced the bandages like knife-blades, and the blood flowing from the wounds re-opened, marked my foot-steps. It being a hot day, the sun shone upon me very oppressively. I endured it for half an hour, when I became deadly sick at the stomach, and, for the want of strength, sunk down under the pain and weakness. The old gentleman, who was in the field at the time, seeing I was exhausted, took me to the house. Scarcely had we arrived when Preston heard of it, and started for the house. We could see by his step that anger was burning in his bosom. The old man took me up stairs, and he himself stood in the stairway as Preston rushed in at the door, all in a passion, and demanded me to be given over into his hands. The old gentleman refused to do so, and stoutly resisted to the last. Preston at length went away, swearing and muttering he would kill me the first time he laid his hands on me. Considering my feebleness at this time, I do not know what would have been the result had I been surrendered into the hands of Mr. Preston, for he was a very large, muscular man.

This was on a Saturday. Something must be done immediately. The old folks said they could protect me no longer, that Preston would vent his malice on me the first opportunity which presented itself, that my life was in his hands. My heart sank within me at this intelligence. It was more than I could endure as I reflected on my helpless condition, and of going out in the world alone. The good old folks deeply sympathized with me, but that was all they could do.

The Sabbath at length arrived. It was as radiant a morning as ever dawned upon this world. There was just breeze enough to stir the foliage overhead. I retired to a shady tree by the bank of the river which was not far away, and, there in my retreat, with heart too full of sadness for utterance, I thought of the days of long ago, of a home on the mountain, of a kind mother whom I left standing in the doorway of that home weeping over my departure, of brothers and sister. Thus I sat for a long time, my heart filled with sorrow and my eyes with tears. Weeping over my misfortunes, I felt the distance was great, and that it would be impossible for me to return East. All the pleasant associations of former times crowded through my mind. The thought of the cleft in the rock, the sweet songs of birds, my playmates, the Sabbath-school, the smiles of the good woman that led me there, and a thousand other things, came up before my mind's eye, and only added to my despondency. While thus all pensive, a drove of cattle passed me. The owner halted and urged me to help him drive his cattle. I told him what had befallen me, that my foot rendered me unable, that I was very feeble, and feared I would be of no use to him. He said he had failed to get a boy, and it was impossible for him to drive his cattle, and, if I would go, he would let me ride his horse. I replied that I would try it.

What little effects I had were tied up in a handkerchief, and I stepped out into the wide world, a homeless boy. For four days we journeyed. In the meantime he inquired into my history. I told him the simple story. He replied that he would give me a good home, if I would go with him. I gladly accepted the invitation, and agreed to go. On the fifth day we arrived at Sauk City, upon the Wisconsin river. While waiting here for our turn to cross the bridge, a peculiar fever came over me and I sank upon the ground. The gentleman took me across the bridge to a hotel, and called in a physician, who, upon examination, said I had the fever and ague. I was unable to go farther, and the man could not wait with his herd of cattle. So he paid me $4.50 for my services, and left me to my fate.

The next morning, feeling much better, I went in pursuit of the drover. I went through every street and inquired at every street corner to learn which road the drover had taken; but my search was fruitless. Tired and in a strange city, what could I do but return? With a heavy heart I recrossed the river, for the purpose, if possible, to find a home somewhere along the road. I had proceeded but a short distance, when another chill came upon me, and I was compelled to lay down beside the road. After the chill had passed away I arose and went on my way, but it had such a weakening effect upon me that I felt faint and hardly able to walk. Upon arriving at the first house, I stopped and asked if I might rest myself. The lady gave me permission to do so. Feeling my lonely and destitute condition, I thought of mother, and tears filled my eyes. The lady, seeing me weeping, asked the cause of my sorrow. I told her what had befallen me; that I had a kind mother whom I never expected to see; that I was an outcast in the world; that a snake's bite had almost brought me to the grave, and now the fever and ague was consuming me. She tried to encourage me to hope for better things.

I stayed there two days, and the lady was very kind to me. How I wished it was my home. But the lady was so good that I did not have it in my heart to ask her, for fear of asking too much.

On the third day I felt so much refreshed that I renewed my efforts in trying to find a home. Whenever I asked a man for work, he would look at me and say "What can you do?" The sufferings I had undergone had left their traces upon my person, and plainly suggested that I would be of no service. Being frustrated in my efforts, I gave up to desponding feelings, caring but little what I did, or where I went, or what became of me. At length, having wandered some three weeks, and traveled over two hundred miles on foot, I returned again to the old folks, telling them my efforts had been without success, and that I wanted them to shelter me until I could find a home. The old folks, with sadness, yet with good reasons, and with sympathy for me, told me I must not let Preston see me, or "he would whip me within an inch of my life." I left the house more discouraged than ever, and my aching heart found solace only in tears.

CHAPTER IX.

Longing for a Home—A Night in the Wild Woods—A Dream—A Long Journey—Incidents by the Way—Arriving at West Stephentown, New York.

It must be remembered that the reason why I failed to find a home was because I was rendered a cripple for the time being by reason of my ankle, and because I was suffering under that consuming and life-wasting disease—fever and ague. Truly all things seemed against me, and the world looked very dark and discouraging. The wide, wide world had no home for my aching head and broken heart. I had tried, oh, so faithfully, to find a home, but all in vain. The people did not care to have a sick boy. In this new country only healthy persons were wanted.

These circumstances, added to the fact that I was over a thousand miles from home and friends, rendered my condition distressing. Being worn out by pain and sickness and the continued travels on foot, under an August sun, and frequently deprived of my meals, for people were not always thoughtful to invite me to their tables, and I was too bashful to ask, I was little prepared to undergo the ills before me. Thus I had little encouragement or strength to continue my search. I was wandering I knew not where. In short, there was but a step to the grave. Thus was my heart filled with a sadness that cannot be described. The reader need not be surprised if I was a long time in going a short distance.

I had scarcely passed out of sight of the house which could afford me protection no longer, when it was most sunset, and the nearest house before me in the way was three miles distant. I was now, for the first time since my misfortune, passing the spot were the monster gave me the almost fatal wound. As I crossed the bridge, I paused for a moment upon it to look down into the dark, purple waters of the sluggish stream; then I raised my eyes toward the spot where the snake bit me. Oh, it was such a dark hour to me! Oh, the desolation, the bitter anguish of my sad heart and lonely life! Giving ᴌ deep, farewell sigh I passed on. I had gone but a short distance, when I felt the fever coming on. Being weak and faint, I laid down by the roadside.

Already the sun was sinking behind the western hills, mirroring its golden light on the bosom of the not-far-off river. As twilight was shrouding the night in darkness, I felt a peculiar terror creep over me. I thought of my help-less condition, how I was now out in the wild woods of the far West, helpless, that only a few rods intervened between me and where the deadly serpent did his cruel act—and the thought suggested to my mind that perhaps another dread monster might be hid in the grass and come upon me before morning, made the blood run cold in my veins. My tongue parched, my body being consumed by the burn-ing fever, my mind filled with longings for some kind pro-tector, with nothing to cover me but heaven's blue vault, glittering with the stars of night, my mind was wild, and the horrors of fear seemed more terrible than death. Every rustling sound or undefined object peering through the dark-ness, added new terror to my excited imagination. The dole-ful screeches of the night birds, the faint and far-a-way how-lings of the prairie-wolves, every flutter and sound, caused my hair to stand on end. In the bitterness of my desolation I cried out for very fear: O my God why am I thus abandoned? But no help came. I was beyond the reach of human sound. For hours I turned first on one side and then the other, and called for help. Then I prayed. In the depths of my helplessness I wept until exhausted with fear and terror. Oh, what a terrible night! Overcome with weariness at last, and the night being calm and warm, after quieting my fears as best I could, at length I fell asleep, sweetly reposing upon the ground, under a kind and heavenly Father's protection, forgetting all my ills and sorrows.

From the depths of my heart, dear young reader, I can but pray that you may be spared such distress. If you have kind parents, love and honor them; if you have a good, comfortable home, stay in it contentedly, whatever the temptations may be to leave it Had I known what was before me, when I turned away from the weeping group in the doorway of that mountain home, nothing could have persuaded me to have abandoned it for the abuses I had and was undergoing. Enjoy childhood and youth while you may, for sorrow and care and calamities of some kind may come upon you full soon. Few know or can fully realize the bitterness of the world until they are left destitute, friendless and among strangers. There is a deeper meaning in the story of the prodigal son coming to himself, than we are wont to give it. In my case it was not profligacy, yet, had I remained within reach of my home, I would have been spared much of that desponding distress which my pen fails to describe. It must be felt to be realized, for in the depth of my desolation the memory of the past ever haunted me. I once had a happy home. And to what place on earth does the heart cling so fondly, and with such pleasing and indestructible recollections? The home of our early childhood; the playground of youth's sunny period. Home! a word which lies very near the heart of us all—imbedded in tender and sacred associations. All that is endearing in the relation of parents and children, brothers and sisters, a mother's watchful love, a father's protection—all cling around the word *Home*, and over it always is spread the

radiance of those remembered joys, such as the morning
of life only knows. The man most to be pitied is he who
has no home. Having lived a homeless life until prosperity and hard toil have reared my beautiful and attractive
home, I write the language of my inmost nature in these
lines, and would impress it upon every young man. The
man who makes for himself a happy home has the chief
means of all earthly comfort and blessing. What need he
care for the world's favors or frowns? If his home is
happy, there is always a place of refuge in adversity and
prosperity. When the world goes wrong, when misfortune
overtakes you, when friends turn away, when the disgust
of your fellowmen follow you through every walk and
by-path, when you are wronged, misunderstood and neglected, what a blessing, what a balm, to enter the doors of
your happy dwelling—shutting the cold world out, and the
warm affection of what is more than all the world to you,
in. Here is the one place where you are welcome, the one
place where you feel that you are understood and trusted,
the one place you love above all others, and where you are
sure of meeting with sympathy. Yes, make your home
happy, and you have an ark of safety amidst the storms of
life. A happy home! with what cheerfulness does it wing
the steps of duty! What other blessing does a man need
who has this? And he who has it not, what blessing does
he not lack? Home! the one word of all others the most
thought of, the most often on the lips, and the most dearly
loved.

But to return. In that night I had a strange dream.
I thought I was in a beautiful garden having all manner
of trees, and bowers, and plants, and fruit, and blooming
flowers, and fountains jetting forth pure, sparkling water,
and music seemed to fill the air, and, presently, I came to
a streamlet rolling its sparkling waters over pebbles in a
merry, laughing mood. On its green banks was a table

filled with a great variety of eatables. Smiling faces and happy voices seemed to be all around me, and presently, mother came up to me and threw her arms around my neck and was so glad to see her long-lost boy, and wiped sorrow's tears from my eyes, and bade me sit down, eat and drink; and the water from the brook looked so pure and tasted so refreshing that it seemed to heal all my ills. Everybody seemed so kind in tone, in looks, in sympathy, in loving attention, that I forgot all my sorrows and was happy amid these associations. My brothers and sister were in the company; I also saw Mrs. Wait, and Warren and Addie; presently the whole Sabbath-school was before me. They listened with wrapped attention to the story of my suffering, which it appears I related to them. They all deeply sympathized with me; then they broke forth in a sweet hymn—oh, such heavenly voices! I had occasion to drink very often of the sparkling waters from the jetting fountains. And every time I drank, I seemed to be stronger. All around me was brightness and good cheer. Flowers in endless variety bloomed on every hand, and bees and insects were flying from shrub to shrub; from branch and bower the birds were pouring forth their songs; there was such a strange combination of the earthly and the heavenly. I seemed restored to health and strength— and heaven could have presented no brighter charms than were spread out before me. Truly the good angels must have kept watch on that night over the slumbers of a poor, helpless child.

At length, I awoke! My tear-stained cheeks were dry and hot, my tongue swollen in my mouth, and my lips parched. Half confused I looked all around me. I could not make out where I was. The dream yet hung in my memory, and I could not reconcile the contrast between what I had just passed through in my sleep and my actual surroundings. But the dream had a wonderfully soothing effect upon me. All the fear and terror was gone, and, like a sweet song, the dream would come up before me all that day, and for a long time after. While thus musing over my thoughts, rosy-fingered dawn heralded the approaching day, while the merry birds, waking from their sleep, made glad the morning with their cheering songs. Wet with the dew of night, I arose, feeling that the good Lord had truly sent a protecting angel to watch over me through the night, for my sleep was sweet and refreshing. A prayer from a truly grateful heart went up to high Heaven on that morning. After which I continued my efforts to find a home. but meeting with no success, I resolved to go home; for what else could I do?

I went to Albany, and the following morning I took the stage for Footville, having money enough to pay my fare, which I had obtained from the cattle drover. Why I took the stage for Footville, I know not; for on our way West we came through Milwaukee and Janesville to Albany; and as I had never seen such a thing as a geography, it would have been most natural to retrace the route we came, unless a divine Providence guided me, for so it would seem by what followed.

As the stage drove up to the postoffice to receive the mail, Mr. Nichols, the owner of eight or ten stage lines that center in Albany, took passage. On our way, Mr. Nichols, who was a noble-hearted man, asked me where I was going. I told him. He was surprised to learn I had undertaken such a journey alone, and asked me if I had money enough. I was embarrassed to reply, for I did not wish to tell him I had none, yet I wanted to speak the truth, so I told him I had paid the last cent that morning for my fare to Footville. He wanted to know how I expected to travel without money. I could give him no answer, so I told him my history, and that I did not know what to do. He was moved in sympathy for me, pulled out his pocket-book and gave me some money, saying he was on his way to Chicago, and he would pay my passage on the cars. Oh, how glad I was! and I could not thank the good gentleman enough for his kindness.

We arrived at Footville at 10 o'clock, where we took the cars for Chicago. Upon arriving in Chicago, he took me to the office of the Michigan Central Railway Co., where he was the means of obtaining a free pass for me to Detroit. Thus this generous gentleman assisted me about 500 miles. I was sick most of the way. While waiting for the departure of the train in Chicago, I was not able to sit up. After I entered the cars, I thought I should die from the terrible gripes in my stomach. I was very sick while in the cars between Chicago and Detroit. At Detroit I took a steamer for Buffalo. After the boat landed at Buffalo, I sought the New York Central Railway Depot. Thus far I had found no difficulty. But my money was now all gone, and there was no alternative but to foot the remainder of the way, which I proceeded to do. Some days I hardly made any progress on account of attacks of fever and ague and the weakness of my ankle, which was not yet half healed. Nights I would crawl into freight-cars or wherever I could pass the hours. One day, toward evening I arrived in a beautiful village. Sitting down upon the platform of the station-house to rest, a number of boys gathered around, some to make sport, while three noble-hearted fellows gave me all the money they had, which amounted to twelve cents.

While here, a boy who sold apples upon the arrival of trains, told me he made from $2 to $3 per day at the business, and urged me to go into partnership with him. I was pleased with the offer, for I thought I could make money enough in a short time to take me home. He said he would see that I had all the apples I needed, though he did not tell me where he got them, nor did I think to ask him. I hastened to buy me a basket, for which I spent the money which the noble-hearted youths had given me, and prepared for business.

Long before day he had me up wading through the wet grass towards a large orchard. When I saw that, he was intent on stealing them, I hesitated and turned back. Upon this he swore at me, called me a coward and many other hard names.

Taking the basket back to the store, I wanted the merchant to take it back and return me the money. This he would not do, but I could take its equivalent in anything else, so, as he had nothing eatable, I took a cheap pocket-book, utterly regardless as to whether I would ever have any money to put into it. Thus ended my experience in selling apples.

After some two weeks' weary traveling, I arrived at Rochester. Here I was dragged to a station-house by the police simply because they found me in a freight-car, about midnight, for where else could I find a place to sleep? In prison I sat down upon the marble floor, for there was nothing in the cell, and passed the remainder of the night in breathing the filthy, noxious air, and in being compelled to listen to horrid imprecations on all sides. The weary hours slowly passed, and in the morning I was taken before the police court to give an account of myself. The room was filled with idle spectators, and I felt very much ashamed of myself. The Judge took his seat, opened the court, and I was the first criminal on the docket. I trembled like a leaf as he eyed me and asked me of what crime I was guilty. I related the circumstances, how I was put in prison. Upon this he set me at liberty without note or comment. But I could never understand why I was taken to the prison for no other crime than simply being found asleep in a freight-car. As soon as I gained my liberty, I took the shortest way out of that city.

I prosecuted my journey as best I could. I was often caught in passing storms. I suppose I did not travel more than six or eight miles a day. Indeed, it was impossible to do more. Frequently I had to lay down by the side of the railroad and wait until a chill or a fever passed. Only those who have experienced the ravages of this disease know how I suffered under it, exposed as I was to rain and sunshine, heat and cold, to night air and cloudy days.

One day the ague came over me, as it was wont to do, so I laid down upon a plank beside the railroad. After "shaking" for over an hour, I fell asleep with one of my ears down upon the plank. Suddenly I heard a terrible crash as if the world were convulsed to its center. I was so paralyzed, I could have felt no worse if the train had run over me, and on rushed the "lightning express," shaking the earth beneath its ponderous weight. I did not lay down on a plank again.

One evening a boy invited me home. I accepted the invitation and followed him. Upon arriving, he told his mother he had a homeless boy. She treated me very kindly — gave me all I could eat and a good bed. I slept so soundly that I did not wake up until they came to the room to see what was the matter with me, and told me it was nine o'clock! I was surprised; it seemed as if I had slept only an hour.

At another time, as I was approaching a village, I felt the ague coming on, so upon arriving, I laid down upon the stoop of the depot. A railroad man coming along ordered me off. I replied that I had a "shake," and was unable to walk. The expression led him to inquire as to what I meant by having a "shake." I explained myself, and told him where I came from, and where I was going, that I had no money and was performing the journey on foot. He said a couple of freight trains were shortly due,

and, as it was getting dark, I could steal a ride by getting
on the " bumper " of a freight car. This filled my mind
with such hopes of soon putting an end to my struggles,
that upon the arrival of the first train, I hastened to take
my place on a bumper. Scarcely had I seated myself,
when the train backed up, and I barely escaped having my
legs crushed between the cars. At this instant the conductor came along, and seeing me, swore at me, telling me
to get off or he would " break my neck." The man who
had instructed me to get on, stepped up to the conductor
and told him my unhappy condition, upon which the conductor told me to get into the " way-car." Oh, how my
heart leaped for joy ! After the train had " started up,"
the conductor came to me and inquired farther into my
history. I repeated to him my story. His heart was
moved, and he bade me to lay aside all fear; he also divided
his supper with me. Oh, how grateful I was to him for
his kindness.

The next morning found us at Utica. The morning light
was fast dispelling the shades of night; and ere the train
started up again the sun had lifted his golden brow and
was flooding the world with his light. The grand old
Mohawk was never more calm than in that summer hour,
and in the quiet of that Sabbath morning. Leaving Utica,
we had proceeded but a short distance when the train was
brought to a halt by the breaking of an axle. After considerable delay the train again proceeded. About one
o'clock we reached Schenectady—only 16 miles from Albany
—and but 32 miles from dear old Stephentown. I now began to be very much excited. My heart beat with hopes.
Slowly the long freight-train held its way over the serpentine track which has some remarkable turns east of Schenectady. When within about eight miles of Albany my
eyes were permitted to behold the mountains of my own
dear home, rearing their lofty brows to the heavens, and at

their sight all the associations which clustered around memory were awakened.

We arrived at West Albany about four o'clock. From here, as the freight went no farther, I footed the remaining two miles. But language fails to describe my gratitude to that whole-hearted conductor. I thanked him over and over again. May heaven reward him for his kindness to a poor, helpless boy.

The following day, for three miles, I passed over the same road on foot and alone that I passed over with my parents when we first came to this country.

Here as I passed was the spot where we children sat down to rest our aching feet; yonder is the house where we took dinner: farther on is the place where stood the straw-stack just over the fence where I nearly perished one cold November night.

Three miles more, and I enter the beautiful village of West Sand Lake, nestling in a beautiful valley environed by hills. Time and again I have been to every house in this village asking for bread, and there are some noble-hearted people here. I pass through the village, and shortly came to East Sand Lake, and then to the village of Alps, and lastly, when the sun was yet an hour high, I arrived at West Stephentown. The journey was accomplished, though it required nearly two months and suffering untold in the performance of it.

O young reader, thank God that you are blessed with kind parents; love them, honor them, and may you never meet with such misfortunes, nor experience such sad hours!

The first place where I made myself known was at the home of my brother Peter. He was still living at the same place at which I left him upon my departure West. I appeared like one from the dead. I had been absent nearly a year, and I was so changed that they could hardly believe that the poor, dust-covered, care-worn, emaciated boy, was none other than John.

Ah! yes, it had been a hard year with me, and the recounting of my trials and sufferings brought tears to the eyes of all who listened to the story. After a few days' rest I went to work for a man.

Though I greatly desired to see my mother and the children, yet the fear of father, which overruled every other consideration, prevented me from going home.

CHAPTER X.

A Surprise—At Home—Reduced by Fever and Ague—
Fleeing for Life—Wandering—Sitting on a Stone by
the Roadside Weeping—Relief—A Good Home

The following Sabbath, with a joyous heart, I went to
the dear old Sabbath-school of which I had so long been
deprived, and for which I had so often longed. Oh, how
glad I was to again look upon the faces of the dear, good
people whom I had learned to love so much, and whose
kindness to me was cherished through all my wanderings.

It may seem almost incredible, but nevertheless it is true,
that I had not been to a Sabbath-school nor had I heard a
sermon preached during all the time I had spent abroad.
Hence this was one of the most refreshing Sabbaths of
my life.

Then the hearty welcomes I received on every hand, and
the friendly smiles, these were as a medicine to my desolate, aching heart. But all this was only a gleam of sunshine through the rifted cloud.

The news of my arrival, though I tried to keep it suppressed, had reached the ears of my father. Scarcely had
the sound of welcome died on the air, after the services of
the Sabbath, when, while on my way home, I was startled,
and terror caused me to tremble like a fawn, as father very
unexpectedly came upon me. The cold chills ran over me
as he said, "I have come to take you home." I now thought
I was doomed to go home and commence where I had left
off.

Upon arriving at home, mother met me at the door and was
very glad to see me. That evening I recounted all my

struggles to my mother. She was greatly affected. But I told her I was glad she was ignorant of my sufferings, as she could have rendered me no help. For a few days father treated me with great kindness. Mother did all in her power to break up the ague, but her labor was in vain. I was very feeble for the abuse on the way, the exposure to hunger, to damp night air, to rain storms, depression of mind, and the consuming fever, had reduced me to such a degree that my frail body was scarcely able to perform the functions of life.

I had hoped for the better, but father thought I ought to work, and I was willing to comply with his request.

The blackberries, which are very bountiful in this part of the country, were now ripening, so my little sister Mary and I went to pick berries. The heavy dews kept the bushes wet half of the forenoon, and in crowding through the brush to pick the berries I would get wet through, and remained in this condition until the sun dried my clothes. Getting wet so often augmented the disease under which I labored.

However, I struggled on without complaining, though many times I would be so exhausted that I had to sit down, My little sister, in her childlike simplicity, would remonstrate with me for not telling father that I was unable to work. I told the dear child it was of no use; I would do the best I could and leave the result with God. As a result, when night came I returned home with but little accomplished. This excited father, and he threatened to punish me if I did not accomplish more. I felt sad and discouraged, and resolved to run away.

I longed to unfold my purpose to mother, but dared not for fear she would not approve of it.

On a beautiful afternoon in October, when father was away, I carried out my purpose. Taking a farewell look at mother and Mary and the baby, which was innocently sleeping in the cradle and under the tender watch of little sister, I departed; they little thinking what a step I was taking, nor did I realize that I had looked upon mother for the last time.

O " sweet home," where are thy endearing ties for me? Slowly and reluctantly I turned away from the parental roof never again to be sought or visited. Gladly would I have remained, but I felt if I had I would only have sunken into an untimely and premature grave. Although there was nothing in this cold, friendless and dreary world which I craved, yet it is human to cling to life, and what little I had was dearer to me than any one else.

I was so weak that I had to stop and rest every half mile, yet I felt that in order to make sure my escape, I must get out of the neighborhood, and to that end put forth every exertion. I continued my journey for several days, when I commenced looking for a home. I kept up a good heart all the third day, though I met with no suc-cess. The fourth day I renewed my efforts. All day I traveled from place to place, but no one wanted a boy. It looked discouraging enough. I could not help but feel apprehensive. Perhaps it was because I was a run-a-way. It troubled me. It might be possible that I did not do right, and my failures might be visitations upon my way-ward course. At all events, I had a very heavy heart. The day was far spent. Meeting with no success, and being faint, I sat down on a large stone by the roadside. While resting, my mind wandered out over the past. I thought how I had now wandered about for three months, having not where to lay my head. All prospects of obtaining a home looked doubtful. With a troubled heart I looked forward to coming events. Perplexed and troubled in mind, and feeling my lonely condition, poor human nature could refrain no longer, and I gave vent to my sad feelings and desolate heart in tears. Would not some kind person have compassion on me and give me a home, or must I wander an exile from shore to shore in vain?

While thus lamenting, a gentleman passed along, and seeing me weep, halted and asked the cause of my tears. I told him I was a homeless boy; had wandered many miles, and that no one wanted me. He bade me in a gentle and sweet voice not to despair, and invited me home with him.

Upon arriving at his residence, the lady of the house offered me some supper. My heart was too full of grief to eat, and she seeing I ate nothing, asked if I was sick. I choked back my feelings and told her my great sorrow. Though I had eaten nothing all day, yet I was not hungry. I craved a home. As I saw those children in that home of plenty, beauty and comfort, sweetly loving each other, and so attentive to each other's wants, my lips quivered and my soul longed to be one of them. The lady seeing the tears, which I tried to choke back, stealing down my cheek, spoke kindly to me, and told me to be of good cheer, the good Lord would provide. These words were spoken in such a kind and motherly way that they entirely unmanned me, and I sobbed like a child. I could not help it. Oh, how lonely and forsaken I felt! Could it be possible I was abandoned? The whole family gathered around me and assured me they would aid me to a home.

In the meantime the gentleman had stepped out, and presently returned with the intelligence that he had found a good place for me. At once the sunshine beamed through my eyes and I quickly brushed away the tears, and hope and expectation took the place of depression and despondency. He told me to follow him and he would take me to the house. This I was glad to do, and, bowing to the good lady, followed him down the road to a farmhouse, where he introduced me to a pleasant-looking farmer and his amiable wife, These people were well, advanced in years, and I found them to be good-hearted, and they were very kind and good to me.

I shall never forget the first night spent with these people. I retired very early, and though I was tired, yet I could not sleep for a long time. There I was in a chamber all by myself, comfortably tucked up in a clean, fresh bed — a real luxury. Was it possible that I now had a home? I could hardly reconcile myself to the fact. How refreshing was the sleep of that night.

But I fail to describe the strangeness I felt to be once more in a home. Oh, how my heart leaped for gratitude! At last, after I had wandered from the middle of July to the first of October, after traveling fourteen hundred miles—from Albany, Wis., to the Wisconsin River, thence back, thence the long distance to Stephentown — thence hither and thither until within three miles of Nassau — had spent most of the nights sleeping in freight-cars, barns, and not a few times in the open air; had been exposed to the chilly night air, to cold rains, to exhaustive travels, to abuse from heartless railroad men, to hunger, to suffering by sickness and disease, after all these buffetings, at last I am in a home. Does the reader wonder at my appreciating its hallowed sweets?

I did not only have a home, but I found that I did not have to work very hard. Up to this time, I had been a slave to toil since landing on these shores. This seemed strange enough, and I hardly knew what to make of it. I had become so used to being kicked and pounded and shoved around that I thought I must receive such treatment as a matter of course. But it was so different here. Then again, I was spoken to in a kindly manner. This made me so grateful that I was constantly on the watch ts anticipate their wants. In short, it seemed as if I was living in a new world.

The good old lady was real motherly to me, and doctored me up, so I soon began to look and feel happy. The fever and ague which had clung to me all these months was broken up about the middle of November. The wound on my ankle also healed up, so I became active and full of life—a real boy—such as I had not been since the days of my happy home upon the Rhine.

There was a defect in the man of the house, a defect I had often seen in other men, and nearer the paternal roof, but my high regards, and my gratitude to these folks, forbids me to name it. God bless them! The name of the man was Richard Vanalstine. Some twenty copies of the CENSER go into the neighborhood where I then lived, and doubtless as the eyes fall on this part of my narrative many will remember the events here narrated.

It would appear, from a spelling-book purchased while living here, and which I retained until after I could write and had learned how time was reckoned, that the winter spent here was 1854–5, as I find that written in the book. It is from this date I have been able to establish the approximate year in which I was born, though I have not depended wholly upon it. But having faithfully compared it with others upon the books where my father had worked, I find they agree.

But I was not slow to show my gratitude for their acts of mercy toward me, for I was nimble on every errand.

Then the reader should have seen me coming out in my new suits of clothes. He would surely have thought I was somebody,—at least, I felt that way.

The richest of all was, there were two orchards upon the farm. Upon the mountain and out West they don't have orchards. But here were two, and, of course, I had all the apples I desired. Never, since the days of long-ago, having enjoyed such a luxury, it was sport for me to climb the trees and pick the great red apples.

But the golden autumn days, with their vernal sun, gentle rains, clear, crisp mornings, ripening nuts, falling leaves, rich, changeable landscapes, were crowning the year with their blessings. At no season of the year has the heart of man more reasons for joy and thanksgiving than when the bountiful fruitage of the year rewards the sower and the reaper alike, and makes the heart sing for joy for the mercies of that God who sent the sunshine, the showers and the winds, and who has caused the

> Valley and meadow, hillside and mountain,
> Dearth of the desert, wealth of the fountain

to fill the great granaries to overflowing.

Then the field, the smooth-cut meadow, the beautiful lawn, varied hill and dale, the forest grandeur, the woodland shadows, the murmuring brook, the sluggish river that

> Lulls itself to sleep,

all seem to " clap their hands " and " sing for joy."

The cheerful looks of the farmer, the quiet enjoyment in the domestic circle, the festive gatherings, " our young folks " with rosy cheeks and sparkling eyes, tell of plenty and of " good times."

The full-orbed moon lends her silvery light, as the well-shocked corn with golden ears affords pleasure to the busy huskers, while the aged sire exclaims :

> Come, my boys, come,
> And merrily shout your harvest home!

All these things I had the privilege and pleasure of experiencing in my beautiful home. Oh, such grand times as we had at husking-bees under the full-orbed moon, the gathering of the buckwheat, or the going to the village mill, or to the picnics in the groves, or the gathering of nuts, or rambles through meadows, by the sides of the streamlets or over the hills.

7

CHAPTER XI.

AT SCHOOL FOR THE FIRST TIME—TERRORS OF DISCOVERY—
FLEEING AGAIN—ON THE CANAL—STARVING IN BUFFALO
—ON THE LAKE—A WEARY JOURNEY—ANOTHER HOME
—BURNING THE BIBLE.

Full soon the vernal days of autumn gave place to cold frosts and rains, and tempests wild, which traversed mountain and plain, leaving the forests disrobed, and desolation in their track. But even the storm-king this winter had a grateful welcome, for I was comfortably sheltered, and the glow of the cheerful fire and genial rays of the evening lamp dispelled all the gloom, drove away every care, and my soul was filled with grateful thoughts to Almighty God.

But to crown the whole, when the district school opened, the good lady trimmed me up with another new suit of clothes, filled a neat little basket with a bountiful dinner and some of the red apples I had picked, and, with a smile, said she was going to send her boy to school. My heart leaped for joy and my eyes sparkled as I thought of the privilege.

A school-boy! Was it possible? There was no voice among that group of children as they wended their way to school on that clear November morning more merry than mine. At school everything was new to me. It was true I was a big dunce, but I had a disposition to learn, and took hold with a resolute will. The alphabet was all I remembered of my Sabbath-school instruction; hence I felt the importance of improving this my first opportunity at school. I studied very diligently, scarcely ever going out at recess or playing more than half an hour at noon. As a result, I made rapid progress—read in the third reader before I left school.

Late in the fall I sought and obtained permission to visit my brother Peter, to let him know of my whereabouts. I was careful to enter the neighborhood after nightfall to avoid being observed. From him I learned that a Mr. Turner (if memory serves me), had been to my father to have me bound out to him. Mr. Turner was a wagon manufacturer, and a fine Christian gentleman, and no doubt would have treated me well, for he greatly admired me for my industry, readiness to learn, and for my honesty and frankness. But I had such a horror of being bound out. I loved freedom. Give me freedom of soul and body, or give me death. So I hastened to his factory, and in excited language told him never to make another attempt to secure me by being bound over to him by my father, for he would not succeed; that he could not force me to live with him, and that I did not thank him for calling upon my father for the end of thus securing me. He looked greatly astonished at my sudden and unexpected appearance, and, doubtless, was equally astonished at my sudden departure, for, having finished my errand, I rushed out of his factory and disappeared, no one knew where save Peter, who would sooner die than reveal my whereabouts.

I returned to my place revolving the events in my mind. What if my retreat should be discovered?

The winter, however, wore away without further molestation, and the event had quite passed out of my mind, when, as I was returning from school one evening, I was overtaken by the same Mr. Turner. The cold chills ran over me, and I was horror-stricken at being discovered.

He stopped his team and talked a long time with me. He said I liked Stephentown and the Sabbath-school, and that he would send me to the day-school if I would come and live with him. But it was of no avail. I could not be persuaded to go with him. I dreaded being bound out. After he left me, I was exceedingly uncomfortable. I now feared that father would learn where I was. And what would he do to me—a run-a-way? I feared he would whip me within an inch of my life.

As I look over this part of my life from the standpoint of a maturer judgment, I think, had I accepted Mr. Turner's proposition, I would have received far better treatment than I received at the hands of brutal men. I had confidence in his integrity, and he would have given me every advantage possible to improve my mind; besides, he lived under the very shadow of the dear old meeting-house on the heights of West Stephentown. But there was that ever-present fear of falling into father's hands, which over-ruled every other consideration. And it was this fear which led me to take the steps I did.

Thus it was not for me to long enjoy the blessings of a good home. How could I bear the thought of leaving these good people? The very idea was crushing to me. It troubled me night and day. But the terrible news was broken to me at last, for one of Mrs. Wait's sons informed me that father had learned of my whereabouts and was coming after me.

Upon the announcement of this intelligence a tremor of fear came over me, and I thought father must be so enraged because I ran away from home that, should he be able to lay hands on me, he would punish me with greater severity than he had ever before, and I resolved, though I deeply regretted to give up my happy home, to try the fortunes of a homeless life, that I might not fall into the hands of an unrelenting father.

It was a severe struggle for me to give up my home and associations, and again try the realities of the wide world. However, it was in my mind to place myself beyond the reach of father; so I set off for the West again. Going to Albany, I sought a berth on a canal-boat as a driver, hoping by this means to earn enough to take me across the lakes.

This was the roughest place I ever was in. There was no regard for the Sabbath, nor sympathy for man or beast. And a boy had to fight his way. Sunshine or rain, cold or heat, I had to be on the tow-path, and not unfrequently was I knocked into the canal or down the embankment by drivers coming in the opposite direction, when right of " tight-rope" was questioned. The reader will understand that two boats meeting each other, it was the duty of one to drop the tow-line into the water, so that the boat could pass over the line, and this was done by slacking the speed of the team. When new boys—green hands—enter upon the tow-path, the experienced ones would often make them drop the line, when by the rules it was their own duty to drop the line.

The first day out it rained very hard, and there was not a dry thread on my person. I usually had to get up at 3 o'clock in the morning, and not unfrequently drive until 10 or 11 o'clock at night. I was so deprived of sleep that I could scarcely open my eyes when I was called in the morning. But whenever I failed to get up, a pail of cold water poured into my bunk, usually started me.

At several places along the route, I was urged into disgraceful fights, and usually came off worsted—I never made any claims to fighting—but here it was a necessity. Quite a number of times I was pitched into the canal, where I had to swim for very life. These abuses were practiced for the amusement of my superiors. Doubtless other boys met the same usage. Some looked even rougher than I did.

I drove from Albany to Hawkinsville, N. Y. I do not sufficiently remember the names of the branches of canals, after leaving the Erie, which was at Rome, N. Y., to give them. I made two trips from Hawkinsville to Utica, N. Y., and I must say that of all the mountainous country traveled by me, it was found about two days out from Rome in the direction of Hawkinsville.

I was to receive eight dollars a month. So, at Rome, the second time up, and after driving for two months and a half, I thought I had enough money to take me across the lakes, but great was my surprise when, upon asking the captain for my pay, he refused to give it to me, and I lost all. From Rome I drove on another boat to Buffalo, but received nothing for my services. Of all the places, the canal is the worst a boy can fall upon.

I should mention that on this trip my brother Peter accompanied me, as he firmly resolved to try his fortune with me, and he suffered the same as myself. We arrived at Buffalo early in the morning, but no boat for Detroit left Buffalo until 8 o'clock p. m. We had eight cents, which purchased one loaf of bread and three cookies. And these were to last us for that day and on the trip across the lake. We had been driving all night, and were hungry when discharged—and this without breakfast or our wages. Of the three cookies, I gave two to Peter and ate one myself, saving the loaf for the trip on lake Erie. Oh, what a long day it was! Peter cried for very hunger, and I could have done the same. While we were leaning up against a building, Peter's eyes red with weeping, an Irishman, passing by, asked what was the matter. I told him we were starving. Upon this he gave us five cents, and, after thanking him gratefully, I hastened to purchase a loaf of bread with it. And such a feast as we had ! We did not need any butter to make it go down.

At length the hour arrived. Nothing daunted, we went aboard a steamer bound for Detroit, purposed in mind to tell the man who collected the fare, that we had been wronged out of our wages; but to our astonishment, no one ever troubled us. From Detroit we set out on foot for Chicago. After leaving Detroit we sat by the side of the railroad, faint with hunger. But we resolved to beg. The first night we slept in a "water-tank." The next day we obtained a ride on a freight-train to Ann Arbor, Mich. In due time we arrived at Jackson, Mich. From here some kind conductor of a freight-train carried us to Marshall. Here, because we were found in the morning sleeping in an empty freight-car, we were locked into it and kept there till noon to the infinite amusement of heartless passers-by. Then we had long weary travels, arriving at Niles, Mich., about 4 o'clock on a Sabbath. Here a kind landlord—God bless him—gave us a bountiful supper. They must have excellent people in Niles. We have always remembered the kindness.

Somebody told us to get aboard the emigrant train which would be along in the night, and as it made long runs without stopping, we would be carried some distance before being put off. We followed out the suggestion. But, no sooner on board, than a sleeping Dutchman, arousing from his nap, grasped the little bundle from Peter's arms, which contained our united worldly goods, under the impression that it was his, and that we had stolen it from him. But, with true grit, Peter hung on. However, the Dutchman was stronger than us both, as I turned a helping hand when I saw our worldly effects in danger, and the handkerchief was torn to shreds, and its contents strewn over the car floor.

We were put off the train at some station the name of which I do not remember. At Michigan City, Ind., a kind lady gave us a bountiful supper. We traveled two days more on foot, when, from some way station, we obtained a ride to Chicago. Here, as everywhere else along the route, we made a freight-car our sleeping quarters.

From Chicago we rode to Turner's Junction, Ill., on the bumper of a rear car of a freight-train. From this place we footed it to Elgin. Here we spent half a day in resting, when, going to sleep in a freight-car, we woke up the next morning in Freeport, Ill. During the night I thought the car was in motion, but was so sleepy and tired that I did not realize it. It appears that a freight-train took the car during the night. As soon as we learned where we were, we left the railroad and went across the country in a northeasterly direction, and, after a long walk, we each of us found homes west of Magnolia, and about two miles southeast of Albany, Wis., and about four or five miles from my former home.

We had undergone such hardships that we were quite sick. Having so often been deprived of food and sleep, the return to civilized life was more than our enfeebled frames could stand. The feelings endured were something similar to those experienced by shipwreck. Our stomachs were not strong enough to take solid food. Neither we nor the people knew this, hence it went pretty hard with us. It seems that I was reduced the most, for I was subject to fearful vomitings for several days, and was deadly sick at my stomach. All this, I was told, was the result of being deprived of food. We suffered very much the whole journey for the want of food.

I do not know how long we were on this trip, but when we left the East it was shortly after the canal opened, and when we arrived here it was almost past harvest.

I cannot describe the sensations I experienced in the change—in having three meals a day and nights of undisturbed sleep. It was all so different from the canal-boat, the tow path, and the rumbling of railway trains.

But there was another chapter in human experience which I had not learned, nor did I ever dream of doing such things as I did while in this home. It turned out that these people were infidels, and they soon succeeded in shaming me out of my religious impressions, by ridiculing everything of a moral nature, and by encouraging me in all kinds of wickedness. The Sabbaths were spent in such amusements as the seasons offered. One Sunday a minister—and ministers I was especially instructed to hate—was on his way to some appointment, when, meeting me in the midst of my Sabbath-breaking, he stopped and talked with me a long time in regard to my wicked actions. I answered all of his questions in the most impudent manner possible. In conclusion, he said that bad boys always came to a bad end. I replied by asking him if it was any of his business if I did come to a bad end.

I have the pleasure of informing the reader that this very minister is now a subscriber to the GOLDEN CENSER, and has called upon me at the office. He also knows all about that part of my history narrated in chapters eight and nine. His name is J. J. Johnson, and he is a minister in the Church of the United Brethren, and lives at Eleroy, Ill., and he it is who requested Hon. J. H. Vinton, of Broadhead, Wis., to call on me.

I had become so imbued with the spirit of these folks, that I thought it was of no use to keep that Bible which the kind lady had presented to me at Sabbath-school, any longer—especially if it was full of lies—so I tore it in pieces, and was in the act of plunging it into the flames when a lady, seeing me in the desperate act, rushed up and wrested it from me. I was sincere in this act. I believed everything that was told me, and I thought I was doing right.

Oh, happy is the youth who has a kind father and a loving mother to shield him from the powers of infidelity and sin! Oh, how many poor, homeless boys are ruined for the want of proper influence and guidance.

CHAPTER XII.

Through Floods—Facing a Storm—A Good Lady—Another Home—Better Days—News of the Death of my Mother and Two Brothers.

But this was not a happy home for me. The man was so oppressive and unreasonable that I ran away. There having been much snow during the winter, the recent heavy rains had swollen the streams and flooded the prairies to such a degree that I found my flight almost impossible. Sometimes the roads were so filled with water that I had to walk fences, and where there were no fences, wade through ice-water knee-deep. But I was bound to make my escape, if I had to swim. Passing Broadhead, I wandered out on the prairie south, which at that time was almost uninhabited. There were no houses, nor fences, nor roads, and every now and then I had to wade through a flood of water. The sun going down, and the atmosphere becoming much colder, I became alarmed, for I was wet through, and my clothes began to freeze on my person. To the right the lowlands of Sugar River were a sea of ice and water. At length I saw a friendly light about four miles distant, and I resolved to make my way to it. After wading nearly half of the distance through water, I arrived, almost chilled with the cold and wet. The good people took me in, cared for me that night, and in the morning invited me to stay until the water receded.

After three days' delay I set out to find a new home. In the evening of that day I arrived in Beloit, weary, hungry and discouraged, for I had been unsuccessful that day.

The following morning, failing to find a home in Beloit, I wandered southward. The day was very uncomfortable, for there was a high southeast wind accompanied with snow and sleet, and the pelting snow beat into my face all day. In the course of time I arrived at Belvidere, and being tired, cold, wet, and hungry, I went into the depot to warm myself. While sitting by the stove, pensive and weary, a little boy came in, who, seeing how depressed I was, asked if I had a home. I replied that I was homeless. Upon this he invited me to accompany him to his house. When we arrived, he told his mother, Mrs. Raymond, that he found me at the depot weeping, and asked her if she would keep me for the night. She smiled and told me to come in. She was very kind and sympathetic; gave me a bountiful supper, and said she would find a home for me. The next day one of her sons, being a grain merchant, heard of a place two miles west of the city. He went with me to see the man. Mr. William Swardwood agreed to take me for one year, promising me seven dollars a month during the working months, and schooling during the winter.

The man with whom I went to live was a Methodist This was the first Christian family it had ever been my fortune to live with. The man, it is true, was one of those Christians who never read the Bible or prayed in his family; he had an excellent wife, however, who was a real mother to me. The man was firm, sometimes harsh. When he told me to do anything, I might just as well obey, for there were no "ifs" in the case. But, on the whole, I had as good a home as I could reasonably expect. As fast as I earned the means I clothed myself up and attended church and Sabbath-school regularly, and life began to present a more sunny side. Though I had to work hard—and this I was willing to do—yet the good lady treated me kindly, gave me right instructions, taking great pains in having me form correct habits, and keeping me neat and clean. She had

so far succeeded in restraining me in the use of profane
and vulgar language, and in instilling right principles into
my mind, that during the summer and autumn I attended
a young people's prayer-meeting, which had a wholesome
influence over me, and made a lasting impression for good.
Oh, how much I owe to this good woman in forming a
Christian character! She had unbounded confidence in
me, and whenever I did make a mistake, she always would
overlook it and kindly say, "Never mind it; we all make
mistakes."

My nature is such that harshness always repels me from
those who have exercised it over me, making me feel
depressed and gloomy, for I never cherished revenge, but
when one spoke kindly to me, then my heart would pulsate
warmly towards such, and my life was sunlight. Now this
good woman had the peculiar gift of appealing to my
heart—to my manhood. I was awkward and uncouth,
and yet she never magnified my faults, but always
set before me the good qualities. And this is the
secret spring of all good. I have somewhere read of a
criminal in prison being visited by one minister after
another, who came in all the Pharisaical dignity of their
office, and coldly talked *at* him, telling him what a great
sinner he was. But one day a minister called upon him
in whose very face love beamed, and in his tone sympathy
flowed, and instead of saying, "I am sorry to see you
here," opened his conversation by saying, "What a mercy
it is that *we* poor sinners are on mercy's side of the
grave." This entered the heart of the poor heart-broken
prisoner. Here was one man—a minister, who confessed
himself a sinner, and the chord of sympathy was struck,
and the heart opened its door. It is this kind, gentle
spirit that won me from my infidel notions. Ah, noble
reader, learn a lesson in this. God knows we all have our
burdens of sorrow to bear, and a smile, a kind word, a bow,

a look of recognition, an act of mercy, may save a soul from giving up in the struggle of life. Let us cultivate sympathy, for it is one of the noblest and most God-like emotions, or as we may say, qualities, of the heart. It is a fountain in the soul, jetting forth those sprays of love for our fallen race, that makes green the valleys of earth, and causes the barren desert to bloom. There is a power in sympathy which will move the iron heart when all other instrumentalities fail. It melts down the frigid icebergs that are found along the voyage of life. You may reason with fallen and depraved man, and show to a demonstration that he is a sinner, yet his heart will be as unyielding as a rock, and your arguments be wasted on the desert air. But go to him with your heart swelling and all aglow with tender sympathy, and enter into his fallen condition; sympathize with him as an eternity-bound brother; plead with him in kind, loving words, and in nine cases out of ten you will break up the fountains of his very being and win him to Christ.

This trait was very largely developed in the life of our Savior. ·Behold him feeding the starving thousands, healing the sick, restoring the blind, giving life to the dead; in short, his almost every act was pervaded with sympathy. Some think it unmanly to weep, but the weeping Christian has this consolation, that it is Christ-like. Behold, as Jesus stands at the grave of Lazarus, his great heart throbbing with emotion and the pearly tears falling from his eyes to the ground. Does he weep for the bereft sisters? Not altogether that, certainly, for he was about to restore to them their dear brother. His tears flowed in behalf of the blind and bigoted Jews who had assembled there. His heart was moved in sympathy for those to whom he would gladly have given life eternal.

Who can ever forget the tears and sympathetic words of a kind, praying mother? The grass may be green over her lonely grave in the churchyard; flowers may have bloomed and withered with the coming and waning years upon her resting-place, but her influence will never die, her prayers never be lost, her sympathetic and noble counsel never fade from the memory. Oh, precious sympathy; how it sustains the burdened soul and helps to build up a pure and holy life.

Sympathy, like every other emotion of the heart, can be cultivated, and the objects of its exercise are manifold. Go where you will, and you can perform the kindly office of the good Samaritan. The child of poverty claims your kindness, the unfortunate and friendless your love, the fallen and disgraced your forgiving look; in short, bleeding humanity as it passes onward to the yawning grave, in piteous agony extends to you a cry for sympathy. A symathizing heart is the secret power of all successful philanthropists, and ministers of the gospel especially should cultivate it, and seek to infuse its spirit into the people among whom they live and labor.

Sympathy is permanent as well as salutary in its effect. The lofty mountains may decay, the flinty granite dissolve, the mighty ocean ascend the sky in vapor, or the earth pass away like a phantom, yet the influence which sympathy exerts over immortal souls will be eternal. Its beneficial effects will reach into the coming world, and those who were drawn up out of the haunts of vice and the pit of destruction will make the heavens vocal with thanksgiving and praise to the King of Glory.

Seek, then, gentle reader, this gracious emotion of the heart, and let its light shine out in your life. Go, in the spirit of Jesus, like an angel of mercy to those who crave your love; kiss away the falling tear from sorrow's cheek, and angels will record your noble deeds in the Lamb's Book of Life, and the dear sympathizing Savior himself will welcome you to the "evergreen shores"—the home of the redeemed.

Surrounded with these hallowed and restraining influences, the summer and autumn days passed quietly and pleasantly away. Winter again returning, I was permitted to go to school once more. Here I learned to write, and as soon as I felt competent enough to write a letter, I did so, writing it to my dear good friend, Mrs. Laura H. Wait, West Stephentown, N. Y. In due time it brought a response. But oh! how sad the intelligence, for it announced the death of my dear mother, the sweet baby which sister Mary was so tenderly tending on that afternoon on which I left home, and my youngest brother Joseph, a boy of but four or five summers. Oh, how heavily the sad news sank into my poor heart! For the first time had the grim messenger of death entered our family circle, and in that visit, selected three of the fairest flowers and transplanted them to the evergreen shore—in the paradise of immortality. What a strange feeling came over me! Was it possible that I should never, oh, never see my dear mother again? Oh, could I only have received her dying blessing; could I have felt her loving hand upon my head, and heard her encouraging me to look toward that home to which she was going; could I only have been permitted to plant the flowers of springtime over her grave, it were well! Alas! even these were denied me. On the mountain, where the winds weep through the hemlock and the pine, are three grass-covered graves, and the golden leaves of each returning autumn fall noiselessly over them, and the rain, falling on the crisp foliage, sighs a mournful story how she died of a broken heart; how she wept over her children and would not be comforted because they were not; how neglect and cruelty had laid in the cold chambers of death her two latest born. Oh, sigh on, ye

wild winds of the mountain! Eternity can only reveal what
it does not become me to write here.

I was so overcome that I could not study, for as often as
the thought recurred to my mind I would burst into a flood
of tears. All was dark and lonely, and in this sad hour I
could not "refrain my voice from weeping." I could not
play with the other children at recess, nor eat my dinners,
for the merry laugh and innocent glee of the school-
room only added sadness to my sorrowing heart.

The bitter sorrows, heartaches, sighings to look upon the
sweet face of mother once more, led me to think of heaven
and heavenly associations; of that realm of light where is
known no sorrow, nor death, nor night; of that beautiful
city, home of the angels, abode of God, whose streets only
by the sinless are trod. Truly my life had been one of
tears, but now my light had suddenly gone out, and it was
dark—oh, so dark! The weary traveler up life's steep and
rugged mountain, covered with sweat and dust, thirsting
and hungering, his eyes often suffused with tears, and his
body racked with pain and suffering, is wont to imagine
whether there is anything better beyond, and as the dashing of the river at the boundary of the land falls upon his
ear he anxiously inquires, How will it be beyond the river?
Is there no better land beyond yon swelling stream? Oh,
is there truly a rest remaining for the good in the long,
long forever? When I pass across the mist that rises from
the river, shall I rest where there is sunshine without a
shadow, employment without fatigue, perpetual youth without old age, and joy without a tear? Tell me, inhabitants
of eternity who have dwelt near the great white throne for
ages past, ye white-winged angels that never sinned, is
there rest for the weary in the land beyond the blue? Do
they live forever on your side of the river? Are the
inhabitants never sick, but always happy there? The
answer comes back from one of the elders: There is no

night here. No sun lights on the inhabitants here; and they hunger no more, neither thirst any more, "for the Lamb which is in the midst of the throne shall feed them, and shall lead them unto living fountains of water: and God shall wipe away all tears from their eyes."

> "The world above is not like this—
> So dark, so sad, and drear; ·
> Oh, no, for there the years of bliss
> Roll on without a tear."

A land without a tear, exempt from causes of sorrow, and without want, every desire perfectly filled, infinitely supplied, is a thought full of richest consolation and joy to the tired and foot-sore traveler in life. To him

> "Sweet fields beyond the swelling flood
> Stand dressed in living green."

And his heart and his treasures are there. He looks up with joy and sings as he trudges on toward the river, "There's a better day coming," and " I soon shall be done with darkness forever. There remains for me light and pleasure without ceasing when I get home. And home is not afar off; I soon shall be there."

In heaven are no such scenes, heart-aching, heart-lacerating. Death dispeoples none of its mansions, diminishes none of its loving groups, robes in mourning none of its inmates. In that world the shroud, the undertaker, the hearse, the sad procession, the cemetery are unknown. What a world, without graves, funerals, tolling-bells, obituaries, records of mortality—how different from this! There is eternal life. Connections there, friendships there, are inseparable. Not a ligament which there binds heart to heart shall ever be ruptured, ever weakened.

This life is a repetition, in some form, of griefs and troubles. Like the waves of the ocean, they follow one

8

another with only brief intervals. Tears repressed to-day burst their confines to-morrow. But when we reach that heavenly rest, our struggles, and perils, and sorrows are ended. Oh, for more frequent and sweet, refreshing views of that blissful land where all tears of affliction shall be wiped away!

How true it is that God's people, however dear to him as elected, redeemed, regenerated, adopted as heirs, educated, provided for, preserved, are not in this life exempted from personal troubles. "Many are the afflictions of the righteous." "Through much tribulation" they "enter into the kingdom of God." But, blessed thought! "There is no more curse. And there shall be no night there; and they need no candle, neither light of the sun; for the Lord God giveth them light, and they shall reign forever and ever." Light springs up in the grave, and tears are wiped from their faces with the thought that there is a better land over the way, and that they soon shall rest there, safe at home.

What a thought! A land without a cloud, and without a tear; life without a pain, and no death-step upon its track. To drink with ravishing joys immortal pleasure, with wings to transport through all the works of God and look into the mystery of eternity, with all its unseen wonders and pleasures, will be quite enough for the soul all saved, and the body all purified during endless years.

Thank God for a home beyond the river for all the good and pure. May we all pass the river in triumph, and rest forever in the home of the soul "over there," where

> They roam through the gardens of endless spring,
> They crowd all thy portals on rushing wing;
> While the echoing domes of the palace ring
> With the hymns of the angels that shout and sing.
>
> The life-fires brighten and burn and roll
> Over diamonds that sparkle, o'er sands of gold,
> Where to breathe the sweet air yields a bliss untold,
> And the dwellers immortal shall never grow old.

I have heard in the city they wait for me;
That its gates stand open wide and free,
That the ransomed the King in his beauty may see,
And live in his presence eternally.
       Beautiful city!
In royal state blest mansions wait,
And beckon on through the pearly gate.

I shall go where the summers will always bloom;
I shall walk no more amid trial and gloom;
I shall bid farewell to the withering tombs;
I shall deck my brow with the conqueror's plumes.
       Beautiful city!
Let me enter in a crown to win!
Our words but half tell of the glory within

CHAPTER XIII.

In Rockford the First Time—A Mean Man—Swindled out of my Wages—Discouraged—Seeking Another Home—Better Results—A Good Old Man—Living in a Universalist Family—On the Farm—A New Experience—Bad Luck—On the Farm again—Another Misfortune—Weeping for very Sympathy, and there was None to Pity.

I was now a motherless boy, far from her final resting-place, and more than ever did I feel that I was abandoned and alone in the world. Added to this there were unanticipated trials before me, for, about two weeks after receiving the intelligence of my mother's death, the school closed, and the man with whom I lived, not wishing to hire me another year, told me to find another place. I would fain have remained, but could not help it; go I must.

This was March 1; 1858, and a bitter cold day it was. I requested Mr. Swartwood, as there were yet twenty dollars due, to pay me. He said he could not as he had no money with him. Once more I must go out into the cold and friendless world, the very thought of which crushed me. As I traveled over the prairies looking for a home the northern blasts almost lifted me from the ground. All day I looked in vain. In the evening I arrived in Rockford, cold, tired, hungry, and discouraged.

Having no money, I asked at private residences the privilege of staying for the night, but being refused I was about giving up in despair when I found a place in the south-western part of the city, west of Winnebago street and

south of the railroad. But the wife and the children
—two in number—were sick. I did not discover this at
first. Being too bashful to back out, I accepted the situation. It being past supper-time, and I being too bashful
to ask, went without anything to eat. When bed-time
arrived, to my discomfiture I learned that I would have to
sleep in the same bed with the sick children. I was distressed. I did not know what to do, for I was now without
a home, without friends, and without money, and I thought,
should I contract some disease it would go hard with me.
So I made believe that I wanted to go out, and taking my
comforter and hat started for the door. Once out, I started
for parts unknown. Just then I heard the night train approaching the city, and the thought flashed into my mind
that I would go to Belvidere, so I started full speed for
the depot and for the train. This was my first entrance
to Rockford, my present home.

When the conductor came around I told him my circumstances, but he did not believe me, and took my comforter
from off my neck, and ordered me to get off at the next
station. This I did, and footed it from Cherry Valley to
Belvidere in the bitter coldness of that night, and was almost frozen. Arriving at the station, I sat up in the engine-
house the remainder of the night. Being faint with hunger and tired by the toil of the day, and as I sat there all
alone, the past—which ever haunted me—with its sorrows
brooded over my mind, and with deep sighs I thought of
the unjust act of the man who professed to be a Christian,
in turning me away without a cent of my wages to help
myself with. Alas! where is there any confidence, when
those who profess to be Christ's turn me from their door,
with not even the means to buy a meal to satisfy hunger?
Let those refrain from weeping who never had a want nor
knew a tear; but upon that dismal night, while the wild
tempest made a sad, mournful noise as it swept around the

building and piled the drifting snow against the window, I wept as only a child of misfortune is compelled to, and felt that there were neither any good nor justice in the world, and longed to be at rest in the eternal sleep of death, where sorrow, cold, hunger, and the vicissitudes of life are unknown.

But the morning dawned at length, and I continued my efforts to find work, and succeeded in finding a place near Genoa, DeKalb County, with a Mr. Ira Ketchum.

This time I fell into a "cod-fish" aristocratic family— the meanest and most overbearing class of beings God ever suffered to live. They treated me more like a dog than a human being. But I performed my tasks, endured their haughty insults, and lived a miserable and unhappy life, and was only too glad when my time expired. But, to my astonishment, Mr. Ketchum heaped insult upon injury by giving me a worthless note. Gathering up what little of this world I had, I sought me another home.

The morning of my departure was a lovely one. The birds, the grassy plains, the lowing herds, the leafy groves, the balmy atmosphere, the smiling sun, in short, all nature seemed to chant a joyful song to the Author of the universe. Upon the zephyrs floated the sweetest fragrance of prairie flowers. All around me seemed to be gladness and song—a strange contrast with my own sad heart. It was the month of roses, June, the loveliest of the year, combining in it the freshness of spring and the gladsomeness of the summer hour, when bright skies and soft air cause nature to fully awaken to new life, beauty, and joy. Earth's emerald carpet was begemmed with richest and most lovely flowers. As I walked along the meadow-path, for I preferred the company of the singing-birds, flitting from fence to branch, and from branch to heaven, to the faces of men which I might meet every few minutes on the highway; I preferred to be fanned by the gentle breezes redolent with the fragrance of blossoms, to the dust and the rumbling of wagons. Ah, my sad heart wanted to be left alone to commune with nature and to drink in its health-giving power. The freshness of this morning was unusual, and the sights and sounds. beguiling; only a few white clouds like hills of silver rising from an azure plain are piled against the deep blue sky. The bright beams of the golden orb of day penetrate each spot of the new-born earth, bathing it in a new flood of glory.

The sparkling stream and the mountain-born rivulet flow melodiously along o'er many lovely spots, and at the musical whisper of the breeze the smiling and honey-laden flowers bow their fragrant heads, and softly kiss the murmuring waters as they behold their beauty reflected in the mirror-like stream. As a cheerful, smiling face always carries a charm wherever it goes, and makes around itself a light that clears the clouded brow, and sparkles in the dull and listless eye; so the cup of joy, borne on by laughing Summer overflows upon all animated beings. How gladly the birds chirp and sing and dance on the budding trees! The song of each happy warbler is full of praise and thanksgiving to God. Kind Summer, how I love thy golden hours, for thy gentle hand has strewn the wild flowers like radiant pearls upon the grass, that they may kiss our feet, look lovingly into our faces, and scent our path with a rich perfume! The wild flowers are scattered in rich boundless profusion and infinite variety. Peace, harmony and beauty dwell among them as they nestle lovingly side by side on the far-extending plains. The bee, as it hums its summer songs, flies from one flower to another to extract their sweetness; and the cheerful child treads them inadvertently beneath his feet, plucks them with his tiny fingers and weaves them into the sweetest posy for his mother. At least, thus was it with me, when other happier years were mine, and in glee I roamed the valleys of another and milder clime.

But the remembrance of these things only seemed to
mock me. And as I raised my eyes and looked over the
undulating prairies waving with golden grain, I wondered
if it would be always thus with me, whether my efforts to
gain an honest living by hard industry would long continue
to be frustrated.

But I had to look me up another home, which I did, and
went to work again for Mr. John Mordoff, three miles west
of Belvidere. This gentleman treated me kindly, and paid
me every cent he agreed to.

The winter of 1859 was now fast approaching, and I
found an excellent home with a good old gentleman, Mr.
Cornelius Vandebourgh, Kingston, Ills., who sent me to
school, first at Kingston, and then at Sycamore.

While attending school at the former place, we were required to write a composition to be read before the school
by two young ladies. I had never written anything except
one letter, and my skill with the pen was not very great.
However, I made the attempt, doing the best I knew how.
But my composition was so poorly written that it did not
bear reading before the school. Some young ladies, who
had been to school all their lives, learning of the facts in
the case, composed essays in which they ridiculed me for
my ignorance by all kinds of funny expressions. These
they read before the school, which excited laughter at my
expense. This cut me to the very quick. I bowed my
head, buried it in my hands upon the desk, and wept. It so
discouraged me that I could not gain confidence enough to
try again during the term, but my soul was set on fire with
indignation, and I longed and hoped to see the day when
I should have as much knowledge as my lady friends (?)
possessed.

Here was the grand turning-point of my life. Up to
this time I had lived recreant to moral conviction of sin;
though I can say with all sincerity that I never took

pleasure in wanton vice. My heart was always tender and I could never treat harshly anything that had life, but inclined toward the noble, the beautiful, the lovely, often retiring to pray to God to guide me; yet I had never openly confessed Jesus as the sinner's friend; feeling that I had no claim on the merits of the all-cleansing blood of the Redeemer of the world.

The Rev. Thos. R. Satterfield was holding a protracted meeting in Kingston, and the truth was brought home to my heart with such force that I thought myself to be a great sinner. For some time my mind was sad and gloomy. One evening as I was returning from the meeting, I felt so depressed in mind that I kneeled down beside the fence and plead with God for Jesus' sake to forgive my sins. All at once a great weight was lifted from my heart. Calm as a peaceful river were my thoughts, and my spirit breathed as it were in a new atmosphere. Truly I found Jesus precious to my soul.

I was regular in attendance upon all means of grace, and rapidly grew in spiritual strength.

The school closing in February, the man thought I ought to attend until Spring, so he procured me a place with Mr. Arnold Brown, Sycamore, where I went to school for two months. The family in which I lived were most excellent people, but they being Universalist in belief, and I an Orthodox convert, they puzzled me many times, for I could not reconcile their interpretation of the Scripture with mine, as I had been taught under the preaching of Mr. Satterfield. This set me thinking, for it was now manifest that there were two sides to understanding the Bible, and I could not tell which was the right side, so I determined to investigate the matter for myself. Eagerly I read everything in my reach, and my mind for a long time was alternating between faith in Christ as the Savior, and open infidelity. The struggle was a hard one, but I resolved to cling to my faith in Jesus until I could clear up the other side so that conscience could be reconciled.

Spring now returning, I again went to work. I had now learned to read, and to comprehend what I read, and was anxious to cultivate my mind. The man with whom I now lived looked with contempt upon literature, and was stoutly opposed to my reading. Of course I never thought of taking the time which belonged to him, and told him if I worked sixteen hours each day for him, he ought not to begrudge me one hour out of the remaining eight, and if I felt like reading, that was my affair. But he was one of those kind of men who thought that "larnin' spil'd pe'ple." However, the horses at noon had to have time to eat, and as I could eat a little quicker than they, I would take my book and sit in the manger and read. I chose this place so I would not have my mind so absorbed in reading as to forget myself, for the moment they were done, I went to work again. The man seeing I was bound to read, told me to cut wood while the horses were eating. Refusing to comply with this unreasonable request, he was offended and drew the cords of severity so tightly that they snapped. I told him he was not the only man in the world, and all I wanted of him was my wages, and he might do his own work. He refused to pay me, so I told him if his heart was so hard, mean and stingy as to cheat a poor boy out of his twice-earned wages, he could keep them. And I left him.

While on my way to Belvidere, I fell in with a curious genius. He said he made five dollars a day in selling medicines, and wanted to know if I did not want to go into the business. I told him I would try it. So he fitted me out with a basket full of medicines. The following morning I started bright and early, with fond expectation of soon realizing a fortune. From house to house I went offering my curatives, but the people were all well and did

not want the medicines. I persevered until in the afternoon, when, becoming hungry, tired and discouraged, I
came to the conclusion, inasmuch as I had not sold a cent's
worth, that it was not a very money-making business, so
I took out my bottles and smashed them, medicine and
all, against a rail fence, sold my basket to an Irishwoman
for a meal, and went to work again.

Again I found me a place. As fate would have it, this
was another Universalist family. But the man did not
trouble me much, as he did not have much religion himself, even such as he professed. Patiently I toiled through
the summer's sultry hours, in hopes of earning money
enough to buy me some clothes, as I was now very destitute. When my time expired, I went to Mr. Taylor for
my wages. Alas! was it possible! Again I was the victim
of misplaced confidence. Oh, it seemed so hard to have
heartless men wrong me time and again out of my hard-
earned wages! What could I do? There was no one to
defend or protect me. In despair and anguish of soul I
sat down by the roadside and cried like a child. Oh, how
bitter the cup so often pressed to my lips! But I could
not live on tears or sighs, so I had to go to work again.
Discouraged to work by the month, I obtained such
employment as I could, and thus earned means to buy
clothes.

Passing through Kingston, an old neighbor was about
to clean his well, and wanted me to go down into it. I
did so. After taking out some eight feet of sand and
mud, while a large stone was being elevated, the chain
around it began to slip when about thirty feet above my
head, and on looking up I saw the stone giving way. My
hair stood on end. Oh! what shall I do, or where can I
escape? One moment more and the stone would crush
me beneath its weight. Calmly as I could I awaited the
issue. Those above me strained every nerve to reach the

stone, and succeeded just as it was in the act of falling. The reader may be assured I drew a long breath.

For four days' services in the well I asked four dollars, and obtained two. After cleaning two more, receiving nothing for one, and only fifty cents for the other, I concluded that my health was of more value to me than their wells, and refused to go into more.

During the remainder of the season I worked for Mr. Foster, of North Kingston, Ill., for my board and school

CHAPTER XIV.

SCHOOL DAYS — OFF FOR OBERLIN, O. — A SAD DISAP-
POINTMENT — IN CLEVELAND — ON A FARM AGAIN —
INJURED FEELINGS VINDICATED — ON THE WAY TO
ILLINOIS—CHANGE OF OCCUPATION.

This winter I studied very diligently. The people seeing I had a mind to learn, and that I was devoted and
earnest as a Christian, suggested to me the propriety of
preparing for the ministry. I replied that I had often
thought of it and that I· would gladly go anywhere the
good Lord directed, but I had given up all hopes of ever
attaining such a position, as I had no money to get an
education with, nor would be likely to have any if I met
with no better success in the future than I had in the
past. In conversation with a neighbor upon this subject
I was informed that there was a school in Oberlin, Ohio
where, by working three hours every day, I could work
my way through college. I received this information with
gladness; and at once made preparation to go, for I
thought this was a grand opening for me. No sooner
had the school closed than I set out for Oberlin with
hopes of a bright and glorious future burning brightly in
my bosom, for the store-house of knowledge with all its
mine of wealth would now be unlocked and its rich
treasures placed within my grasp; in brief, I was going to
have the longings of my whole being satisfied, if energy
and study could do it.

Oberlin had been pictured in· my mind as a lovely,
sunny village, renowned for its classical lore.

The second night after my departure was tempestuous,

and the storm-clouds hung frowningly in the sky of the approaching morning. As the train neared Oberlin I was all excited and noted every object of interest. Upon arriving, the morning was dark, cold, and rainy. With quick step and hopeful heart I hastened to the school in high expectation of being soon initiated into its duties.

But, oh! how bitter the disappointment when with a heavy heart I learned that it had been misrepresented to me, and that nothing could be done for me other than that I could go out into the forests and cut wood for three shillings a cord, and thus earn money to pay my expenses.

The following morning I left Oberlin amid rain and snow, and pressed my way on foot to Eleria, at which place I went to nearly every house and asked for a home where I could work for my board and go to school, but no one wanted me. Having tried in vain, and as night was fast approaching, I made an effort to procure a place for the night, but, as it was in times of old, "they began to make excuses," saying that they had sickness in the family, and therefore could not keep strangers. Having been out in the rain all day, my clothes were wet through, and the weather changing, it was so cold that they began to freeze on me. Being faint with hunger, weary by my fruitless efforts, and discouraged, I sat down by the side of the swiftly rushing stream to drown my sorrow. All pensive, my heart burst forth into weeping. While thus mingling my tears with the waters of the brook, a man passing along the street noticed me, and coming up, asked why I was there weeping. I replied that I had not a cent of money, that I had no friends, that no one would give me anything to eat or keep me for the night, that I was tired, hungry, wet and almost chilled, and did not know what to do or where to go. Upon this he gave me twenty-five cents and took me to a hotel where I was kindly provided for. I very gratefully thanked the noble gentleman for his generosity.

The next morning I left Eleria very much refreshed and feeling that there were some wayside angels in life's thorny pathway. May God bless them. But, oh! how **meager** is charity when disrobed of the praise of society. On to Cleveland I pressed my way for the purpose of renewing my efforts to find a place to go to school. Toward evening I again made application to stay all night, and found a good place. They were so kind and gentle that I sighed and longed to live with them. Upon arriving at Cleveland, I made another fruitless effort.

After leaving Oberlin and while footing it the eight miles to Eleria in the rain and mud of February, I revolved many things in my mind. I thought of the past, and how I had been wronged out of my wages. Oh, how could I think of going to work on a farm under such discouragements? What could I do? This I purposed to do: I would first try to obtain a place and go to school. If I failed in that, then I would try to learn a trade. Then the question arose, what trade would be best for me? I ran over in my mind the merits and demerits of the various trades. I wanted something that would satisfy this long ing after knowledge. I must have an education or die in the attempt. And what would help me to obtain this desire of my life? All at once it flashed into my mind to learn the printer's trade. But, as above observed, there was no place for me at either going to school or learning the selected trade. What could I do? The way was hedged up. Disheartened, I retreated as far as Berea, and on the Monday following sought employment again on the farm. Wandering out into Columbia township, I found a place with Mr. Brunson and went to work.

Well, here I am on a farm again. Wonder what success I will have this time? Though I had become discouraged in working on a farm, yet necessity compelled me to. At all events it afforded me a home, and I went to work with a good will, trusting in God and making the best of my position I could. I found it here as I had in some other places—grinding the most possible work out of a poor boy for the least amount of money. I had to get up at four o'clock in the morning, and often work until nine in the evening. I endured this unceasing toil until July, when I was taken sick. I asked the man for my wages, telling him that I was unable to endure such hard toil. Looking frowningly and contemptuously upon me, he replied that I would have to wait his convenience. Just my luck again! Sadly I left him exulting over his victory.

Passing along the road, a young man, who had been witness to my slavish life, asked me if I had received my pay. I replied that I had not. He then pressed me to sue Mr. Brunson, and thus collect my pay. I told him I had never done such a thing in my life, and did not know how to proceed. He replied, "You pitch into him, and I will back you up; get out a warrant, and a writ for me and one for neighbor Snell; we will see that you will have justice done you, for he has made it a practice for years to go to Cleveland and get some ignorant foreigners to work for him, whom he would grind down with labor until they would leave him, as you have done, and then refuse to pay them." I followed the suggestion of my friend; went to the justice of the peace and stated my case. The justice said I must first choose a guardian—as I was under age—and then he would give me the proper papers. Mr. Brunson, to the great amusement of the whole neighborhood, was brought to terms, and had to pay every cent.

While living with this Mr. Brunson my mind had become discouraged, and my heart ached for something better. Like a bird in its cage, it fluttered for liberty. The world looked empty enough to me. This state of things led me

to contemplate the home in heaven. My mind dwelt so
much upon that theme that often while in the field, away
from mortal eyes, I would stop my team and up upon
my knees in the furrow, and pray to Almighty God to pity
me and to help me. Then the good angels—for so I called
the sweet and heavenly thoughts which filled my soul—
would drive away all my sadness and longing. How many
times I thought my sainted mother stood before me and,
with that sad, sweet look in her face, would say, " Be of
good cheer, my boy, the future will bring brighter days."
The meetings, too, gave me much comfort. Oh, what
powerful prayer-meetings we used to have in the little
meeting-house standing on the bank of the river in the
suburbs of the village of Olmstead! What mighty men
of God used to pray in the prayer-circles! Those Ohio
people really had the kind of religion that suited me.

My faithful attendance upon all means of grace, and the
secret, prayerful reading of my Bible, I think, were the only
things that kept me from giving up in despair, and plunging
headlong into vice and ruin. I would read and re-read the
story of those worthies in sacred history until my own
heart seemed touched with a live coal from off God's altar.
To my mind there was something so grand, so God-like,
in the actions of these moral heroes. Amid my discouragements and my tears I sought to write upon my own heart
the actions and lives of those Hebrew worthies who even
dared to go down into the heated furnace of affliction. You
remember it pleased Nebuchadnezzar to set up a golden
image in the plain of Dura, and he bade all nations and
people assemble to witness its dedication. The historian
tells us that thirty-six nations were there represented, and
it would seem that none of that vast concourse, save three,
questioned the propriety of bowing down to the golden
image. It is so easy to go with the multitude. Men
sometimes even now make a similar mistake. Look upon

9

that plain filled with devoted subjects prostrating themselves at the sound of musical instruments and the cry of
the herds.   Ah, Shadrach, Meshech, and Abednego, do
ye well to stand up boldly before the God of heaven in the
face of this multitude and under the consequences of the
royal decree?   Noble youths!

Mark the modest and calm reply to the king's question-
ings: " If it be so, our God will deliver us from the burning fiery furnace, but if not, *be it known unto thee, O king,
that we will not serve thy gods nor worship the golden
image which thou hast set up.*"   Did mortals ever utter
burning, living words that conveyed more resolute determination to do right though the heavens fall?   It is true
that these words brought upon them the displeasure of that
wicked monarch, and they were ruthlessly thrust into the
fiery furnace, but in the midst of the flames the form of
the fourth appears!   Well might that heathen king, as he
looked down into the glowing lake of living fire, turn back
pale and exclaim: "Did not we cast three men bound into
the midst of the fire?   Lo, I see four men loose, walking
in the midst of the fire, and the form of the fourth is *like
unto the Son of God.*"   Yes, when God sends his angels,
earth and hell shall not prevail against us.   To the admiration of all that assemblage of people, these three noble
youths came forth from the flames with not even the smell
of fire upon their persons.   When God delivers there is
no mistaking—it is signal and complete.

Notice the unassuming modesty, yet firm confidence of
these youths.   Their determination to be true to God did
not relieve them from the fiery furnace, but once in it, God
was with them.   So it may be with us.   To have God with
us we must go down into the furnace of affliction.   There
is no great sorrow but good will come out of it.   When it
it is dark—very dark—the stars shine all the more brightly
above us.   When the storm sweeps over us, then in the

dark storm-cloud appears the beautiful rainbow of safety and peace. After the winter come the gentle showers, springing grass, bursting buds, and the unfolding flowers, and we say, "How delightful is spring!" Oh, ye aching, longing hearts, in the furnace of affliction, can ye not see the form of the Fourth?

Again, it could not have been a very agreeable or a very pleasing thought for those youths to contemplate as they saw the soldiers preparing the fiery furnace. The thought must cut them to the heart, but they stood the test How men dislike to have their hearts probed where the deepest sin is lodged! The besetting sin is about the last one acknowledged; that is the one most unwillingly submitted to the Healer for treatment. It is easy to indulge in virtuous indignation against sins which are loathsome to the sight. It is easy to berate the drunkard, or to cudgel the prostrate wretch whom everybody cuffs and kicks. It is fashionable to hate the abandoned. But when it comes to looking home—to taking measurements of our own inclinations and impulses—to analyzing the sin that approaches ourselves, then the question takes on a new and terrible significance. The insinuating evil that approaches us dressed in the garb of expediency, recommended by some plausible circumstances, is the peril which must be felt to be escaped. It is easy to keep out of the range of other men's sin, to stand clear of certain crushing crimes which scathe the moral nature; but to stand guard over one's own tendencies, to fortify the soul against the silent and secret attacks of the tempter—this requires the grace of God and the soul's best courage for ever. Unless the heart be fully consecrated to the Savior, and all the impulses and influences of the life controlled by the Spirit, a mere profession of religion is nothing more than a bandage for a whithered hand, or a sling for a helpless arm. No, no, mere heartless profession is an insult to the Al-

mighty.   He wants men who will stand the test—who
hesitate not to go down into the furnace.

Then there is another significance to this furnace trial.
All valuable jewels have to stand the test of fire.   Indeed,
the more precious and valuable, the severer the tests.
All know this, how the refiner sits by the fire to watch the
transforming process.   And then these jewels as they come
from the furnace are made very desirable.   It is said that
the white topaz of Portugal has an untold value.   Philip
of Spain bought a gem worth fifteen thousand ducats, and
Leo kept a pearl valued at eighty thousand crowns; but
God's jewels are worth more than these.   The plainest gem
in his casket costs more than they all, for it cost the blood
of his Son.   But the price was paid, the covenant sealed,
and " they shall be mine, saith the Lord of hosts."   Who
can even compute the moral worth of those brave youths!
Ah, they were a thousand times more valuable than fine
gold!   Oh, if we only had such brave young men to-day—
young men who would stand up in the face of every opposition and stem the tides of sin.   Had we such moral
heroes in every department of life, in less than ten years
we would bring a conquered world and lay it at the feet of
Jesus.   He that hath God on his side, though single-handed
and alone, is always in the majority.

But there is the furnace.   How men will shrink from
it.   Yet in the furnace is the test.   The Pharisees and
hypocrites will not be likely to venture in.   However,
every jewel in the casket of God must be genuine.   Imi-
tation stones and paste diamonds may deceive the eye of
man until they are *tested;* so a firm creed and studied art
may pass for loyalty to God until it is touched by the magic
fires of persecution.   The diamond must be cut and polished before its worth is known; the chrysolite and topaz
must be passed through the fire before they get their luster;
the dark spots in the amethyst must be cleared away in

the flames. And so of God's jewels. "I have chosen thee in the furnace of affliction." His diamonds are ground and finished by suffering; his gems are cleared of flaws in the fires of persecution. The purest stones, if not cut and polished, are unfit for the Master's use. Never was Christian hope so strong that it suffered not by worldly honors; and never Christian faith so firm that it faltered not in the hour of success.

But when the morning is gone and the night has come, the fires of faith are re-kindled. When earthly hopes are stricken down like stars from the sky, we cast ourselves upon the anchor that never fails the tempest-tossed heart. When friends forget their vows, and the mountains and islands of human trust are moved from their places, we remember him who hath said: "I will never leave thee nor forsake thee."

Every Christian virtue gleams, like the chrysolite, more brightly in the flames of affliction. Every loyal friend of God is as firm in the hour of affliction as the diamond in the hand of the lapidary. Every crystal tear from his children is a pearl in God's casket. Every loyal, suffering heart is a gem in his coronet.

"They shall be *mine*, saith the Lord of hosts." Earth may hold them now; persecution may fling her poisoned arrows, temptation may assail and disease may waste,—yea death may even hold them,—but in that grand, triumphant morning when he maketh up his jewels, every star and every gem shall gleam in the crown of the King. None are forgotten, for he who seeketh them cannot fail in his search. They come from the burning sands of the south and the ice-bound hills of the north. The forgotten graves of forest wild and mountain height shall break before the eye of the King and yield his jewels up. His voice shall cleave the ocean walls of pearl and sapphire with the cry, "Give up the dead," and then

Death's reign on sea and land is o'er,
God's treasured dust he must restore,
God's buried gems he holds no more
Beneath the wave or clod.

The world has seen the crowns of her petty princes and tyrant kings, but she shall yet witness a coronation of which her princes have never dreamed—a glory they have never sought. The music shall be the glad songs of the redeemed of every nation, kindred and tongue. The crown jewels are they that have passed through the furnace of affliction to gleam in the kingdom of God, and behold, he who weareth the crown is *"King of kings and Lord of lords."*

Ah, my young reader, it was such reflections as these that fired my heart to endure the furnace, to prove myself a hero, even amid the obscurity of a farm life. Like the bird in its cage, my nobler feelings and aspirations were fettered. I was down in the furnace, but God sat as the refiner. Oh, blessed thought! Oh, precious hope. Is there one who may read these pages that has had a similar experience? If so, God bless you. Be brave. Dare to do right. Dare to be true. Behold the form of the Fourth is in the midst of the furnace with thee, "and the form of the fourth is like unto the Son of God."

It has been expressed to me that it was a wonder I did not give up, and say it was of no use. With such thoughts in my heart how could I? Would it be the part of wisdom, that because I was frail in body, poor and discarded, and because heartless men oppressed me in my helplessness, that therefore I should blacken my soul with sin, or stain these longings of my being with crime? Did I thus read my Bible? Had I not seen its terrible fruits in all its naked deformity? And was not the sight enough to cause me to loathe it with all the intensity of my nature?

Oh, young men, you who may chance to read these lines.

Stop a moment and reflect. Do these thoughts meet your approval? If so, then amid the darkest hours of your life hang on to your manhood, and, God's word for it, you will not be abandoned by Him who was touched by a sense of our infirmities. Would that I had the gift of language and the flow of thought, to inspire you to noble action, to a proper sense of the grandeur of your own being, and the grand possibilities before you. Let us arise in the strength of these God-given powers, and bless the world by the noble impulses that throb through our very being.

But I was in the furnace. Perhaps I did not behave as heroically as did those noble youths on the plains of Dura. And perhaps I ought not to relate my actions here. But I give them as they took place, and would not recommend them to others. I lived up to the light I had, and can only add that it may serve to illustrate human nature under trying circumstances, and seemingly insurmountable obstacles.

This Mr. Brunson was decidedly opposed to reading. But read I must or die. Despite of the sixteen hours of work which I had to daily perform, I took time—yes, I took it from my sleep—to read. And to give the young reader an idea, I will give the items as I find them for that year.

I commenced work on the 3d of March — had many cold days accompanied with snow and raw winds from the north. I have a poor opportunity for self-culture, as Mr. Brunson believes the more ignorant a man is the more work he will do. This holds good so far as brute force goes, but I can not subscribe to the belief. Give me intelligence. However, I found time to read "Christ and the Apostles," 1,250 pages; "Indian Wars," 400 pages; a medical work, 200 pages; "Fifty Years in Chains," 500 pages; some three hundred pages in Fox's Book of Martyrs, and the Cleveland Weekly *Leader*, which I read upon my knees while

the old man Brunson performed the morning devotional
exercises.   This may seem irreverent in me, but I take no
stock in the old man's prayers, as his soul would not cover
the point of a needle.   The old lady also mistrusted that I
burned more of her tallow candle than I ought to, just to
go to bed with, but I took good care to keep my books out
of sight.

But they purposed to put a stop to this reading business by pressing me more hours into work, and, as the
rye is just ready to cut, the old man expects me to keep
up in binding.   This I can readily do, as the grain stands
good and tall on the ground.   The first day the old man
sweat and tugged away to get the start of me, but I kept
up.   About 4 o'clock he "bushed" and set me to "shocking" while he went to the house.

But on the next day came sweet revenge.   He went into
a piece of oats on a side-hill.   It was very short and I had
to "pull my bands," and often, after I had bound a bundle
it would "quash out" and fall to pieces because the grain
stalks were so short.   As a result, the old gentleman
cradled away from me with ease, to my great discomfiture,
as I was ambitious to keep up.   This afforded him sweet
revenge for yesterday's vexation, and, because I had been
guilty of reading against his expressed command.   So
every time he cradled a swath, he would urge me to greater
diligence in the most imperious and aggravating manner
possible.   I tried hard to keep up, but in vain.   I worked
patiently, and without replying to his oft-repeated urgings
until about 11 o'clock, when, disheartened and vexed beyond
endurance by reason of the fruitless efforts to bind the
grain and by the un-called-for urgings of the old man, my
soul was set on fire with indignation, the hot blood mounted
into my face, I threw down the rake with such violence as
to break it into many pieces, and turned to the old man
and told him he could bind his own grain, and left the

field. He was astonished and confounded at my daring
to do such an act. But he saw that I meant what I
said, and began to apologize, and to call to me to return.
I turned -around, and firmly told him he did not have
money enough to hire me for another hour, that he was
not worthy of my service, that I would see him and his
crops perish, and then I would not help him. He then
replied that if I left him in harvest-time, he would not pay
me. To this I rejoined that if he was so contemptibly
mean and his soul so little as to cheat me out of my wages,
he might keep them, that he was not able to employ me
longer, that no decent man could treat a brute as he had
treated me. Upon this he tamed down, and said he would
use me better if I only stayed. But I was firm, went to
the house, took my things and left, and obtained my pay,
too, as before related.

But then I did not regard it as a victory. It cost me
over a month's wages to go through the process of choosing a guardian. I would never of my own accord have
appealed to the law. It is my nature to suffer and to forgive. I envy not the selfish man—of all men he is the
rather to be pitied. This man could have paid without
trouble. He was rich and I was poor, but he was as selfish as
he was rich. And what a miserable depravity selfishness is.
It can see nothing but its own good. The man who is ruled
by it is a miserable slave. He does not seem to comprehend that the All-wise Father, who sitteth in the circle of
the heaven, did not make the beautiful world, and fill it
with the sources of exquisite enjoyment, and arch it over
with the blue sky and bright sun, solely for the selfish
man; yet he acts as though every water privilege ought to
turn his wheel—every wind be fair for his ship—every
shower invigorate his crop, and every enterprise enrich his
coffers. He cares not who starves if he fares sumptuously
every day. He cares not who sleeps on the unsheltered

highway, so long as he has a home. Gold is a god, and he
will have gold, if he has to coin it from the blood of his
fellow-men. He will spoil the harvest in breweries and
distilleries, and then ruin his fellow-men in taverns and
hotels, in order to gain gold.

I hardly know what to do. I was sick at heart. It
seemed to me that there was nothing good or true in the
world. I worked a short time in the neighborhood, by the
day, and then concluded to return to Illinois. So I went
on foot to Afton, where I took the cars for the West.
There were some very beautiful towns and cities on the
way, which, perhaps, are too well known for me to describe
here. Norwalk, Toledo, Adrian and South Bend especially, attracted my attention as very handsomely built
cities.

As I was walking along the streets of Chicago, going
from one depot to another, and, while opposite the door of
a saloon, of a sudden I heard a crash, and the next moment a poor fellow lay bleeding at my feet—he had been
pitched out head first upon the pavement. There he lay,
helpless as a child. If it would have done any good, I
could have cried for him, for he looked as if he was a victim, from some happy home—made drunk, robbed of his
money, and then thrust out. What an unenviable position
the saloon-keeper occupies—a more pitiful, a more unworthy, more degraded, and more sinful position cannot be
conceived! To prey upon the shame, the crime, the poverty, the body, the soul, the time, the eternity, of a fellow-
creature, is awful! To prepare the way of bankruptcy,
pauperism, disease, prison, death, is not to be coveted! To
assist to ruin character, murder reputation, sink position
and circumstances, filch a man's crumb of bread, is odi-
ous. To beggar families, break the hearts of wives, scatter
domestic firebrands and death, break up happy homes,
divide united hearts, dissolve family links of the closest

tie, is a baseness indescribable. To rise into riches by such a course is not to be rich; to be honored is to be dishonored; to gain place in the world is to have no dignity; to stand forth in the cause of religion is to daub Zion's walls with untempered mortar. To swell out in portly dimensions, by the sale of strong drink is the price of poverty; to rise into luxury is a gain from wretchedness; to walk abroad in ease is a purchase from perspiration and toil; to assume high airs, and gad about all bespangled and bejeweled, is an elevation wrung from shame, degradation, misery and death. How infatuated must the drinker be to a class of men rolling in every comfort and luxury, possessing wealth and property, and all purchased at the poor infatuated inebriate's expense. The saloon-keeper well clothed, while he is in rags; the saloon-keeper's wife jeweled, but the poor drunkard's not where to lay her head; the saloon-keeper's children clothed, fed, educated, head and feet preserved from the inclemencies of the season; but mark his customers, cold, starved, ragged, wet, diseased. What a difference between the state of those that support and those that are supported by strong drink! Surely, if reflection was left in the drunkard's mind, the sketch I have just given would banish forever the drinker from the saloon.

Arriving at Kingston, I worked through the remainder of the harvest by the day, and in the autumn again went to live with Mr. Vandebourgh.

While here, I learned that Mr. J. R. Howlett, editor of the *Lane Leader*, wanted an apprentice. Having had so many reverses, I now felt that I could do no worse than I had done; besides, learning to be a printer would almost be as good as a school, and what I stored away in my mind no man could take from me.

Reasoning thus with myself, I resolved to go and learn the printer's trade.

Accordingly, on the 16th of September, 1860, I set out for Lane—now Rochelle—full of hopes for better days and a brighter future. On, over the undulating prairies, the iron horse held its course.

This step was truly a marked one, changing as it did, all my plans and purposes. It was more an act of desperation than of deliberation and forethought. I must confess I had my doubts and fears. I was troubled in mind. I was out on the ocean of life all alone. No one to guide my mind or give me the counsel I so much craved. I had faith in God, yet like the disciples of old I did not fully understand its nature. The apostle declares that "faith is the substance of things hoped for, the evidence of things not seen," and in this declaration I could see, as in a mirror, my whole past life. Amid all my misfortunes, I always hoped for something better in the future. And in this event I hoped that my life would not be a failure.

CHAPTER XV.

A Printer's Devil — Studying—A Fire—Another Fire —A Man Hung—A Dark Day— On the Way to Rockford — The First Night in my Future Home Passed in a Freight-car — A New Place — Incidents —War Times—In Camp—Soldier Life—Dark Days —A Misfortune.

No sooner had the train halted at the station, in Rochelle, than I alighted and sought the office. Mr. Howlett received me kindly and set me to work in the office. I was highly pleased with my new occupation. How different life seemed to me. Instead of being compelled to work from fourteen to sixteen hours each day out in the heat and cold, sunshine and rain, I had to work only ten. What a grand opportunity for self culture! Truly a new era had dawned upon my life; and I felt that a kind Providence had opened a way for me to gratify my eager desire to study; nor did I undervalue or slight these privileges. And I did not only have the evenings and mornings to myself, but occasionally spare hours; all of which I prized. Ah! how I loved those winter hours, when, with some good book, I sat by the cheerful fire, while the tempest wild traversed mountain and plain, and dismal night winds and drifting snow sighed in the barren branches.

The editor, finding me so anxious to read, threw open his library; and I had a feast of good things. So eager was I to improve the golden moments, that I constructed a little shelf on the wall close by where I worked, on which I had a book, and I was found reading when a leisure moment presented itself. And roller-boys in a printing office have many such moments. Volume after volume was thus read.

While Rochelle was a lovely village, and many good people lived in it, yet the gate-ways to hell stood open on every street-corner, and poor whisky often made night fearful. Being in such a public place, and noticed by all for my quiet, thoughtful turn, and withal, fearless in my religious convictions, I was subjected to many taunts and sneers. Nor could my infidel opponents get much the advantage of me; for while their breath was fragrant with bad whisky, mine was fresh with the contents of many a volume. As a result they watched me from every street corner, if possible to lead me into temptation. But I resisted with an iron resolution.

As a new mode of attack, some would come to the prayer-meeting for the purpose of picking up some of my remarks, and then, when they met or saw me on the street, they would sing out, "There goes the pious devil;" and then would repeat in taunting ways some expression they heard me use in meeting.

While here I was sexton of the church of which Rev. Calvin Brookins was pastor; so one night I was suddenly awakened by the cry of "Fire! fire!" and a terrible rattling at my door. As I had the keys to the only church in town which contained a bell, I sprang out of bed and hastened to ring the alarm. There was a strong wind, and the fire-demon, in about three hours, laid eleven stores in ashes. This was a severe blow to our village.

The following June we were again visited by a conflagration, sweeping away four grain warehouses, and leaving 40,000 bushels of grain in ashes. The next morning after the fire, men could be seen hastening along the street, wringing their hands and exclaiming in bitter anguish, " I am a ruined man!"

Shortly after, a man by the name of Burk was suspected, and one dark, dismal morning was taken into an upper room, and, ere 1 o'clock, was hanging, a corpse, from the third story window. Oh, what an hour this was in my experience! It would be vain to describe my feelings as I attempted to gaze upon the aged, gray-haired man struggling between life and death. The day was dark and gloomy. Storm clouds chased each other athwart the sky, and anon poured out upon the earth torrents of rain, accompanied by thunder and lightning. All nature seemed draped in mourning. As the man was being thrust out of the window, a chain of lightning flashed across the lurid sky, and shone on the ghastly form, and a peal of thunder shook the crowded hall as if the Almighty had frowned on a deed so dark. The vast assembly swayed to and fro like a reed in the wind, panic stricken at the work of their own hands. At sundown the corpse was conveyed in a pine box, and this in an old lumber wagon, to its final resting place. Thus ended the most tragic and fearful day of my life.

As usual, my mind was busy with the true causes of such an act. The man, beyond a doubt, committed a great crime and brought distress to many homes, and also did those commit sin who took the law into their own hands. Sin expresses it. How short the word. Only three little letters; and yet in that one brief syllable are compressed all the woes of earth, all the agonies of perdition. Sin—all the crimes and follies, the wrongs and miseries of six thousand years of human history epitomized. Sin—three tiny clicking types express it. But how gigantic, how fearful a monster! Sin—black with countless millions of horrors, and red with oceans of gore. On all God's beautiful earth there is not a spot unpolluted by its hideous footprints. On land or sea, from pole to pole, there's not a breeze whose wings are not laden with its poisonous breath. Sin—where has it not entered? It crept into heaven in ambitious guise. Its baleful whispers were heard amid the fragrant bowers of Paradise. It bathed the hands of earth's first-born son in fratricidal blood. It rolled the destroying billows of the deluge over a world steeped in its wickedness. It reared and razed the proud battlements of Babylon and Nineveh. It has poured out enough human blood to fill the ocean's mighty reservoirs, and float all the navies in creation. It has wrung from anguished eyes tears enough to feed all the rivers and lakes on our planet. It has extorted every groan and sigh that ever pierced the pitying ear of Omniscience. It has inspired all the Neros, Herods, Caligulas, Napoleons, and Quantrells. It has swept with carnage-crimsoned, desolating tread beneath the banner of Cæsar and Tamerlane. It has brought down fire from heaven·upon Sodom and Gomorrah and Jerusalem. Beneath the aged olives of Gethsemane it crushed the gentle spirit of the Son of God. What wonder is it that God hates sin, or that men sometimes shudder at the acts of their own hands? And in this is the solution why that crowded hall of human beings turned ghastly pale and their hearts were terror-stricken.

But it was now midsummer, and I wanted to make a visit among my old associates and friends at Kingston. My employer readily granted my request.

Accordingly, having perfected my arrangements, I set out to visit Kingston. Taking the night train, I arrived at DeKalb Center about midnight. The air was so bland and the heavens above me so lovely, that I purposed walking over to Kingston, a distance of twelve miles, the after part of this night, for I loved to meditate in the quiet hours when the world is hushed in silence.

God has created us rational, intelligent beings. He has

endowed us with powers of perception. He has imprinted upon our souls the love of the beautiful. He bids us to drink deep of the manifold displays of His wisdom. On every hand may be seen the hand-writing of Omnipotent power, and we lose much of the real enjoyment of life, if we never step out into the grand temple of nature and "consider"—study—our Creator's beneficence, not only in the grandeur of the lofty cedars of Lebanon and the trees of the forest "clapping their hands for joy," but in the "lilies of the valley." Often, when my soul was with anguish riven, have I found a sweet solace, a heavenly balm, by plucking some wayside flower and admiring its beauty, its loveliness, its fragrance, until my heart seemed to forget all its ills.

Passing through the slumbering village, I hastened along the country road until, all absorbed in admiration, I gazed upon the vernal fields, foliaged groves, waving grain. The moon shone upon meadow and fields and woodlands, with her mild, soft, silvery light. The bright, twinkling stars, golden gems on night's blue page, looked so fair and pleasing that I exclaimed, "How wonderful, O God, are thy works!" It was a fitting hour for meditation. I raised my eyes heavenward, and beholding the display of infinite goodness, I thought of the welcome time when the blessed Savior shall come again in his own glory, accompanied by the angels, and with a voice that shall wake the sleeping nations, bid the weary pilgrims of earth throw off their mortality and rise into newness of eternal life. Oh, welcomed time, when, disrobed of mortality, we shall be transported beyond the sorrows of life to the fair Eden of immortality, where the throne of God and of the Lamb is established on the ages of eternity! Oh, the rapturous gaze, as we shall for the first time behold the angels and just men made perfect, the crystal fountains and the sea of glass, the river of life rolling down its golden sands, the ambrosial fruits upon its vernal banks, the emerald fields, and the tree whose fruit shall be for the healing of the nations! There we shall live in eternal youth. No malady of earth shall fade or mar our beauty! On angel wing, with the speed of the swiftly-rushing wind, we shall take our flight to those worlds that shine so lovely upon me to-night, and explore their continents, look upon and admire their lofty mountains, extensive rivers, deep-foliaged forests, wide oceans, inland seas, fertile plains, and converse with their inhabitants, who, perhaps, never passed the fiery ordeal of sin; and after spending a million of years—if time in that better land is measured by years—we shall return to the Father, our hearts filled with wonder and joy, and, casting our crowns at the feet of Him who is worthy to receive honor and power and dominion, we shall exclaim, "O God, how manifold are thy works, and thy wisdom and goodness passeth knowledge!" While thus meditating, " Aurora, leaving the saffron bed of Tithonus, first spread the earth over with early light," painting on the morning sky such hues as no artist can paint, striking with her golden tinsel the stars from the azure sky; then awoke the feathered tribes, and made the heavens vocal with their oratorio; whilst forth from the gates of the east issued the orb of day. I arrived at my destination well repaid for my night's adventure.

In August, 1861, Mr. Howlett sold his office and set up a saloon, to try his fortune in dealing out poor liquor to depraved appetites instead of sound truths to the minds and hearts of men. I felt very bad over this change, as Mr. Howlett was an excellent man, and was worthy of a better business. Being thrown out of my situation, I came to Rockford—making the distance on foot under an August sun. I arrived about 8 o'clock in the evening. This time I asked for no accommodation, but passed the first night in a freight car. Thus I passed the first night in the city of my future home and the home of the CENSER, in a, freight-car, having nothing but a small bundle for a pillow, and the car floor for my bed.

The next day I applied at every office in the city for work, but without success. At last I resolved to work for my board, and my services were accepted by the Blaisdells, of the *Republican*. But this was not the place of my choice, yet I made the best of my circumstances possible. The first night in my new quarters I had to spend in a saloon with the roughs until midnight, when I had to carry telegrams for the paper until one o'clock, and at last about four o'clock in the morning, was shown to a miserable apology for a bed—it was not as inviting as the car floor bed of the previous night.

I will here observe that the reason why I sat in the saloon was that I was anxious to hold my situation and wanted to be on hand when the foreman—who spent the evening there—saw proper to send me for the night dispatches. Both the language and the silly card playing were repulsive to my nature, and as for the liquor, I would no more have been persuaded to drink, than to destroy my own life. Whatever failures in life I might make, I purposed never to become a drunkard. This resolution I observed with such firmness that I allowed myself to drink nothing but cold water summer or winter through all the years of my apprenticeship and school-days.

But my stay with the Blaisdells was only for three days, at the end of which time I found another situation, and continued my apprenticeship under the instruction of E. C. Daugherty, editor of the *Register*. Mr. Daugherty was a Christian gentleman, a member of the M. E. Church, and his office was a desirable place in which to work—it being the largest establishment in the city. Upon the whole, my opportunities and advantages for becoming a thorough printer were much better than at Rochelle. I

was also highly pleased with the city, for I found it not
only beautifully situated on both banks of Rock River,
with wide and handsomely shaded streets, but it was a city
of churches—of which there were fifteen.   It also contained many beautiful buildings, both public and private.
The industry, enterprise and intelligence of the people
was also marked.   In such a home as this, the reader may
well be assured, I improved both my time and opportunities.   All my leisure hours were occupied in pursuing my
studies.   While here I had access to the city library, and
while other youths spent their time and money in visiting
saloons, smoking cigars, attending shows and having a
good time generally, I was in my room storing my mind
with useful knowledge.   I would very often be so absorbed in the contents of a book as to study past midnight.
I read the histories of Greece, of Rome, of Germany, of
France, of England; I read Josephus, histories of the
Oriental cities; works on philosophy, astronomy and the
sciences; biographies of eminent men in the past and
present.   These were my pastimes.   Indeed, I had a book
in my hand from the time that I entered the house until I
left it, and I never went to any place unless to meeting
or to hear some lecture; hence I was comparatively very
little known.

I have often wondered as I look back on the mine of
wealth and real enjoyment there is in perusing the histories of other times, and living as it were in the golden
ages of the past, how people possessed of a sound mind
and right reason could fritter away the precious moments
of life in reading shallow and sickening tales.   Could I
but persuade our youth, who are fast growing up into
manhood and womanhood, to choose wisdom's part, I
would feel amply rewarded for this faithful admonition.   I
am pained to see so many of our young folks giving themselves up to light, trashy reading; spending the golden

moments of early life in perverting their tastes, weakening their mental powers, unfitting themselves for solid, substantial reading, exciting a morbid sensation—feeding their immortal souls on the vain and empty imagery of some love-sick, brainless, dissipated maniac, who might do a better service to his generation by going to work and in earning an honest living.

Oh! Christian fathers and mothers, let "eternal vigilance," be written in flaming letters over the tender years of your dear children!

I do not know where the notion first obtained that life now, to be tolerable, must be spiced with condiments of the keenest and most titillating sort. Each fresh gratification quickly palls, and new devices must constantly be brought forward to stimulate the jaded sense. The theater is radiant with voluptuous images, and thousands swarm nightly to gloat on the female charms their clouds of gauze scarcely affect to conceal. Gross pictures are hawked about the streets, and obscene books are offered to boys and grey-beards alike, in the exchange and market-place. The newspapers strain every nerve to outstrip each other in the astonishing, the preposterous, and the extravagant; and those from whose occasional exhibition of care, thought, and scholarship we have learned to hope better things, seem of late to have abandoned themselves to the worst spirit of the hour and to have plunged bodily into the coarse vortex of sensation. Even the pulpit in some localities yields to the vulgar tendencies that mar nearly all the sacred things, and some of the most influential and successful preachers, who, in a purer and more cultivated age would be simply laughed down as greedy and sensual charlatans, are producing in every direction their legitimate effect. We see on every hand false views of life usually ending in bitter disappointment, minds and bodies prematurely broken and withered.

Perhaps I went to the other extreme, but if I did it was because I felt the need of informing my mind. I don't know how I appeared to the young people, or in what estimation they held me, for, during a two years' stay I was only found at one church sociable, and then I came across one of Prof. Upham's works, and was so charmed with the contents of the book, that I sat down and became oblivious to all around me until people began to go home. And, while the young men went home with their "girls," I obtained permission and went home with the book.

It may not be out of place to state that few discovered that I was a self-educated boy. I overheard people several times saying that I was remarkably well-informed. Indeed, more than once did I write compositions for scholars in the high school who passed them off as their own. This was not honest in them, nor perhaps in me to write them, but I obtained the training, and had the benefit of whatever criticisms the principal of the school saw proper to pass upon the compositions, and I was not slow to profit by them.

Permit me to add here, lest I be misunderstood, that I cannot justify the above. It was dishonest, though at that time I had no particular conscience in the matter. To every young reader we would say, Be yourself, write your own compositions, be natural, act yourself, do not pretend to be smarter than you really are, for then will there be a chance for improvement. A lazy boy or girl will never make a bright scholar. For to be a scholar requires long application, patient study, and unflinching determination to succeed.

I do not know what unconscious impressions I was making upon the young people at that time, for it is well known by those who are most intimately acquainted with me that I am very cheerful in spirits, jovial in conversation, and often have a real unbending time in social chats;

fancy then, how surprised I was when a young lady asked me, since my return from college, if I "was as sour as I used to be?"

While I believe with all my heart in sterling piety, and in a proper deportment before the world, yet I have no sympathy with hypocritical canting. What! the gospel gloomy, its fruits sour? It cannot be. It is an anthem from the harps of heaven; the music of the river of life washing its shores on high, and pouring in cascades upon the earth. Not so cheerful was the song of the morning stars, nor shout of the sons of God so joyful. Gushing from the fountains of eternal harmony, it was first heard on earth in a low tone of solemn gladness, uttered in Eden by the Lord God himself. This gave the keynote of the gospel song. Patriarchs caught it up and taught it to the generations following. It breathed from the harp of the psalmist, and rang like a clarion from tower and mountain top as prophets proclaimed the year of jubilee. Fresh notes from heaven have enriched the harmony, as the Lord of hosts and his angels have revealed new promises, and called on the suffering children of Zion to be joyful in their King. From bondage and exile, from dens and caves, from bloody fields, and fiery stakes, and peaceful deathbeds, have they answered in tones which have cheered the disconsolate, and made oppressors shake upon their thrones; while sun and moon, and all the stars of night, stormy wind fulfilling his word, the roaring sea and the fullness thereof, mountains and hills, fruitful fields, and all the trees of the wood, have rejoiced before the Lord, and the coming of his Anointed, for the redemption of his people and the glory of his holy name. When the glad tidings of salvation have thus rendered universal creation joyful, the gospel of peace can never make any one sour, but it does make one calm and hopeful.

A young man living in a city without the gentle restraints of the home circle, is necessarily exposed to many temptations and allurements of the devil. Though, perhaps, I was not so sorely tempted as many are, because I did not put myself in the way of the tempter, yet I had to resist him sometimes, for he would unbidden throw himself in my way. I will only give one or two illustrations, and pass:

One beautiful evening in June, as I was walking down Court street, I met two young ladies, one of whom with a smile said, "Oh, Mr. Lemley! we are so glad to see you, we seldom see you on the streets. It's such a warm evening, do come with us down to the saloon and have a dish of ice cream!"

I replied, "I would be much pleased to accept your invitation, but as I never visit saloons, I cannot comply with your wishes. I am on my way to prayer-meeting, and would be pleased to have your company thither." They turned and left me.

Upon another time, as I was on my way to hear a lecture, a young man rushed up and accosted me as follows :

"How in the d——l do you make out to keep cool on such a hot evening as this ?"

I replied, "Be patient and I will give you the secret."

"Be patient !" he shouted, "how can any one be patient when their insides are melting ?" Thus saying, he took me by the arm, and dragging me towards a saloon, continued, "Come, let's take something to drink, I be d——d if I'm not burning up alive."

"Keep cool," I kindly replied, "down yonder is Rock River. I will watch for signs of fire, and if you should ignite, with your permission I will plunge you into it, only do not go near a saloon to-night."

"Oh, excuse me!" he exclaimed, "I forgot that you are a deacon; but suppose you stir up your spirits by taking a 'horn;' your a d——n good fellow; the only fault you have is your old fogyism."

Of course I stoutly refused, and went to the lecture, while my friend stopped at the saloon, as have thousands of youths, to get cool.

But the summer was a wonderfully lively one. From the hills and from the plains, from palace hall and cottage home, the nation's noblest boys were falling into line and marching to bloody fields of battle. As Rockford was one of the headquarters for this section of country, all this summer and autumn the marching of troops, the rattle of drums, the display of flags, kept up a continual excitement. In those dark, terrible days of war, when the nation was wrapped in mourning, and so many homes were made desolate; when from the Rocky Mountain's eastern slope to the Potomac's swiftly-flowing stream, God's green fields were black with battle smoke; when rivers ran red with the blood of slaughtered thousands; when the earth drank in life's crimson current, it would hardly be in keeping with the purpose of this narrative to enter into the account of the many thrilling scenes which were constantly being enacted all over the land. In passing, I can only add that our city sent many brave soldiers to the field, and frequently was it called upon to pay its last tributes of respect to its fallen heroes.

Times change, and boys during the days of war sprung up, like Jonah's gourd, in a night to full manhood. At least so it seemed. For I was astonished when I learned that Warren Wait, one of my playmates in my mountain home, had become a soldier, marched to the front, was taken prisoner, and was now in Camp Douglas, Chicago. Upon learning this I hastened to see him. And there, in that camp, we spent six of the shortest hours of our lives in recounting the past, noting the changes, and relating events. Then together we partook of a soldier's meal, after which we took our farewell, and have never seen each other since.

Notwithstanding I spent all my spare hours in study, yet I never lost an opportunity when it presented itself to earn a little pocket money. And this I often did by sticking up posters or handbills. My fellow-apprentices often derided and upbraided me for my improving small opportunities. They would spurn the quarters and half-dollars thus earned. They had set their mark high, and would only do the great things. How often I reflected on their words, and wondered if in after years they would bless the world with their learning or genius. I had observed well the characteristics of great men, and I found that he who would rule well must first serve; that the young man who scorns to do little things may never have the opportunity to do the great things, for the things that are deemed great are often actually small; and things that seem small are often great in their bearings and consequences. Trifles lighter than straws are often the feathers that turn the scale of character and destiny.

The vast events and phenomena of the earth are gradual in their progress and slow in their growth; whatever comes to pass suddenly commonly passes away suddenly. Jonah's gourd grew up in a night, but perished in the morning. Startling theories and speculations that break forth upon the world like the sun from behind a cloud, or like the lightning that turns the cloud and night into a flame, soon sift upon the earth their expiring ashes. Excitements in church or state that spring themselves upon the world, and dash or flash along the times like meteors or the lightnings, are soon followed by denser darkness. We shall find, by careful noticing of things, that great and valuable results are usually of gradual growth, from slight original causes; the little leaven in its gradual operations, leavening the whole lump. The least of all seeds becomes a great tree, under the branches of which the birds of heaven come and shelter themselves. The vast river rolls on to the sea; it leaps cataracts, floats navies, impels mighty machinery, and inundates wide regions of country; but it started, it may be, in the crevice of a rock, or in a dewdrop not bigger than a tear. Great islands and archipelagoes, the seat, perhaps, of mighty empires, are the work, often, of very little animals, that build them up slowly from the bottom of the sea. It is said that a whisper slightly stirs the air around the globe. Touch the restless sea anywhere with the tip of your finger, and you move relatively the whole ocean. Nothing is more certain than that our every word, and act, and whisper, in its influence upon the moral world and upon eternity, is like the results just named. Such is the moral and social machinery, that there is needed often only the touching of a match, the pressing of a spring, or turning of a valve, to start a tremendous train of consequences. The pebble from the sling of the shepherd boy, which he picked up out of a little brook, was a little thing, but it decided the fate of two armies and of two nations. The eating of an apple led to the world's fall, and the falling of an apple to the world's philosophy. The mariner's needle and its play are little matters, but the discovery of great continents, and the carrying on of the world's commerce are not little matters. The nice touches and shades given by the skillful artist to his painting are little matters, but little here makes perfection. The sculptor does not mold the human countenance at once. A thousand blows roughcast it, says one, and ten thousand chisel points polish and perfect it, and bring out the exact features and the living expression. It is a work of time. So do human influences and actions chisel out slowly our fixed character and habits. Every day adds something to the slow work. The little dropping insensibly wears the solid rock that laughs at the storm and defies the surges of the sea. Achan's wedge of gold was a little thing, but it led to vast results. The two mites of the poor widow were a little sum, but, measured by their motive, they were perhaps the largest contribution ever made to Christian charity. The colors in Joseph's coat were little things, but his reigning over Egypt was not. The ark of bulrushes was a little thing, but the giving of the moral law was not; leading the Israelites from bondage to Canaan was not. There is power in littles.

> Think nought a trifle, though it small appear;
> Small sands the mountains make, atoms the world,
> Moments make the year, and trifles time, and this eternity.

A tract, if no more, it may be, than two leaves, from the hand of a servant girl, perhaps, lead to the conversion of no less than Richard Baxter. He awoke to a world of usefulness. Among the library of books he wrote was the "Call to the Unconverted." It fell into the hands of Philip Doddridge. It led him to Christ. Doddridge too, awoke to a world of usefulness. His "Rise and Progress" was the means of the awakening of William Wilberforce. A book of his writing led to the salvation of Leigh Richmond. He wrote the "Dairyman's Daughter" that fell upon the world like a leaf from heaven. Hundreds have been brought to Christ by that one sweet tract. Is there no power in littles? Whoever waits to do wonders in this world, forgets or never knew how God does his wonders, how he made the world and the great waters, by the doing of a well-nigh infinite number of little things; and how he empowers us to do little things; to wit., by doing little things always and well. He who waits to do wonders in this world, in any other way than by doing little duties well, will have to bewail at last a life lost, a soul lost, an eternity lost.

Little acts are the elements of true greatness. They raise life's value, like the little figures over the larger ones in arithmetic, to its highest power. They are the tests of .

character and disinterestedness. They are the straws upon life's deceitful current, that show the current's way. The heart comes all out in them. They move on the dial of character and responsibility significantly. They indicate the character and destiny. They help to make the immortal man. It matters not so much where we are as what we are. It is seldom that acts of moral heroism are called for. Rather, the real heroism of life is, do all its little duties promptly and faithfully.

During the following winter as I was on my way from the office one evening, my attention was arrested by a crowd of boys on the opposite side of the street. Curious to know what afforded them so much sport, I crossed over, when I beheld a shocking sight. A young man, scarcely out of his "teens," lay upon the sidewalk intoxicated. He was a noble-looking youth, and as he lay there, a ruthless lot of boys kicking snow in his face, I felt so sad, for upon his brow seemed the imprint of innocence. As I passed along I thought of the misery and sorrow this dire demon—this destroyer of our peace—had brought upon me. Oh, had I the power, I would write over every saloon in the land in letters of fire, *"This is the ante-room of hell!"* Oh, youth! touch not, handle not, taste not this destroyer of your manhood; for at the last it biteth like an adder.

Oh, why should our young men seek to find happiness in such degrading stimulants? As I slowly walked to my boarding place I thought of the burning and eloquent words of Paul Denton, the missionary, who, to appease the people, and in answer to "Where is the liquor?" answered in a tone of thunder, and pointing his long, bony fingers at the matchless double spring gushing up in two strong columns with a sound like a shout of joy, from the bosom of the earth:

"There," he repeated, with a look terrible as lightning, while his enemy actually trembled at his feet, "there is the liquor which God the Eternal brews for all his children. Not in the simmering still, over smoky fires choked with poisonous gases, and surrounded with the stench of sickening odors and corruption, doth your Father in heaven prepare the precious essence of life—pure, cold water. But in the glade and grassy dell, where the red deer wander and the child loves to play, there God brews it; and down, low down in the deepest valleys, where the fountain murmurs and the rills sing; and high up on the mountain tops, where the naked grandeur glitters like gold in the sun, where the storm-clouds brood and the thunder crashes; and out on the wild, wide sea, where the hurricane howls music, and the big waves roll the chorus, sweeping the march of God—there he brews it—beverage of life, health-giving water. And everywhere it is a thing of beauty, gleaming in the dewdrop, singing in the summer rain, shining in the ice gem, till they seem turned to living jewels, spreading a golden vail over the setting sun, or a white gauze around the midnight moon; sporting in the cataract, sleeping in the glacier, dancing in the hail-shower, folding its bright curtains softly around the wintry world, and weaving the many-colored bow, that seraph's zone of the air, whose warp is the raindrops of the earth, and whose woof is the sunbeams of heaven, all checkered over with the celestial flowers of the mystic hand of refraction—that blessed life water. No poisonous bubble on its brink; its foam brings not madness and murder; no blood stains its liquid glass; pale widows and starving children weep not burning tears in its depths! Speak out, my friends; would you exchange it for the demon's drink, alcohol?"

But then I had aspirations which I fear were beyond my years. For I purposed to start a printing office as soon as my trade was completed, in the fall. I had selected Dixon, Ills., as a suitable place in which to commence business. I had $140 on deposit in the bank, money I had earned by extra work and careful savings. I thought Dixon to be a good place, as at that time there was but one printing office, and it was the county seat of Lee county. I believed that industry would bless a humble beginning. To this end I purchased presses and other materials of Richard Blaisdell, of the Rockford *Republican*, which had quite recently discontinued. But instead of reserving part of my money for incidental expenses, I paid it all over to him, and the end of a long story is, I was never able to move the material. As I had not paid for all, and as I had been over-reached by the keen-sighted lawyer, E. W. Blaisdell, his brother, who made out the papers, I lost every cent. I went to J. E. Fox and I. S. Hyatt, men in whom I had confidence, for they were my instructors in the *Register*, and told them my misfortune. They saw at once my mistake, and that legally I had forfeited my money. They went to Mr. Blaisdell and told him that mine was a boyish act, and that if he would not refund all of the money he ought to give back half or two-thirds. But he neither listened to them nor ever gave me back a cent.

This was my first experience in establishing a printing office. I felt so bad over my loss—my hard earnings of three years—that I could not eat for several meals, and for three or four weeks was very much disheartened and distracted. However, I had the sympathy of all who knew the circumstances, and I took courage and hoped for better fortune in the future.

CHAPTER XVI.

CHANGE OF PURPOSE—AT SCHOOL—IN EVANSTON—ON THE
WAY TO MIDDLETOWN—NEW ENGLAND LIFE—CURIOUS
PEOPLE—THE NEWTONS—AT SCHOOL AGAIN—DISTRESS
—UNEXPECTED RELIEF—FAITH IN GOD.

I continued as an apprentice until fall. In the meantime it was impressed upon my mind more forcibly than
ever before that I ought to prepare for the ministry. Indeed I regarded my loss recited in the last chapter as a
visitation of Providence for not heeding the voice of conscience.

Sometimes it is said that after we fail in everything else
we turn to the preaching of the gospel. But this can
hardly be said of me, as I was a successful printer, and
loved the printing art, and had I consulted my own ease
and pleasure I would have continued at my trade, especially as I had just completed it, and the prospects and
inducements of good wages were before me. But I really
felt that God called me to the ministry. , This was no sudden change of mind, but I had the conviction more or less
since my Oberlin disappointment.

With these things revolving in my mind, I came and told
my employer my conviction of duty, and after consulting
with D. P. Kidder, D.D., Professor in the Theological Institute at Evanston, Ill., and with Rev. J. H. Vincent, my
pastor, as to my suitableness for that position, and the cor-
rectness of my convictions—whether I was really called of
God—I gave up all, and prepared to go to school.

I was advised first to graduate from the public schools of
Rockford. Having at least seven years of hard study be

fore me, and neither money nor friends to aid me in my
efforts in obtaining an education, I resolved to throw myself entirely on Providence, feeling that if I was called of
God he would open a way somewhere and lead me into it.
The thought suggested itself to me, that as I now had a
trade, I could adopt my Oberlin plan of working several
hours each day; so I went to Mr. Daugherty and told him
what I had purposed to do, and asked him if he would
give me employment, and how many hours of work each
day would be a fair compensation for my board only. He
replied that he would board me if I would work four hours
each day and all of Saturday. I stopped a moment to reflect, then said I thought it was too much, for allowing me
only at the rate of twelve dollars a week, it would amount
to six dollars a week—rather dear board. But he did not
feel disposed to lower his figures, and as this was the best
I could do, I had to comply. But after some six months'
trial, I found it impossible to do so much work and keep
up with my studies; so I purposed going to Evanston,
which place held out great inducements to poor, struggling
boys.

Accordingly, the last of January, 1864, giving up all
the dear associations which I had formed, and which were
ever prized by me, I set out for Evanston. As I passed
down Main street I was both surprised and cheered by the
friendly encouragement received from those who knew my
studious habits. As one and another extended their friendly hands and wished me success, I was led to reflect that
one scarcely knows how many friends he has until he comes
to leave them. So it was in my case.

Reaching the depot in advance of the train, I had a few
moments for reflection. I thought of the many happy
hours I had spent in this beautiful inland city; of the
social and mental privileges it afforded me; of the religious
instruction I had received; of the joyful pastimes in the

11

quiet summer hours, when all nature laughed for very gladness; of the morning or evening walks in the groves, along the meadow brooks, or along the banks of the river; the freshness of the flowers, the sweetness of the sylvan orchestra; the enchantment in looking upon fields of waving grain, or the groves clad in their vestments of green. But all these associations must now be given up—and all to prepare myself for a life of more extended usefulness in my Divine Master's service. While thus musing, the shrill whistle of the approaching train announced to me that my "departure was at hand."

After a short ride I arrived at Belvidere, where I purposed spending the Sabbath with my brother Peter. Strange as it may seem, just four years previous I spent the Sabbath in this city under very similar circumstances, then on my way to Oberlin, Ohio; now to Evanston, Illinois.

Monday morning, upon going aboard the train, I very unexpectedly fell in with two Rockford students, who were on their way to the same school to which I was going, so I had company which made my journey very pleasant.

Evanston, by rail, is about 100 miles from Rockford, and one must needs go through Chicago. But the trains made close connection, so we arrived at our destination about 1 o'clock. Upon stepping from the cars I was quite curious to take observations of Evanston, my future home, and found it a very beautiful village, situated on the western shore of lake Michigan,.and twelve miles north of Chicago, and is the seat of the Garrett Biblical Institute, Northwestern University, and Northwestern Female College.

Having previously been invited by letter to call on Dr. Kidder, I at once sought his residence, was kindly received, and enjoyed the comforts of his beautiful home for two days. I found Mrs. Kidder an excellent lady, possessing many spiritual and mental attainments.

While here, waiting for the term to open, for I had arrived two days in advance, I went down to the lake shore to look upon the grandeur and creative powers of the Almighty as seen in the deep. If one wishes to have a sense of his own littleness and insignificance, let him walk along the sea-shore and look upon the dark blue waters, and listen to the roar of the far-sounding waves, as they come, white-crested, sweeping in and crashing along the beach. Truly the voice of many waters is at once grand and awe-inspiring. At least so it seemed to me.

It has beautifully been said that every mountain, valley, river, garden, hillside, flower and tree reminds one of the Divine Master; for the mountain was his wonted place of prayer, the river, where he was baptized; the garden, in which he suffered; the hillside, where he taught the lesson of the vine and the branch; the flowers of the field and the lilies of the valley, his illustration of true grandeur; the fig-tree received his curse because it was unfruitful, and the sea was hushed by his "Peace; be still." I thought as I walked along the shore of the lake, what a grand sight it must have been to see omnipotent power exercised in calming the troubled sea. What a consolation to have the Master in the ship. Doubtless the earth was laden with fragrance and melody as the radiance of departing day faded on the Judean hills; the shadows gathered in the valleys, and crept up the vine-clad heights, and the hush of night rested reverently upon fair scenes, hallowed by the footsteps of Jesus. A beautiful lake, embosomed amid verdant loveliness, sparkled beneath the starry brightness of an eastern sky, and a little bark glided over the silvery expanse, bearing the Master and his disciples on an errand of mercy, to the fierce captive among the Gadarean tombs. Suddenly the shadows deepened and darkened, and the blackness of the tempest cast a threatening gloom over the uncertain way. In nature's weariness Jesus slept, unmindful of the wild unrest of the stormy sea whose waves rolled over the frail vessel, as if to hide tnose trembling watchers in their cold and pitiless embrace, forever away from the light and the joy of life. With fearful hearts they awoke the sleeper with the anxious inquiry, "Carest thou not that we perish?" Calmly he rose and looked out upon the troubled waters, and "Peace! be still," thrilled the darkness and the tempest. Nature, in her wild commotion, acknowledged the voice of her Master; the fair lake reposed as quietly as a sleeping child, for "the wind ceased and there was a great calm."

The cloud and sunshine of eighteen hundred years have passed away, and still the words of the loving Master are echoing upon the shores of Time. The blight of sin dims the loveliness and mars the music of earth, but the discord of many a soul is hushed into the music of the redeemed, as they come out of the darkness and lay down the weapons of rebellion for the peace "which passeth understanding." And they who bear the consecrated cross often need the gentle message. There are murmurs because of ungranted requests, when denial is a blessing; there are impatient waitings, when waiting is to serve; there are fiery trials, purifying mercies of the great Refiner, and there are hours of danger when it is well to "stand still and see the salvation of the Lord."

After being duly initiated, I found good associates, kind instructors, and everything moved along pleasantly as far as study was concerned. But what a time I had in being shut up in a student's room poring over Greek roots and Latin endings! Then I was so homesick! I could think of nothing but Rockford, and the associations I had left. However, I received many letters and copies of the city papers, which were read and re-read. My excellent pastor, Rev. J. H. Vincent, now editor of the *Sunday-school Advocate*, wrote me some cheering and encouraging letters. These were treasured in my mind.

While here many incidents occurred which I must pass. One thing seemed very strange, and that was the mournful, subdued sounding of the waves against the strand each morning when first waking from sleep when all was quiet. It was a long time before I became accustomed to it. My room was in the third story, and overlooked the lake.

On as beautiful an April morning as ever dawned on Evanston—after a severe storm—a cry of " A wreck! a wreck! I see men afloat! Hasten to the rescue!" rang through the Institute. Books were abandoned, rooms were emptied, and the students gathered on the shore to see the wreck driven before the waves toward the shore. But the wreck grounded some ten or fifteen rods from the shore. The weather was clear and crisp, the water cold as ice, and the waves were breaking against the sides of the vessel and threatening destruction to the four survivors. But help was of no avail. The whole village had learned the news and were assembling. But there was no one brave enough to stem the waves and the cold. The men on the wreck were perishing. They appealed to the people on the shore for help. One had just expired. They held his frozen and lifeless body up to the full view of the hundreds on shore. The appeal was enough to sicken the stoutest heart. At length a student from the senior class in the Institute, Mr. Hartzell, now editor of the *Southwestern Christian Advocate*, being muscular and an excellent swimmer, plunged into the angry waves, and, though nearly losing his own life, rescued the perishing from the wreck. It was a noble, a brave, a daring deed, and cheer upon cheer followed him in his humane efforts. As a suitable testimonial for his bravery, the students and people of Evanston raised a purse of ninety-two dollars, and presented him with an entire set of the American *Enclyclopædia*.

I had advanced far enough in English branches to pass

examination for the Freshman class in the University. But I had never studied the languages. Hence there were two full years of hard study before me before I could enter upon the University course. But I was full of hope, and study was my natural element. I could study 14 and 16 hours out of the 24, and then regret to lose time in sleep.

Poverty—bless the Lord for his expressions of sympathy for this class of humanity while in his incarnation—was ever casting anxious thoughts in my mind. It is no disgrace to be poor, but it is wonderfully inconvenient sometimes, and I found it so while here.

The school year was now drawing to a close. The reader will understand that I came to Evanston at the opening of the third or last term of the school; but there was another item I would have to meet, and which perplexed me, viz.: my board bill; for it will be remembered I had no means. How should I meet it? What could I do? This I resolved to do: As there were no recitations on Saturdays, I conceived the plan of going to Chicago and working at my trade. Having obtained letters of introduction to some of the offices, I went down to the city, and after several applications, obtained work in the *Christian Times* office, now *The Standard*. I continued working thus on Saturdays until the close of the University school year in June. But living so far from my work, I had to travel by rail to reach it, and as the train did not pass through Evanston until between 8 and 9 o'clock in the morning, it would be quite late before arriving in the city. As a result, in order to pay my railroad fare and to meet my other expenses, I had to work until the night train left the city, fifteen minutes before twelve at night. Thus I worked from nine o'clock in the morning until fifteen minutes to twelve at night. During these working hours I made from four to five dollars, and thus met my college expenses.

An incident and I pass. While working one evening, I

was unusually busy, when the court-house bell admonished me that I must hasten to the depot in time for the train. But I thought I could make the time, and kept at my work a little longer. Turning down the gaslight, I hastened to the sidewalk, and ran most of the way to make up for lost time, but arrived just in time to be a little too late. I could hear the ringing of the bell of the out-going train, and thought perhaps I could overtake it—the trains in the city usually run slow—so I doubled my speed, and after the train I hastened. I ran for a mile or over, and almost overtook it, when its speed became too great for me, and I sank down completely out of breath. Well, I was left. What next? Put up at a hotel, and thus spend the greater part of my hard earnings? No; that I could not consent to do. Where could I go? The thought flashed into my mind to return to the office, and see how I could pass the remainder of the night there. Upon reaching it to my surprise I found some bundles of paper. I took them down, and though but little softer than the floor, I was thankful for even such a bed. As Jacob, when he pillowed his head upon the stones, had refreshing sleep, so I sweetly rested. I was driven to this extremity several times. Of course I always had to foot the twelve miles from Chicago to Evanston in time to have my lesson prepared for the first class on Monday morning.

However, experience taught me that this was too much for poor human nature; for after studying hard all the week and working Saturdays on blind, puzzling manuscripts—which were often more trying than the Greek verb—until midnight, I would be very much exhausted, and suffered from violent headaches. And what alarmed me most was, Saturday nights, after retiring I would be troubled with fearful dreams. I would dream that my whole day's work, in printer's language, " pied;" that is, all the type I had set I thought suddenly fell down. These dreams, which I could not shake off, so worried me that my rest was much broken. Feeling that my health would be ruined if I continued over-taxing nature in this way, I came to the conclusion that either I must abandon my efforts in trying to get an education, or try some other method which would be less taxing to nature. But how could I think of abandoning my heart's fondest desire and the only ambition of my life!

As the school year was drawing to a close, I thought of another expediency, viz.: to write to editors of newspapers in places where institutions of learning were located. Accordingly I wrote to eight or ten editors; but receiving no responses, at the close of the school I set out in person, for where there's a will there's a way; and if there is not God will make a way. Bidding farewell to my classmates, to the blooming prairies—the scene of sunshine and shadow—I set off for Ann Arbor, Michigan, as the first place to make application for work.

It was a hot day in the last part of June, and it was a dusty, fatiguing ride. The passengers kept good spirits. In front of me sat two young men. As the cars stopped at Jackson, Mich., one of them said to the other, "Let's take a drink." And so the boys did, and re-entered the cars with their language and persons marked with the bar-room color.

Take a drink! The young men were well-dressed fools. Years hence a thousand woes will bloom in the footprints now made in their life. A false light gilds the deadly miasma which dogs their footsteps. They see not the smoking altar towards which they are tending. A host of shadowy phantoms of vice and crime are flitting on before. Red-handed murder laughs at their folly, and death is in waiting at the freshly-opened grave. There are tears to be shed by those who this hour dream not of the sorrow which these false steps shall bring upon them.

Take a drink! All the uncounted hosts of drunkards whose graves in every land mark the pathway of intemperance, took a drink. Three out of four of the murderers of the past year took a drink. Their steps were toward the dram-shops, and then from the scaffold out upon the fearful waste beyond. The palsied wretches who totter in our streets all took drinks. Families are beggared by single drinks. Hell is peopled with them.

I involuntarily shudder when I see young men crowding the deeply beaten paths to the dram-shop. They are all confident of their own strength. With the glass in hand where coils the deadly adder, they ha! ha! about the fools that drink themselves to death. They boldly leap into the tide where strong arms have failed to beat back the sullen flow. They dance and shout in the midst of the grinning and ghastly dead, and riot upon the reeking fumes of the grave's foul breath. They boast of their strength. And yet they are but the reed in the storm. They wither like grass under the sirocco breath of the plague they nourish. A time, and they are friendless, homeless, and degraded. Another day, and the story of their lives is told by a rude, stoneless grave in potter's field.

Don't take a drink! Shun the dead Sea Fruits which bloom upon the shore where millions have died. The baubles which float along the breakers' brim hide the adder's fang. The history of ages have offered themselves, body and soul, to the demon of the cup. The bondage of iron galls but the limbs. That of the dram fetters the soul.

Upon arriving at Ann Arbor, I sought and obtained employment in the *Argus* office. However, this was only transient, as they could not give me a permanent situation.

While here I had the pleasure of visiting the museum, the library, and other departments of the State University.

I spent some six weeks in this beautiful city, and gladly would I have accepted work if I could only have obtained it. From here I purposed going to Delaware, Ohio, and thence, if I failed, to Meadsville, Pa., and so on until I found a situation.

Having stayed as long as I could obtain work, I was on the point of starting for Delaware, Ohio, when, to my great surprise, I received a letter from Middletown, Conn., which was addressed to me at Evanston, and forwarded by one of the students to Ann Arbor, stating that my proposition was accepted. As soon as I had noted its contents, which was on Saturday evening previous to my departure, I could hardly contain myself for joy, and accordingly prepared to at once set out for Middletown, Conn. So overjoyed was I that I could sleep but little either Saturday or Sunday nights.

Monday morning, at the early hour of 3 o'clock, I set out for the depot. About 40 minutes later I heard the rumbling of the approaching train among the hills and vales, and a few minutes later I was on my way. Passing Ypsilanti, where the State Normal School is located, we arrived in Detroit while it was yet early. This time I passed through Canada *via* Sarnia. The face of the country as seen from the cars from the Detroit Junction to Stratford (perhaps Stanford), was in great contrast with the undulations of the western prairies; for most of the distance extensive forests and stumpy fields, with here and there a farmhouse, only relieved the eye.

At the above-named place—being the junction or crossing of some road where we changed cars for Buffalo, N. Y. —the country looked somewhat more inviting. Paris had the appearance of a beautiful town. The vicinity was also picturesque. After leaving this place we had a fair view of grain fields filled with the "Canada thistle," known the country through as the pest of the farmer. Indeed it must be discouraging to have these pests year after year absorb the nutrition and strength of the soil to the detriment of the crops.

I also experienced while passing along this road, that it took considerable United States money to purchase a little. At that time, if memory serves me right, only forty cents in Canada money could be obtained for one dollar of ours. About 8 o'clock we reached Buffalo, and thus ended my travels on British soil.

From Buffalo to Albany I could not help but note the places and scenes of suffering I had passed through when I footed the distance years before. Though I was poor now, yet my condition was infinitely better, and something tangible was before me. Then, I was some four weeks in making the distance from Buffalo; now, less than twelve hours.

At Albany I left the railroad, as I purposed passing overland by way of Stephentown, and striking the railroad at Pittsfield, Mass. I could not pass within sixteen miles of the scenes of other days, the home of my father and the graves of my mother and brothers, without visiting them.

This was about the 10th of July, 1864. And, as near as I could count the years, just ten of them had passed away since my flight from home. For ten years had I suffered and wandered from place to place seeking to better my condition. But how changed all things were! The boys I knew then were now on bloody fields of battle, and some of them, say it softly, were sleeping in Southern graves, some where the Potomac's silver wavelets break on the shore, others by Richmond's sunny hills, still others, in Libby and Andersonville prisons, while unceasing prayers from Northern homes of desolation, wrung from mothers' aching hearts, went up day and night for the soldier boys, and for the country's safety. O sad hours! O distracted

country! O disconsolate mothers! Heaven pity! Almost
every home in Stephentown had consecrated a father, a
brother, or a son upon the nation's altar.

I made the home of Mrs. L. H. Wait my first stopping-
place. But, my playmates! where were they? Warren
was in the army; Addie was living a hundred miles away.
My Sabbath-school companions were grown up to manhood and womanhood, and another generation of children
was filling the school. Many of the older people had died.
Some had moved away. In short, great changes had taken
place, and it made me almost homesick to depart—for it
was nothing to what I had anticipated.

Ten years ago! What changes! I was a mere lad then,
and who can tell the glory and blessedness of boyhood.
My home then was in an obscure valley. Lofty hills rise
on each side and throw long shadows on each other alter-
nately as the day dawns and ends. The old log cabin has
fallen into decay; tall weeds have taken possession of the
flower-beds; the meadow has become a field of briers, and
the mountain paths so often trod by me are now obliterated.
All things are changed. This dear spot had once the gladdest music of earth to me; no birds ever sang so sweetly
as those to which I then listened; no sun ever shone so
lovely as the one which lifted his brow over the grand old
hill. But the years give not up their treasures. 'Tis
well: keep them O ye loving years. The dream is mine;
the flowers were mine then; the fruit is mine now. Angels of the household, how they follow us, smiles of gladness, tears of affection, songs of the heart; they live with
us still.

I went to church in the adjacent village. All is change;
however, the dear old church is much the same, but they
who worship there, how different! A few only seem famil-
iar. Old songs, but new voices. Many sing the new song

now on the mountain of beauty, in the land of the morning.

We are journeying to other years. Shall they be years of sunshine? Shall they be years of peace? We go to the coming years; shall they be the long, long years of autumn glory following a life of faith and goodness on earth?

Shall we all be home again in our Fatherland? Short years of earth, long years of heavenly joy. Short years of seed sowing, of tears, of crosses, of duty and love, shall they lead us to the eternal and blessed years, where Christ is the shepherd, and leadeth his own forever?

One of the last things received at Ann Arbor was a long letter from my dear friend beneath whose roof I was now stopping. She little thought when she wrote that letter, of seeing me so soon, and on the first evening of my arrival I sat down and recounted the events of my life to the dear, good lady, Mrs. Wait, who all these years had befriended me and encouraged me to manly deeds. She it was who had so faithfully corresponded with me, overlooked all my deficiencies, and expressed unbounded confidence in me, and had so often encouraged me to struggle on, assuring me that I would yet be a man—a self-made man. Precious mother in Israel, God bless you in the declining years of life, and may the golden shores of eternity bring to your brow a crown of glory! Pen fails me to write down the lasting gratitude that springs up in my poor heart toward this noble woman. She has been a real mother to me. And, under God, I owe much, if I possess any moral worth, to this servant of God.

On that evening I learned the story of my poor mother's death, and the unhappy circumstances attending it. Charity towards my father, and the sacred memory of my angel mother, whose good hand never had anything but blessing for her eldest-born, forbid me to dwell upon this subject.

The reflective reader will not be lost for the reason why it is best for me not to say more.

The following day I visited my father. He was greatly surprised to see me. But my visit was a sad one—it was one of tears. As solemn as was the occasion to me, when I could scarcely keep back the tears of an aching heart, he had the effrontery to offer me a glass of beer. With chills of horror and loathing, followed by the hot blood rushing through my veins and mounting into my face, I stood until the goblet was filled, and then took it and dashed it into a hundred pieces upon the door-stone, exclaiming as I did so, "Oh, demon of hell, thou art the cause of all this sorrow, and the ruin of this family!" My father looked astonished at the daring deed, and said something in an undertone to himself about the waste of the beer. In the home I found a stepmother, my sister Mary and brother Jacob. This constituted the family. Jacob was an own brother, born since I had left home, and hence this was the first time I had seen him, though eight or nine years old. Both of the children were abused out of measure by the cruelty of the stepmother, though I did not learn the full extent of the abuse at this time. I will recur to this farther along in this sketch.

The reader will remember that when I received the intelligence of my mother's death, while living with Mr. Wm. Swardwood, Belvidere, Ills., it contained the news of the death of two of my brothers.

That the reader may catch a glimpse of the entire family I will here recapitulate: namely, the writer, on his way to Middletown, Conn.; Peter, a soldier in the army, wounded at Murphriesboro, Tenn.; Mary, at home; Joseph, the oldest of the two above spoken of, died of scarlet fever; Leopold, living at the steam saw-mill, and whom I have never seen; Jacob, at home, and the baby brother never seen by me, died of scarlet fever. This constitutes the whole family.

Two I have never seen, one having died while away from home, and the other I have lost traces of.

Suffer me to add here, that I have learned since publishing this sketch in the CENSER, that both Joseph and my baby brother (whose name I have never learned), had the best of treatment and care while sick at the hands of those noble-hearted women of West Stephentown. It made the tears come to my eyes as I learned that they were so good and patient. The motherless babe never murmured as it lay on its bed of suffering. Joseph, who must have been a lad of ten at the time of his death, was given away just as I had been, but was more fortunate in that he fell into the hands of a Christian family. He was loved by them, and was gentle and obedient. But the sweet angel of death garnered the budding flowers for a fairer clime.

To these good people, should I never be able to see them in the flesh, I would extend my lasting and heartfelt gratitude. God bless them for showing kindness and mercy to two of a helpless and scattered family of unfortunate children. Yes, with tears streaming from my eyes as I pen these lines, I know there are wayside angels scattered up and down this earth of ours, who have large hearts. I have found some in the way. May heaven reward them for the kindly words spoken to this wounded, aching heart, filled with unutterable sorrow.

The next morning, in company with Father, Mary and Jacob, I visited the graves of my mother and two brothers, Joseph, and the youngest-born, whose name I have not learned. They are in a neglected and seldom-used burial-place, on the southeastern slope of a hill almost three miles from the village of Alps. The whole is enclosed by a stone wall which is broken down in many places. It made my heart ache to see the generally-neglected and un-cared-for condition of the burial place. We had to enter by a pair of bars. Scratching our hands several times with

briers, we at last arrived at a grass-covered mound which
father pointed out as the grave of mother, and by the side
of this were two smaller mounds, which were the graves
of my brothers.   Mary, Jacob, and myself kneeled down
by the graves and wept.   " Oh, loved one, precious mother,
grief-stricken, heart-broken mother!   Are you conscious
of our presence?   Do you hear the falling of our tears
upon the sod?   Oh come back to us, if but for a moment!
Speak to us as of yore!   Alas! alas! the zephyrs of the
quiet summer hour bear our moanings and our sighings
away to the echoless shore, and no voice returns to us!
Sleep on, blessed, sainted, angelic one!   earth has no sorrow that Heaven cannot cure!   And these, thy latest-born,
shall never battle in the bitter, ah, thrice bitter struggle of
life!"   I bowed my head upon the grave, and would have
given the dearest object of my life could I have looked
upon the face, and received a token from the peaceful sleeper.   But, alas! alas! it was too late now.

It was in my heart, if I could do no more, to plant a
few flowers over the sainted spot, but even these I could
not obtain, so I had to leave the place as I found it.

Fourteen years later, in 1876, I was again permitted to
visit the place, and to erect headstones over the graves of
mother and brothers, and to secure a substantial fence
around the whole burial plot.   Joseph, however, upon
careful investigation, was not found buried on the mountain, but in North Nassau.

I have always cherished the memory of my angel mother,
and have grieved much over the thought that added to all
her sufferings in the last hours of her life, she would repeatedly call for her children, and they were not.   At the
last she exclaimed, " I could die happy if I could only see
my children once more;" and then she would moan in the
most pitiable tones, as if in great agony.   It was the memory of these things that made the visit at her grave such

a sad one. Alas! the sorrows of a drunkard's home, who can tell them?

But mine is the Christian's consolation. In this world we may expect sorrow. We must suffer as well as do the will of our Father which is in heaven. And this we cannot do without meek, submissive patience. The cross first, and then the crown. Sowing in tears it may be, yet, doubtless, if we faint not, we shall return bearing our precious sheaves, with the smile of heaven upon our faces. The storm may rage over mountain and plain, and terror fill our fainting hearts, but behind the tempest is the radiant sun whose genial rays picture through the sparkling tears of nature the beautiful bow of peace in the very cloud we so much dreaded. We may cry out when the deep fountains of our nature are broken up: "Oh, why do afflictions cover me over as the waters cover the deep?" Be patient, these sorrows are only stepping stones to the higher life. Over the turbid waves of life's tempestuous sea come angel voices, bidding us be calm, for Jesus drank of the cup pressed to our lips. Behold, what sorrows did he undergo, and with what patience did he suffer them! Patient when Judas unworthily betrayed him with a kiss; patient when Caiaphas despitefully used him; patient when hurried from one place to another; patient when Herod with his men of war set him at naught; patient when Pilate so unrighteously condemned him; patient when scourged and crowned with thorns; patient when his cross was laid upon him, and when he was reviled, reproached, scoffed at, and every way insulted. Lord Jesus, grant us patience, after this example, to bear thy holy will in all things. Thy patience, thy gentleness, thy love, shall stop these murmuring lips. Oh, lead us through sorrow's vail up to the golden city of our God.

I remained in the neighborhood about a week. I gathered up all the items relative to my mother's death I could,

12

and the good people told me many sad things, all of which it does not become me to relate here. God pity the wife and family of the drunkard!

From Stephentown, I went *via* New Lebanon Springs to Pittsfield, Mass. Coming from the prairies, the reader may well think I appreciated and, as much as the burden of my heart permitted me, enjoyed the ever-changing scenery along that mountain road.

It was a real luxury to once more breathe the pure mountain air, and to look upon those giant sentinels of the ages rearing their rugged brows towards the heavens. And then it was the most lovely time of year to travel among the varied sceneries of New England. Would that I had space to describe the impressions made upon my mind as I passed the villages, hamlets, and stately farm-houses, with their orchards, their flower-gardens, beautiful lawns; how enchanting to view the undulations of the country between the mountains with their foliaged forests, to look upon the distant lakelets shimmering in the noon-tide sun of the quiet summer hour, to catch gleams of the sparkling rills, rolling their cooling streams over pebbly beds; to gaze upon waving fields, or low-lying meadows, filling the air with the fragrance of the new-mown grass. Then all these objects were relieved by deep ravines and lofty hills. It was a district of country thus diversified I was now traveling in company with a friend.

Passing Stephentown at a time in the morning when the milkmaids were out, when the flowers were breathing their sweetness on the air, when the birds from rose-bush and shrub and distant grove were carroling forth their best songs, when the peasantry were coming from their cottages to enter the sunny fields of labor. Truly these objects diverted my mind, and I was glad in my heart that I was permitted to traverse these places remembered of long ago. There was not a street nor house but what I had visited time and again in the person of the poor, despised and oft-rejected beggar-boy. But times change, and we change with them. I was now a youth, and on my way to college. Could it be possible! or was it only a dream? Yes, it was a veritable fact.

Leaving the village of Hancock about two miles to our left, we presently came to the somewhat noted New Lebanon Springs. The reader will remember that here is located perhaps the largest community of Shakers in this country. While they are a quaint people, with their long coats, their broad-brimmed hats, their flowing locks; yet they are as honest as the day is long. Then their village, their extensive farm, their vast seed-beds, and thrifty-looking horses and cattle, are models for any farmer. But I guess I would not make a very good Shaker, from the fact that I love liberty too well. Yet these New Lebanon Shakers have one of the most sunny spots in eastern New York.

From here we ascended a lofty hill for about four miles, from the summit of which we beheld Pittsfield, Mass., nestling in a plain as lovely as must have been Shinar of old. To the north, surrounded on two sides by groves, we espied a lake rippling in the morning breeze.'

One that is as charmed with God's beautiful world as I am, could drink in deeper enjoyments than my pen could describe. Our blessed Lord loved to retire to the mountain top, and it was on the side of the mountain he said to his disciples, " Ye are the light of the world." Thus he seized upon a figure of speech at once natural and tangible. But then his words are among the marvels of the incarnation, especially when contrasted with the cumbrous and frivolous diction of the religious teachers of his day and race. All the imagery which he employs reveals not only such purity and divinity of thought as befit the Lord of glory, but attests such an indwelling in the material world as we should expect from the Lord of nature. His illustrations are taken from the objects and events of every-day life; the pendant lily, the broken bulrush, the smoking flax, the piece of money, the pearl of great price, the lost sheep, the sower and the seed, the leaven, the salt, the fish and the net, the red glare of the approaching tempest, the sunrise and the sunset, the lightning and the wind, the neighbor aroused at dead of night, the boys piping in the market-place, the steward and the laborer, the willful prodigal boy, the bridegroom and the bride, the wicket gate, the broad road, the stony ground, the burning lake. There is nothing improbable in the supposition that the objects and events thus employed were either present or near while the Saviour spoke; so that they were not only the vehicles of truth, but the means of arresting attention. So that we are at liberty to believe that those who first heard the words of the quotation above, heard them under circumstances never to be forgotten. Our Lord had passed the whole night in prayer upon the lofty peak of that saddle-shaped mountain which rises by the shore of the sea of Galilee. When the grey of the early morning was paling the deep blue of the midnight sky, he came down from his lonely eminence, and calling to him his disciples, appointed the twelve apostles. The tableland on which he stood was high above the level of the inland sea, and upon it was gathered a great multitude of people, whom he taught concerning his kingdom, having first healed their sick. Facing to the east as the spot did, the time soon after sunrise, perhaps even while the sun came forth from the chambers of the east, the scene and the sermon must have been deeply impressed upon the minds and hearts of the observers. It was the month of April, when the air was vocal with the matin song of the birds, and all vegetable life was strong and fresh. It was a region famous for the purple tints of the mountain-side; for its profusion and luxuriance of green;

for the brilliant plumage of its birds; for its masses of growing grain, dotted here and there with the rich scarlet and pink tints of the native oleander; a region of silver fountain and waterfall above, of the dark blue lake beneath. As the sunlight, first tipping the mountain peak with rosy radiance, stole gradually down the purple mountain sides, bringing out a new world of beautiful form and rich color, reflecting itself in a million drops of dew, and in every watery spray; no one that looked could fail to have a vivid conception of the dignity of the disciples to whom the Master said, " Ye are the light of the world."

Thus the very mountains were used by the Saviour as pulpits, and the rising sun as illustrating divine truth. If our Redeemer thus used every object in nature—from the "high mountain" to the "lily of the valley"—to illustrate and enforce his sermons, should not we, for his sake, associate them in our life whenever we come in contact with them?

About nine o'clock we reached Pittsfield. Having about two hours to wait for the train, I took a hasty ramble through this beautiful inland city. It certainly is one of the most lovely I was ever in. Its streets are wide, and shaded on either side by large trees; the business part was thrifty, and every home seemed a mansion or a cottage of peace and happiness. Here the widely-known, and now lamented Dr. Todd spent a life of untold usefulness. His church is a model of New England architecture. While I was thus drinking in the enchantments of this place, I heard the approaching train that was to further me on my journey, and I hastened to the depot.

After leaving this place, we passed through the southern spur of the Green Mountains. And for picturesqueness and novelty of scenery the student of nature will seldom find a more varied tract of country traversed by rail. We passed several villages and towns, but the cars don't stop long enough for one to get a good look, though we were constantly on the alert. At Springfield, Mass., I for the first time saw the Connecticut River, about which I had read so much, and the beautiful valley stretching to the south as far as the eye could see. As in admiration I looked upon that enchanting stream, and the valley through which it flowed, I could only exclaim, "Behold, the half had not been told me!" As I will have occasion to refer to Springfield again, I will hasten along in my sketch.

Here we changed cars, and the iron horse soon carried us through the valley along the river's bank to Windsor Locks, where we re-crossed the river, but continued along the bank of the same to Hartford, Conn. Those who know, say that this valley, stretching from Springfield on the north to Hartford, and perhaps Middletown on the south, is the richest and most fruitful of all New England. Fancy my surprise then, as I noticed the red, and, to all appearance, parched soil, as viewed from the car-window. There was such a contrast between it and the black, alluvial soil of the prairies. And it did not seem possible that such soil could produce anything. But such are the contrasts the different sections of our own country present to the traveler. Stopping at Windsor and Hartford, I arrived at Middletown, and at once sought out the *Constitution* office and reported myself. Mr. Newton received me kindly, and was ready to set me to work. But I was now out of money, and in a strange place. The manners of the people, even their very speech, was different from that of the West. I confess I was homesick. But I kept a stiff upper lip. Mr. Newton suggested that I should first look myself up a suitable room. So I went out and wandered all over the city, but not one could I find within my limited means. I could not see my way. At evening I returned to the office well discouraged. It was now supper time. He invited me to go and take tea with him.

But I could eat little. My mind was sorely depressed. They suggested one place and another. But I was a stranger and could find no one who would trust me. But I found Mrs. Newton a pleasant lady, whose cheerful face did much to drive away the depression of my mind. And as they listened to my voice, and as I related the events through which I had passed, a better spirit prevailed. They at once saw that I was now helpless, and they did really cheer me up. They had plenty of rooms—empty ones too—in the house, and they gave me as good a one as they had.

This was on Saturday evening, Aug. 6. The next day was my first Sabbath in a New England town. And a lovely morning it was. I arose quite early, and for over an hour I sat by the open window looking out upon flower-gardens, palace homes, stone sidewalks; and meditated on the contrasts of my present with my former surroundings.

While I thus sat in the cool of the morning, resting from the fatigue of a long journey, and as my senses were invigorated by the flower-scented air, I thought of that home in heaven, that rest which remains for the people of God, of meeting the King in his glorious apparel, and of uniting with redemption's hosts in singing the "new song," for

In the sweet by-and-by,
We shall meet on that beautiful shore.

How cheering to the Christian heart is that sweet "song of Zion!" How it thrills the soul with emotion unutterable! How it lifts the bowed head, and brings fresh inspiration and strength to the fainting spirit! How it points the languid eye of faith to brighter scenes and fairer realms and untold felicities "beyond the river." Oh, how its matchless melody brings into play our noblest aspirations, raises upward our highest hopes, and gives us new vigor to labor on, and travel on, and fight on, until our labors shall end, our journey shall be over, our warfare shall be concluded, and we shall mingle our voices in the strains of that still sweeter song of "Moses and the Lamb." Fellow Christian, traveling through earth's dreary solitudes, how is it with thee? Art thou toil-worn and footsore, and are thy garments soiled with the dust of travel? Has the weary march over mountain and plain and through the dangerous "enemy's country," weakened thy faith and chilled thy hope? And is the confession daily extorted from thy lips that thou art a "pilgrim and a stranger on the earth?". List, my brother, to the great apostle as he speaks of the pilgrims who have gone before you! Hear him: "They that say such things declare plainly that they seek a country. Will they reach that country?" Hear him again: "Wherefore, God is not ashamed to be called their God, for he hath prepared for them a city." Be encouraged weary one. Travel on in the King's highway. The "sweet by and by" is coming. A few more hills to climb, a few more valleys to pass through, a few more dangers to surmount, and then, oh, then, Zion's towers and "heaven-built walls" shall be full in view, and, crossing in triumph the intervening flood, thou shalt reach and enter the pilgrim's eternal rest. Then let the music of the sweet by and by ring out in hopeful cadence through the chambers of your souls, until we get out of the "wilderness, and beyond the desert, and across old Jordan;" and then, in higher notes and loftier strains, we will unite our voices in the sweeter chorus of Moses and the Lamb.

At the hour of ten I was startled by the united peals of half-a-dozen deep-toned church bells. They were rung with such precision that they struck together; then their vibrations would float on the air and grow less and less until lost to the hearing. For a minute all would be silent, and then crash came the united volume of the far-sounding bells. I had never heard the like before. But then this is the way they call the people to church in Middletown.

The Sabbath ended, and I entered upon my duties in the *Constitution* office. I agreed to work for Newton two hours each day, and half of Saturdays for my board. I now felt that I had been amply rewarded for all my efforts. However, as there were some six weeks before the school year opened, I worked all this time in consideration of board, in addition to the time as above stated. When the time for the opening of the school arrived, as I was not far enough advanced to enter the University, I attended the Connecticut Institute, and applied myself more diligently, if possible, than ever before, in order that I should be able to enter the University in 1865.

While the weather was warm everything was as comfortable as I could desire. The autumn passed agreeably away, and the cold weather was approaching, and as I had spent most all of my money in the purchase of books, I was quite in need of some to purchase clothing, and I did not know where it was coming from; so I went in prayer to Jesus, as I had often done, and unfolded my heart's burden to him, for the true believer has the blessed assurance that the Lord will withhold no good thing from those who love him, and that he doeth all things well. And I trusted, if I had not mistaken the leadings of Providence, that my humble prayers might in some way be answered. So one morning while unusually industrious over the then perplexing and tangled passage: *Sic ait: et dicto citius tumida æquora placat, collectasque fugat nubes, solemque reducit*, in the first book of Virgil, I was surprised with a message that a couple of ladies in a carriage wanted to see me. My heart was all in a flutter. Who would care to see a poor student in a strange city? Revolving in my mind as to what it could all mean, with uncovered head I approached the carriage, when two ladies, with sweet, smiling faces handed me a letter, saying that it contained good news for me, and then drove away. Wondering in astonishment what it all meant, and eager to learn the good news, I burst open the envelope, and six dollars and seventy-five cents met my eyes! Truly these two ladies were angel messengers of mercy in this my hour of need. But my astonishment was still greater when in the evening the post brought me a letter from Mrs. J. B. Skinner, Rockford, Ill., containing five dollars, and shortly after another from the same lady containing twelve dollars. Oh, could it be possible that the Lord was so kind as to answer my feeble prayers with such signal displays of his goodness.

CHAPTER XVII.

College Days—A Strange Letter—Wonderful Deliverance—A Bright Future—In New Haven—On
the Connecticut—In New York—Startling Intelligence—Finding my Only Sister—A Resolve at a
Great Sacrifice—In Racine, Wis.—Out of Employment—On the Road—Vain Efforts—Discouraged.

As truth, and nothing but the truth, constitutes the
merits of this sketch, I must here relate the facts as they
transpired, though I was even grateful for the privilege of
obtaining my schooling under the adverse circumstances
in which I was placed. In some respects Mr. Newton befriended me, and my gratitude to him for this almost per-
suades me to pass over some things, but for the good of
the young reader for whom I write this sketch, I must
adhere to my purpose, but I do so with malice toward
none. I know eyes will fall on this narrative that may
now wish it could be changed.

When winter came I suffered much from cold, for I had
to perform my task in the morning, and as the proprietors
did not deem it economy to permit me to build a fire, my
fingers almost froze in setting type. When I first arrived
I worked some six weeks for the Newtons, all of which
was applied on my board arrangement, and during that
time there was ample accommodation at their residence;
but when school opened somehow the proud and selfish
aristocracy of the Newtons could not tolerate me in their
family. A kind lady, seeing this, offered me a neatly furnished room, but her husband objected, saying that he did

not build his house for the accommodation of Newton's outcasts—he was helping the Newtons, not me. It appeared that they tried, after they had obtained the six weeks' work, to cast me off, but I held them to their agreement. Hence, being at their mercy, they gave me such accommodations as they chose, and during the cold winter evenings I had to sit in the kitchen without a fire, and study by a tallow dip, as that was a cent or two cheaper a week. I was not permitted to sit with the family around a comfortable fire, and could take up with their haughty actions or leave. Silent tears flowed, but no one saw them; my cheeks burned with indignation, but no one knew it.

The room might have been kept quite comfortable if the outside doors had only been kept closed, but these were swinging open every few minutes, and as I was not permitted to replenish the fire, which was usually suffered to go down as soon as tea was prepared, the room often became very uncomfortable as early as seven or eight o'clock. I would put my over-coat on, and then the cold chills ran over me. Often my hands would get so cold that I could scarcely turn the pages of my lexicons while looking up the meaning of words. The reader will of course notice I was at this time studying Latin and Greek. Students will know what turning the leaves in the lexicons means. The result was I had a cold fastened upon me all winter, and was nearly sick once or twice. But I could not think of giving up my studies, though I suffered more than pen could tell. I must go through the University or die in the attempt. There was no such thing as giving up on account of physical pains.

Thus firmly resolved, I was even grateful for the cold kitchen for my studio, and a tallow dip by the light of which to dig out Greek roots. While thus engaged, a scene which reminded me of other and earlier days took place. One cold winter night as I was bending over my

Greek, I thought I heard a faint tapping at the kitchen door. I went to the door, where I found a girl, her tattered garments all covered with the drifting snow, and her chilled person shivering with the cold. My heart was moved in sympathy for the sufferer, and I tried to lighten her sorrow with a cheerful smile. She, looking up into my face, broke forth in a low, plaintive voice: "Please give me some bread, mother is sick and destitute." I asked her to come in, but she refusing, I hastened to call the folks of the house. Upon their coming to the door, they questioned the poor child until tears stood in her eyes, just as I have been questioned a hundred of times, and then, giving her a cookey, turned her away. Oh, how it made my heart ache! Oh, what angels such folks will make in heaven! Poor, miserable selfishness! it blights the soul in this world, and damns it in the next.

Now, Mr. Newton and his family professed to be Christians. They had devotional exercises every morning. Mrs. Newton had baked that day, and in turning the child away they not only closed their hearts against a charity which ought to have made them glad for the very opportunity, but actually told a lie to make it seem, reasonable. But pride and selfishness did not belong to the Newton family altogether, but has its devotees all over the world. We can trace it as far back as Cain. In a thousand forms it has cursed the world. Look at those two men who went up to the temple to pray. The bold, proud, well-dressed Pharisee, satisfied with himself, stands in the center of the court and prays with well-made sentences, and surely those who look upon him will say, "There is the gentleman of the age;" just as we short-sighted creatures fondle and advance to honor many a hypocrite, because he has the ability to put on a fair exterior. But as Jesus comes into the hall, he points to that plainly-clad publican, who stands with tremling knees and bowed head in that obscure cor-her near the door, and prays in broken words for mercy, and Jesus tells us that this one, " rather than the other," is the Christian.

The gospel of our Lord certainly draws the lines so plainly that no one need be mistaken in this Christian grace, without which it is impossible to please God. Why, just look at that Samaritan act. On that wild and rocky path that leads from Jerusalem to Jericho lies a man near that dark pass in the mountains who has been left "half dead" by robbers. That well-dressed Levite who looked upon him a few moments ago, and found that he was one of the common people, and passed on, showed his breeding as a gentleman in saving himself from the touch of such a man; that priest, who glances scornfully upon the penniless sufferer as he passes by on the other side, shows that he is of high blood that must not be contaminated with the common crowd. Surely, they are gentlemen complete! But Jesus, by some strange oversight of their Jewish rank and fine clothes, points us to that low-born Samaritan, bending over the suffering man, softly wiping the ugly clots of blood, binding up his wounds, turning back from his journey, mounting him on his own beast, and paying for him at the inn, and tells us that this Samaritan is the true neighbor of the three. In public highways of the world you may see his monuments; on a thousand hospitals you may see his name. Where are the monuments and hospitals that honor the manhood of the priest and Levite?

Around that box at the temple into which the people drop their gifts of charity, you can hear the rustle of silks and see the twinkle of jewelry, as those well-dressed ladies drop in their gold; but how they knit their brows and draw back their dresses as that poor widow, in her threadbare garments, with her poorly-dressed little one in her arms, crowds up toward the box and drops in those two mites. No one thanks her, although it is "all her living;" but

Christ tells us that this poor, meek, gentle giver has done a greater act of self-denial "than they all."

We discover in these examples that it is not the form or parade which is well pleasing in God's sight, but the motive and the heart, for no trait can so adorn and dignify nature as kindness. When we know a man to be kind, we instinctively feel that he is noble, no matter how humble his circumstances, or how rough his external appearance. If he has a warm and generous heart we value his good opinion, we seek his society, we secretly put him down on our list of friends. How often do we hear the expression concerning some one whose manners lack polish, who has been frowned on by fortune, or who has stepped aside from the path of rectitude, "Well, after all, he is a good-hearted man." The tongue of the traducer is silenced, and the mantle of charity falls on the child of misfortune, so instinctively do we recognize the worth and beauty of this heavenly virtue.

To be kind, is to be Godlike, for he is kind to the evil and to the unthankful, and sendeth rain on the just and on the unjust. It is in vain that we call on God to draw near to us so long as we ignore those works of practical goodness by which we can draw near to him. He requires no loud self-services, no tinsel glitter of priestly forms, but the silent incense of the heart, poured out in behalf of struggling, aspiring humanity. One of the sublimest sights that can engage the attention or gladden the hearts of mortals or immortals, is that of a good man, holding fast his integrity amidst corrupt and hardening influences, and never losing sight of the fact that we are all equally dear to the common Father. Such a man is a center of social and moral influences around which cluster the affections of an entire community, and from whom rays of fraternal sympathy shoot far and wide into the surrounding darkness. May this noble virtue, my good reader, be your profession. I have seen a great many things in my life, but I have never seen a man come to want because he spent his fortune doing such acts as the Samaritan did. God will certainly bless and prosper the generous, sympathizing heart. They who water shall be watered again.

Well, I struggled on, wading through difficulties and over obstacles, and at last came to the close of the school year—to the last recitation under the tuition of Dr. D. Chase.

As the respective standing of each student was read before the school, I was surprised and astonished to hear my name at the top of the list! It was all unexpected, and I cannot describe my feelings as I received the first honors of the Institute, the principal remarking as he gave it me, "All must have marked the industry and manly deportment, as well as the studious habits of this boy." Of course it was gratifying to reflect that a green Illinoisan should, under so many adverse circumstances, bear away the first honors from a Connecticut school.

The reader who has carefully traced my wanderings from my Rockford home up to this, my first triumph over difficulties, cannot fail to notice that every step was contested. Indeed, I could have given up many times, had the inclinations of nature been followed. I was told more than once I could never succeed, as it took money to go to school with. But I kept a brave heart and a faith in God. Here is the rock on which I planted my destiny. The most beautiful of all truths, the great and crowning truth of all truths, is that there is a God—a God whose power and love perfectly adapt him to man. Man is a needy being, and God alone can meet his need. In other words, God is exactly what every man wants. It is of more importance to have a clear perception of this truth, than to see and clearly apprehend all other truths. Indeed, it underlies all others, and all others will one day sink into insignificance before it. Art and science may make it their boast that they can raise a man to a great height; that they can develop and cultivate, to a wonderful degree, his intellectual nature; and so they can. But when art has done all it can, when science has done all it can, man still has nothing worth possessing if he has not a God of power and love to meet his highest need. A human being divorced by his own willfulness from God, and trying to take the long and perilous journey from the cradle to the grave without him, is one of the most pitiful of objects. A human being trying to remodel and reconstruct himself, and bring himself up from a wreck to a perfect man; a rational, intelligent existence trying to make headway in this world, and hoping to keep clear of rocks and quicksands, and make a prosperous voyage, and sail safely and triumphantly into port, simply by the use of his own powers, and without faith in God,—shows most amazing folly.

But it seems to be a great and not fully answered question in these days, what it is that God does for a man, and how much he does for him, and what is really the result of his faith in God.

If faith in God brings nothing whatever to needy men, then it is only a fanciful idea, a chimera, a delusion, a something to talk about and write about, if we choose, but of no earthly use to anybody. I, however, am of those who believe that faith in God brings something to the needy, and that its results are glorious and everlasting. I believe that in answer to this faith, God walks with man; walks by his side, and works in him and for him most powerfully and wonderfully. And therefore I would say to every man: Have faith in God. But let us not for a moment dream that because we have faith in God we may leave God to do everything for us, while we do nothing for ourselves.

No: God works for no man who can, and yet will not,

13

work for himself. This is freely admitted by everybody to a certain extent. It is acknowledged that God does not give to any one the luxuries, or even the necessary things of life, such as shelter, food, and raiment, unless he works for them. If a man, grown weary and impatient of toil, should conclude to spend the rest of his days in idleness and ease, and live by faith in God, he would probably have pretty poor living, and a pretty sore experience of poverty. Comfortable homes, fine palaces, fine equipages, rare gardens, and rich fields, all things that men desire and enjoy, come only through toil, and not God's toil, but man's toil. What people want in this world they must work for. They must enter heartily and energetically into some field of labor, and work in it patiently and perseveringly if they want what money can buy. This is God's law. Toil and the fruits of toil are inseparably connected, and it is only those who help themselves whose faith in God as a helper is worth anything. Probably no one will say that this is unsound doctrine. No man in his right mind expects ease or even ordinary comforts, however great may be his faith in God, without working for them. And human as well as divine effort is necessary in education, whether of the head or the heart. Let a man pray: "O God, make me a scholar! Reveal unto me all the beauties and mysteries of art and science, and teach me all languages, and spare me the labor of study." Let him offer such a prayer, and the amount of his education would soon be told. But let him ask God to bless his efforts, and to help him grow in that practice and perseverance so necessary to the pursuit of all knowledge, and let him have faith that God will answer, and he will then see exactly when and where faith in God comes in to help a man. He will see how beautifully and perfectly this faith chimes with human effort.

Now, in nothing is human effort so much needed as in the education of the heart and head, and it is the duty of all who want to be made better, not only to believe in God, but to work with him in the greatest of all labor, the cultivation of the heart. Here, as in all other things to be gained, faith in God will avail nothing if a man does not use all possible means for the cultivation of the mind, and reach his eager hands after all helps, and open his eyes wide, that he may see whatever tends to pull him down or raise him up. And yet it is taught by many, in these last days (we hope they are the last days of ignorance and folly) that men may see anything but themselves; that they must not know their own mental and moral constitution; that if they want to grow better — in other words, want to grow in grace — all they have to do is to have faith in the God of all grace. But if men knowingly and willingly reject any knowledge that would help to make them better, I can not see how they can consistently ask God to make them better, nor how they can expect him to do it, any more than they can expect him, without their own effort, to build their houses for them, and lay out the grounds, and cultivate their choice flowers and rich fruits. God helps men, not by doing for them what they can do themselves, but by directing them to all the help that is within their reach.

A few weeks later the school year of the Wesleyan University opened, and on the 31st day of August, 1865, I became a student in the University. My expenses necessarily increased, and, as I had given the time and labor of all my vacations for the past year to the Newtons in order to retain my position, I was in more straitened circumstances than ever before; but I was willing to deprive myself of every comfort of life, and actually suffered for the want of sufficient clothes. With a firm resolution I determined to meet every difficulty, and yield only when compelled by necessity. As I now had a room in the college buildings, I spared my employers the trouble of giv-

ing me their back kitchen for my study; and, when cold
weather set in, I had a quiet comfortable place in which to
study.   Though I was troubled in my mind and put to my
wits' end to find out some honest and honorable means with
which to meet my expenses, yet I did not lose my confidence in God, but lived a life of simple trust; feeling that
he never requires impossibilities of his creatures. Besides, other students were struggling, some of them living
on potatoes and corn bread.

Oh, could our men of wealth only look into the cold, cheer-
less, dismal rooms to be found in almost every college in
the land, and there see noble but indigent young men ruining their health in the effort of obtaining an education
to prepare them for future usefulness, I think their hearts
would be touched! But then, young men that would rise
in the world, must be hewers of their own character, and
such are always honored.

But my distress was gaining upon me, and, looking at
it from a human standpoint, it did seem that I must give
up, at least, until I could earn a little money with which
to purchase clothes and books,

During those discouraging days, many an hour I spent
on my knees asking God to help me. Hitherto the good
Lord had been merciful to me. I had already passed two
of the six years. I had felt that I was under the leadings
of Providence in this matter. I had hoped, almost against
hope, that I should not at this point be compelled to yield.
If my clothes would only last, I could manage in other
respects to go through the school year. I resolved to go
just as far as I could, and leave the rest with God.

But the eye of Jehovah was upon me, though, short-
sighted and faithless as I was, I could not believe. I was
like the disciples of old praying for the deliverance of
Peter, and when he stood at the outer door knocking they
did not believe, but thought it was his angel. Thus I

prayed. However, on this wise the Lord answered my prayer.

During all this time I had charge of a Bible class in one of the city churches. For several Sabbaths I noticed an elderly lady dressed in deep mourning, sitting in a pew opposite my class apparently very attentively listening to what was said. One Sabbath, in particular, I noticed her, and invited her to take a seat in the class. But she very respectfully declined.

The school closed, and I went to my room thinking nothing more about the lady — as visits from strangers were of frequent occurrence. Shortly after this I received a note requesting me to call on the writer at such a time and place. I was much puzzled and wondered what it all meant. Anxiously I waited for the evening to arrive, and, upon the appointed time, I hastened to the residence of the writer of the note, and, to my surprise, the same lady above referred to answered the door bell, and invited me into the reception room.

Looking upon me pleasantly, she said, in substance, that for over a year she had seen me pass her residence to my work as regularly as clock work; that she observed my clothes were becoming threadbare, that she knew what kind of men I was working for; she had observed me at the meetings and had watched my conduct for some time and as she thought I was worthy of whatever she should bestow upon me, she now purposed giving me my board free of charge. She added some other words, but I do not know what they were, for I was so surprised that I was almost overcome. I could hardly believe that she really meant all she said. Was it possible? My board free for over three years? Yes. That was not all. She said she would take me as a member of her family. I almost fainted under this intelligence, and replied to the kind lady as best I could, that I deemed myself too unworthy of so great kindness yet, if it pleased her to bestow it, I would most thankfully receive it. The name of this lady is Mrs. Joseph W. Hayes.

I returned to my room with heart overflowing with gratitude to the kind lady for her generous act and to God in dealing so mercifully with me.

The next morning I related the incident to Messrs. Newton, supposing that they would certainly be glad to get rid of me; but on the contrary they reproached me; telling me that they thought I was more of a man than to accept such an offer, and from such a source; that it was very uncertain, and if she turned me away, they would never take me again. This made me feel uncomfortable, for I knew nothing of the woman; but I made up my mind to accept her hospitality, their admonitions notwithstanding, for I had suffered much at their hands, and I was now almost destitute of clothing, and there was no opportunity to earn any while working under my present contract, for they not only had two hours of each day, and half of Saturday, but all of my vacations. Yet, rather than to give up my school privileges, I would have suffered any deprivation. But there was now a change in my favor, and I resolved to avail myself of so good an opportunity, and trusted in Providence for the future, for it seemed to me that God would not thus mock my efforts and frustrate my purposes. On the contrary, I acknowledged the good hand of the Lord in it all. So bidding them good-bye, I started for my new home.

I found Mrs. Hayes to be a kind-hearted woman and a most excellent Christian lady. She not only gave me my board, but had several suits of clothes made for me, and gave me money to meet my other expenses; in short, Mr. and Mrs. Hayes did a great deal for me, and may God bless them for it. I now could not help but feel that God was with me, and that he had done for me far more than I ever expected. Life now presented a sunny side, and everything looked as if the remainder of my college days would be crowned with uninterrupted prosperity.

Though these kind people did so much for me, yet I did not give myself over to idleness, for the good Lord only helps such as are willing to help themselves. So during the vacations I went out and worked at my trade. One vacation I spent in Springfield, Mass., which is one of the prettiest inland cities in the United States, and noted, the country through, for its morality and literary culture. While here, I worked in the *Daily Union* book room. I found Springfield a very pleasant place to live in. Its inhabitants were remarkably active, intelligent, and thrifty. One of the leading objects of interest to the visitor is the U. S. Armory.

While here I had the pleasure of listening to the preaching of Dr. Ide, a Baptist minister of great ability, both as a preacher and a writer. And he was a host in himself. His pungent utterances carried everything before them. I thought as I listened to his convincing arguments, eloquent appeals, and logical reasoning, as well as earnest entreaties, that he was a representative man the age needs. Yes, we need men of action, intensified action, and, therefore, men of influence and power, to enter the arena of this world and fight the battle of truth against error, and of righteousness against sin. Men are needed who will strike fast blows and hard ones—men who have a purpose and an indomitable will; men who will yield to no discouragement and who will not allow themselves to suffer defeat. Men are needed who would rather die—suffer martyrdom—than to submit tamely and passively to the absurd state of things which too generally obtains in the social, civil, ecclesiastical and moral world. Men who go forth in the might of God to uproot, and tear down, and utterly overthrow and cast out all these formulaes, conventionalisms, legal enactments, and selfish aims and artifices which stand in the way of gospel freedom and the proper development of redeemed human nature. The world is everywhere in perishing need of men who cannot be scared, bought, or sold —will tell the truth fearlessly and take the consequences.

We have had enough of hair-splitting theology on points of minor importance, of subtle metaphysics, of practical atheism, of fawning and of general time-serving. The people are being surfeited with these things, while the "weightier matters of the law, judgment and truth," are being too much overlooked, or purposely ignored. It would seem as if the great pendulum of the moral world has been swinging hellward until it had reached that extremity of its arc, and must again from this time vibrate heavenward.

The people, vast multitudes of them, are ready for the pure truth, and will receive it if it be spoken in the fear and love of God—no matter how plain, the plainer the better. "The harvest of the earth is," in this respect, "fully ripe"—at least this is true in multitudes of places—and all that is necessary is for the right kind of men to "thrust in the sickle and reap."

A sickly sentimentalism, abstract creeds, dry forms, numbers, position, and wealth, cannot accomplish the work to be done. These are sufficiently prevalent and in vogue almost everywhere throughout the wide extent of Christendom, but the world grows no better for their existence. They do not reach the evil, but stop short—very far short. A vitality must be infused into all—a vitality which comes only from God, and which is conveyed through men who are wholly consecrated to his will.

The great need of these times is power, *power*, POWER—more power, moral power, omnipotent power—power to stir men and devils—power with God, power to prevail against all opposition—power to stand and withstand persecution; to flourish, like the burning bush, unconsumed in fire. This is the power that comes of moral purity, of

a single aim to please God. It is the art of hitching on to
Omnipotence by faith, and making the power of God our
own—available to us for the work to be done.

In spite of all the means usually resorted to to reach
and save men, they will sleep on, dream on, die in their
sins, and perish everlastingly, Something more, something
different, is needed. God holds his servants to the real,
stern, old-fashioned, soul-subduing and soul-saving truths
of the Bible as the *sine qua non* (i. e. the indispensible
condition) of success in this work—those truths so unpal-
atable to the carnal heart, and yet so powerful to save men;
so much resisted, and yet so irresistible; so little appreciated, and yet so indispensable.

If they do not preach these truths he will not receive
their services, he will not own them as his workmen nor
accept their work. God always has, and always will, set
his seal to his own truth when it is uttered plainly, fearlessly, and in faith. He will ever accompany truth thus
uttered by his mighty power in such a manner as to convince gainsayers, confound skeptics, and show the people
that he is God, and that they are but worms. Men are
therefore needed who will thus expound God's Word, who
will thus preach his truth—men who will not, who dare
not.

> Smooth down the sacred text to ears polite,
> And snugly keep damnation out of sight,—

men who will eagerly enter any and every open door of
usefulness, and where no door is open, force one open.

Earnest, self-denying men, who count not their own lives
dear unto themselves, only so they may do their whole duty
and finish their whole course with joy, are wanted in every
department of moral enterprise. Of pigmies there are
plenty; but where are the moral heroes? A very few there
are, bless God! But how few and scattering, and how in-

adequate to the moral want of the age. Lilliputian souls
are numerous; but how few are great, noble, generous,
magnanimous, self-sacrificing laborers, overflowing with
love to God and man. A few names there are who have
not defiled their garments in the stagnant pool of time-
serving, nor in the filthy waters of self-complacency. And
how they shine! How precious and valuable they are; of
what priceless worth in such a world as this! Oh, that
their number might be greatly augmented! This is the
pressing want of these days.

Oh, that a multitude of such men might be raised up to
stay the ever-increasing tide of wickedness. Souls here
and there are perishing by the million for want of the
bread of life. Who will break it to them? Who will rise
up and feed to these poor souls the "true bread from
heaven"? In many places the Macedonian cry is raised,
"Come over and help us." Thousands, yea millions, of
souls are perishing for want of gospel light. Sinners are
heedlessly pursuing the broad road that leads to endless
ruin, and many are standing at the very brink of the grave,
soon to be hurled into eternity before a just God, to appear
at his inflexible bar unprepared, without a hope in Christ.
Oh, how much these souls need competent spiritual guides
to point them to the "Lamb of God who taketh away the
sin of the world!" No one to tell them of the power and
willingness of Christ to save—of the all-cleansing blood;
no one to warn them effectually to "flee from the wrath to
come!" Everywhere the fields are white to the harvest.
and what is wanted is more men and means. How the
precious cause languishes because there are not more zealous laborers. We need enthusiastic men—men who are
willing to sacrifice their all, and consecrate themselves to
the work of the Redeemer, to spread the everlasting gospel
of Jesus Christ to fallen and perishing humanity.

We are thankful that every denomination has its fearless

exponents of God's word. It is the blessed privilege of every minister to have power with God and with men. What a blessing such men are to the world. How they raise the aching, longing heart up towards heaven. When I listened to such men as Ide, Holland, Cumings, Vincent, and others, I wanted to light my torch, be it ever so feeble, from off the altar fires of their hearts, and with devotion proclaim the everlasting gospel in great love, yet fearlessly and with unction that would reach the heart.

To this end I redoubled my energies, re-consecrated my life, and counted it a privilege to make any sacrifices if I might but obtain the needed mental training.

Being greatly refreshed I returned to the school to resume my studies for another term with increased industry and diligence. To me study was a pleasure, and books were more pleasing companions than the idle, kid-gloved, fashionable snobs who think themselves somebody because their parents are blessed with a few dollars. But so goes the world.

I spent three vacations in Hartford, noted for its pretty women—but then the ladies all are beautiful.

I suppose this city has more insurance companies than any other in the country. Here I worked on the Hartford *Daily Post*. This city was only some sixteen miles from Middletown, and hence I visited it quite often. But by the river it is about twenty miles, and it was my pleasure to skate the entire distance once in two hours. Perhaps it would be no more than fair to add that I skated with and not against the wind. I must add that Hartford is one of the neatest built cities in all New England. Indeed it is a place I would very much desire to live in.

For culture and refinement few cities in this country present greater advantages than Hartford. The colleges, schools, and churches are among the most attractive buildings in the city. The old Center Church is historically known as one of the Puritan landmarks.

But this beautiful place, like every other in the land, is cursed with the minions of ruin. There is a locality in the eastern portion of the city which presents a picture of human life at once dark and sickening. As I beheld the demoralized condition and the depraved and vicious looks of those people steeped in sin, I wondered if it was possible that any of them ever would enter heaven. Doubtless it was such sights as this represented which called out the great sacrifice of the Son of God. When we take in the magnitude, even from a finite standpoint, of so great a salvation, we can but exclaim: Oh, the love of Christ! The abounding, unmeasured, unspeakable love of Christ! Who shall sound its depth, or ascend to its height, or search out its breadth? A shoreless sea whose depth has never been fathomed! A tower of strength to whose summit none have ascended! A land of liberty and joy whose boundaries are unknown! It is like water to the thirsty, like food to the famishing, like home to the wanderer, this all-embracing, all-sustaining, all-sufficient love of Christ.

It is like the shadow of a great rock in a weary land. When the soul grows fatigued and faint with her journey over the barren sands, that every life-path at times leads over; when the garnish glare of earthly splendors that gleam and dazzle but do not satisfy is become a weariness to both flesh and spirit; then how sweet to rest in the shadow of the Rock of Ages.

The love of Christ! It makes the wilderness to bud and blossom as the rose; it makes the arid deserts of care and toil gush with lucent springs, and gleam with silver-tongued and shining streams! It smoothes the roughest path, it lightens the heaviest load; it softens the hardest blow, and brightens the darkest way. It adds higher luster to the brighest hours, it brings a purer joy to the happiest lot; the fairest days were dark without it, the gladdest thoughts are sad beside it.

Crowd all the charms of this beautiful earth into one favored spot, pour all the blessings of beauty, all the pleasures of taste and intellect, all the sweetness of human love, all the honors and splendors and comfort of this world upon the fortunate dweller there, but withhold from him the love of Christ, and he walks unsatisfied, with a void in his heart that nothing can fill! Isolate him instead within the darkest dungeon, deny him the light of day, the sound of human voices, the sight of dear faces—but leave him the love of Christ, and behold the darkness is light about him.

A love that never fades, never fails, never wanes, never changes! A love that never wearies of our follies and feebleness, that calls for no charm in us to win it, that lends his own strength to our weakness. A love that delights to bless, that asks naught but faithfulness to itself, and forgives a thousand lapses in that!—that rejoices in doing good even to the unthankful and the evil.

A love that comforts the mourner, and points beyond the pall and the coffin and the open tomb, beyond the daisied mound and the shut door of the vault to the shining shore beyond the river, where the ransomed walk, saved through the love of Christ, where the parted meet, re-united in the bonds of peace. A love that cheers the dying and saves the trembling soul, that opens the gates from this land of the dying to yonder land of the living! Who shall describe it? Who shall do it justice? Not I. "For I am persuaded that neither death nor life, nor angels, nor principalities, nor powers, nor things present, nor things to come, nor height, nor depth, nor any other creature, shall be able to separate us from the love of God, which is in Christ Jesus our Lord!"

While this love is precious to the Christian, and a consolation amid the darkest clouds of human trials, yet how little is it appreciated or valued by those whose lives are in open rebellion to the divine government!

While traveling between Springfield and Hartford I for the first time saw the tobacco plant growing in the field, and if the tobacco users could see the filthy green worm that chews it before them, I think they would turn from the disgusting and filthy habit. If there is anything that would grieve the heart of God, it is to see the beautiful and fertile valley of the Connecticut between Hartford and Springfield—the garden of New England—all given up to raising that filthy weed—tobacco. Another sad thought struck me very forcibly, viz: The poor students—such as have no regular trades to work at—usually find employment—about the only work they can find—in these tobacco fields. I have heard them say that it used to make them very sick to pick off those filthy worms from the leaves of the plant. But necessity forced them to become unwilling laborers in the production of this unmitigated nuisance.

I also had the privilege of spending one vacation in New Haven—the city of elms. I never saw a more beautiful street than Arch. The branches of the elms on either side, interlacing, form a perfect arch. There is a pump on the campus whose waters are so pure, sparkling and sweet that it is the wonder and admiration of travelers; and I have gone a mile in order to drink at its fount. Truly, the waters flowing from Siloam's shady rill could not have been more healthful than these.

I have since learned that the pump has been removed, and the well filled up. One such fountain is worth more to any city than all the saloons in the land. It is my opinion that if suitable fountains were constructed in public places of our towns and cities, and made free and inviting to all, there would not be half the drunkenness that now curses the land. In Germany, I remember, they had such fountains erected on almost every street, and thousands, during the summer hours, came and slaked their thirst.

Here, it was my first privilege to live by the seashore.

And there was a marked difference both in the temperature and smell of the atmosphere. Here was a rare opportunity for me. I used to go down to the sea shore and pick up curiously formed shells on the beach, listen to the music of the wavelets falling in silvery spray on the pebbly shore, and enjoy the pure sea breezes and bathe in the dark blue waters. Oh, happy were these hours as I roamed along the shore of the far-sounding sea and looked out over its darkling waters! If one wishes to witness the display of Almighty power, let him behold the angry billows lashing their fury on the shore with a noise more terrific than bursting cannon, when the depths of the ocean are agitated and waves mountain-high roll their crested brows shoreward, sweeping everything in their pathway. Such a sight is both sublime and awe-inspiring.

There was a lofty cliff over against the city, to the summit of which I was wont to climb in the cool of the summer evenings and sit on its brow and note the busy rush of business of Connecticut's metropolis in the valley below, and then raise my eyes and look out over the waters as far as the eye could see. In the far distance, the outlines of Long Island could be seen—a mere black line along the horizon. To the west, hill on hill arose while fertile valleys with fields and meadow brooks spread out between. Being weary, I sat down to rest and meditate. From the brow of the uplifted peak before me, the sun has just flashed back to earth his last parting glance, and out from the gloomy caves of night, dark shadows are gliding like spectres grim and grey, creeping silently across fields of blooming clover and verdant grass, tripping lightly over flowery vales and mossy knolls; darting swiftly up the woody hillsides, and folding all this weary world in one broad robe of darkest grey. Pressed by unseen fingers, the flowers unclose their jeweled doors, and pouring forth a flood of fragrance fill the air with richest perfumes. The songs of the merry little brook, seem set to a minor key, so soft and subdued are its murmurings. A state of dreamy languor pervades all nature, and in the blessed hush of this holy hour, unbinding the galling shackles of toil and wrapping about my weary frame the soft mantle of quiet repose, I yield to the gentle influence of peace, that falls like the silvery drops of a summer shower on my weary, aching heart, washing therefrom the accumulated dust of another day's march in the great highway.

All day conflicting thoughts have thronged my brain. On the troubled waters of fear and doubt I have drifted up and down, while the chilling spray fell thick on my trembling soul. Surging high above my head the gloom-crested waves threatened to overwhelm my little bark Hope, with all its holy freight of happiness and joy; but now, safely anchored in the sunny cove of trust, I look back over the foaming sea, and spanning the dark expanse, with colors undimmed, the bow of peace appears, and smiling sweetly down upon me from a sky serene, the sun-rays of Hope flood my soul with pure and holy joy. I seem in a new world. Calm as the rays that fall upon me from the rising moon, are the waters on which I rest to-night. Over the murmuring sea on balm-laden gales, from that not far-away spirit land, whose thrilling strains rouse the slumbering energies of my soul, and from its joy-lit recesses, in answering harmony with the angel chorus, rises a swelling praise to him who maketh it light at evening time, and whispers in my listening ear in accents softer and sweeter than the breath of flowers, "My peace I give unto you; not as the world giveth give I unto you."

After holding with the invisible communion so sweet and soul-satisfying, and beholding with Faith's clear vision the untold glories of the Eternal, what wonder the chained soul longs to break the cords that bind it to earth, and soar on untrained wings up into higher, purer realms;

shrinking from the touch of things terrestrial, and like
the awe-stricken Apostles, wishing never to leave the holy
mount; rather making thereon tabernacles for an eternal
habitation. But life has its sterner duties from which we
must not shrink. There are deep, sunless vales of hard
endeavor, as well as joy-wreathed mounts of peace, for us
to pass in our journey to the Celestial City. "Go work
in my vineyard" is a command resting upon all. None
are exempt, the divine edict extending to every son and
daughter of Adam. It is our duty, then, as subjects of an
all-wise ruler, to labor; it is essential to our happiness and
the fulfillment of our mission on earth. We disobey God
and incurring the divine displeasure, suffer a merited punishment, if, folding our hands in inglorious ease, we eat
daily of the honeyed bread of idleness. But labor hath a
deeper import, a higher and holier object than simply
gathering the perishable things of earth. There is a heavenly manna, the soul's daily food, for which we ought
all to earnestly seek, without which the famished soul
shrinks into an image of deformity, an object of pity in
the sight of wandering angels. Ah! how many are there
starving the soul to nourish and adorn the body; forgetful
of the exceeding worth of the inner above the outer man.

One Sabbath evening I went to a fashionable church,
but, while the ushers in silver slippers and with smiling
faces gushingly received those who had on goodly apparel,
none of them noticed me or offered to give me a seat. Of
course I retired to my boarding place, revolving many
things in my mind. At another time, having obtained
entrance at another church, I was equally astonished in
hearing the preacher, in the course of his sermon, declare
that he had no patience with those who always dealt with
the first principles of the gospel, or that were hunting up
young men to swell the numbers of the membership. He
said his church had got beyond first principles, and as for

14

additions to the church, it was full: it did not need more. I was confounded, for I had never so understood the gospel. Again I thought, and put things together, and again I wondered what it all meant. Only a stone's throw from the church where I heard this sermon, a man told me he could count fifty prostitutes in one block alone. While I was slow to believe this statement, yet, I saw many painful sights. I was working on a morning paper part of my time, which usually caused my work to end at three or four o'clock in the morning, and, at that late hour, I passed a dance house filled with drunkenness and revelry and dancing. What a picture? not wanted at the churches. And who shall be responsible for the loss of those souls?

There is a day of wrath coming. It will come sometime though long deferred. And one of the advantages vouchsafed unto us by the gospel of grace is the tender mercies of a loving Saviour, and the offer of pardon and full salvation to all who will accept through Christ. It is the part of basest ingratitude to resist the heavenly entreaties, expostulations, invitations, and promises so lovingly, freely and mercifully held out to perishing, helpless man. We sometimes think that those who reject so great good, offered to them on so liberal conditions, do not fully comprehend or take in the magnitude of the atonement. Did they realize it in all its proportions, it would seem that no rational mind would give sleep to the eyelids until the soul's safety was secured.

Neither the preacher who does not want the people reached by the gospel, nor yet the deluded and self-deceived will be held guiltless, though the heavens may bend in mercy, and the Mediator stay the arm of Omnipotence. Every soul is required to work out its own salvation with fear and trembling. Let me for a moment pause, and present some of the considerations which will fill our minds and engage our thoughts when the "day of his wrath" shall appear. To enter more clearly into the thoughts under consideration, we recommend the careful reading of the 6th chapter of Revelation. So terrible will be that day spoken of by the Revelator that the physical world shall be convulsed, the sun turned to blackness, the moon to blood, the stars fall from their orbits, the mountains be wrenched from their primal setting, the islands lashed, and the very heavens rolled together as a scroll. Men will be stricken with great fear, and in their terror will run to the mountains and caves and will cry unto the rocks, saying, "Fall on us, and hide us from the face of him that sitteth on the throne, and from the wrath of the Lamb, for the great day of his wrath is come; and who shall be able to stand!" And what the wrath of the Lamb, the meek and lowly Jesus, can be in that day we do not know unless it is to visit on those who have slighted his mercies and spurned his offers the merited and justly deserved punishment.

But is it possible to take into the mind and for the imagination to forecast the terribleness of that day as it shall flash over the world in the twinkling of an eye? It will come at just such a time when men will least expect it; when the world's great workshops shall be peopled with men, women and children. No universal blast of death will have first swept across the earth, and depopulated it of its inhabitants. Living men and women and children will be all over the world when the day comes, as full of strength, health, vigor, activity, thought, forethought, as at any period since God first "breathed into man's nostrils the breath of life."

It will come when men are blind to its coming, each in his own blindness, asleep — each in his own dream. The astronomer will be calculating his eclipses for years to come — the physician will be studying his arts, to add length of days to man's body —the philosopher, with his

"philosophy falsely so called," will be improving and en-
lightening his species—the politician will be planning
beautiful schemes for man's welfare in ages onward—the
man of riches will be saying to his soul: "Soul, thou hast
much goods laid up for many years; take thine ease, eat,
drink, and be merry"—the "man that will be rich" will
be toiling and laboring after his "filthy lucre," rising up
early and sitting up late—the man that "liveth in pleasure"
will be sending for "the harp and the viol, the tabret, and
pipe and wine," to be in his "feast," regarding "not the
work of the Lord, neither considering the operation of his
hands"—blind preachers will be speaking their smooth
things and prophesying their deceits, each in his own delusion, but all of them blinding men's eyes to the day—the
king, and the noble, and the magistrate, and the farmer,
and the tradesman, and the laborer—the mean man and
the mighty man, the married and the unmarried, the people and the priest, the servant and his master, the maid and
her mistress, the buyer and the seller, the lender and the
borrower, the taker of usury and the giver of usury to him
—shall all be weaving their webs of distant years and distant things, turning time into eternity, thinking and speaking of time's world as never-ending, at the very instant
when the day of His wrath shall send the thoughtless and
mercy-rejecting, and God-hating, and Christ-spurning, and
rebellious, and heaven-defying multitudes on their knees
imploring the mountains and the rocks to fall on them.
And what a prayer of self-accusation, of self-reproach, of
despair, it will be!

But who can fathom the human heart save the Almighty?
When the five cities of the plains were about to meet their
doom, it is said of their inhabitants that they offered violence to the very angels who came as monitors of the impending doom. Whether the world shall be better or worse
at that day than it is now, is a question worthy of the pro-

foundest thoughts of the ablest thinkers of the age. At all events it will be bad enough. Doubtless there will be thousands and tens of thousands of living men, eating and drinking, buying and selling, planting and building; fluttering like the butterflies in a summer's day about the perishing flowers of a perishing world; steeping all their senses in the earthly business of the passing hour; making everything a business, whether pleasure, daily avocation, or necessary labor. The farmer will be at his market, the planter with his trees, the builder at his house, the tradesman in his shop, the student at his books, the reveller at his feast, the gambler at his cards, the rake at his revels, the usurer at his gold, the nobleman at his pomp, the king at his court, the soldier in his camp, the laborer at his toil, the idler at his folly, the drunkard at his drink, the glutton at his meat! Each at his sin, each in his day-dream, each in his soul's poison! The Lord bears it no longer. His mouth has sent forth the word of all-desolating vengeance. The vengeance storm obeys, and gathers and thickens, and rolls on, and hangs over. One moment's pause— the preachers are preaching—peradventure the sinners may repent. One moment's pause—hark! the pause is terrible— hark! "A shout, the voice of the archangel, and the trump of God." And the world will roll in flames of living fires, while over the crash of burning worlds, the shrieks of startled and unprepared millions, a voice shall be heard—a voice louder than mighty thunders, louder than the lashing of ocean waves, more awful than dissolving elements: "TIME IS NO MORE!"

Oh, what a day of separation — instant and awful — will that day indeed be! Two of a household shall be in one bed, brothers, it may be, that have grown up together, eating of the same meat and drinking of the same cup— two women of one village, sisters in neighborly love and kindness, shall be grinding corn in one mill, each for her little ones—two men of the same house of worship, dwelling together as brethren in unity, and making their daily labor good and pleasant by sharing it together, shall be working in one field;—and " one shall be taken," "caught up to meet the Lord in the air," and " the other shall be left." Oh, then will be the cry of those who are left bitter and all-consuming: "Rocks and mountains, fall on us!" Our punishment is just, but our disappointment is more than we can endure; hide us, for the glory of the Lamb is but burning wrath to our guilty souls. Oh, the bitter lashings of these awakened consciences so often stifled and crushed; who shall be able to stand? Oh, my soul, believe it not! But oh, be not deceived. The soul that spurned, rejected, and despised the bloody sweat of the Lamb of God in the garden of Gethsemane, upon that eventful night when he cried: "If it be possible let this cup pass from me;" or sneered at the sinless One, as from the cross he cried: "Eli, eli, lama sabacthani," will not be able to stand before the glories of our risen Lord—the King of glory.

But I forbear carrying this thought any farther. God be merciful to us sinners! If these thoughts engaged our minds as they should, and as they will, I cannot see how men who have taken the vows of the church upon them can rest at ease.

In the light of these sublime and awful solemn truths, prepare my heart and head, O Lamb of God, to sound the gospel trumpet until the thoughtless shall pause to reflect on the danger of resting one moment short of salvation in Christ. Oh, it is sad to see this beautiful city given up to sins of the grossest kind, while those who hold the Lamp of Life are satisfied to read moral essays to fashionable sinners. One blessed thought—we are yet on mercy's side of the grave. The day of his wrath is yet in the future; the invitations of the gospel are yet ours to accept. O Lamb of God, help us, help these poor hearts of ours to come to thee, and that early, while it is yet to-day!

But my soul was set on fire with indignation and pity to see God's holy Sabbath profaned all along the shore, either way from the city, by multitudes of men and women either drinking and dancing on the smooth and shady grounds spreading back from the water, or gambling, or swimming by hundreds in the surf. But why do I write these things against New Haven, the city of elms, of schools, of intelligence, of enterprise? Because I saw them with my own eyes, and they made a lasting impression upon my mind, and because I had heard so much about the morality of this city.

Though I spent six weeks here, yet they seemed very short, for I never tired in looking upon the enchantments of the ocean, the coming and going of vessels and great steamers, and the usual bustle of city life. In returning to Middletown, I went by way of the shore road as far as Lime, and from thence by steamer up the Connecticut. And it was a memorable ride along the base of those New England hills, to look upon the villages and antiquated farm-houses. At Lime I had to wait some six hours for the steamer, all of which time I spent in running from one object to another. I thought I could catch another glimpse of the sea by going down through the fields a short distance. So off I started, and went some three miles, but to no purpose; however, I had an opportunity to see some real old-fashioned farm-houses, and the sight of these repaid me for my sea chase.

On the west side of the Connecticut, and almost opposite Lime, is Saybrook, one of the oldest towns in New England, and the former home of Yale College. There is a charm about these Connecticut towns I fail to describe. They must be seen to be appreciated, and Saybrook peculiarly impressed me with this feature of New England. In short the whole length of the Connecticut, from Springfield (as far up the river as I have ever been) to its mouth is lined with hamlets, towns and cities, both beautiful and picturesque.

Upon arriving at home, I was well refreshed to enter upon a vigorous year of hard study. All of which I was glad to have the privilege of doing. This was now my fourth year in Middletown, and I was real happy in the pursuit of my study and the progress I was making, and, humanly speaking, I was expected to enjoy the pleasure of graduating from the University.

But, strange as it may seem, I was cut short in my expectations—it was not for me to enjoy such privileges and blessings as I was then in the possession of long.

While I heard and saw many things I both loved and admired, I also observed many which were not so pleasing. I shall not speak of them further than to say that sin has also marred these beautiful valleys and grand old hills.

I remember upon one occasion of being invited to go down the river on an excursion. The day was lovely in every respect, and many gallant men and beautiful women joined in the festivities. The ride was all we could expect; indeed the owner of the handsome steamer, acquitted himself like a gentleman. But on the return they must stop at Haddam three hours to shake the "light fantastic toe" over the carpet of green.

I retired, and took a three hours' ramble over the woodland hills and verdant valleys. Oh, how charming! How true it is that we walk here, as it were, in the vestibule of life; at times, from the great cathedral above us, we can hear the organ and the chanting of the choir. And not only was the grove made vocal by nature's appointed minstrels, but the earth beneath my feet was strewn with flowers. If there are any wayside angels other than those appointed as guardians over us, then these flowers are angels of refinement and good thoughts. Happy is the person who is early taught a love of flowers. Earth may grow weary to him, life may lose its charms, but he will ever derive consolation from the thousand scources of nature. He may go forth, dispairing and disgusted with the deceptive charms of the world; but when he is alone in the mossy woods, with the flowers all around, and their odor rising in the hushed air, he finds that there is beauty still left in existence. His spirit roves from the beautiful flowers to their maker and preserver, and to the blessed coming-time when he shall wander as a white-robed angel, where the roses of Paradise are blossoming along the River of Life.

The time having expired, I hastened back to the boat, and arrived home about sundown.

But how little do many people realize the true grandeur of life. It seems to be generally accepted that to gratify the social and lower passions is the crowning glory of earthly existence. There is a shrinking from anything that has the appearance of suffering, forgetting that, as the flower when trod upon gives forth its sweetest perfume, so does human life when softened and refined by deep sorrows. Why, just look at the Saviour. Was there ever such gentleness and sympathy? And was he not thus because he was a "man of sorrows and acquainted with grief"? Behold the crowning glory of this virtue in Gethsemane.

It is night. The new moon casts her faint light through the branches of the well-grown olive trees. Not a breath of air is felt; not a sound is heard save the flapping of the wings of some feathered tenant of the grove, being disturbed in its night retreat by some evil-disposed rival. Yonder is the brook of Cedron, winding its way through the valley of Jehoshaphat. Its rippling waters leap from shoal to shoal, murmuring its song of praise to Him who does all things well. Overhead the starry heavens are spread out, lending grandeur to the scene. Opposite is

the city of Jerusalem, and out of one of the gates we see
twelve men issue, slowly treading their way across the
brook. How wearily they walk. Silently, as though some
great sorrow pressed their hearts, they enter one of the
gates of the garden. Proceeding some distance, they sit
down under one of the trees. Eleven of the company are
heavy with sleep, but the other seems to be burdened with
a load that is ready to crush him to the ground. He requests three of the group to come with him some distance
from the rest. Having arrived at a suitable place, he un-
burdens his heart to them: "My soul is exceeding sorrowful; tarry ye here, and watch with me;" and admonish-
ing them to prayer, he tears himself from them. See how
he reels as he advances, and falling on his knees—no, on
his face—we hear the plaintive cry floating on the midnight air: "O my Father, if it be possible let this cup
pass from me; nevertheless, not as I will, but as thou
wilt." See how he agonizes; look! what is it that trickles
down his careworn brow and runs down his weather-beaten
cheeks? Is it drops of sweat? No, no, it is blood that
courses down his sacred face. And who is this sufferer?
And whence this agony? But stop; what is that shining
form gliding through the trees toward him? It is an angel,
sent from the shining courts above to strengthen him. To
strengthen whom? Your Saviour and my Saviour. And
what for, do you ask? To bear your sins and my sins; yea
the sins of the whole world. He was about to drink the
very dregs of our cup of woe. The agony of pain deserved
by me and you, dear reader, caused this sweat of blood to
ooze from his undefiled body. Our woe was breaking
over his guiltless head. He bore our sorrows and our
griefs, and with his stripes we are healed. The punishment
due us was meted out to him.

But why was it that our Saviour, the God-man, thus
suffered? Was it to gain power? No, for he is the King

of kings and Lord of lords. Was it to gain wealth? No, for by him " all things were made." Was he obliged to do it? No, for he laid down his life of his own free will and accord. Was it because we were his friends? No, for we rebelled against him. Was it to gain fame and happiness? No, for he is " Lord over all, blessed forever." What was it then? It was pure disinterested love, love and compassion for his enemies, that actuated him to undergo this trying ordeal. Well may the poet exclaim:

> " Oh, for such love let rocks and hills
> Their lasting silence break."

Oh! how our hearts should melt in humble gratitude to our adorable Redeemer for such unparalleled love and affection. How we should humble ourselves in dust and ashes before him, and how willingly we should unreservedly consecrate all we have to him and his service, for —

> " Love so amazing, so divine,
> Demands my soul, my life, my all."

But do we display any gratitude when we spend our precious time in idle frivolity and senseless levity? And is it at such times heavenly messengers come to us, and pour out upon us benedictions? No. They come only when we are sober and meditative. They came to Jacob while pillowing his weary head upon a stone in a strange land, to Joseph while in the Egyptian prison, to Moses while in the desert near Sinai, to Gideon while in the field, to Elijah while by the brook's side, and to the Saviour while in the garden of suffering. Is there not a lesson in all this for us to imitate and follow? The men and women who have drank deep at the wells of sorrow are the ones who can enter into human sympathy and move us to noble actions. And these, too, are the silent workers. They seek not, and therefore expect not, the adulations of men.

Human butchers, and human monsters such as Xerxes, Alexander, Napoleon, Frederick the Great, whose garments were rolled in blood, at whose tread the nations trembled, and who left rivers of blood to mark the pathway of their career to worldly fame, expected and demanded honors at the hand of their fellows. But these men and their imitators, curse humanity rather than bless it. It is not the great and mighty forces (as men count greatness) that are the most productive of good. The quiet ministrations and acts are the ones most likely to bless and benefit. It is the bubbling stream that flows gently, the little rivulet which runs along day and night by the farmhouse, that is useful, rather than the swollen flood or warring cataract. Niagara excites our wonder, and we stand amazed at the power and greatness of God there, as he pours it from the hollow of his hand. But one Niagara is enough for the continent or the world, while the same world requires thousands and tens of thousands of silver fountains and gentle flowing rivulets that water every farm and meadow, and every garden, and shall flow every day and night, with their gentle, quiet beauty. So with the acts of our lives. It is not by great deeds good is to be done, but by the daily and quiet virtues of life, Christian temper, and meek submission to God's appointing. All our prayers and all our desires should be prefaced: "Not my will, but thy will be done."

But to return. At the end of another school year, I thought I would go to Albany, N. Y., to spend my vacation. I could have found work at Hartford, New Haven, or Springfield, but, as I was not really obliged to work, but doing so from a conscientious motive of helping myself all I could, and at the same time wishing to see as much of the world as I could, I resolved to visit Albany and work during the vacation. Accordingly I laid my plans to take the steamer for New York City, and from thence, another boat up the Hudson, thus giving me a good opportunity to see many things at about the same expense as to go in the cars. Being all night on the water, we arrived at New York about 4 o'clock. But I was up at early dawn and on deck to drink in every object of interest, to see, if possible, if I could recognize the places as I saw them from the deck of the vessel when first I landed on these shores. But found I could not. Doubtless such great changes had taken place that it was not possible for me to trace the objects.

I had no sooner landed than I took the street cars and went from one end of the city to the other, and where there were no cars, I footed it. I also went over to Brooklyn, and traveled by street car and on foot until I was very tired. Already I had spent about eleven hours in looking upon the magnificence of New York and Brooklyn. It would take too much space to give the readers a description of these great cities, besides, they are well known to most of people, but I will relate an incident or two and pass.

What I had experienced in New Haven, I here saw carried out with greater artistic skill. I never visit a city but I try to see and learn all I can, and I anticipated a rich treat the following day. I was up with the sun's first rays. A clear Sabbath morn touched spire and dome with its kindling benizen. Clear and distinct, yet soft and hallowing as the music of the ocean murmur, chimed out the bells of Trinity. A wondrous mingling of the solemn and the triumphant marched out on the hushed air, and the waves of the grand old-time melody poured into the soul with its flood of other-day memories. Up with every trembling note the spirit mounted until it heard them caught up in an exultant anthem in the beyond.

I turned into the throng which swept along Broadway. I noticed nothing of the externals of the living tide, but thought of him who came from heaven to labor, suffer and die, that man should sing this anthem of triumph over death and the grave.

As I lingered by the church door, a poorly-clad woman crept hesitatingly near, and anxiously peered into the dimly-lighted space. A sister in costly robes swept scornfully by her, and the poor one shrunk back. And such a look of agony; so piteous—so terribly eloquent of despair —as rested upon that upturned face. "Pass in," I said, "they'll give you a place." She hesitated a moment, and then stole over the threshold, but was met three steps from the door, and almost rudely told that there was "no room here for such as you!" Just the very experience I had at New Haven, only in a milder form. The frail form shrunk back, reeled a moment, as if under a blow, and passed out.

The chant of the organ within, the soft, rich light in the lofty room, and the costly surroundings, all at once seemed a mockery; the very spire in its baptism of gold, a piercing lie. Sorrowfully, and with cheek hotly-burning, I, too, turned back and followed the retreating figure. She turned into a locality where, on that beautiful Sabbath day, the leprous blight of vice and crime reeked like a consuming plague. Within sight of that lofty spire and within sound of those thrilling chimes, was a seething, burning hell on earth! Everywhere rang out the freezing oath, the obscene jest, and the boisterous, mocking laughter. The curse of rum, and of its twin ministers—vice and crime— was written on all things; stared from signs on dingy, crumbling tenements; floated out from the broken windows; burst up from the stenching cellar-ways; rang sharply from filthy and ragged groups gathered in the sunshine. What a sepulchre of manhood and womanhood; of virtue and truth; of hope of earth and heaven. The sights and sounds smote the soul with sickness. I looked up to the sun, and wondered how it could beam so sweetly on such a scene. Over the grim walls I listened to the chiming of a hundred bells, and asked whether it was true that Christ ever cared for or redeemed such as these? Whether on earth there was one angel of kindness and faith to watch over them? Whether Christ could raise such to the beauty of transfigured glory? Whether those at their worship yonder ever thought of heathen but a stone's throw from their temple?

Heavy-hearted I turned into an alley, and up a filthy stairway, and stood in the presence of poverty.. What a dwelling-place for human beings! Up to the opening in the roof, and hot with the miasma of pestilence, a current of air met me at the landing. Floors, walls, and passages were repulsive with the accumulated dirt of years. With compressed lip I peered about, and finally knocked at one of the doors. Slowly and suspiciously the door was opened and I passed in.

Were this not from real life, passing before my own eyes, not one of my readers would believe that a Christian land had one such place; our brotherhood such degradation. There were, in that small room, twelve persons of different ages, standing, sitting and lying. In single garments filthy and tattered, grown-up girls were crowded into one corner. Children, half-naked, poured out their profane welcome. Gray-haired women stared at me with a mingling of scorn and surprise. Swarthy men, with matted locks, glowered as if in anger. Want, vice, and crime here found a lair.

Ah, my reader, here was the desolation of rum. Oh, had I the gift of expression, I would write so plainly against this enemy of all good until every eye could see it as I now see it in this room—a very hell on earth. From the gilded gin palace on the corner of yonder street, through all the walks of life, its march of ruin is onward. It invades the family and social circle, and spreads woe and sorrow around. It cuts down youth in its vigor, manhood in its strength, old age in its weakness. It breaks the father's heart, bereaves the doting mother, extinguishes natural affection, erases conjugal love, blots out filial attachments, blights parental hope, and brings down moaning age in sorrow to the grave. It produces weakness, not strength; sickness, not health; death, not life. It makes wives widows, children orphans, fathers fiends, and all these beggars and paupers. It hails fever, feeds rheumatics, nurses gout, welcomes epidemics, invites cholera, imparts pestilence, and embraces consumption. It covers your land with idleness and poverty, disease and crime; it fills your jails, supplies your almshouses, and demands your asylums. It engenders controversies, fosters quarrels, cherishes riots, condemns law, spurns peace, loves mobs, crowds your penitentiaries, and furnishes victims for the scaffold. It is the life-blood of the gambler, the aliment of the counterfeiter, prop for the highwayman, support for the midnight incendiary. It countenances the liar, respects the thief, esteems the blasphemer, violates obligation, reverences fraud, honors infamy, defames benevolence, hates love, scorns virtue, and slanders innocence. It induces the father to butcher his tender offspring, the husband to murder his wife, and helps the child to grind his paricidal axe. It burns man, consumes woman, detests life, curses God, despises heaven. It subborns witnesses, nurses perjury, defiles the jury-box, and stains the judicial ermine; it bribes votes, disqualifies voters, pollutes your institutions, and endangers your government; it degrades citizens, debases legislators, dishonors statesmen, disarms patriots. It brings shame, not honor; disgrace, not hope; misery, not happiness; terror, not safety; and as if with the malevolence of a fiend, it calmly surveys its frightful desolations, and insatiate with havoc, it poisons felicity, ruins morals, blights confidence, slays reputation, wipes out national honor, curses the world, and laughs at its ruins. Would to God this were all! It does more. Must we write it? IT DAMNS THE SOUL! Awful thought. Terrible doom. Yet Christians sport with this satanic agency as a harmless thing. As I think these things my very soul cries out for help and safety to the victims of this monster.

Oh, what a sad sight. In the corner and upon rags, was a girl in the last stages of consumption, the still beautiful wreck of early womanhood, smitten in its downward way, and fast wasting unto death. The strangely full and lustrous eye heralded the swiftly-coming change; the hectic burned brightly upon the sunken cheek. The hair, fair as if touched with summer gold, lay out upon the rags, and the thin, transparent hands lay out on either side. The neck and bosom were bared, as if to win a touch of air upon the burning flesh. The bold, sneering look of the leper had passed away, and the face was so gently, so touchingly sad that I wept over the wreck of this once lovely and beautiful person. Some laughed rudely, others hummed snatches of song, others were cursing over their drink.

The girl beckoned to me as I stood with the extended hand in mine. For a long time she looked me in the face, the bosom heaving with short, sharp gasps; and then her eyes slowly filled, the tears rippling over the cheeks and dripping upon the rags.

"Why do you weep in this place, sir? When mother died, oh, so long ago, I wept. I wanted to die then. Do you think I shall die now? I hope so, for I am so tired. I once heard that there was one Jesus, who could make angels out of such as I am; but I have never seen him. Is he good to poor folks? Does he ever come to such places? A man once told me that this Jesus had been killed, and that I should be lost. If He is living, and would come here, He would pity me, I know He would, and take me where mother is! Is that heaven for poor folks? Are you Christ? Did He ever weep? If He had come and wept

15

as you do, I know I should have been good, and not have been in such a place as this. You—Mary—Mother—Jesus—"

I wept in the presence of death. Calmly, as the sun would set, the burden of a weary life had been lifted, the eyes looking out as if upon some sweet vision in the distance, and a smile of unearthly sweetness lingering upon the half-closed lips. Jesus was last whispered there in life; let us hope that Jesus was with her in death. Mary —the woman I had followed from the —— church—and a stranger had held the weary hands as the erring one went out into the dark valley of the limitless beyond. Had she seen a mother—seen Christ? Had that weary soul, made as wool through the mercy of the Redeemer, arisen from that couch of rags and its sin-stained clay, and, with ministering and waiting angels, entered into rest?

The words of the dying girl were a terrible revelation. An orphan, homeless, friendless and without education, the currents of her life had swept her out like a waif and dashed her upon ruin. What fair reader of the GOLDEN CENSER wishes to test her heroism by waging such a battle against such odds?

Motherless, and no common or Sabbath-school instruction; no knowledge of God, or his son! Has heathendom one history so sad? Here was heathenism in a Christian land. Perhaps it was well I was permitted to see and to experience this hour in this great city. The impressions, certainly, are deeper upon my heart, and while I mingle my tears with these victims of sin—sinned against more than sinning—I can but hope the words spoken may spring up unto eternal life. And is it possible that one can profess to be crucified to the world and not be touched by others' sorrow? Can one believe in Christ, remain idle —faithless—while thousands of such are all about us? Leave the costly equipage, now and then, brother, sister, and on foot, as did our Saviour, seek souls among the poor and the unfortunate. There is a power in a living, practical, working gospel; triumphs awaiting the exercise of a Christ-like faith—a faith of works. Among the erring, even, may be found those who may be made heirs of glory. Such do not attend your churches. Go to them, and touch chords which shall vibrate by the throne of God.

The next day I renewed my observations of New York. About noon, being well tired, I sat down upon the steps of the city hall, and wrote a letter to Mrs. L. H. Wait, descriptive of what I had seen in the commercial metropolis of the western world. After this, feeling rested, I again set out to look in upon the great printing offices. I visited several large daily offices, and was offered a situation in one of them, but declined to accept, for I feared the temptations and evil influences of this city might be too great for me, hence I could not be persuaded to accept. I have learned that one way—and a most effectual way it is too—to resist temptation, is to keep out of its influence.

The day being far spent, and being fatigued, I set out for the Hudson, purposing to continue my journey to Albany. Walking leisurely and rather slowly along, a young man rushed up and stuck a bill in my face, which announced the sale of jewelry, and great bargains to be had. I paused to read, and then told the man I did not wish to purchase as I never wore such things. At this juncture another came up apparently very eager to learn the contents of the bill and was also very anxious to make a purchase, and the two urged me to go with them. Still I refused, telling them I had no desire whatever to make such a purchase. At length they said, if I did not wish to purchase, I need not do so, but they would esteem it a great favor to have me go with them. I still hesitated, and only consented to go as a mere matter of accommodation which they assured me would be greatly appreciated by

them. Yet I did not feel that things were quite right.
Another thing that made me regret my having consented to
go was, as soon as we had entered the room, a door attend-
ant locked it after us. As for the jewelry, I would not have
given one dollar for all there was displayed. My two companions purchased freely and one dollar drew valuable
watches—all the sales were in purchasing a ticket, and the
ticket drew whatever the number upon it corresponded
with in the show-case. I still stood and looked on, and
was not at all anxious to invest. But they continued to
urge me to "try my luck," and I as stoutly refused, reminding them of their promise.

But they began to grow more vehement, and almost
compelled me to make a purchase. Finally they asked me
if I had any money. I told them I had enough to pay my
expenses to Albany. Then they wanted me to show it to
them. This I refused to do, at the same time feeling anxious for my safety. They then grew angry and commenced to swear at me. This made me feel still more
uncomfortable and I began to realize that I must be in
some of the "sharpers'" trap.

Finally I told them if they would let me out I would
make a purchase. To this they agreed. I paid one dollar,
and drew a blank. In this I was not disappointed, for I
considered myself lucky if I could regain my freedom at
the expense of one dollar. They urged me several times
to try my luck again as I would have better success. But
I kept reminding them of their promise, constantly telling
them I had no use for jewelry.

At length they unbarred the door and let me out. When
I had reached the street I took a long breath, and resolved
not to be thus caught again.

I continued my way to the boat, purchased a ticket, and
purposed sitting down and taking a rest. Having gone
aboard, and, it being quite warm, I took a drink of water.

While at the tank, a well-dressed, fine-looking and gentlemanly behaved man waited his turn after me to take a drink. While I was drinking he asked me where I was going. I told him. He wanted to know if I lived at Albany. I replied that I did not. Upon this I passed along to a sofa and sat down.

Scarcely had I seated myself than the man at the water tank took a seat by my side, and continued his conversation. He was cleanly dressed, had a duster, and to all appearance looked like a man of business. He said he was a merchant in Albany, had been to the city and made a purchase of goods, and there was only an hour left before the boat started, and he had to see about the shipping of his goods, and wanted to know if I would do him so great a favor as to go up town with him, and accompany his wife and sister to the boat while he attended to his goods, as he had not time to do both, and he feared his wife and sister could not find their way to the boat alone. The request, uttered in all sincerity, seemed to me to be a reasonable one, and, tired as I was, I told him I would go with him and do as he had requested.

He took me through one street and another, occupying my attention by prying into my history and asking very personal questions. I felt somewhat distressed, yet politeness to him forbade my doing otherwise than to answer them.

We had traveled some two miles, and I began to grow anxious about getting back to the boat in time, and had frequently asked him how much farther it was, and was on the point of breaking away from him and returning, when a man, springing out from some unperceived nook, in an angry tone demanded pay for a bill of goods shipped, which he violently shook in the face of my companion. It was for the amount of $600. The merchant pulled out his pocket-book as if he was willing and ready to pay. But here came the "tug of war." He had a great roll of bills, but all ranging from $500 to $2,000. He could not make change so as to pay the $600. In his perplexity he turned to me and asked me if I had any money. I replied that I had. "How much have you?" I said, about $50. He still seemed perplexed, and took out another pocket-book, and, behold! he found $50 in small bills. Now if I would lend him my money he could make change. The man who presented the bill kept urging him to hurry up as his time was valuable. The merchant asked me if I would lend him my $50 until he reached the boat, when he would re-pay me. I hesitated. I did not feel quite right in the matter. He, seeing my hesitancy, offered me a $500 bill for security until he reached the boat. Still I hesitated. He as promptly offered me a $1,000 bill if I would only lend him $50, so that he could pay the man. I had never seen government bills of the denominations above named, and I feared there might be another "sharper's" catch in this, so I declined.

Upon this they both turned upon me and urged me to accommodate them in a matter of so great importance. I put my hand into my pocket, and had hold of my pocket book, when I noticed the merchant give the other a wink of the eye, peculiar and similar to winks exchanged at the jewelry store where I had so recently invested one dollar. The thought flashed into my mind that this was nothing but a confidence game, and, without saying a word, I turn-ed and ran, leaving the merchant to pay his own bills, and to escort his wife and sister.

In both instances above given I was a victim to the "confidence craft." It is worthy of remark that no one molested me during the whole day until near four o'clock, and in the vicinity of the Hudson steamers' dock.

I barely reached the boat in time, though I used great haste in returning. Thus ended the day in New York I was pleased with what I had seen, and could not help but feel that Providence had protected me even while in the hands of those who sought to overreach me. If any of my readers ever. visit New York, I hope they will remember these incidents and look out for the sharpers, for they will always come in disguise, professing the opposite of their designs, and, doubtless will be the most friendly people you will meet—that is, they appear so to be.

Upon arriving at Albany, I learned through parties from the vicinity of my father that his family was broken up, that Jacob had gone out into the world as I had done before him, that Mary, through heartless abuse, suffering and exposure, was in an asylum at Troy, N. Y., and that my father had gone to Philadelphia.

All this was as unexpected as it was sad. Oh, the desolation of rum! Upon hearing this, I at once hastened to see Mary, when I for the first time learned how she had been so misused, since the death of my mother, by my father and a step-mother, as to bring on derangement, and in this condition was thrust into Marshall's Infirmary, where she had been for nearly four years when I found her. She was then gradually recovering, and her physician expressed thankfulness that I had come.

I at once, though not without a severe struggle, gave up my studies to provide for her. I felt this was my duty, and conscience—the monitor of my life—approved of my conviction.

I first thought of finding a home for her until I had completed my education, but her physician thought it would not answer to place her among strangers. So I gave up all my long-cherished anticipations, and took her out of the asylum to provide her a home.

It would seem that all this was providential, and I could hardly realize the fearful reality. It was very hard to give up my good home at Mrs. Hayes's which I had so long enjoyed, and the flattering prospects of reaping the reward of my toil and suffering and unflinching determination to graduate from college, nor could anything else have turned me from my purpose. But this appeal was direct, and her claims on me for protection seemed imperative. I tried to find my two brothers, but these I could not find. There was therefore not one of the family remaining to whom she could go. While at the asylum I further learned that father had sold his mountain home in East Sand Lake, and had started a liquor saloon in Philadelphia.

I think the reader who has followed me thus far in this narrative knows pretty well where I stand on the liquor question. To learn that my father had finally gone into that business made me feel very bad. That soul-destroying occupation has ruined millions. The marks of bloody hands are all over the liquor-seller's fortune. His business is to coin the diseased and depraved appetite of men into money. There is no single moral element of legitimate commerce in it. While other men deal in that which benefits the consumer, he trades in what produces nothing but blight and ruin. Whoever consumes his goods has less of moral character, of social standing, of productive power, of personal happiness, of the respect of men, and the favor of God. Taken into a family they destroy peace, and love, and hope.

His earnings represent that which should be food for hungry children and common comforts for distressed households. His calling blesses no human being and curses most deeply those whose money he receives. As he is successful the sum of human happiness diminishes in the world. His business is at war with all public and private interests. It is the fruitful source of murder, beggary and disease. His business place is the scene of brawls, fighting and profanity. Crime of all kinds increases as he prospers. There is not a home in the land but would be

happier and safer if his business were blotted out of existence. He stands the active antagonist to the churches, the
schools, the laws, the homes, the hopes of the whole community. Mothers pray that their sons may be saved from
his clutches, wives that their husbands may not come near
him. The bread of children depends upon the avoidance
of him. The public is more secure on its holidays if he be↩
compelled to lock up his establishment. The more frequently men visit his place the less likely they are to attend to their regular calling. He sees his patrons die in
the madness of delirium before they have numbered half
their days, because they have been good customers of his.
All this he sees and knows, and yet for money he will per-
sist in the evil work. He is able, as is every other business man, to trace the lines of his traffic. He knows who
are his customers and where his profits come from. He
understands perfectly that his gains represent the homes of
families robbed of their shelter, bread taken from their
mouths, and shoes from the feet of children. That they
are often the earnings of weary and worn women with the
needle or over the washtub. That they represent money
begged in the name of charity by his pitiable victims from
door to door. That his every dollar represents unutterable
agony and is stained with human blood. And yet with the
coolest calculation he accepts the responsibility for the
money it brings. By this cold, fiendish greed for gain he
is led on in this traffic of infamy. But I could hardly believe that my father, once so noble-hearted, generous and
kind had come to this. How sad! To sell liquor, what a
responsibility!

Here I lose sight of my father altogether. I never could
obtain his address, and, at this writing, I do not know
whether he is dead or alive.

As I look over the strange scattering of my father's family, I have often reflected what a wonderful display of the

work of rum it manifests. There are five of us living, and three of us do not know where the other two are, and I suppose father does not know, and, possibly, may not care, where any of his children are. If rum does not degrade natural affections, I do not know what does. The superintendent of the Infirmary also told me that father came after Mary in the spring, but, remembering what she had passed through, he refused to give her up; and advised me to take her beyond his reach.

I again set out for the West, and, after some effort, found employment in the Racine *Advocate* office. As I had nothing to commence with but ready hands and willing heart, every cent of my wages went as fast as I earned them in clothing her up. At first she was much depressed, but our home overlooking the lake filled with many a sail, and the mellow sunlight sparkling upon its glassy surface, soon diverted her mind.

As she had never been to school a day in her life, and fearing to send her to school now on account of the state of her mind, I tried to learn her the alphabet, which, after a great effort, I succeeded in doing.

She told me that after mother's death, she had to work out of doors. In the winter time she was compelled to drive oxen and draw wood, wading through the deep snow all day, and often her skirts and stockings would be frozen around her ankles, and her feet and hands white with frost; in the summer time she had to work on the farm in the hot sun; that she did not get half enough to eat; often she was so whipped that she could not raise her hands to her head for days, shoulders and arms being laid open in gashes; she never was allowed time to comb her hair except Sundays; often sent to bed without anything to eat; that the last thing she remembers, she was sent to her stepmother's brother, whose wife was on her dying bed. It was late in the fall, the weather cold. There were five children in the family, and she had to do all the work of the house. Nights she had to watch with the sick woman until twelve o'clock; was forced to sew while doing so, and in a room without a fire—as the man was too stingy to allow her a fire; and that her fingers would be so benumbed that when she accidentally pricked them in sewing, she did not feel it, nor would blood flow.

I could give many pages of which the above is only to illustrate the general fact, that all the children were treated heartlessly at home.

Kind reader, it was this poor helpless sister I befriended, and left my books to provide and care for, and in so doing, however great my sacrifices, I have always felt I was only doing the duty of a brother.

CHAPTER XVIII.

The Conception of the Golden Censer—Ups and Downs in Starting the Paper—Among the People—Strange incidents.

I was getting along comfortably, when in the dead of winter I was thrown out of employment. As I had no means to stem the tide, I went to Milwaukee to look for work; from there to LaCrosse, stopping at the intermediate towns and cities; thence to Rochester and Owatonna, in Minnesota. From there down to McGregor and Prairie du Chien, and thence back to Racine. Meeting with no success in any of the cities along this route, I came to Rockford, but making a failure here, I did not know what to do next. It seemed I had done all human energy could. Tired, discouraged and sick at heart, I spent sleepless nights thinking what I could do. Do something I must, and that without delay. I went to Freeport, Lyons, Clinton, Rock Island, and Davenport, but to no purpose. Anguish-riven, I gave up in despair, when I conceived the idea of combining both my intellectual attainments and my trade in something that would bring me relief, and the Golden Censer was the result.

The reader will notice that publishing a paper never entered my mind previous to this, since my boyish attempt spoken of in a previous chapter. I was studying for the ministry, and I thought I could do nothing else but work at my trade. Neither do I take any credit for the conception or the bringing into existence of the Golden Censer. The whole thing was unpremeditated, and I was only led to the act by force of circumstances. But is not this God's way? Had it not been for the failures in finding work, and the desperations of my necessities, the GOLDEN CENSER would to-day be unknown. It is the same old story over and over. David, the stripling shepherd lad from the flocks with his sling and pebbles meets the vaunting enemy of Israel; the humble and ignorant—as the world counts wisdom—disciples tell the story of the cross though opposed by Jewish priest and Roman ruler; God-fearing and man-daring Luther takes down the long-neglected Bible and preaches a free salvation obtained through the atonement of Christ; Latimer and the martyrs declared amid the tortures of the burning fagots that the light which they had kindled should never go out; Bunyan behind his prison bars dreams of the royal road cast up for the ransomed to walk in, and gives to the world the Progress of the Pilgrim; Wesley stands on the grave of his father and offers a pardoning Saviour to a perishing world; Whitfield dared to preach though hell arrayed itself against him. Time would fail us to tell of the vast army of revivalists, ministers and workers in our country who poured out the best energies of their lives to save souls. And all these were pressed into their service by the force of circumstances, and were modest and retiring. But the world always looks to great and learned men, while the reverse is God's appointing. Go into any country you please, visit any college or seminary you choose, and the wealthy young men are not the leaders of the people or foremost in the noblest work which can engage the attention of men and absorb their energies. I am aware there are honorable exceptions. But, as a rule, the most eminent divines, the most distinguished statesmen, the wisest rulers, the ablest judges, the most renowned philosophers, the most successful evangelists, came from the homes of poverty, and, to a certain extent, were the makers of their own manhood.

I know of an eminent college president, who, in his college days, for want of six cents to pay postage on a letter,
had to let it remain in the postoffice three weeks; of an
able preacher who, for the want of means while a student,
studied his lessons under a street lamp; of a statesman
whose wisdom filled the land—one whom millions have
learned to bless—who studied his borrowed law books while
walking twenty miles over a March road in the central part
of Illinois. Indeed, this page could be filled with incidents similar to the above, illustrative of the fact that character has to be cut out with hard blows and severe mental
training, and only the few are willing to pay the price.

But God knows his workmen. He prepares them while
they are behind the plow, in the forest with the woodsman's
axe, in the office as chore boys, in the store or bank or
shop as errand lads, and all at once their names flash over
the land as did David's when he had defeated the enemy
of Israel.

But I shrunk from my task. It was a dark, desperate
hour to me. I had my sister to support and no work to
be .obtained. What could I do? Already I had traveled
over five hundred miles—some of it on foot—to find work,
and came to Rockford, with the hope that where I was best
known they would pity me and give me work. But in the
years that had passed since I left it great changes had taken
place. Mr. Daugherty had died, the *Register* was owned
by others who knew me not, and hence I received no encouragement.

Perhaps it may not be out of place to relate some incidents in my travels. They were many, but I can give
only a few. When I left Racine, Feb. 8th, 1868, it was a
bitter cold day, and traveling was very uncomfortable; but
I endured the weather's inclemency, and patiently went
from place to place asking for work. At New Lisbon, Wis.,
while waiting in the depot for the train, I was tired, hun-

gry, and thirsty. I had but little money, and hardly felt warranted to go to a hotel for a meal. As there was no water to be had in the depot, I went over the way, and entering what proved to be a saloon, asked for a drink of water. The bar-tender very politely handed me a glass of water. While I was drinking it the proprietor, a German, upbraided his clerk for giving me water, when if he had refused I might have purchased lager. He said all this in German, which I understood, and when I had set down the glass I looked him in the face and in the German language politely thanked him for the glass of water, and walked away. He looked astonished, but his hard features did not relax.

The train arrived at LaCrosse about two o'clock in the morning. But I was so saving of the few dollars I had that I sat up the remainder of the night. But even this was begrudged me by the hotel-keeper, and I went out upon the streets, and walked up and down until daylight. Thence I crossed the Mississippi on the ice, and footed my way from LaCrosse to Rushford, up the valley of Root river, and from there to Rochester, Minn. While thus traveling I was overtaken by a sudden thaw, and the walking was rendered very bad, as the snow and water in many places flooded the road. From Rochester I took the cars to Owatonna. Here I obtained a day and a half work. In the evening I attended a prayer-meeting for the first time in Minnesota, but my heart was so filled with disquietude, and my mind so depressed, that I could not enjoy it. From here I went to Austin, where I obtained half a day's work. In the meantime the weather had changed, and a great snow-storm prevailed. We waited full six hours for the train, which was blocked in by snow. While thus waiting, I for the first time saw Fred Douglass, and listened to his brilliant wit, and sound common sense.

From Austin I returned to Racine, on the promise of

Mr. Wm. Louis, son-in-law to Mr. Mitchell, a prominent wagon manufacturer. Before I left Racine he said he would employ me as book-keeper, if I failed to find work. In this I was also disappointed. As near as I could learn, he promised me this situation without intention of fulfilling. I waited on him a whole week to answer me, but I have not yet been informed. I came to Kenosha on the cars, but from there the road was blocked up, so I footed it over the drifts, often sinking into them up to my waist, and on the second day met the snow-plow at Genoa Junction, and arrived in Rockford about midnight. Here I obtained work for three weeks. Going to Freeport I took the cars to Port Byron, arriving there at ten o'clock at night. From here I footed the distance to Rock Island in the same night, arriving at Moline just as the sun was rising. I was terribly scared several times during my lonely night journey, once by a ferocious dog, and once by a strange noise for which I could not account, but which appeared to be the waters of the Mississippi washing against rocks in the channel of the river. The reader will understand that the road lay along the bank of the river. Another strange thing was, about three o'clock in the morning I suddenly entered a dense fog, and after traveling some time in it, I as suddenly came out of it. This was accounted for afterward when I learned that it was low, marshy ground. On my return I stopped at Fulton. I was now out of money. I asked several hotel-keepers to keep me all night, but, upon being refused, I sought quarters in some empty freight cars. It was so cold that I was soon frozen out, and had to exercise to keep warm. I undertook to cross the railroad bridge which spans the Mississippi, but after feeling my way in the dark on the extended trestle-work, at the eminent risk of falling forty or fifty feet, I at length reached the bridge proper, when I was compelled to turn back, as the guard would not permit me to pass. Well, I spent the remainder of the night in running and jumping to keep from freezing. Failing to find work at Clinton and Lyons, I footed my way back to Mt. Carroll, where I obtained two days' work, and then returned to Rockford.

These, my good readers were some of the efforts I put forth to find work to provide for my poor sister. I cannot give all the hardships endured, for they would occupy too much space. Everything looked dark and discouraging. It seemed too bad that a living could not be obtained at the price of honest industry. If other young men have the same difficulties in finding situations that I experienced, I pity them. I find that it is a safe rule to follow, where it is possible, to always look up a place or situation, before leaving the old. But of course this cannot be done when one is thrown out of employment, as in my case.

But how was I to publish a paper without a cause, without friends, without money, without credit, or even experience as an editor? I hardly dared disclose my purpose to any one, lest they would think me deranged or a madman. I had obtained a little more work upon my return to Rockford, so I had a little money, enough, perhaps, to pay my own and sister's board for two weeks. With a heart too full of trouble to express on paper, I went to a small job office—then located near the river, but since discontinued—and hired the use of the type for one issue. For this I paid five dollars. With a cloud of doubts, and fears, and anxiety, I set every type for the paper myself, working until two or three o'clock in the night. In the stillness of the midnight hour when naught broke the silence save

The click
Of the type in the stick,

I wondered if people would subscribe for the CENSER. I thought if they could look down into my bleeding heart,

16

they would subscribe, whether they wanted it or not. Thus day after day and night after night, I worked on, until at the end of two weeks, with many prayers, and trembling hands and a fluttering heart, I folded the first sheets as they came fresh from the press.

As a matter of curiosity, as well as to show how faithfully I have adhered to my first assurance to the people, I reproduce the salutatory of the first issue of the CENSER, which is as follows:

"Through various difficulties and over many obstacles, the GOLDEN CENSER comes before the reader for the first time, fresh and full of hope. Questions will arise in the mind of the thoughtful reader as to what will be the policy of this paper; what denomination it is to represent. In meeting these inquiries, it replies: It shall be its life purpose to make the GOLDEN CENSER a first-class family paper. All articles which have an evil and pernicious influence will be carefully excluded from its columns. It is painfully conscious that our beloved country is flooded with a literature which is poisoning the minds and ruining the immortal souls of our young people. To counteract this tide of unwholesome reading, it shall be its aim to place a paper before the youth of our land which shall exert a beneficial influence upon their minds. It shall be a paper for the young Christian and aged saint.

"The GOLDEN CENSER is to represent no denomination, for every denomination is already ably represented by an efficient press. It acknowledges the universal brotherhood of man. From whatever shore or clime, if he has the imprint of Christ upon his heart, we can shake him by the hand as a fellow-pilgrim on the heavenly journey. We expect to associate with the blood-washed throng on the shores of eternity, why not here? God loves the heirs of glory, why not we? They are on their way to a home beyond the river of death, why not join their company? We may not agree upon every point in theology, but for that shall we turn the cold shoulder and point the finger of contempt? God forbid. We worship one God. The same Saviour died for all. We take the same blessed Bible as our guide, and expect to meet in Judgment, where it will not be asked what denomination we represented, but whether we have been workers in the harvest-field of the world.

"But while we take this stand, we do not wish to be understood that we advocate church union. For it is not clear to our mind whether it would be for the highest advantage of the church to become a trunk without branches. We believe that each branch of the Christian church has her mission in this world, and with Jesus as its head, we say, Press on to victory; may God bless your efforts and eternity reveal your works as that of faithful servants. Nor do we wish to be understood that we shall uphold the views of the "liberal Christian," who is riding to heaven in a golden chariot; for without the cross there is no crown. Nor shall we approve of the "isms" which are flooding our land, and by their false and unscriptural teaching are sending deluded mortals to hell by thousands. But we shall be earnest workers; we shall advocate righteousness, temperance, and a judgment to come; we shall stretch forth our hand towards the erring, and with tenderness and love gently raise them up, pointing them to the bleeding Lamb of God 'who taketh away the sins of the world.' To this end we ask that God may give us wisdom, a humble and submissive heart, direct our thoughts, guide us in our duties, and bless the mission of the GOLDEN CENSER to the good of its readers and the world."

But all kinds of rumors were on the streets, which made me feel very much discouraged. However, I summoned courage, and called on seven ministers in this city and gave them sample copies, with a simple request that they take them to prayer-meeting and give them to earnest workers, and encourage my efforts. I also sent copies to other ministers all over the country, with a similar request. In the city I received no encouragement, so far as I know, from the pastors called on, and but one from abroad. Things looked darker still, for I expected some sympathy from those who profess to sympathize with earth's sorrowing ones, who have consecrated everything to Christ. It seemed very dark, for now I was not only out of work, but some $25 in debt for the use of type and press, and my own time and labor lost. Oh, if the people could have looked into my heart and seen the deep anguish there, they would have been moved to compassion. But the conflict was yet before me.

With a heart filled with doubts and anxieties, unheralded, unpuffed, and unknown, I started out on foot to procure subscribers. A few who knew my desperate circumstances subscribed to encourage me, never expecting to see the second issue. Leaving Rockford in the hands of my friends who promised to circulate the CENSER and procure subscribers, I set out for Cherry Valley, Belvidere, Caledonia, Beloit, Rockton, Shirland, Durand, and Winnebago. These places embrace a chain of towns lying in a semi-circle north around Rockford.

At Belvidere, I called on four ministers and plead for sympathy and co-operation in obtaining subscribers. I gave them copies, with a similar request as above. Upon calling on them a second time to learn of their success, I was told by one, that the papers were used to start fire with, by another, that he was not in the canvassing business, by a third, that he had enough to do to attend to his duties, and so on. Not a single word of encouragement did they give me, but did all they could to discourage me. I turned away grieved—and, I could not help giving vent to my feelings in tears. Oh, where was the cup of cold water given in the name of a disciple? where the precept of the golden rule?

I have always held the office of the Christian ministry as sacred, and supposed that of all men the consecrated servants of Christ would be moved in sympathy for me, and the disappointment of my expectations staggered my faith in religion. But this was only for the moment. Though all mankind should deny the power of the gospel, yet "I know that my Redeemer liveth." In the depth of my distress I went to the Fountain of Life for comfort and support. The world's charms may all fade as do the summer flowers, the gems of beauty tarnish, and every prospect be cut off; yet the precious store-house of God's love stands open to the humblest of his creatures. There is the precious blood—precious because he who shed it is the mighty God and the sinless man; because without it sin could never be forgiven, lost sinners never saved, and God never reconciled—precious, because its voice, both within the veil and in believing hearts, ever whispers peace—precious, because every soul sprinkled with it shall be eternally safe from the glittering sword of God's vengeance. Of its preciousness the white-robed multitude will ever sing before the throne of God.

To the aching heart Jesus is precious because he is the brightness of his Father's glory; because he is "bone of our bone and flesh of our flesh;" because all the majesty of Divinity, all the tenderness of perfect humanity, meet in him; because in his person and in his work there is exact suitableness to meet the need of ruined souls and trusting saints. He is the "one pearl of great price"—the "chiefest among ten thousand," the "altogether lovely One." His holiness, his power, his love, his grace, are precious. His living, his dying, his interceding, his second coming, are precious. So exceeding precious is he to believing hearts, that to all eternity they will gaze upon it, and tell it out, and yet leave its depths unfathomed.

This precious Saviour gives us precious faith, and this is precious because it is the hand that clings to a precious Christ—the eye that gazes upon him through the mists and vapors that darken this vale of tears. Precious, because it draws the soul into communion with its risen Head. Precious, because it rests on the sure foundation of the truth of a covenant-keeping God. Precious, because it looks "not at the things which are seen," often so troublesome and so dark, but "the things which are not seen," "the fullness of joy," which is at "God's right hand for evermore."

Added to all these are the precious promises, precious, because they are very many; and their clusters are very sweet. Pardon for the guilty, strength for the weak, comfort for the mourner—yea, every good and perfect gift that weary, hungry, thirsty souls can need, is wrapped up in these "precious promises." They shine forth through the Word, as brilliant stars shine out of midnight. They rejoice the heart as fair flowers charm the weary wanderer over a desert way. Precious, because they are "yea and amen in Christ Jesus." The believer's heritage of promises, in all its rich, unfailing abundance, can never be forfeited.

These precious things all the discouragement of the world could not take from me, and in this time of perplexity were a great consolation, and enabled me through my tears to look up from the world, and beyond its heartless, unceasing cares to the hill-tops of glory. Ah, yes, good reader, beyond this vale of gloom, where cold winds blow and bitter storms beat, is a fair land of delightful scenery and healthfulness. No storms come there. No clouds, no frosts, no heat, no withering of beautiful flowers, no fading of lovely fields—the "evergreen shore," indeed. Here the skies are always bright, the air ever pure, birds ever singing, nature ever smiling. Hilltops are clad in bright green, valleys decked with beauteous flowers. Nature smiles to the inhabitants of that land, and the blessed inhabitants smile back, and say, "Great is the Lord, and greatly to be praised!" The bright beyond is not far off. Over these "hills of time," in the near distance, the hilltops of glory appear; and roaming those "sweet fields beyond the swelling tide" shall be seen those who are now freed from the troubles that crowd in upon my life. I too long to be free, yet I dare not distrust the goodness of my Heavenly Father who is too wise to err. I have somewhere read of a chamois hunter of Chamouni, who, in crossing the Mer de Glace, endeavored to leap across one of the enormous crevasses or fissures by which the ice-ocean is in many places rent. He missed his footing and fell in, but was able, by extending his arms, to moderate the speed of his descent, and thus reached the bottom, a hundred yards below, without a fracture of limbs. But his situation seemed hopeless. He could not scale the slippery walls of his crystal prison, and in a few hours at most he must be frozen to death. A stream of water was rushing below the ice, downwards towards the valley. He followed this, the only possible path. Sometimes he had to bend low in the narrow tunnel; sometimes he waded, sometimes he floated down. At length he reached a vaulted chamber, from which there was no visible outlet. The water which filled it darkly heaved. Retreat was impossible; delay was death. So, commending himself to the help of God, he plunged down into the center of the gurgling pool. Then followed a moment or two of darkness, tumult and terror; then he was thrown up amidst the flowers, and the hay-fields, and the merry songs of the vale of Chamouni.

This illustrates the brief moment of time when compared with eternity. Our path may be often dark and dangerous. Escape may seem impossible. Death may put on its most appalling form. But uttering our watchword, " Jehovah

Jireh," let us still advance. Even if we see no light beyond, let us plunge into the darkness for a moment only. Then we shall be ushered into that world of light and bliss, where we shall prove, in the fullest sense, that eye hath not seen, nor ear heard, nor hath it entered into the heart to conceive, the things which God has provided for those who love him.

While life is brief when compared with eternity, yet it is our duty and privilege to work for God. In this span of existence, though we can touch the cradle with one hand, and the tomb-stone with the other, the highest favor that can be conferred upon a mortal is to be permitted to work for God. The dignity of the calling does not depend upon the work done, but upon the exalted character of him for whom it is performed. The Queen of Sheba regarded the servants of Solomon as objects of envy. His fame was great throughout the world, and his servants shared in his renown.

If those who serve an earthly monarch derive luster from his power, much more are those exalted who do the bidding of the King of kings. They are the favored ones of earth. They are akin to angels. These do the will of God in heaven; the saints do it in the more difficult place—on earth. Their reward is great. It will be bestowed, not according to the nature of the work, but according to the fidelity with which it is done.

God will give employment to every one who will consent to do his will, but we cannot choose our work. God does that. We are very apt to over-estimate our own ability. A railroad could never be run if every man was allowed to choose his own position. The brakemen would all want to be conductors—the conductors, directors—the firemen, engineers, and the engineers, superintendents. There is always confusion in the cause of God when the disciples insist upon choosing their places. Diotrephes is never satisfied unless he can have the pre-eminence. His motto is, "Rule or ruin;" and where he rules he is almost sure to ruin. The foot is a very useful member of the body; but place it where the eye should be, and it becomes a deformity and a nuisance. He who is sulky and fault-finding, unless he can be leader, is not fit for a leader. He who backslides because a license is not given him, stands more in need of saving grace than of a license.

If we really desire to serve God, we shall take our work as his providence opens it before us. We shall not grumble at his allotments. We shall not keep everything in confusion by insisting upon having our own preferences gratified. Some persons, who really appear to want to be good, can never, for any length of time, be contented anywhere. Things do not go as they wish. The wills of others come in conflict with their own. Unexpected difficulties arise. Faith and perseverance might overcome them. And this was the element now called forth by the opposition of those who professed to be ministers of Christ. While I was toiling night and day to bring out the CENSER, I never anticipated that I would meet with opposition from Christians, or that my hard-earned efforts would be used by a minister to light his fire with. But so goes the world. I might have known better had I reflected, for the progress of the Christian religion has been contended every inch of its way, and men sometimes preach for money. But perhaps it was suffered to be so, for it kindled the fires of true devotion in my own heart, and when I saw the deadness of the church it filled my soul with a zeal and enthusiasm before unexperienced, and I resolved to boldly contend for my God-given rights, though all the forces of earth and hell were brought to bear against me. It requires a holy boldness to stand up for truth under every trying circumstance. You remember when Paul with burning eloquence and unparalleled earnestness preached of temperance, of

righteousness, and of a judgment to come, even the learned
Agrippa cried out: "Paul, thou art beside thyself; much
learning doth make thee mad." To meet the forces of sin,
a man must take his life in his hands, and commit his ways
unto God. There is no neutral ground—"either for or
against" is the Divine declaration.

There is a power in this divine consecration, this holy
enthusiasm, this convincing earnestness, this pleading perseverance that carries all before it. One man with God on
his side can put to flight ten thousand of the hosts of hell.
Witness Elijah on Mt. Carmel. All Israel is assembled to
see which should be God. With a boldness, and yet a
humble trust in the God of heaven, he stands up before
the assembled thousands and not only defies the prophets
of Baal to call on their god to consume the sacrifice by fire,
but in language that must have vexed them, he said, "Cry
aloud, for he is a god, either he is walking, or he is pursuing, or he is on a journey, or peradventure, he sleepeth."
There was no cringing fear in that language. The prophet's heart burned with holy enthusiasm to win the people
back to the worship of the true God. The same enthusiasm was manifest on the day of pentecost when Peter stood
up before the very Jews who had so recently crucified the
Lord, and plainly told them that they had committed the
wicked act. Evidently Peter did not preach to please the
people. He delivered God's message though every word
like melted lava went burning its way to the hearts of his
hearers. Oh, for the power of the Holy Ghost in these
days of backsliding and coldness! I want enthusiasm in
God's work, and I must have it if I would succeed. I care
not what the world or sinners may say. The devil would
steal away my very heart if I would but let him. Why
should it be a reproach to a Christian to use this element
of power? We find it in the world. Show me the man
who is not earnest in his secular business, and I will show

you one who does not prosper. Yes, men are sometimes intensely earnest when dollars are at stake, or homes are being lost, or property destroyed. Who could not see this element in action when the great financial crisis was upon us, and banks were tottering? Why, in New York men sat up day and night poring over their ledgers, and on the streets men offered fortunes to but take the place of another in the crowd pushing toward some unfortunate bank. Men were enthusiastic then, and they were not ashamed to let the world see their enthusiasm. So it is on election days. How men will work, and pull, and plead, and argue to secure the election of their men. And they are not ashamed to let men know that they are enthusiastic. But the Christian, he must keep cool, keep his mouth shut, put his light under a bushel. Don't raise a religious excitement. If you do, why souls will be converted, and the devil will be defeated. Ah, good readers, if we would win in the battle of life, we must let the world know that we mean earnest, uncompromising, persevering, enthusiastic efforts! Men are in earnest in business circles, in every department in life The minions of darkness are in earnest in their work of ruin. The saloon, the ball-room, the theater, the places of pleasure, are open day and night to lead the young from the paths of virtue. And these places are fearfully in earnest in their hellish work. So enthusiastic are they in their labors that these gateways to ruin, these side doors to perdition, these ante-rooms to hell, are clothed and arrayed in the most attractive manner possible.

With our church doors locked all but two or three hours in the week, with our faith, if we have any, down in our boots, with our over-coats and furs on, with fear, doubt and hesitancy stamped in every feature of our face, and with a hollow, sepulchral voice, we wail over the declination of religion, we talk about the inroads of infidelity, the rapid spread of the "isms" that are creeping over the world.

And it is enough to freeze the very atmosphere to hear some Christians talk. Oh! my brethren, open those church doors, pull off those over-garments, fling those doubts and fears to the wind, and, under God, go to work with the same faith and enthusiasm that you display in your counting-room, your store, your work-shop, or in whatever department of life you may be engaged, and there is no scriptural reason why there should not be such a revival of religion throughout this land as has not been witnessed for years. "According to your faith, be it unto you." There is more danger of cold formalism than of anything else. We have unbounded faith in the gospel of Christ to the saving of the world. It is declared that the nations would be converted, that the kingdoms should become our Lord's. Why not work for the accomplishment of these desirable ends? Let the children of God but see eye to eye in this great, this common work, and Christianity, like a mighty tidal wave, will sweep all the opposing elements before it. There is as much power in the gospel to-day as ever. The arm of the Almighty is not shortened that he cannot save. We know that man unrenewed by grace is bad, but no worse now than at any former time. He is as bad as he can be. He was bad in Eden; he was bad for two thousand years under the law, and has been bad these almost nineteen hundred years under grace; but there is power in the gospel to save. When men are willing to give their lives to work for God and for humanity, then he takes these men and uses them.

I have always admired Grant's replies. When asked as to the feasibility of a certain military measure he replied, "We will fight it out on this line if it takes all summer." When the brave Garibaldi was on his way to Rome, he was told that if he got there he would be imprisoned. Said he, "If fifty Garibaldis are imprisoned, let Rome be free!" And when the cause of Christ is buried so deep in our hearts that we do not think of ourselves, and are willing to die, then we will reach our fellow-men. There have been in every age brave souls that stood as living witnesses for Christ. And, thank God, there are many such in every community at the present time. Dr. Duff, the returned missionary, once addressed a meeting of his countrymen in Edinburgh, Scotland. As his great heart burned within him for the great mission work, and witnessing the apparent coldness and indifference of his hearers, he grew eloquent, not only eloquent, but earnest, not only earnest, but enthusiastic, until he fainted in the midst of his speech. When he recovered, he said: " I was speaking for India, was I not?" And they said he was. "Take me back, that I may finish my speech." And, notwithstanding the entreaties of those around, he insisted on returning, and they brought him back. He then said, "Is it true that we have been sending appeal after appeal for young men to go to India, and none of our sons have gone? Is it true that Scotland has no more sons to give to the Lord Jesus? If true, although I have spent twenty-five years there, and lost my constitution—if it is true that Scotland has no more sons to give, I will be off to-morrow, and go to the shores of the Ganges, and there be a witness for Christ." That is what we want. A little more—a good deal more—of that enthusiasm, and Christianity will begin to move, and go through the world and will reach men by hundreds and thousands.

If these professed servants of Christ had thus been actuated they would have taken me by the hand and said: " Yes, young brother, your paper has the gospel ring in it, and in so far as you conform to the teachings of the divine Master, God bless your efforts. We will help you. There are people all over these cities that need just such a paper." But this was not said to me; hence, is it uncharitable to conclude that either they were extremely selfish or else they were "wolves in sheep's clothing"?

Being thus taunted and mocked, with a bleeding heart I turned away from these dry sticks, these soulless monsters, these who denied me the crust of bread or cup of water, and put my trust alone in God, and relying upon my own energy, set out on foot, visited all the places round about, and personally asked the people to patronize my humble efforts.

I was two weeks in making the trip. And oh, the weary feet, and trial of faith, the choking back the crushed feelings, and the heart-sighs were known only to myself! But there were wayside angels—God bless them!—who had comforting words even for me. Out of the thousands of homes visited by me—for I worked from the time people were out of their beds in the morning until they retired at evening—I procured some 320 subscribers. About half of these had paid me. Foot-sore and well-nigh sick from exhaustion, I returned to Rockford, paid my bills for paper, printing, etc., and at once set to work to bring out the second edition. This was issued the same as the first—doing all the work myself. By the time this was put to press, four weeks had expired since the first issue.

When I had returned from my trip, and paid all my obligations, some, who were stung because God had helped me despite their contumelies, then misrepresented me. Turning to the file of the second issue, Vol. I., I find the following language in one of its editorials: "The reader is aware that I do all the mechanical labor upon the paper myself, and it keeps me so occupied, that I am compelled to work nights until a late hour. I have been so pressed on this issue, that I have not even had time to write out my editorials, but have put them from the brain into type. As I compose the type on this article, all is still as death around me. The noise and bustle of "busy life" has ceased; the "world's great workshop is closed;" you, gentle reader, like the lily of the valley, have gone to rest. Sweet sleep is refreshing your weary body and mind, while the stars above you in beauty smile-on the darkness of night, and the dewy shades mantle mountain and forest and field. I fain would enjoy your luxury, but patiently I toil, while the deep-toned bell in yonder church spire measures off the weary hours, to bring forth a paper which might interest you. As I work on, doubts and shadows flit before me, I wonder if sympathy for me fills your heart to the extent of spending one hour, only one hour, in getting sub-scribers, while I give not only day after day, but night after night. It is hard for me, I admit, but, dear reader, you would weep over me if you knew the anxiety which weighs down my poor heart. God knows I am honest as the day is long, yet hundreds, for no other reason than simply because I have kindly solicited their patronage, have expressed their suspicion as to my motive, and I am grieved when I meet such. For could they look down into my heart and see the motive they would insult me no more."

Oh, it was so hard. I was sorry many times I was so foolish as to enter upon such an undertaking. While thus lamenting I received the following letter:

148 MADISON ST., CHICAGO, ILL., MAY 6, 1868.

FRIEND LEMLEY:—I feel that I am no stranger to you, for I love all that love my Savior, and I write to encourage you, if you are unselfishly doing God's will. But why not put your paper on higher ground than to support self? Why not propose to do all in your power and all in the power of your friends, with the help and blessing of God, to try and win sinners to Christ—and that short word "sinners" includes us all—to try and make Christians Christ-like, to make them better, to show them the possibility of a better Christian life in this world?

Your life has not been of sore trouble for naught. Man did it, but God allowed it, and allowed it for good He has good in store for you, if you will reach out your hand for it. May God bless you and guide you and show you himself.

There are two ways of starting a newspaper. The first, is to spend from $20,000 to $50,000 to establish and find a circulation. That is man's way, and it shows the usual wisdom of man in its extravagance. The other way is, to be sure you are doing God's will, and in faith rely upon him to find for it a circulation. God's blessing is worth more than $50,000 or $100,000.

I believe in Providence, and I do not know but God has been training you for just this work, and that your paper, so unattractive to bigoted men, set in sects like men in plaster cases in order to get their " busts," may yet be the power of God unto salvation. I pray God that it may be a spiritual paper, and that its tendency may be to draw a backsliden people nearer their God, from whom they continually confess they have departed.   H. D.

This letter from (to me) an entire stranger was a beam of sunshine through the rifted clouds. It put new ideas into my mind. I had thought of nothing higher, except in a general way, that is, it was not the burden of my heart to make it wholly a simple matter of faith in God, and look to him for my daily bread, but I was desperately struggling to relieve my temporal wants. I thought if God should bless my humble efforts, why not throw myself upon his bounty? But I was slow in learning this lesson.

As soon as the second issue was from the press, I again set out on foot to procure subscribers. This time I visited New Milford, Byron, Oregon, Mt. Morris, Polo, Dixon, Franklin Grove, Ashton, Rochelle, Creston, Malta, DeKalb Center, Courtland Station, and Sycamore. I was about two weeks in completing this circuit, and returned to Rockford with my boots literally walked out, worn to shreds, but I had four hundred names.

One of the most fearful nights I ever passed was in footing it from Sycamore to Belvidere, across the country, twenty-two miles, in a terrible rain-storm. There was not a dry thread on my person, and I thought I should give up before reaching the latter place. But I succeeded, and was in time for the night train west.

I could fill this page with incidents in my canvass, but I must hasten along in this sketch. Doubtless many will remember the care-worn and discouraged face of the writer as he for the first time modestly asked them to subscribe for the CENSER.

In all of the above-named towns the CENSER has had a good circulation from the beginning, and many names, I remember them still, now stand on my lists as landmarks of those days.

I remember entering a house in Oregon, when the lady looked me in the face and exclaimed; "Why, young man, you are sick?" I replied that the hot sun constantly beating down upon my temples caused me to suffer continually from severe headaches, but I could not help it.

But why do I prolong this scene? Pen cannot describe the hardships and the struggles and the weary, unceasing tramp, tramp, from daylight to late in the evening. But in all this I was establishing my credit, if nothing more. Farther, I learned lessons worth their weight in pure gold. I noted every word and criticism uttered or made, and I obtained the expression of the people as to their idea of what a religious paper ought to be, and I said to myself, God being my helper, I would incorporate the ideas of the people, and bring out just such a paper as they had indicated. Thus the reader will see that I took my first lessons in editorship while tramping from door to door, and listening to the criticisms, which sometimes were severe and humiliating.

With the experience, the money, and the seven hundred

17

and fifty names, I began to feel encouraged. I bent all my energies to my task, and issued the third number about the 10th of June, and every two weeks after this issue through the year!

I also received several encouraging letters of which the following is one:

BELOIT, Wis., June 7, 1868.

DEAR BRO. LEMLEY:—In looking over the GOLDEN CENSER, to-day, I see so much food for the Christian I can truly say that my heart burned within me while reading your blessed paper. I would say, brother, go on, and may God bless you, and may you succeed in your noble enterprise; you shall have my feeble prayers, influence and support, and I doubt not that you will soon have the prayers and support of all good Christians. I feel that your paper is just what we all need in our families where we have children. Keep up good courage and let your noble paper circulate; it will be bread cast upon waters; it will return with double blessing to you. If you ever should hear that one precious soul has been saved through God's goodness by reading your paper, it would well pay you for all the trouble and trials you have had. I hope you will succeed; you must not get discouraged, knowing that you are in a good cause. Yours respectfully,

M. D. CLARKE.

While working on the third issue, I purchased type enough to set up the entire paper, but the press-work had to be done at another office. At the end of six months the circulation reached one thousand. But I persevered with an iron determination, and with an energy that bid defiance to impossibilities and that would make a failure a success, I surmounted every obstacle, and carried out my purpose. I confess it required firmness and a stiff upper lip, but I could not for a moment entertain the thought of giving up.

As the reader might expect, I made many blunders. But there was always some one ready to send me a cutting, stinging letter. These I would read, and re-read, bitter though they were to my sensitive feelings, until the lesson was stamped upon my mind. I cannot express the discomfiture I experienced when somebody, being offended at an article, ordered the paper stopped. I surely thought my business was ruined, for I expected the next mail flooded with similar letters.

In the midst of my perplexities and doubts, I received the following letter from the Rev. Isaiah B. Coleman, West Stephentown, N. Y.:

"'What meaneth this?' Thus inquired the wondering multitude, when with the sound of 'a rushing, mighty wind,' God manifested himself to his disciples—the Holy Ghost resting upon them in 'cloven tongues like as of fire,' inspiring them with power to speak with other tongues the wonderful works of God. Not at some mighty, rushing wind, not at cloven tongues of fire, nor of the speaking with other tongues, have we stood in wonder and amazement, but at the wonderful power of God, in taking instruments of humble birth, and transforming them, as it were, into angels of mercy. So thought we, as we took up the GOLDEN CENSER, addressed to another, with its pages all aglow, with its sweet-burning incense, fragrant with its well-timed soul-food, adapting itself to the wants of its many readers. The inquiry and amazement becomes more intense, as the mind goes back only a few years. When its editor, as yet but a boy, stood at the door of the writer, shivering with cold—from his scanty clothing—asking alms, with his little brother, driven under fear of the lash from the door of that humble home, by him, who of all others, should have provided for and comforted those poor worse than orphan boys.

"Again, by the influence of one whom he has since chosen to adopt as mother, he stands in the vestibule of the old church at West Stephentown, N. Y., trembling lest none should care for the poor outcast boy. But he is welcomed and soon stands in the Sunday-school class, with the boy teacher, whose head comes little more than to the shoulder of his pupil, to learn his first lesson of the way of life; and to be told, that though driven out from home with none there to love him, that the ever-blessed Jesus loved and would care for the poor friendless boy.

" It is a wonder that he, abandoned by home friends, did not abandon himself, and drift down the ways of death, instead of climbing the rugged steeps of light and life, and then seeking to rescue from the asylum a dear sister, motherless and deranged, forsaken and driven there by ill-treatment at home; that for her sake the GOLDEN CENSER springs into life. All this is a matter of thanksgiving if not of surprise. That it still lives with its fast-increasing patronage and prosperity, reminds us of the comforting words of an inspired writer, ' When my father and my mother forsake me, then the Lord will take me up.'

"I. B. COLEMAN."

Notwithstanding the ups·and downs, the sunshine and the shadow, the joys and depressions, the CENSER lived through its babyhood, and its misgiving editor had the satisfaction of closing volume first in triumph. The CEN-SER was a success! And not only did the CENSER live, but the editor lived, and so did his sister for whom he was providing, and I paid cash for paper and printing at the end of every issue. And over and above all expenses, I realized six hundred and fifty dollars, which I invested in a little home.

CHAPTER XIX.

DISCOURAGEMENTS — OPPOSITIONS — PATIENCE UNDER PER-
PLEXITIES — SUCCESS — PULPIT EFFORTS — DISAPPOINTED
EXPECTATIONS — A NEW PRESS — THE PAPER ISSUED
WEEKLY.

Fresh with the bloom of springtime, when beauty smiles
in the valley and on the mountain, when blossoms whiten
the orchards, and birds flit in air, when the martin builds
her nest, when flowers distill their fragrance in the air, the
GOLDEN CENSER entered upon its second year full of hope
and expectation. I select the following brief extracts from
the first issue in Vol. II., to illustrate the mind that guided
my pen editorial at that time:

" We come telling the ever-pleasing story of the cross,
the love of a precious Saviour; exhorting the indifferent
to a higher life, encouraging the desponding, soothing the
sorrowing, gently and tenderly pointing the lost to the
Lamb of God that taketh away the sins of the world;
preaching temperance, righteousness, and a judgment to
come; standing up for the truth though the heavens fall;
denouncing sin in high places and low; seeking to know
nothing save Jesus and him crucified. Full of hope and
childlike trust in the promises of Him who owns the cattle
on a thousand hills, we are resolved, if possible, to live
more devoted—throw our whole energy into our life-work.
We feel the importance of our work; the harvest-field is
vast, the laborers few, and thousands all over the land are
perishing for the want of spiritual food, that bread which
cometh down from heaven. Our struggle at the throne of
grace shall be for that earnestness which will never falter

amid discouragements—when the storm-clouds hover darkly over our pathway. In all this we seek no honor, except the approving smiles of heaven. If we are successful in doing good, we wish no applause; to God be all the glory, for we are only an unprofitable servant at best.

With the experience of the past, the cheering prospects of the present, simple trust in the Master for the future, and the prayers of God's children, we strive to press forward unto higher attainments, holier lives, purer purposes, more devoted and consecrated energies. With these resolutions before us, we extend our hand editorial to all our patrons' for another year, hoping that our visits will be profitable. We crave your sympathy; being but a mere youth, we are more liable to err than we will when riper years crown our brow. May God bless our good readers, and may Israel's tender Shepherd lead you by the fountains of living waters, are our sincere prayers."

The reader cannot fail to notice in this extract that my motives were the same then as now; that I sought with all my heart to do good and to bless my fellowmen, and doubtless this was one reason why the CENSER lived dispite my bitter enemies—for enemies I had, and why I had them I know not. Yet, it grew and was gaining favor with God and man. The local press, however, did not want the CENSER to live, and the editors of two of the three papers then published in Rockford took it upon themselves to read me lectures through their respective periodicals. At first I was scared and surely thought I was a ruined man, for I believed the people would credit the malicious lies. God, however, sometimes does use the devil for good. Their editorials did bring some more filthy serpents—snakes in the grass—for they gave no signatures to their articles—to the surface, but all well-meaning people, especially those who personally knew me, considered the articles as malicious and uncalled-for, and hence they brought me friends and more patronage.

Thus, contrary to the hopes and expectations of the over-confident, and those who used their influence against the paper, it continued to survive their hatred, yea, it was permitted to behold the springing flowers of another May, to witness the abundance wherewith God has provided us, and to gain precious lessons from his bountiful goodness.

The new-born year smiled upon my anxious heart, and cheered me with its unfolding charms, for who is not made glad in beholding the flush of the morning, the golden sky at sunset, the falling showers, the tree-tops rustling with the music of myriad leaves of gold, and emerald, and crimson, the meadows rejoicing in multitudes of blooming flowers, and the valleys singing praises in the far-stretching fields of waving grain when the balmy winds, wafted from the orange groves of the South, kiss our lips and fan our brows; when the mountain rills sing for joy, in short, when all nature pours upon us a perpetual tide of blessing, in obedience to the command of unstinted beneficence?

Ah, good reader, when we reflect that God crowns every season with his goodness, should we not come to him with glowing hearts, bounding hopes, and confiding trust? Oh, can we live and receive all these blessings at the hands of a kind and merciful God, and still be ungrateful? Then let our hearts break forth in admiration and praise to our Father in heaven. And if our springtime down in this world of cold, dreary storms has such attractions, such beauties, what will it be on the other shore, where eternal spring with its vernal fields, flowing rivers of living waters, with its summer sheen and cloudless skies, is ever in bloom, and where beauty never fades?

However, I found it harder to sustain myself the second year than the first. I used the "credit system," that is, I sent the paper as long as it was taken from the office.

Hence all who failed to send in their renewals I was carrying, and they served only as dead weights. But I hoped on, and trusted they would remember the CENSER.

To give the young reader an idea how I hung on when discouragements pressed me on every hand, I will here relate an incident which illustrates the invincible pluck which only saved the CENSER from an untimely grave. A gentleman living in Beloit, Wis., held a note of $10.00 against a farmer living three miles west of Harrison, Ill., which he sent me, saying, if I would collect it, I could appropriate it on the paper. Accordingly, I wrote a letter to the man in Harrison. But no reply came. I wrote a second time, and no reply was made. So I let the matter drop for a time. But through harvest my receipts on the paper were so light that I knew not how to meet my bills. I thought of that note. It would help me a little if I only had the money. So I set out on foot under the noonday sun of an August day, and traveled over the dusty way nineteen miles, to collect the money. I was successful, receiving fifty cents additional as interest. This greatly cheered me, and with a stronger heart I returned to Rockford, and the paper was saved a little longer.

But there is no success without effort, and if hard, persevering toil would bring success, the CENSER would yet be a success. I fully understood that many a brave boy had come up through great discouragements and perplexities, and I was not going to give it up. History is full of men who bent circumstances to their condition, and surmounted every obstacle. When I look at Johnson, poring over words; or Kitto, spelling out his Greek and Hebrew; or Goldsmith, bearing his literary attempts from publisher to publisher; or Joseph Hume, during his years of parliamentary persecution; or Cobden, in the free-trade conflict; or Faraday, washing bottles and retorts; or Stephenson, mending the men's watches, and enjoying his herring under a hedge—I can but be reminded of the words of Sir Fowell Buxton, and find myself compelled to subscribe to them: "The longer I live, the more I am certain that the great difference between men, between the feeble and the powerful, the great and the insignificant, is energy—invincible determination—a purpose once fixed, and then death or victory. That quality will do anything that can be done in the world, and no talents, no circumstances, no opportunities, will make a two-legged creature a man without it." The fact is, nothing can be done without labor. Poets, they say, must be born poets, and the same holds good with mathematicians and lawyers; but we may be quite sure Milton did not write "Paradise Lost," Blackstone his "Commentary," or Newton his "Principia," without intense study. Michael Faraday learned something of chemistry over his bottle-cleaning; George Stephenson something of mechanics over his clocks; and Elihu Burrit something of languages over his anvil; but neither would have reached eminence without prodigious labor. Let every young man take it for granted little can be done without it. Cæsar, we are told, studied in a camp, and swam rivers holding his "Commentaries" out of the water with his hand. Alfred, King of England, Frederick the Great, and Napoleon, though guiding empires, found time to converse with books.

Newton was in his eighty-fifth year when he improved his "Chronology;" Waller wrote poetry at eighty-two; and the present Earl of Derby, when long past sixty, could translate Homer to relieve the tediousness of a sick room. Whitfield, during a ministry of thirty-four years, preached upwards of 18,000 sermons, and traveled many thousands of miles. It is said that when he found his powers failing him, this great man undertook to put himself upon "short allowance," and that was to preach only once every day in the week, and three times on Sunday! For more than fifty years John Wesley delivered two, and frequently three, sermons a day, and preached during that time more than 40,000 sermons. He traveled about 4,500 miles every year on the average, and so, during his ministry, he could not have passed over less than 225,000 miles in pursuit of his Master's work.

Every young man should cultivate habits of industry, before he loses the power by contact with the worthless and the impure. A little time in pleasure, and a little more money in books, would not deprive you of much enjoyment, and might confer upon you much profit. Leave off dreaming and set to work; one hour every night after business would be more than two whole days a month, and enough to accomplish feats of learning. All have the chance; they only want the inclination. A little time, like a little money, if expected to be serviceable, must be laid out well. We are not all born with a genius, but we each have faculties, and without sighing for what we have not, let us make the best use of what we have. At the same time, when we find out for what we are intended, we must take care we do not go beyond it; and as Sidney Smith says: "If Providence only meant us to write posies for rings, and mottoes for twelfth cakes, let us keep to posies and mottoes. A good motto for a twelfth cake is more respectable than a wretched epic in twelve books." It is when people get out of their depth that they become laughable—not before; and so it is wise for a young man to talk of nothing but the flavor of a cigar and the tie of a cravat, if his studies have gone no deeper. "If there be one thing on earth which is truly admirable," said Dr. Arnold, "it is to see God's wisdom blessing an inferiority of natural powers, where they have been honestly, truly, and zealously cultivated."

Above all things, my young men readers, forget not the words of the wise man: "The fear of the Lord is the beginning of wisdom," and in acquiring the wisdom of this world, neglect not the things pertaining to that which is to come. You are men of business—be Christian men of business. The thing is quite possible. Daniel was the prime minister of Persia, and had to manage the affairs of a hundred and twenty provinces, and yet he could find time to go into his chamber three times a day, that he might pray and give thanks to God. Alfred the Great, Martin Luther, John Thornton, William Wilberforce, and Fowell Buxton were all men of business, and yet they were all men of God. And so should it be with every young man who pretends to true wisdom. Among your studies let one book have your attention—the Bible; that old book, which in spite of infidelity, has stood its ground for centuries.

I often think how little we use life thoroughly; how little we really live our life; how seldom we are in the humor to carry out its great and solemn purposes; how we let its opportunities fly by us, like thistle-down on the wind. Why are we not always denying ourselves, taking up the cross and following the Master? Why are we not always on the watch for every occasion in which a word may be said, or a deed done, or a thought thought, that shall be a protest for Christ, in the vain and sinful world? Why is God's love but a rare, wintry gleam, and never a steady summer in our souls?

Actuated by such examples, I held to my task, and was permitted to close Vol. II. But, financially, it was a failure. It was a hard year with me, I had met with severe losses, and was beset with rare discouragements, and in the midst of these disasters, I felt more than once like sitting down and saying, it is of no use: I never can make the CENSER a success. But success is not always counted by dollars and cents. It might have been much worse. Even wealthy corporations sometimes fail, and, in this respect, the Censer was ahead of them, for it was not a failure. I had paid all its debts, if I did have to do without the needed clothing in order to meet my obligations, for I had rather wear patched pants and coat, and honestly look men in the face, than to appear in fine clothes and owe everybody.

But let me pause here and bring up another thread of my sketch. In the autumn of 1868, I was licensed by the church to preach. The Rev. Samuel Oates, of Belvidere, Ill., gave me the first invitation to preach in his pulpit. As a matter of course I took great care in the preparation of my sermons. I wrote them out carefully, revised and trimmed them to the best of my ability, and, with the two in my pocket, I started for Belvidere. The Sabbath was to be an eventful day. I kept praying that I might not make a failure, yet the thought that there was a possibility, made me feel very uncomfortable—but I continued raising my heart in silent prayer. At length the Sabbath dawned. It was a beautiful September day. I wanted to retire for secret prayer, but could find no place. So I went to the outskirts of the city, entered a large corn-field, and there, away from the world, I bowed in prayer for strength and success. While thus communing with God, the church-bell sounded through the air, my heart fluttered, and my mind became more depressed. I felt it was a solemn thing to preach the gospel. I arose, and went to the church, entered the pulpit and opened the services. The Spirit was with me, and, though I read my sermon, yet I had great liberty, and preached with satisfaction, at least to myself. When I sat down I felt quite confident the people were not disappointed in me. Something kept saying in my heart, You did well, John. But there was no vanity in this. Indeed, in the hundreds of sermons since preached, I never could feel proud over even the best of my pulpit efforts, for I felt that I was but a poor worm of the dust, and but for God's grace the meanest.

To return. My writing was in a condensed style and in a small letter and in the preparation of my evening's sermon in my study, I did not anticipate lamp-lights, nor the trial before me. However, when the hour arrived, and, after the preliminary services, I announced my text, and started off, as I had done in the morning, by reading. But, oh, such light! I looked, I strained my eyes, I crouched down nearer my manuscript, I hesitated, I mispronounced my words, I stumbled, I began to sweat, great drops stood on my forehead, my clothes were wet with perspiration, the good people saw my embarrassment, and, doubtless, pitied me, the young folks snickered, and knowing ones wagged their heads. I was the smallest man in all God's creation, and if there had been a knot-hole in the floor I felt as if I could have gone through it. But there was no such easy escape. There I was—all alone. The minister absent, and no one to take my place. To sit down would have been a disgrace from which I could never have recovered. What could I do! I gave my sermon a fling back to the sofa, gathered up my presence of mind, recalled the general heads of my discourse, and, silently pleading for wisdom, I rallied. My lips were unsealed; somehow I grew strangely eloquent, my voice was astonishing to my own ears, and such a sermon as I there preached, I never have had the privilege to surpass. For months after I grieved over this unpleasant circumstance. However, it forever broke me of reading my sermons. I have read but two sermons since that day—one in New Milford, and one in Rockton. Thus opened my ministerial labors, and Belvidere has the honor—if honor it is—of listening to my first efforts.

After this, for the next two years, in addition to my office labor, both editorial and otherwise, I preached nearly every Sunday, and sometimes two and three times on the Sabbath. There is scarcely a church from Lena on the west to Chicago on the east but what I have preached in.

One day a good brother called on me and wanted me to preach down in his church—only eight miles from Rockford. I agreed to go, and, accordingly, on Saturday evening, after the labors in the office were completed, I set out on foot and alone, expecting to be overtaken by some team going that way which would give me a ride. In this I was not disappointed, and reached the neighborhood about eight o'clock in the evening. As I was a stranger, I thought I would call on the man who invited me to preach. Going to the house, I knocked. The door was opened. I asked if I could stay for the night. The lady thought not. I then asked how far it was to the next house. She said it was over half a mile to any house where they would be likely to keep me. I then asked her again if they could not keep me for the night, assuring her that a lounge or carpet would satisfy me. She looked toward her husband who by this time had come to the door. He said that the main part of the building was new and had just been plastered, and did not dare to make up a bed in any of the rooms as there was great danger of taking a severe cold. I replied that I was very careful of my health and did not wish to expose myself to danger, and asked how far it was to Mr. Burk's house. Upon my giving this name, the man opened the door wide so that the light fell full into my face, and then recognized me. Covered with mortification and making all kinds of apologies, he bid me come in—the fire was replenished—a bounteous supper was soon ready —a comfortable bed was in readiness against the hour of retiring, and I never found more hospitable people in all my travels. I preached the next day, and was assured by my host that he had never listened to a sermon which brought such conviction, though I took no advantage of the circumstance of the preceding evening.

At another time I was invited to another place to preach. I withhold names out of regard for my friends, as the

CENSER is largely circulated in the places about which I write. I accepted and went. I stopped at the residence of a local preacher—a saintly man. In the evening he invited me to go down town with him and he would introduce me to some of the brethren who desired to look upon the face of the CENSER editor. I complied, and was introduced to one and another. Having made several purchases, he was about to return. I followed him out of the store, when he remembered another article needed, and returned to purchase it. I remained on the sidewalk, and just one side of the door, out of the observation of those within. Now, all who have seen the writer know that he is not very large; and, in those days was beardless, and had a boylike appearance. Fancy then my astonishment, when heads crowded together and eagerly asked of my local brother, "What! is that the editor of the CENSER? Why he don't look as if he knew enough to say boo! He will disappoint the congregation to-morrow! We made a mistake in getting that boy here! We are in for it. Why, we supposed we were going to have somebody." Our local brother quietly told them to come out and hear me.

All of the above conversation was not intended for my ears, as a matter of course. Our local brother having returned to the side-walk, we started for his home, he never intimating the nature of the conversation, nor I to him that I had unintentionally overheard it.

But the Sabbath came. As the Sabbath-school was held at nine o'clock, in company with the local preacher I attended. During nearly the whole session an excellent brother, a leading member, took it upon himself to lecture me, telling me of the intelligence of the congregation, of the culture of their pastor, of the pulpit efforts, and that I would not meet the expectation of the people if I displayed any vanity or ignorance. This, and what I had heard the evening before, made me feel uncomfortable, and

I began to wish I was at home. However, I thanked the brother for his timely warning and suggestions. With these things on my mind, I entered the pulpit, opened the services, and preached my sermon. Whether poor or otherwise, I could see that the congregation was not disappointed. When I came down I was almost thronged with hearty hand-shaking and congratulations. But then all the difference was between a success and a failure, and not so much because of the unpretending youth before them.

At another time I had an appointment at a school-house. The Sabbath-school held its session before preaching. I was expected to preach. They had heard of the editor of the CENSER, and expected some great personage. In the meantime I had entered the room, but no one suspected the unassuming young man sitting by the stove as the expected editor preacher. School closed, and one and another were asking whether the expected preacher had arrived. No one knew whether he had or not. And then, as is usual in some places, I received some compliments which were not intended for my ears. Of course I looked serious, and at a crack in the stove, in order to keep my face straight. As soon as the tumult subsided and the room became quiet, I took my seat in the desk, and I never saw such an astonished and confounded congregation in my life. But the preacher met their expectations, and after the sermon the good people crowded around me, and begged that I should not remember their remarks against them. All of which I took as a good pleasantry.

Had I space, and were it interesting, I could give many incidents similar to the above. But these must serve. There certainly is a lesson in each one of them. Yet, poor human nature, we have to watch these tongues and these actions of ours all the time. They certainly had a good effect upon me. Doubtless other ministers could give a similar experience.

While I am giving my experience in the ministry, to make this a complete autobiography, it may not be out of the way to give place to one of the many discourses delivered, which I do, selecting the following:

TEXT: Refrain thy voice from weeping, and thine eyes from tears, for thy work shall be rewarded, saith the Lord.—JEREMIAH. xxxi, 16.

The chosen people of God were at this time in Babylonish captivity, far away from their native land and the associations of childhood and endearments of friends. While in the valley of the Euphrates, five hundred miles from the Holy City, many gloomy thoughts and desponding fears filled their weary hearts as they reflected on their hopeless servitude in a foreign land. After laboring hard through the day under the cruel lash of the task-master and a burning sun, at evening, when the bustle and tumult of the city was hushed, the orb of day had descended behind the western hills, and the quiet of twilight was hovering over the earth, the Israelites were wont to retire to the verdant banks of the Euphrates, without the city walls, where they could worship God in the beauty of holiness. The Hebrews had psalms which surpassed those of all the heathen nations around them in melody and sweetness, and, indeed, they cannot be equaled by the productions of the present day. But their hearts were too sad for music. Hanging their harps upon the willows that grew along the river's bank, they cast their weeping eyes over the dark purple waters of the swollen stream toward their dear native land. While thus sighing with broken hearts over their unhappy lot, the natives, with insulting taunts, pressed them to sing some of the sweet songs of Zion, thus making them feel more keenly, if possible, the anguish of their souls.

The Jews, prior to their captivity, were prosperous in all their pursuits. Their fields glowed with golden harvests, and the vines hung heavy with the purple clusters.

18

While in the full enjoyment ef the bounties of their beneficent Creator, they forgot God and gave themselves up to
idolatry and the lusts of their own evil hearts. They had
forgotten how the Lord brought them up out of the land
of Egypt with a strong arm and established them in the
promised land flowing with milk and honey, and how he
had made them a mighty people—a terror to surrounding
nations. They had discarded the warnings of Jehovah and
stoned the prophets sent of the Most High to warn them
of their impending fate. Although they had been the subjects of God's especial favor, yet his unwavering adherence
to justice suffered them to be carried away into bondage
that they might repent of their folly in servitude, where
we find them with penitent hearts and eyes suffused with
bitter tears. Nor are their sobbings unheard, for God,
with the tenderness of a loving Father, says, "Refrain thy
voice from weeping, and thine eyes from tears, for thy
work shall be rewarded, saith the Lord."

We learn, then, in the first place, that God's retributive
justice will overtake those forgetful of his benevolence and
loving-kindness. Seated on his throne in heaven and looking down upon the kingdoms of this world, he knows no
nationality, nor does he display especial regard for one class
of persons to the neglect of another. And, secondly, God
will hear the prayers of the true penitent and avenge the
oppressed.

1. We may observe that the Lord is very kind to all his
created intelligences, showering upon them blessings with
an unsparing hand. He sends the gentle rains to refresh
the parched earth and to revive the wilted and drooping
crops. He causes the sun to shine that it may mature the
coming harvest. He spreads before us tokens of his regard for which we never thank him. Among these are
life, the air we breath, health, kind friends, the products
of foreign lands which afford us so many table luxuries,

the changes of the seasons with their varied atmosphere, the merry songs of birds, the sweet fragrance of flowers to cheer our drooping spirits, the clothes we wear, comfortable homes to shelter us from the winter storms, light of day in which to execute our purposes, shades of night that we may repose our wearied limbs,--these and numerous other expressions of God's kindness towards us, are taken as a matter of course, and hence we never thank him for them. On the other hand, we receive his bounties, accumulate wealth, build houses and barns and fill them with treasures as if earth was our eternal habitation; find fault if the ways of Providence do not coincide with ours; we feast at sumptuous tables while Lazarus, all wounded and bruised, lays at our gate asking in vain for the crumbs that fall from our tables; we ride in carriages, gratify our vanity in useless ornaments and expensive dress, cultivate a proud and haughty spirit, oppress the poor, despise the admonitions of a tender conscience, reject the counsels and warnings of the messenger of God, cling to the vain delusions of a transitory life, reveling as it were over the reeking fumes of the grave's foul breath.

It is not reasonable to suppose, while God is thus beneficent on the one hand and men ungrateful and extremely selfish on the other, that he is not grieved and wounded in heart. Although prosperity may crown our efforts for a season, and the Creator exercise his patience and forbearance, yet be not deceived, God is not mocked—sooner or later he will pour out the wrath of his indignation and whirl his shafts of justice at our proud and selfish hearts. Jesus, while on earth, told us to seek first the kingdom of heaven and his righteousness and all things else needful would be added unto us. But our lives practically say, "We will first seek the vain and transitory things of this world, and then, if we have time or inclination, the things that pertain to our soul's salvation." God did not create and place us in this world of natural beauty for the sake of having us lay up our treasures where moth and rust doth corrupt and thieves break through and steal, but to honor his name and prepare ourselves for eternity. It is the neglect of these duties which bring upon us all our woes and afflictions. The Lord knows what is for our highest good, hence, when he sees us bowed down to idols and the pursuits of this world, he comes to us in tribulation and sorrow—he cuts off our friends and plants them on the eternal shore for the purpose that we might lift our eyes from the associations of earth to those of heaven—he suffers calamities to come upon us that we might learn our dependence upon his Almighty arm for support—he removes our property to humble our pride and to show us the uncertainties of temporal possessions—he prostrates our vigorous bodies upon couches of sickness to remind us that the bloom and beauty of youth is liable to wither and fade and our physical frames subject to decay. God does not send these misfortunes to revenge his slighted mercies, but simply to teach us the lesson of humility which we ought to have learned without them. Thus when the Lord sees us down by the river bank of humility, as were the Hebrew captives, weeping with penitential tears over our sins, and entreating to return to his favor, he comes to us with the tenderness of parental affection, pouring the oil of consolation into our wounded spirits, and whispers in our longing ears in tones sweeter than honey or the honey-comb, "Refrain thy voice from weeping, and thine eyes from tears."

The Creator is a beneficent Being, who has given us these faculties of the soul and intellect, not to prostitute them to base and ignoble purposes, but to employ them to reclaim the world from sin and the power of hell. Ah! dying mortal, have you ever asked, "What will all the pleasure, folly, vanity, sin, riches, or wisdom of this world

avail a rebel sinner in that awful day?" What can the
devil then do for his victims? Where will he and they be
through all eternity? Oh! the anguish of such a thought.
In that awful day the wicked will cry unto the rocks and
mountains to fall on them and hide them from the face of
Him that sitteth upon the throne, and from the wrath of
the Lamb—rejected and despised upon earth—for the great
day of his wrath shall have come, and who shall be able to
withstand? Oh! the bitter sting of sin. Well might the
prophet Jeremiah exclaim, "Oh! that my head were water
and mine eyes a fountain of tears, that I might weep day
and night for the blindness and sins of my people! Mine
eyes run down with rivers of water! Astonishment hath
taken hold of me! Oh! that I had in the wilderness a
lodging-place! Be astonished, O ye heavens, at this! See;
O Lord, and consider my affliction!"

Says one, "I would gladly spend all my time and means,
if I only had the ability and knew how to direct my energies." To such an inquirer we reply: In the name of
God and common sense, do not let the devil deceive you
longer while the world around you is writhing in sin and
bleeding at every pore under the galling fetters of hell. If
I were to tell around your neighborhood that you were de-
ficient in common sense, you would arraign me before a
court of justice before the going down of to-morrow's sun,
for slander. But you yourself say before God's people you
have no abilities to do kind offices for the Prince of Peace.
Behold the great harvest-field of the world all white for
the reaper. Thrust in the sickle and gather the sheaves
into the granary of the Lord. Look around you on every
hand and you will see the poor to be relieved, the orphan
to be cared for, the widow in her sad and disconsolate condition to be comforted, the homeless little wanderers in
this cold world of selfishness to be clothed and fed, the outcast and erring to be reclaimed, noisome dungeons and

prisons to be visited, to administer kindly offices to those wasting and pining away in filthy cells, in short, to communicate happiness throughout all the ranks of our fellow-men with whom we mingle, to sooth the disconsolate and the desponding, to relieve the distressed, to instruct the ignorant, to expand the intellect, to animate and direct the benevolent affections, to increase the enjoyments of the lower orders of the community, to direct the opening minds of the young, to lead the froward by gentle steps into the paths of wisdom and holiness, to administer to the wants of the wayfaring man, and to promote every scheme which has the grand object in view of ameliorating the sufferings of humanity and advancing the Redeemer's kingdom. God has given this glorious work into our hands, that, after we have been co-laborers in saving the world from sin, we might enjoy the reward he has in store for those that love and honor his cause. Then weep not, my hearers, over the perishing things of this life, but rather weep over our young men and women who are pressing forward to the grave without a single hope of a future life, weep over those whom intemperance has bound with its cruel fetters and is dragging down so many thousands of our noblest youth to an untimely and a drunkard's grave, weep over those whom the evil genius of vice has decoyed and led from the path of virtue. Oh! fathers, weep over your wayward sons that they might return and save their feet from the snares of ruin. Oh! mothers, weep over your lovely daughters, who, through misgivings, are still rejecting the dear Saviour—the friend of sinners—who left the glories of the sky, coming forth from the bosom of the Father, made bare his own breast to receive the wounds from the shafts of justice which were directed against our own guilty lives; Oh! weep over the nations in foreign lands and the islands of the ocean, who are groping in heathen darkness bowing down to the devices of their own hands. Then, when brotherly love shall flow in full fruition, when the star which arose over Bethlehem's plains shall shine in his full luster, when sin shall have received its mortal wound, when 'all nations, tribes, kindred, and tongues on this terraqueous globe shall lift their voices in praise, and shall join the sacramental hosts of the elect, when the golden banner of the gospel shall wave on every breeze, and the cross of Christ be upborne by millions of redeemed souls, the Lord shall say to the laborers in this great and noble work, "Refrain thy voice from weeping, and thine eyes from tears, for thy work shall be rewarded."

This is a life work and requires a firm, resolute and an unwavering purpose. We must refrain from outward show or pomp,—the humble Publican, not the haughty Pharisee, went down to his house justified. We must be earnest, enduring the heat and burden of the day manfully, remembering we shall reap if we faint not. We must be calm and composed. Like the ship holding her course over the watery paths of the dark and tempestuous sea while billows roll over her deck in mighty surges, while the lightning's shaft and the fierce storm-cloud threaten death to her crew. Tossed on the troubled sea she weathers the storms and accomplishes her journey. So it should ever be with the Christian on the sea of life where the billows of sin, mountain high, at times lash his wearied efforts, yet if calmly, firmly resisted, they will break harmlessly upon the rock-bound shores of time. A fanatic is a positive injury in this life work, because his inconsistencies more than neutralize all the good he may do. God is omnicient, and, therefore, is not dependent on finite efforts for the accomplishment of his purposes in this world. But it hath pleased him to honor man in the great work of saving sinners. That Almighty Being who doth according to his will in the armies of heaven and among the inhabitants of earth, and who is carrying forward all the plans of

his government to a glorious consummation, will bountifully reward us in this life and in the life to come crown
us with immortality.

We trust that the period is fast approaching, when the
breath of a new spirit shall pervade the inhabitants of every
clime, when holy love shall unite all nations of earth in
one harmonious society, when the messengers of the Prince
of Peace " shall run to and fro " from the north to
the south, from the rising to the setting sun; when the
sound of the gospel trumpet shall re-echo through every
land; when the light of divine revelation shall diffuse its
radiance on the benighted shores of idolatry; when its sublime doctrines and moral requisitions shall be fully understood and recognized in all their practical bearings, and
when the energy of that Almighty Spirit which reduced to
light and order the dark and shapeless chaos shall be ex-
erted on the depraved minds of this world's population.
Then the death-like slumber which has seized upon Adam's
race shall be broken; the dead in trepasses awake to new
life and activity; this confusion of the universe and garments rolled in blood be restored to reason and intellectual
freedom and to the society of angelic being; the face of the
moral creation be renewed after the image of its Creator.
Then wars shall cease, anarchy and disunion convulse nations no more; violence and oppression come to an end;
liberty be proclaimed to the captives and the opening
of the prison doors to them that are bound. Then the
order and beauty of the celestial system will be restored.
"Holiness to the Lord" will be inscribed on all the pursuits of man   Kindness and compassion will form the
amiable characteristics of every rank of social life.   Love
will spread her benignant wings from shore to shore, and
reign in the hearts of the inhabitants of the earth.   For
thus saith the voice of him who sits on the throne of the
universe, "Behold I make all things new—I create new

heavens and a new earth, and the former things shall not
be remembered, nor come into mind.   Be ye glad, and rejoice forever in that which I create; for behold, I create
Jerusalem a rejoicing, and her people a joy, and the voice
of weeping shall be no more heard in her, nor the voice of
crying."

And secondly:

God will hear our prayers and pour out the wrath of his
indignation upon our oppressors.   It is true that the Lord
may not visit our adversaries always as we, under their re-
vilings, might desire.   You know the Israelites in their
Babylonish captivity wept and sighed to return to their
native land for a long time after they had repented of their
folly; but when deliverance came it was signal and salutary.

While the old heathen monarch with a thousand of his
lords was at the drunken feast, and pouring out libations
to his gods, and, to insult the God of heaven still more,
ordered the sacred vessels of the temple to be desecrated,
"then came, in the self-same hour, forth the fingers of a
man's hand, and wrote over against the candlestick upon
the plaster of the wall of the king's palace."   Belshazzar
was confounded.   He called all the wise men to read the
writing.   They came, looked, turned pale, and confessed
that they were unable.   In his distress and terror he sends
for the prophet of Israel.   Daniel hastens to the king's
palace.   He turns to the wall of the banquet-house, bril-
liantly lighted, and slowly reads: "*Mene, mene, tekel, up-
harsin*," and with God's appointed authority, unfolds the
mystery of the writing, and turns and leaves the royal
feast.   Scarcely had the footsteps of the retiring prophet
ceased to sound through the richly-carved corridors of that
palatial mansion, ere the soldiers of Cyrus, having entered
the city through the channel of the river in the self-same
hour, rushed into the royal banquet-hall, and slaughtered

the king in his own palace; and Babylon, the terror of
nations, fell, and her courts have become the hiding-places
of venomous serpents and the retreat of the wild men of
the desert. So with us. The heavens above us may seem
like brass, the earth beneath us like burning iron; we may
be vexed by evil, designing persons; the sneers and frowns
of this life may sink sadly into our hearts, and almost cause
us to waver in our purpose, yet the Lord hears our prayers,
although we may not realize the answer in this life, or
may not see why afflictions have been brought upon us,
but when we shall have broken from this prison-house of
corruption, and winged our flight to the eternal world, we
will see from the celestial shores that our misfortunes were
blessings in disguise, that God was using our feeble instrumentalities for the accomplishment of some great purpose. Dear friends, let us be patient in this world of tribulation. What though the world deride our efforts, throw
barriers into the way of our usefulness, sneer at our feeble
endeavor, and despise our prayers; oh, remember the servant is not above his master, and if Christ was insulted
and even put to death by rude hands, how may we, who
profess to be his followers, expect to escape the poisoned
arrows of the enemy of our souls? This is the hour of
conflict. This world is a battle-field. The armies of the
redeemed are marshaled against the powers of darkness.
The conflict may be fierce and bloody, and the earth bathed
with the crimson flood, yet the forces of the aliens shall be
defeated and victory crown the gospel banner, and the Lord
of hosts will ride forth in the chariots of heaven, and establish an everlasting peace. Then that glorious scene
presented to the view of the apostle John shall be fully
realized: "Behold the tabernacle of God is with men, and
he will dwell with them, and they shall be his people, and
God himself shall be with them, and be their God. And
God shall wipe away all tears from their eyes, and there

shall be no more curse, neither sorrow nor crying, neither shall there be any more pain; for the former things have passed away." Glorious promise! God dwell with his people! All tears be wiped away! No more curse! The red dragon sin be put in subjection! Glorious day! when the angels, swift-winged messengers of the sky, shall minister to our happiness! When the "morning stars" that shouted for joy when this fair creation arose into existence, shall be filled with unutterable delight and shout even with more ecstatic joy than they did on that memorable morning, "Glory to God in the highest, peace on earth, and good will among men!" Press on, O ye heirs of salvation! "Refrain thy voice from weeping," O disconsolate ones, "and thine eyes from tears, for thy work shall be rewarded, saith the Lord!" Yonder, in Eden's fair bower, where the ambrosial fruits ever bloom on the tree of life, where rivers roll down their golden streams of sweet nectar, and the crystal fountains and sea of glass shimmer in the summer sheen of the heavenly Jerusalem, will be thy eternal home as the reward of perseverance and patience, my brother, sister, friend. And this for Jesus' sake.

It is needless to add that the good Lord blessed my humble efforts. It was more than my meat and my drink to do my heavenly Father's will. While thus laboring, my friends often told me I must be careful, or I would soon wear out. But to these fears I replied, "Better wear out than to rust out." When I beheld the desolation on every hand—of the young wasting the precious years, I felt as if I must cry out, and spare not to proclaim the love of that Saviour who had done so much for me. O Father Divine, help me ever to set in motion, if it be in the humblest way, those streamlets of influence that gladden the hearts of humanity, and honor my God and my Saviour. May I see the smile of heaven resting upon all the fruits of my life work when I step through the portals of eternity. May it then be said: "Well done, good and faithful servant, thou hast been faithful over a few things"—eternity's blessings shall be thy reward.

At this time I was also receiving many calls to fill pulpits while the pastors either absented themselves by visiting other places, or by taking a rest at my expense. I was always glad to go, and the only consideration I asked was the privilege of presenting the CENSER to the congregation. This they usually granted me very freely. And I must here say that I found in the ministry a general disposition to aid me. All of which was truly and thankfully appreciated by me. However, I found some inconsiderate persons, as the following will illustrate: At this time it was my practice to write to pastors of the churches I desired to visit, asking them if it would be agreeable to them to have me come. These letters were very generally favorably answered. In response to such a letter I set out for a village southwest of Rockford. I could make about half the distance by rail, leaving about seventeen miles to walk. I obtained a ride the first six miles, and footed the remainder over ice and snow, and arrived in time, but strangely and unaccountably to me, the pastor not only did not offer me the common courtesies, but did not even recognize me, though I was well known to him. Hence my labor was in vain, and traveling expense out of pocket.

At another place the pastor urged me to preach. I did so, and made a favorable impression. After the sermon, the pastor very unexpectedly proposed to take up a collection for missions. I at once saw the design and trusted in God for results. The collection amounted to forty-five cents, while every head of a family present subscribed for the CENSER and paid for it, besides several subscribing for copies to be sent abroad. I never saw such a confused pastor in my life. But I was not at fault. He had invited me.

At another place I was written to by the pastor to con-

duct the services for him in his absence. I accepted and
filled the appointment. But to my surprise, after the sermon, a deacon arose, and pressingly urged a collection for
church incidentals. I said not a word, though I felt there
was selfishness somewhere at work to divert the thoughts
of the people. The collection was taken, and two dollars
and forty cents was the amount. I never took a larger
subscription for the CENSER, considering the size of the
congregation, than I did that beautiful May morning.

But I preached many times and in many places where
the objects of the paper were not presented, and it is astonishing how inconsiderate some good people are. An excellent brother at one time urged me to come. I went; paid
my railroad fare, believing my expenses would be refunded,
and labored hard and earnestly on the Sabbath. At the
close the brother thanked me and that was all. I felt so
bad and so poor over it that I footed it back to Rockford
the same night, arriving at daybreak. At another place
I happened in the evening at a village in company with
some friends; did not expect to preach, but the pastor
learned of my presence, and preach I must. I did so. The
people who brought me to the village lived in the country,
and I was on the way to Rockford, and they supposed the
preacher would see me provided for the night. The
preacher shook my hand and thanked me very heartily for
the sermon. That night I went down to the depot and sat
up until 3 o'clock for the night train. I would have stayed
with the minister or any member of the church had I been
invited.

On Christmas of this year—which was on Saturday—I
traveled on foot through a deep snow to Mt. Morris—thirty
miles. I arrived in the evening about eight o'clock, tired
and foot-sore. But I was kindly received and well cared-
for. The good people also patronized me very freely, so
much so that I footed it back to Rockford on Monday with

a cheerful heart. This was toil, but it was a matter of
stern necessity to keep the paper from sinking—and all because I carried so many unpaying subscribers.

Thus, while the good people were happy in their beautiful homes during these holidays, I was tramping through
the deep snow, and facing cold winds asking people to subscribe for the GOLDEN CENSER. Oh, it was so discouraging. But I had heart-cheering reflections as I thus trudged
along my weary way, on foot and alone. Ah, indeed, every
ruined son of nature, however desolate and depressed his
condition, on this gladsome festal week, the week in which
we commemorate the advent of the Lord of glory in his
incarnation, should shout for joy that salvation, like a
mighty river, encompasses the entire earth. See its wid-
ening stream. It winds around the hills of Asia. It flows
across the sandy plains of Africa. It rolls hard by India's
coral strand. Across the European continent its gentle
waters swiftly roll. Over Greenland's icy mountains it
melts the frozen regions into love and good will. And
through the length and breadth of our own dear land it
dances like pearls, beneath the sun, as it flows on in silent
murmurs. Wherever a human body is wrapped around an
immortal spirit, there the stream flows in all its freshness.
And all along this stream are innumerable voices of invitation, crying "Whosoever will, let him take of the water
of life freely."

"Whosoever will." Ah, yes, it takes the will. There
must be a willingness to take salvation on God's own terms.
And what are his terms? It reads, "whosoever will, let
him take the water of life." His way, then, is to take.
You cannot buy, you must take. Poor mistaken souls who
expect to buy salvation with their penitence, their tears,
their sighs and groans. Away with them, it takes us back
to heathenism, where, to purchase salvation, long pilgrim-
ages were made to the temples of imaginary deities—track-

ing the path to their shrines with their own life-blood. Where the Hindoo threw himself beneath the wheels of Juggernaut and the mother cast her child in the Ganges. Where the blood flowed from lacerations by their own hands.

Not so with God's free gift to man. The terms are simply, "take of the water of life freely." If there were a price on the gospel, then would we despair, for only the learned, the refined, the rich and the noble would be its favored objects. Poverty might then sit down and weep, while the rich and the learned worshiped within marble temples and at golden shrines. But that is a true saying. worthy of all acceptation, that "the poor have the gospel preached to them." The great Physician came not to heal the well, but the sick. He came not to save the secure, but the lost. What Jesus giveth, he giveth, and that freely. All things that we can do with the view of purchasing salvation are an insult to Christ in the garden and on the cross, and an abomination in the sight of God. He who would seek to merit salvation by his own good deeds and inherent virtues, attempts to steal from the brow of Jesus the crown that he so dearly purchased in his sufferings for the "sins of many."

But, good reader, did your thoughts ever wander back over the years to that Bethlehem scene, to the incarnation, the songs of angels, to the appearing of a new star, to the journey of the Magi? If so your thoughts readily take in the surroundings. Out upon the hillsides of Judea, in the silent watches of the night, when all nature was hushed in repose, and the twinkling stars shone the brightest, a band of humble shepherds are tending their flocks. The night is calm and clear. Below them, on a plain, surrounded with palm-trees, lies the quiet village of Bethlehem. Upon an eminence above them slumbers the proud daughter of Zion—Jerusalem, the chosen city of the ever-living God.   On either side of them rose the ever-lasting hills, extending their hoary brows toward heaven; while at their feet the woodland streamlets murmur their cheerful songs to drooping nature; upon their banks bloom the lilies and violets—precious types of purity.

In the dead hour of the night, while their flocks are ruminating beneath the pale beams of the moon's silvery light, the shepherds, in the stillness of the hour, recline themselves upon the flowery mead, and with upraised eyes are meditating the wondrous works of the firmament, when lo! far up in the deep blue sky a golden light, as if the jasper gates of heaven were opening, met their as-tonished gaze.   A vast company of angels at length were observed, winging their flight through the etherial deep, as if on some mission sent.   Passing orb after orb, they are nearing the furthermost boundaries of this earth. With breathless silence the shepherds watch the angelic host.   Nearer and still nearer they come.   Darkness takes its flight before the matchless brightness of the heavenly messengers.   Now they break forth into sweet, choral songs —such as human ear had never before heard—filling sky and earth with melody, while from the golden city comes the chorus which, in deep sublimity, shakes sea and land.

Forthwith the King descends from his eternal throne, and in awful grandeur proceeds to the battlements of heaven, and all the inhabitants of that world follow. Out upon the space of time he flings the brightest star of his matchless crown.   Then with a voice that shall reach the sleeping dead, the angels break forth: " Glory to God in the highest! on earth peace, good will to man!"   For Shiloh has come, and his star appears in the east, which shall never go down till the kingdoms of earth shall be-come the kingdoms of Christ the Lord!

Glorious morn! Wondrous gift! Precious Saviour!   All along down the ages let thy merry birthday ring in gladsome song, for in it is the promise of the better life, a nobler inheritance, a crown, pure robes, palms of victory! Thus, while my thoughts were drinking in the glories of the heavenly world, though only imperfectly conceived, I was despised and rejected of men because humbly struggling to point humanity to its imperishable realities. While my body was weary, my soul feasted on its manna and drank deep at the Fountain whence flow the healing waters that are a medicine to the aching, longing heart.

At another time I set out to reach an appointment. It rained on Saturday afternoon, and the roads were so poor that I had to stop ten miles away from my appointment. The man with whom I stopped would have taken me Sabbath morning, but was sick and could not. So, nothing daunted, I set out on foot over the snow-drifts, ice, and swollen streams to reach the place ten miles away in time. I arrived about fifteen minutes late—was so tired I could hardly walk. The preacher who had expected me, had opened the services, and conducted them to their close without noticing me. At the close I made myself known. But to my utter surprise, he merely passed the compliments of the day, went out of the church, and to another appointment without saying a word to me. I was in a strange place, and among strangers. No one invited me home. As there was no hotel in the place, I had to go without dinner, and this was quite an effort, as I had traveled ten miles on foot since breakfast. In the afternoon I was invited to preach in another church in the village. I did so, and it was one of my best efforts. But the preacher refused to let me present the CENSER to the people. It was now about four o'clock. I lingered at the church until the congregation had nearly all retired, in hopes that some one would invite me, for I was faint with hunger. But no one gave me an invitation. So I set out on foot eight miles to a friend where I obtained food and shelter.

19

But oh! the weary limbs and heart-aches, who can tell them.

I bring up these incidents to show how inconsiderate some people are. Doubtless, if I named the congregations above referred to they would be stung to the very heart, but I looked upon it as thoughtlessness on their part, and not as selfishness. And I would here add, if you have a strange preacher for a Sabbath, see that he has a place to stay, and, if you can give him no more, see that his traveling expenses are all paid. Now it costs time and effort to prepare the sermons, and then it takes energy and strength to deliver them. To do all this for the good of a community for no pecuniary consideration, is very liberal on the part of the preacher, but to be obliged to pay four or five dollars as traveling expenses out of the preacher's meagre purse, is simply an imposition and an insult. But then I was learning human nature—though some of the lessons were dearly paid for.

Passing constantly through such experience, of which the above is only illustrative, the reader need not be surprised if some of the editorials were written plain, and right at the heart of a class of people in every community. Of course I took good care not to be personal. My labors were frequently rewarded with, "Stop my paper," "I don't want such a paper," and many other personal flings and insults. I felt hurt, the lips often quivered, and I hardly knew what to do. Then again, I was too severe in striking at certain national sins, such as intemperance, corruptions, defalcations, and the like; others again objected to it because the CENSER exposed the sin and folly in croquet-playing, theater-attending, and church lotteries, and its brood of minor sins.

The great cry raised against me in my earnest, uncompromising efforts, was that I was too severe. It made my heart sick to see the church slumbering in idleness, while those who made a profession thought it unfortunate that so much stringency and rigidity are put into religion. But is it indeed? Whose fault is it? Who put it in? Who made it what it is? Who said, "Be ye holy, for I am holy"? Who made the holiness of God the standard and the motive of holiness? Who bade us to be perfect, for our Father in heaven is perfect? It is obviously impossible to put any more stringency and rigidity into religion than God put into it, when he made his own character the measure of that perfection to which his creatures must aspire and should be always tending. Systems of theology, creeds, or catechisms, or doctors of divinity, do not make religion. The Christian religion is of God. It was taught in the New Testament by the God incarnate and his apostles, and practically illustrated in the life of Christ. And is the religion of any sect of intelligent, orthodox Christians more *strict* or *rigid* than the system which requires the church to be separate from sinners, not to be conformed to the world, to be pure in heart, to be perfect, to be holy, as God is holy? That is the requirement of the gospel, that is the old-fashioned doctrine of the church, and if there is anything more rigid than that put into religion I have never heard of it.

Well, my brother, you who think the good old way marked out by the Lord himself, taught by his apostles, and enforced by the early church, too straight, what do you propose to do about it? Are you going to lower the standard; to sew pillows under all arm-holes; to call evil good; to boil the peas in the shoes of penance; to make beds of roses for soldiers of the cross; or substitute the songs and shouts of a fashionable meeting for the self-denials and toils and penitence of a life of conflict and of faith, by which Christian heroes conquer through Christ and win heaven at last?

It is said that when Rubenstein, the great German musician, was in this country, he went to hear a famous preacher. In answer to the inquiry for his opinion of the preaching, he is reported to have remarked:

"The tendency of what I heard was to bring religion down to the people, not to bring the people up to religion."

Precisely such is the tendency of much which goes for gospel preaching. It aims to inculcate a perfection that accommodates itself to the imperfection of the sinner. It is a system that regards it a great misfortune that religion is so rigid and stringent, and would excuse the short-comings of the Christian by the failure of his judgment and the exceeding strictness of the law. Did Christ ever lower the claims of religion to meet the infirmities of men? Did the apostles, in their letters or their sermons, dilute the gospel or the commandments that it might be easier for men to be conformed to the image of God?

The idea of lowering the standard in order to adapt religion to the taste of the age, or the views of this leader or that; the idea of making religion popular by making it possible for a sinner to compromise his sins; the idea of holiness less holy than that which the Bible requires—is the dry rot of the church in our day. It is the essential element of that sentimental religion which substitutes joy for repentance, and "feeling good" for faith. "The religion of gush" is born of it. Worldliness, licentiousness, and all manner of concupiscence, flow from it as naturally as water from a fountain. Meetings that once were pentecostal seasons, when men were pricked to the heart by pungent preaching, and were turned by hundreds from sin to holiness, are now powerless to convict of sin. In my judgment the religion of to-day needs power more than anything else. The practical preaching which the age requires must exalt the requirements of the divine law to the high standard of the gospel, showing the inconsistency of sin,—any and all sin,—sins of omission and commission, of thought, word and deed, with that holiness which is of the heart; shrinking from fraud, falsehood, unfaithfulness, impurity in thought, speech, or behavior, as from the plague, and seeking after God and his righteousness as of the goal of the soul's aspirations and hope.

Let the pulpit inculcate the doctrine of holiness, for God demands it of all his creatures. And it is because the church has lost its confidence in the verities of Christ that it is so lean and powerless. Speaking upon this very subject in conversation with a minister I asked: Have you got it? Got what? Power from on high? No. I do not believe in physical religion—in this power, as you call it. Ah! But there is a power in religion that neither earth nor hell can withstand. One saint with God on his side is more powerful than them all. How was it with Jacob at the ford Jabbok? All night the weeping man struggles in weakness with the mighty God, saying, "I will not let thee go, except thou bless me." And God blessed him there, even at daybreak, and called his name Israel, "for as a prince" he had power with God, and with man, and prevailed. The disciples were instructed to remain at Jerusalem until they were endowed with power from on high, and when the baptism of power and of the Holy Ghost was upon them, they began to speak with such holy tenderness, with such incontrovertable logic, with such burning eloquence, as to send the arrows of conviction right to the hearts of the very men who so recently crucified the Lord of glory, and they cried out, "Men and brethren, what shall we do?" Peter is in prison, a little band are assembled at Mark's house on a retired street in Jerusalem to pray, and they did not have very great faith either, but somehow they must have had enough to move the throne of heaven, for at midnight, the angel smote off the chains from Peter's hands, opened the great iron gates and

led him out.   There was power in all this, greater than the
strength of prison walls or dungeon gates.   Why, listen!
Do you hear that terrible earthquake down there in Phil-
ippi?   What is the matter?   Oh, nothing much, Paul and
Silas, at midnight are praying, and, though their feet are
made fast in the stocks, and they in the inner prison
guarded by soldiers, yet so happy were they that they
"sang praises unto God, and the prisoners heard them."
Oh, how sweet the music of their voices must have sounded
to those prisoners!   But while Paul and Silas were enjoying their little prayer-meeting, the keeper of the prison
awoke out of his sleep, and seeing the prison doors open,
he drew out his sword, and would have killed himself; poor
fellow, he ought to have kept awake.   He knew it was
death to a Roman soldier to sleep while on duty, hence the
desperation of his purposed act.   But Paul, the noble-
hearted, cried with a loud voice, saying, "Do thyself no
harm; for we are all here."   Ah! there was power in that
prison prayer-meeting—even the subduing of heathen soldiers.

    We see then, from the above examples, quoted from the
Scripture, that saints of old believed in power.   And when
we see what this power has done for holy men of old, it is
very desirable, for it so energizes the whole man, soul,
intellect and all.   But to have this power we must meet
the conditions—live a holy, pure life.   The Word and
Spirit not only agree in being quick and powerful, but
sharp—hear it—sharp—piercing, discerning; here is one
of the signs of this purity and power.

    Whoever is under the inspiration of the Holy Ghost,
will be marked with a definiteness and steadiness of aim,
and at times will pierce, and cut, and cleave, and anatomize
with a daring and precision that is awful.   Is this the
power you want? or is it the power to present only things
lovely and of good report?

Again, what is it? Well, it is not power to talk loud.
It don't mean the high swells so much, nor even a gifted
tongue, though this shall be touched as with living coals.
True greatness is a humble attitude. It is power when
called a fanatic by your neighbors, with others in doubt
but that it may be true, to stand calm and serene in the
recollection that you have eternity to contradict them in,
and can afford to wait for the argument. Moral power is
not a superadded quality of holiness—a separate gift tacked
on to that state, which may be lost off; it belongs to purity
and can never be taken out of it. If you have holiness,
you have religious power just as you need. And there are
men and women girded in God's own armor, who ask leave
of nothing if they may but triumph over all things through
Christ who strengtheneth them. Their moral power and
holy grandeur are enough to charm angels.

Now what is the philosophy of this power? It lies in
that faith which is of the operation of the Holy Ghost.
We are strong, as religious beings, just in proportion to
our faith. But the question arises, What is strong faith?
It is not a faith so great in the scope of its actings, as in
its firmness. It is unmixed faith; in opposition to some
believing, some reasoning, and the rest of human probabilities. Faith as a grain of mustard seed is strong, if it is
faith only. This supplementing faith with outward signs
vitiates what faith we have. This reassuring the immut-
able promise, by sights and dreams, by hopeful appearances
and human probabilities, is like requiring the Almighty to
give bail for his character.

Real faith makes the Infinite master of our impossibilities.
Some of our teachers seem to think that faith may be coax-
ed and caressed along to victory, if one only knows how to
do it. But there is more motive to faith in one gleam or
the two-edged sword than is found in all persuading or
platitudes.

Bring on a necessity for God's help! Dash into the bruised reeds—make every human prop reel before the emergency—bereave the soul of home help and home hope, reduced to a spiritual foundling on the door-steps of the kingdom, too starved to knock, and faith will go to Christ, and go alone too. Go to the wreck if you would see the life-boat shooting over the swells. God don't touch a soul till it founders. The chief doubt of human salvation, everywhere, lies in the deceitfulness and mockery of home remedies; all of which must be abandoned in despair, before Christ, the great Alternative, is accepted; for no man trusts his all on the credit of the poor man's Saviour with two hopes on hand. Hence it requires more faith to disbelieve in ourselves than it does to believe in God. Looking to God comes natural to despairing eyes. Who dare sink, taking all his props with him, at the bidding of Jesus Christ? That is faith! God can lift us up on our sinking faith, for the conditions of our exaltation are met in our going down, for man's extremity is God's opportunity, the weakest of all God's saints on his knees is stronger than the whole unbelieving world beside.

Again, this spiritual power would subdue all opposition. With God all things are possible. It is the lack of our confidence or faith to claim the promises that make us mere babes in the faith—mere religious dwarfs. Why are some churches praying for the outpouring of the Holy Spirit, and no Holy Spirit is outpoured, while other communities with similar petitions are blessed with gracious refreshings from the Lord? Is it because God is partial? Ah! no. God is no respecter of persons. One soul is just as precious in his sight as another. But it is because of our faith. We don't meet the conditions. For when we offer the petition, "O Lord, revive thy work," we ask for a blessing that cannot be over-estimated, and which must sweep every string of the heart. If that petition comes from unholy or faithless lips it is worse than mockery—it is an insult to the Almighty. But the faith-power pleads with God until its "violence" takes the promises by force, until the windows of heaven are opened and the blessing poured out. Then ministers and people would be agreed as touching "the one thing," harmony would prevail in congregations, empty pews would be filled, ministers would preach with more unction, hearers would listen with deeper attention, precious souls would be converted, churches would be built up and strengthened, thousands of the ungodly would be arrested in their wickedness, the most abandoned would be stricken with awe and inquire after Christ, skeptics and infidels would bow before the truth and admit that verily there is a God in the earth, the causes of benevolence would receive a fresh impulse, the debts of boards would be easily paid and their treasuries would be filled, the parched and desolate places would bloom as the garden of the Lord, the acceptable year of the Lord would hasten apace when prison doors would open, chains fall off, captives be liberated, swords beaten into plowshares, wars and rumors of wars cease, childhood escape the dire consequences of sin, old age walk to quiet, peaceful graves with the golden shores of eternity in full view, all earth resound with the knowledge of the Lord, and every heart be filled with joy unspeakable; in short, the very God of heaven would come down and dwell among his people to the everlasting joy of Israel's hosts; all places of vice and temptation would be swept away as the vapor of the morning; the rum-shops, and dance houses, and billiard halls, and pleasure gardens, would go down before a refined and Christian principle; taxation, extortion, government subsidies, great corporations grinding the face of the poor, would be things of the past; the Golden Rule would be in every transaction, and every phase of the work of Christ would put on a new and vigorous life!

Would that my pen had the eloquence to move the hearts of all my readers towards the attainment of this power. This is no ideal picture, but a grand possibility. O God help us to cast these dead weights from us; help us to arise into that newness of life which will enable us to exercise that power which shall raise a fallen, helpless world heavenward! May we never be satisfied to live at this poor dying rate, down in the damp valley of doubts and fears, but let us climb the mountain heights and bask in the clear sunlight of heaven, and live in full view of the promised land,—then shall our years be crowned with a halo of glory worthy the name of Christians whose God is the Lord of hosts.

But it is "hope deferred that maketh the heart sick" In the spirit of my heavenly Master, I tried to advance these old-fashioned doctrines of the Bible, but people despised me for it. I was unpopular, and the weekly issues of the GOLDEN CENSER, burning with these truths, only made it obnoxious to the dead, formal professor, whose heart was a whited sephulcher, and whose life daily displayed the pharisaical prayer, "I thank God that I am not as other men, even that poor publican," the CENSER, which is trying to disturb my peace of mind. I won't read it. I'll just stop it.

Thus I found it necessary to canvass for the paper just as I had done at its commencement. I visited Madison, Janesville, Edgerton, Stoughton, Milton, Delavan, Elkhorn, and many other towns in Wisconsin. After having spent nearly a week on one of these trips, upon Saturday night I arrived in a most lovely village—I withhold names. I sought the pastors of several churches, and asked them if they would let me present the paper to the people. They refused, and also gave me no encouragement to stay over Sunday. I left the place about sundown. Having traveled and canvassed for some distance, as it was getting late,

I asked at one place and another to stay for the night. But they all began to make excuses, and some even told me to leave their premises. I was tired, sick at heart and discouraged. People were retiring, and I became alarmed that I should receive no shelter. I stopped at one place and very politely and entreatingly asked them to keep me, assuring them I would sleep on the floor, if I only could be protected from the dampness of the night air. The man told me to "clear out." I then asked him how far it was to the next house. He told me "eighty rods." I replied that I would go and ask at the next house, and if they refused me, I would return and sleep in his barn or under one of his straw stacks.

I had gone but a short distance when he called to me to return. I did so gladly, and I received very kind treatment from the good farmer and his wife. The next day 1 preached in the church of the village three miles distant (not the one I had passed), and had the most of these people as my auditors. Somehow a strange feeling came over me, and I was eloquent and earnest, and used the gospel sword in love and tenderness. Half the congregation were in tears. I trust they were benefited. Now all this may seem very strange to some of my readers, yet this is my simple experience.

But, oh, it was so hard! Why are people so slow to help a poor struggling mortal? The only consolation I had was the reflection that this mortal life was but for a little while, and I looked up, through my tears, and asked, " How long, O Father!" But then these " little whiles" of God—do they comfort us as God meant they should, or do we look one another in the face, wondering and saying, What is this that he saith? For faith's and comfort's sake, let us seek the meaning and the consolation of God's "little whiles." The mystery of the "little while" is a legacy to the universal church. Christ's discourse on his second coming, in Matt. 24, certain passages in the Epistles, and the closing words of Revelations, "Behold I come quickly," may all have had, and will have their influence in awakening and keeping alive this, the sweetest hope that the church can cherish—the little while of human life. "For what is your life? It is even as a vapor that appeareth for a little time and then vanisheth away." Whence this doleful confession of human frailty, that man, made in God's image, gifted with God's reason, heir of God's immortality, fades from existence like a summer cloud? The scriptures declare, "Our days are swifter than a weaver's shuttle; our years are spent like a tale that is told." Man is "like the grass, withered by the heat so soon as it is sprung up; his days are an hand-breadth." We are really living by the day. We are born every morning, we die every night, and with the dreadful uncertainty that any day may intercept our plans and dash our hopes. We are impressed with the brevity of our days, not so much from their absolute fewness as from our constant liability to death.

Look at the "little while" of earthly sorrow. "Our light affliction, which is but for a moment." Surely he is a stranger to human grief, who thus can speak lightly of life's woes. But listen to his own confession: "Of the Jews five times received I forty stripes save one, thrice was I beaten with rods, once was I stoned, thrice I suffered shipwreck, a night and a day have I been in the deep, in journeyings often, in perils of water, in perils of robbers, in perils by my own countrymen, in perils by the heathen, in perils in the city, in perils in the wilderness, in perils in the sea, in perils among false brethren, in weariness and painfulness, in watchings often, in hunger and thirst, in fastings often, in cold and nakedness; besides those things that are without, that which cometh upon me daily, the care of all the · churches." So far, then, from being a novice, he is an old veteran, battle-scarred and tried. But

by what magic scale does he weigh such momentous experiences, that he can call them "light afflictions"? By what
unknown standard of time does he gauge their continuance, that they seem "but for a moment"? His afflictions
were not light in themselves. There were times when, to
use his own language, he "was pressed out of measure,
above strength, insomuch that he despaired of life," but
whenever the heavy sorrow of life bore down the scale he
threw into the balance a weight so mighty that the beam
was instantly reversed, and that weight was the eternal
weight of glory. Paul's public life was by no means brief,
and during the period he might well say, "I die daily."
As the weight of glory made the affliction light, so the eternal weight of glory made it seem but for a moment. It
was then, from the time-view of the eternal, that Paul
looked upon life's woes, and felt that they were only for "a
little while."

Rightly estimated and improved, our afflictions are our
greatest mercies. They are the credentials of sonship,
they are seals of the divine love, and in proportion as we
strive, with God's grace, to become partakers of his holiness, shall we find the world sinking in the distance, and
ourselves poised on the wings of faith, and rejoicing in
God's time-view, estimating earth's painful hours by the
eternal standard, and comforted by the thought that the
sufferings of this present time are not worthy to be compared with the glory that shall be revealed in us. From
the remote ages of that eternal future we shall look back
and see our entire earthly life to be but a point, a speck in
our immortal career.

To you, my fellow soldiers, I have these words to say:
These are not times for fainting: these are not times for
idling. All the world is active; the wheels of commerce
are revolving at a greater rate than ever. Everywhere
events march with a giant stride. We have seen what our

fathers dreamed not of. Now, if ever, the church of God ought to be awake. The demands of souls require our utmost diligence; the enemy is active in deceiving; we must be active in instructing and saving now, by the precious blood of Christ, who bought us. O ye believers in Christ, bestir yourselves, if the blood divine be in your veins, and if ye be soldiers of that great Captain, who unto death strove against sin; and if ye expect to wear the white robe and wave the palm of victory, in the name of the eternal and ever-living God, seek ye his Spirit and the divine energy, that ye may labor yet more abundantly and faint not.

How many are crushed because their best efforts are not appreciated. The labors of the CENSER were often spurned because its editor was poor and depressed.

However, God plants his angels in the most barren and waste places. It is a beautiful thought, whether true or not. I love to make it so. It is related that among the things that are said to have come down to us from paradise uninjured by the fall, the "Beauty of Flowers" stands foremost; and this relic of Eden is, happily, within the reach of all. The rich have no monopoly in this; rank and reputation are not necessary to its possession; for, true to the touch of the divine pencil, the flowers will open with as gorgeous beauty by the side of the poor man's cottage as by the palace of the millionaire; and the lowliest dwelling may be surrounded with that which in beauty of adornment outrivals Solomon in all his glory.

What the flowers are to the poor cottager, God's "little whiles" and "light afflictions" are to the sons of sorrow and of toil. The humblest may share the precious promises held out to us in the Word of Life. Many times could I have sat down discouraged, and said it is of no use; but I would not thus yield. I preferred to suffer honestly with debts paid, than to swindle my creditors by failures.

To thus meet my obligations, in order to save every dollar possible, I often had long journeys to perform on foot, as I could not afford to travel all the distance by cars. At one time I footed it from Forreston—about forty miles —to Rockford in the afternoon and night; at another time from Beloit, Wis., in the night; several times from Rockton in the night. All these travels were performed after three or four days' canvassing, and when I was tired, hungry, and often discouraged. But I was a poor boy, struggling against adverse circumstances to provide a home for my poor, unfortunate sister. Oh, if the good people could have looked into my heart and seen the bleeding record there they would have taken the CENSER! But if human energy could prevent it, I determined that the paper would never fail so long as life and health remained.

About this time the Rockford lottery was in full blast. The CENSER exposed the villany in all its naked deformity. As might have been expected, the local papers, who were reaping their harvest out of it in the way of advertising, and in doing the printing for the swindlers, opened their guns on the poor CENSER. I literally fought my way. It was hard. I had my idea of what Christianity consisted. I was painfully sensible that people lived not only far below their blessed privilege, but below positive duty. The CENSER showed the people their sins, and they called me severe, and many did all they could to discourage me in my efforts.

In my poverty and gloomy prospects, I felt like giving up. Many times I repented of my purpose in trying to continue the CENSER. I really envied the ditch-digger and the street-scavenger as mortals far happier than I. Oh, it did seem so hard! What a vast amount of selfishness I unearthed in opposing and exposing the sins of the times. Under these perplexing and unpromising circumstances I completed the second volume of the CENSER. I had realized not a cent, though I worked hard every day and every evening in the week, and most every Sunday preached two or three times; met with disappointments; traveled hundreds of miles on foot through rain, wind and snow; canvassed from house to house, actually pleading for patronage in my deep poverty and under pressing circumstances; I had slept in the open air, in the woods at the foot of some large tree, in barns, under straw and hay stacks, in short, anywhere night overtook me. It is true I asked at houses to be kept for the night, but was often refused. I do not know as I ought to relate these things, as I have kept them locked up in my own heart until now, and am only led to do so to encourage the young and those who have to struggle with the untoward circumstances of life. As from my beautiful home and pleasant surroundings, I look over these years of trial and heartaches, it seems almost impossible that there is such a wide contrast. And I do think any person less used and inured to hardships than the writer would have broken down in health and resolution. God, however, led me by a way I knew not, and it is just like God to be so good and merciful as he has been to me.

And let me say for the encouragement of the young reader, never despair. Be sure you are right, then go ahead. God on your side is always a majority, though the whole world oppose you. I have confidence in the young man who is actuated by a laudable aspiration. Man's desire for greatness has ever been conspicuous in the history of the past. It has frequently brought upon him suffering in body and mind, and blighted his prospect of future success simply because it was misdirected. Because a noble faculty is abused, is no reason why we should not obey its promptings, especially when it would lead us to the higher and the better development of our natures. The desire to rise above the commonalities of life is one of the noblest aspirations implanted in the human heart by the Creator, if properly directed; but when misguided, it becomes a twofold curse, in that it brings wretchedness to its possessor, and inflicts sorrow and misery upon those to whom his influence extends. Man without a desire to excel in what he undertakes would be a mere drone—a being without motive, and hence without action. No great enterprise would be undertaken; no ships would plow the ocean's waves; no cars traverse the fertile plains. The farm, the shop, the counting-room, the studio, the pulpit—all would be abandoned, had man no higher motive than merely to exist.

Yet man, through misconception of heroism, has perverted his desire for greatness, and brought about untold evils.

Aspiring to be gods, angels fell;
Aspiring to be angels, men rebel.

The world again and again has been shaken by the advent of some so-called mighty hero. Armies, like a fatal pestilence, have devastated empires, dethroned kings, and slaughtered multitudes in their march to conquest. The pages of history are stained with deeds of blood and polluted with the record of crimes. Earth has been a vast arena, on which military champions struggled for glory. Alexander overturning dynasties; Hannibal invading Rome with fire and sword; Cæsar crimsoning the fields of Gaul and Germany with human gore; Napoleon sweeping over the burning sands of Egypt,—are but illustrations of a false conception of true greatness.

True greatness never writes its achievements on the tablet of fame with the sword. Like the sun in his meridian splendor, it brings blessings to this world overwhelmed by the powers of darkness. It binds up the broken heart, pours the oil of gladness into the wounds of oppres-

20

sion, visits the prisoner in his dungeon, strikes the fetters
from the captive's galled limbs, fills the ocean with snow-
white sails, spreads the network of railways and telegraphs
over continents, causes the barren plains and desolate regions of the globe to bloom like the rose of summer.   It
penetrates the bowels of the earth, and brings up its glittering treasures: it detects the microscopic inhabitants of
the dewdrop; it unfolds to us the countless charms of
nature; in short, it leads us to admire the wisdom and glory
of God throughout his boundless dominions.

Although every age has furnished men who have vainly
sought the pathway of greatness by subverting kingdoms
and empires, yet there have also been men who have actually found it.   Socrates, the great moral philosopher of
the heathen world, proclaimed under the very shadow of
temples consecrated to idolatry, the eternal truth—there is
but one God.   His greatness seemed like the rising sun
over Helicon's cities of blind superstition.   Cicero, the
central light of Rome, saving that mighty empire from
civil dissension by his eloquence and wisdom, has engraven
his name on a monument which shall never decay while
ages fill their appointed course; Howard, whose heart
yearned with sympathy for the poor and imprisoned, who
spent his fortune and life in visiting noisome dungeons,
will be held in grateful remembrance, not only by Conti-
nental Europe, but by all mankind;   Newton, to whom
we are indebted for those fundamental truths of natural
philosophy by which we have been enabled to compute the
distances and ascertain the motion of celestial bodies, far
transcends, in true greatness, the noblest of Oriental heroes.
The name of Mr. Peabody, the great benefactor of the
poor of London, will go down to the latest generation with
the everlasting gratitude of orphans and widows.   Who
can adequately extol the influence of such greatness of
heart and such nobleness of purpose?   The monument he

has erected, not in the park of the great commercial metropolis of the world, but in the hearts of thousands who have been the recipients of his princely gift, will survive the wreck of time.

God has given this emotion of the heart to man, that he might do good in the world in which he has been placed. Were he ambitious to relieve the destitute, to cultivate the arts of peace instead of war, to send Bibles to every region, to proclaim the glad tidings of good will to men in every place; all nations, kindred and tongues, long before this, would have been marshaled into the sacramental hosts of the Prince of Peace. If aspiration for greatness were directed to suppress intemperance, to ameliorate the sufferings of the unfortunate, to reclaim the outcast and erring, there would not be a land in the course of the sun, nor an island washed by ocean waves, but would glow with industry and beam with gladness. The Creator is a beneficent being, and he would not have implanted in the soul a desire for greatness, a yearning after immortality, if he did not intend it for man's highest good both in time and eternity.

The beneficent results which would flow from true greatness, were it universally exercised as God intended it should be, are beyond finite conception. Wrangling and contention would cease; the earth would rejoice in golden harvests, prisons would fall into decay, crime and corruption would be suppressed, brotherly love would flow from heart to heart, childhood would be full of cheerfulness and early learn the name of Christ and the way of life, and age with hoary locks would serenely walk to the quiet tomb. Then the dreams of poets and predictions of prophets would be fully realized, the golden age would again be restored, the " desire of all nations" would dwell among men, and under Christ's beneficent reign the real glories of the universe and the character of our God be more clearly known.

This is a world of conflict in which the nobler faculties of nature are at war with evil passions and with the powers of darkness. Our feeble efforts and short-sighted plans are inadequate for the successful prosecution of the warfare. It requires a firm will, clear mind, invincible determination, pure and truthful hearts, to aspire after that greatness of which God approves. Could we fan these thoughts into a living fire in the hearts of the young, then would a moral reformation roll across the land, such as has not been witnessed since the days of pentecost. Ah, my young reader, the possibilities before you are grand. Will you grasp them?

But I resolved, God being my helper, to go just as far as I could; do the very best I knew how; spend much time in secret prayer, asking for true wisdom, that in all my writings there might be the real gospel spirit, that everything might be written in love and with a pure desire to benefit my fellowmen. I worked early and late, and faithfully, and could not help but feel if a pure motive, honest industry, and conscientious dealing were ever rewarded, I ought to succeed financially.

I also looked more carefully into my publishing interests. While thus investigating, I found that I was paying money into a wealthy but unscrupulous corporation. So I at once determined to get from under this unjust oppression, and moved from the *Register* office into a small room, 20x20, in Metropolitan block. I also purchased my own print paper. But here I found another difficulty, namely, to take the CENSER forms from one end of the city to the other to get them printed, as I had no press of my own. However, it would not do to give it up, so I suffered the inconvenience, and notwithstanding my inconveniences, issued the paper with great promptness.

At this opportune moment I learned that the office of "*The Church*," a religious paper published at Palo, Ills., was for sale. I purchased the whole concern, running in debt for it. The reason why I took this unwarranted step was, by the transaction I secured a hand-press upon which I purposed to print the CENSER. But, after moving the press to Rockford, and after expending considerable money in procuring the necessary fixtures, and setting the press in position, upon trial, to my great disappointment, I could not make it do as good printing as I found it for the interest of the paper to do, so the great bulk of the office was dead property on my hands.

I became very depressed in mind, and the cold sweat started from every pore of my body as I thought of the certain ruin which would crush me when my notes came due. If a man wants torture of mind, let him have all his expectations fall to ashes, as did mine in the trial of that hand press, and he will know what it is to suffer. It is somewhere related that there was an ingenious torture which consisted of a cell, which at the prisoner's first entrance presented an air of ease and comfort. After a few days' confinement he began to see that its walls were gradually contracting. The discovery once made, the fact became more appalling every day. Slowly, but terribly, the sides drew closer, and the unhappy victim was at last crushed to death. What an emblem was this of my condition. Every day was hastening the crisis when I would be crushed by debts hastily assumed, and the purchase which would prove worthless. Well it would not do to give it up, so I worked still harder, and canvassed for the paper with a determined will to succeed, and the good Lord opened a way, and I was able to continue the paper and meet all my obligations.

During the early part of this summer the office of " *Words for Jesus*," a monthly magazine, published by the Lamont Bros., in the city of Rockford, was offered for sale. I purchased this also, paying cash. The CENSER now had the united material and strength of two additional papers. In the meantime I was paying, as fast as I could, for the first office above mentioned. With close economy, careful financiering, and by paying cash for everything purchased, I began to gain a little financially. But the greatest need was a printing press. I would never permanently succeed until I cut off the expense of hiring my printing done out of the office. Besides, it was a great inconvenience, and an injury to the general interests of the paper, for on mailing days the office had to be shut up while the CENSER force —editor and all—were at the *Register* office, folding and mailing the CENSER. Of course, when patrons visited the office on these days, they found it locked, and did not know where to find us, hence I lost patronage through this seeming inattention to our business, though I could not help it. A press I needed, a press I must have, and a press I resolved to have. For a long time I made it a subject of prayer, and when the opportune time presented itself I laid the matter before the CENSER readers. They—God bless the dear, good people!—responded liberally, in contributing $474.76. The most of this came in small sums, and some of it from the little boys and girls, but all of it was very gratefully received. About $800 found its way into the bank to my credit. I thought that this might possibly be enough as a first payment towards the needed press. Accordingly it was ordered, and expressly built for the CENSER by the Cincinnati Type Foundry. Though it was ordered in August, yet it did not arrive until October. This was a great event in the history of the CENSER. The press cost $1,500. Of this, $800 was paid upon delivery, and the press mortgaged for the remainder. The press once in position, I found it to be a most excellent one, and it made the CENSER look bright and clean. I also saved $27 a week in doing my own work, and all the inconveniences to which I had been subjected. With the aid of the press, and the added experience in financiering, and studied economy, the prospects seemed more cheering to me, and I took fresh courage, thanked God for the good success, and with a braver heart bent to my work. As soon as the people learned that I had a press, subscriptions poured in upon me from every direction. It did seem to me that the tide had now turned, and even the enemies of the CENSER believed the paper would live for "certain." The months glided swiftly along, and by the 15th of February the mortgage was lifted, the press paid for, and the CENSER once more out of debt. Under these favorable circumstances the 3rd volume was brought to a close. The year was a very successful one, for I had paid for two offices purchased—the two costing $550—and $1,050, $450 being donated, on the new press; paid all my financial obligations, and had $1,150 to my credit in the bank. All this was accomplished by an unwavering trust in God, hard work, determined perseverance, and without advertisements in the paper.

The discouraging question is often put, " What can you accomplish? The world is very large, how insignificant a fraction of it can our best words directly affect. The minister preaches on Sunday, say, to three hundred hearers; how meager, therefore, seems the result!" Evidently to calculate the effect is not our business; we are to do our duty. Whether men heed our word, or whether they scoff at it, still we try to speak it. A man should labor just the same as if assured that the salvation of the whole world depended on his individual efforts. I once heard a politician strike the key-note, when he exclaimed: "I go into this campaign as if I fully believed that on my effort the issue of the election depends!" Thus, in the three years of labor on the CENSER, did I labor, regardless of results. I could have sat down many times and given up had I consulted results. Of all men to be pitied, it is that class who are always looking for results. What is that to them or to me? Our duty in this world is to work. God will take care of results. Work, work, early and late, with a brave heart, a strong arm, and a firm faith. God will honor such work, and reward the laborer, and it matters but little whether we see the reward of our labor in this world or not. This is the law of our being, yea, it is the voice of God to every man—not work, not eat. God gives the soils, the seeds, the sun and the rain. He makes man do the rest—to till, to sow, to gather in, to harvest. God goes on with the work to the exact place where man should take hold, and there he stops. God will not plant one hill of corn nor build one mill to save man. The whole human family may perish if it will not work. The bird must use its wings and the fish must stir its fins, to secure their food. The bee must leave its hive for honey; and man must use his hands and brains to some useful purpose. This is the law of Jehovah; and this rule holds equally good in religious things. God builds no church edifices—throws no wall of partition around a church because it claims to be his. He commands every church to work; and it must work or die.

But I had other higher incentives to labor for God. It was to bless my fellowmen, and to glorify my heavenly Father upon the earth. I often get tired and discouraged over these feeble efforts; then comes the thought that eternity will be long enough to rest in, and I take new courage, and renew my efforts.

Heaven! What a word! It comprises within its syllables all the ideas of bliss, and is the perpetual synonym of every term of rapture or delight. It is the highest meaning of whole families of delicious words. It is home. It is rest. It is refuge. It is glory—the glory of achievement, of victory, of wealth, of authority, of personal splendor and ineffable beauty, of strength, of exaltation, .

of wisdom, of honor, of unimpeachable truth and purity, and of an unspotted holiness.

Heaven is salvation—salvation from guilt, from fear, from sorrow, from pain, from death; a salvation positive as well as negative—fruition of joy as well as deliverance from penalty; salvation from the body as well as the soul. It is a house, a mansion—rather "many mansions"—a country, a city, a kingdom. It is the general assembly, the family of God, the church of the first-born. It is the casket in which Jehovah treasures his jewels, the divine pasturage where the Almighty feeds his flock, and leads them to fountains of living water, and it is the marriage supper of the Lamb. It is the joy of the returned mariner, the shout of harvest-home, the triumph march of the Redeemer, the coronation of the Son of God. It is another Canaan with another Joshua; another Eden with the second Adam; the real holy of holies, with its priests forever after the order of Melchisedec.

Heaven is conscious, personal purity during each moment of eternity; it is blissful association with the moral heroes of every age,—with patriarchs, prophets, apostles and martyrs,—and it is the smile of God forever. It is youth perpetuated without indiscretion, and it is age living on to everlasting years without infirmity. It is the homestead of the holy, the family mansion of the universal Father, the fatherland of Gabriel and Michael. It is the goal of the racer, the rest of the pilgrim, and the exceeding great reward of the faithful; the country where none die, or are sick or sorrowful, or unfortunate, or friendless —a better country. A land in whose soil grows indigenous the tree of life; a scion of which flourished in Eden till the fall; where there is a day without night, and light without the sun, and ceaseless action without fatigue.

Heaven is the congregation of the glorified; the one hundred forty and four thousand of the tribes of Israel, united with the great multitude which no man can number, of all nations and kindreds, and people, and tongues, standing before the throne and before the lamb, clothed with white robes and palms in their hands, and crying with a loud voice saying, "Salvation to our God which sitteth upon the throne, and unto the Lamb;" while all the angels which stand around about the throne, and about the elders and the four beasts, fall before the throne on their faces, and worship God, saying, "Amen, blessing and glory, and wisdom, and thanksgiving, and honor, and power, and might, be unto our God, forever and ever, Amen."

Heaven is the great supper, spread by the Almighty for his family; it is the everlasting union and repose of the saints; it is the Sabbath of eternity; and its seat is the metropolis of creation, the council-chamber of the celestial senate, the court and throne of Jehovah.

All terms used in the Scriptures to set forth " the glory that shall be revealed in us," are so used as to convey a weight of meaning beyond their usual signification; but still, " eye hath not seen, nor ear heard, neither have entered into the heart of man, the things that God hath reserved for them that fear him;" for he is able to do in this world, exceedingly abundantly above all that we ask or think, and to bestow upon us in the next " a far more exceeding and eternal weight of glory."

With these glorious anticipations in full view, let me toil in the vineyard, let me die in the harness, let me fall on the field, let me climb to the high lands of Eden, let me stand with the blood-washed, let me sing redemption's song, let me see the tree of life whose leaves are for the healing of the nations, let me see that immortal stream issuing from the throne of God, rolling its crystal river over beds of gold, let me see the angels on snowy wings, let me see my blessed Lord,—and all my toils, and tears and trials, and heart-aches will pass from remembrance forever, for the Lamb shall wipe all tears away and lead us by fountains of living waters.

But to return, volume fourth was opened under very favorable auspices, with a new title, new type, enlarged, and otherwise improved, and was issued weekly. Up to this time it had been issued only once in two weeks. From the salutatory of that year I give the following extract:

"For the first time does the GOLDEN CENSER appear as a weekly periodical. We have long and patiently toiled to this end. The object of our ambition is now attained, though we do not now lay down the oars and flow with the tide. We shall throw all the energy of life into our work. It is dear to our heart, and we are awfully in earnest in this work. We shall hew to the gospel line, let the chips fall where they may. This is our purpose, and we mean, God being our helper, to carry it out.

We are glad the CENSER was born in the springtime, in sweet May, the loveliest month in the year, when over the hills and through the valleys the rays of the sun come streaming, while on the mountains and in the forests nature's orchestra pours forth its sweetest song. Had we the gift of the poet we would 'paint the beauties of the new-born year in colors of living light; for we never weary of the springtime with its refreshing showers, balmy breezes, and sunny hours. How we love to watch the growing grass on the lawn, the unfolding leaves in the grove, the flowers springing into beauty all around us. Oh, the raptures as we revel amid the apple and cherry blossoms, and breathe the air all redolent with their sweetness!

It is amid this universal resurrection of nature into life, and the glee of gladsome hearts wafted on the morning air, that the GOLDEN CENSER comes to its numerous readers, scattered from shore to shore, living in city, village, and hamlet; on the farm, by the inland rivers, in the forests, and on the prairies. We come with the flush of youth upon our check, and the beacon of hope in our heart. We glory not in ourself, but in the cross of Jesus. Our purposes all center •there. Had we a thousand lives, they should all be consecrated to our Divine Master. It is the old, old story we shall repeat. We are earnest and zealous—shall exhort, persuade, entreat, and invite the wandering, strengthen the weak, cheer the faltering, encourage the desponding, and speak words of sympathy to the sorrowing. We shall be bold and fearless in combating intemperance and the popular amusements of the day.

It was the firm, unwavering adherence to the plain old truths that made the CENSER so unpopular and despised. But I could not help it. I would not lower the standard to please a pleasure-loving world. It was the glory of one of the apostles to boldly declare, despite the unpopularity and the contumely, that he was not ashamed of the gospel of Christ. Would that the same thing could truthfully be said of all ministers and religious editors. Doubtless the reader has not failed to notice the unrest and feverish anxiety on the part of some theologians of to-day for a better form of stating truth than we have always employed. Even the president of a college under the patronage of one of the most reliable branches of the church, recently labored to show that Christianity needed "new phases," a gospel "which asks nothing of faith which reason cannot grant," or, in other words, a religion of reason, a religion of the head. And thus our professedly-acknowledged teachers take butterfly chases after the milder forms of infidelity and evolutionism, seemingly forgetful that the gospel of Christ is not to heal men's heads but men's hearts. It would seem that the religious world is laboring to find out some new way to salvation other than repentance and faith in the Lord Jesus Christ. But there is none other way. The Scriptures declare that there is no other name under heaven than the name of Jesus Christ whereby we can be saved. He that seeks some other entrance into the kingdom than by the door, the same is a thief and a robber.

I am simple enough and trustful enough to desire none other gospel than the one in which the apostles glorified, the one which saved the early church, the one promulgated by the reformers, the one that has cheered thousands of souls now in glory, the one that our fathers loved. I know it hurts the proud, sinful heart; but it hurts only to heal. It convicted the erring Peter; it struck blind the bold and defiant Saul, while yet breathing out threatening and slaughter against the church at Damascus; but it healed them. It is the two-edged sword that pierces the heart, but it only cuts out the root of bitterness. I am glad that it has virtue enough to heal the most depraved sinner. This world of sin needs just such a gospel. Its severity in handling sin is exceeded by the peaceable fruits of righteousness which it always brings forth in the heart upon which it operates.

When I experimentally know what this gospel can do, and what it has done, I'm grieved at these theological trimmers whose crime is not so much that they abolish hell as that by their religion of reason they destroy the prospects of heaven—for heaven is not a place of rest for reason as a rest from *sin*.

It is to be devoutly hoped that the "ism" period is about at an end; that the religion of science, of reason, of geology, and of speculation will soon have finished their career in disturbing and distracting the minds of the people.

An eminent writer of extended observation says: "The masses are beginning to turn from nostrums to the old, old story, and to ask for something genuine. Rhetorical chemists and book-making naturalists have coined their hypotheses into currency, and are retreating from their rash opinions. Now is the opportunity for the weak-

kneed Christians to come back, repent, believe and cling
to the old gospel. Preachers who have made capital out
of abusing scripture and slurring Christ and trimming for
skeptics, are feeling the influence of the tidal wave, and
begin to tack for the change of wind.

There is nothing so powerful or enduring as truth. It
wins respect and retains it. The Christian army needs to
be advanced all along the line. Indifferentism is not
liberalism. Men of straw must be displaced by men of
grit and godliness. The sinfulness of sin and its inherent
damnation must be fearlessly set forth. It is the highest
use of the element of fear to halt a man until Christ's love
can lay hold of him. We need the unadulterated Bible
spirit—the gospel Saviour." It is this gospel that will
save the nation, and not another.

If men would only lay aside their speculations, and give
their united and hearty support to this gospel, what marked changes would take place! Instead of the cold and
heartless formalism, a new life and a new energy would
pulsate through the Christian church, selfishness and indifference would give place to warm, glowing hearts, unfruitful lives would be baptised with the Holy Ghost,
closed lips would be unsealed, tongues touched by the altar-
fires of Jehovah would permeate every community into life
and beauty. Instead of the unbelief, the distrust, the
doubts, the hesitancy on the part of those who have never
come to this gospel fountain, there would be confidence,
faith and ready and open hearts for the inception of the
truth.

These are no idle speculations, but verities attested by
all past history, observation, and experience. Let us then
glory in the gospel of Christ, and not be ashamed to confess it before the world. And why should we be ashamed?
Shame is the first and surest evidence that we have not the
genuine article. Ashamed of my Lord! God forbid.

Ashamed to confess before the world that I an heir to the kingdom to come! Heaven forgive the offense. O God help us to throw open wide the doors of these stifled and almost lifeless hearts of ours, and let the sunlight of right-eousness come in, that its heavenly beams may energize them into new life and beauty.

During this summer I built me a residence at an ex-pense of $1,400. The reader will remember that I invest-ed $650 the first year in a house. The whole at that time cost me $1,200, which, added to the above, made my resi-dence worth $2,600. And right here let me say that, al-though a homeless wanderer up to this time, yet no one loves a happy cheerful home more than the writer. I al-ways hoped I would be prospered enough to procure the longing of my nature, and now I was living in the full re-alization my hopes.

But, let me pause here and bring up another thread of my narrative. In the autumn of 1870, I became ac-quainted with a young lady whose general bearing—for young men must receive their first impressions from gen-eral views—were in keeping with my ideas of what a wife should be. I sought her company, and was favorably re-ceived. After a pleasant acquaintance and courtship of nearly a year, we were united in the bonds of matrimony by the Rev. C. Brookins, September 20th, 1871. The reader will remember that Rev. C. Brookins was my pas-tor while living at Rochelle. He also received me into the communion of the church while at Rochelle. In this age, when many young men seek wealthy fathers-in-law, rather than to work out their own character and fortune by hard, honest toil, and to enjoy the industry of their own hands, let me add that I considered it beneath the dignity of true manhood to thus court the lap of indolence, and hence I sought my companion from the humble walks of life, who was thereby qualified to struggle with me amid adverse circumstances. And in this I have not been disappointed, for in the events which I am about to narrate, she stood up bravely, denied herself, and in a womanly manner bore our common distress with fortitude, often cheering me when it looked so dark without by hopeful words and rigid economy, preferring to suffer with me, to lamenting her sad choice in the selection of an editor for a husband, who was blessed with nothing but poverty.

But the CENSER was growing and our quarters became too contracted. Hence, as a matter of necessity, the CENSER was removed to Shaw's block, into a room 22x30. This was not quite what I wanted, but was the best I could obtain.

The summer passed into autumn, and autumn in turn gave place to winter. When the cold, bitter days came, I found my quarters most miserably calculated for a printing office, and more than once I had to let my employes abandon their work, and seek warmer quarters, and hence, I was greatly hindered in my work, especially through the holidays.

And this brings us to another New Year, when we are wont to pause in the journey of life and look back over the year, and note the progress we have made. What a wonderful personage is old Father Time, with his remorseless scythe and hour-glass, measuring off the years and cutting down the flowers, no matter whether just unfolding or full-blown. How insignificant is a year to him. Grim with age, and gray with the frosts of sixty centuries, he sits, deep in the dim and misty aisles and sepulchres of the past, where the white tombstone marks the mounds raised over the buried years, weaving the shrouds of departed ages. Around him stand the now unheeded years, filled with the memories of long lapsed deeds of centuries of crime, of blood, of wrong; memories mingled with hopes and fears, with cares and joys, with the history of our meek and lovely Saviour, with his perfect love and walk, with salvation full and free for a perishing world, with prophesies and thoughts too vast for comprehension.

The dying year is but a grain of sand to time's vast ocean, but one journey around the sun, but a link in the chain of eternity, yet how full of human frailties, of fields of blood, of untimely graves, of midnight revelry, of cold assassins, of ruined lives, of lost hopes, of tears bitter and heartbreaking, of untimely graves, of sorrow and anguish —all the natural fruits of dire sin, the fell monster of darkness—the destroyer of our happiness.

But hark! upon the gale, the wintry demon bears a doleful sound—the funeral tones of death. The year is dying —is going with the moldering relics of unnumbered ages to rest beside antiquity, to be forgotten, to be forever dead, though freighted with the souls of those who have taken their flight to yonder world of light and beauty to live with him who giveth the waters of life freely. Oh! shall we not pause to drop a tear in the ashes of the dying year? Oh! how hard to die unwept and unlamented. The year hath wrought its mission, hath given us bountifully of nature's productions, hath filled our store-houses with grain, hath cheered the hearts of the children of men. Yes, we will raise our hearts in grateful thanks for the fruitage and vintage of the dying year.

Midnight's solemn silences come o'er the slumbering world, the hour hand moves on the dial, and the pendulum swings forward into the New Year! We know not what will be the history of this youthful visitor—whether good or bad. But as we stand upon the threshold of this New Year, let us pause for a moment and brush away the cobwebs of selfishness which may have gathered around our lives; let us step out into nobler actions, let us think less of self, more of our fellowmen, more of Jesus and of God, let us live for a purpose which shall draw down heavenly

21

benedictions upon us; let us open our hearts, full and free, and extend a friendly hand of mutual greeting. Thus will the dawning year make glad the pure and true-hearted, the constant and the good.

And what a time is this in which to form resolutions of amendment—and to carry them out too—to guard well our words, to set in motion such a train of influences as shall bless us in the day of eternity. It is said of a dying prodigal, when he found the last grain of sand had slipped through the hour-glass that he exclaimed: "Gather up my influence and bury it with me!" Alas! vain request, this were a thing impossible. There is no winding-sheet so strong as to hold the forces of influence let loose in our lives; no graves so deep that they can cover the ever-increasing and ever-ripening fruits of our lives' actions. A pebble tossed into the ocean moves, though imperceptibly to us, the world. The influence of the voice of the chirping birds stirs the aerial ocean in all its vastness. A word spoken, a frown or a smile, a look or a token, a silence or an utterance, lives on throughout all time, ever onward and increasing in its influence for weal or for woe. If the dying youth had requested that the free winds be bound in gossamer, the mad waves of the ocean be chained with cords of ether, the lurid lightning to be chased down by the sloth, or any other impossible thing, his wish would not have been more absolutely unfeasible. "Bury my influence!" Ah! 'twere impossible! Blot out my markings from the bulletin board of human actions! It cannot be done. No stream of influence, whether it be the filtering vein of obscurity or the torrent of popular power, shall ever be wholly restrained. All! all live on, and live for aye! O Great Father, what a responsibility falls upon me! Who is able to render his account! The words of my mouth sound forever along the aerial aisle of trackless ether, the stroke of my hand produces an impulse that will be felt through all space, and all time. The things done in secret shall be sounded from the house-tops of the judgment. Men, angels, and God shall know all my doings. If the results were confined to myself and to my direct acts, I might be less careful as to my course. But all that I am and all that I do is multiplied and intensified a myriad times upon earth's present and future population. My influence, however humble my station, will sweep on forever. Eternity alone can measure the full-grown results of my smallest action.

With such reflections as these I try to be very careful in the editing of the CENSER, to let its pages be consecrated to gospel truths and a holy Christianity.

But the year passed pleasantly away. I was able to meet all my expenses, and publish the paper weekly at $1.00 per year without a single advertisement. This was considered quite an undertaking, and I must confess I had some doubts as to my ability to give so much reading at such a small cost, but I felt my way cautiously and trusted in God for results. It was true, at the close of this year I could not show so large bank credits, but I was quite satisfied with the results, for I had established the fact that a religious paper can be sustained without advertisements, and at a subscription price within the means of the poorest. By turning to the last number of Vol. 4th, I find these words in its closing editorials, " It will be remembered by those who read our salutatory four years ago, that in the first number of the GOLDEN CENSER issued, we lifted up a standard against worldliness, formality, card-playing, raffling, church lotteries, dancing Christians, theater-going church members, wine-bibbing professors, the horrid rum traffic, and all the follies and extravagances that follow in the train of fashion. That we have not lowered our standard or tempered our words to please worldly professors of religion, but have, to the best of our ability, fulfilled our pledges, we are sure our readers will attest. Our views remain unchanged. We still believe that a cheap paper in the interests of Christianity, pure and free from all worldly interests, is a want which the age demands, and that plainness of speech in regard to the vanities and follies that are eating out the spiritual life of the church, is needed, and that it has pleased the Master to call us to this important mission."

Volume fifth opened under discouraging circumstances. The paper was so radical upon many points that it lost public favor. For my faithful, earnest appeals to a pure, holy life, I received hundreds of insulting, coarse and obscene letters. But I toiled patiently on amid my discouragements, trusting in God.

Despite the perplexities of office cares and troubles in meeting my financial obligations, I still continued my labors among the people, preaching the gospel. A service always given gratuitously on my part—and sometimes paying my traveling expenses besides.

One Sabbath I had an appointment some fifteen miles away from Rockford. I had to take an early start in order to reach it in time for the morning services. My way was along the west bank of Rock River. In the quiet of a Sabbath day, myself and wife set out in a carriage to the place of preaching. The morning was lovely. The sun shone never more brightly on spire, dome and dwelling. The great machineries of the world were hushed, the streets deserted, and the smoke of furnaces had cleared away, and Rockford quietly rested embowered with the foliage of her shade-trees, her beautiful flower gardens and creeping vines. Truly this is the Sabbath, and our citizens respect God's command, "Remember the Sabbath, to keep it holy." On through the city and out into the country we held our way. Oh, how fresh the morning air! how sublime the country! Behold the

Fields stand dressed in living green!

Far to the southwest stretch away the rich, varied, waving plains. Passing farm-houses, lawns, orchards, fields, ruminating herds, and pasture lands, we entered a beautiful grove, and, presently, we came in sight of towering cliffs, at once grand and sublime. At our left the river winded away until it was lost to our sight among the hills. Its bordering slopes, like a frill on the green robe of the earth, rolled back on either side in their undulations until earth and sky kiss each other; gurgling brooks hummed along their channels; flowers bloomed and breathed forth their fragrance; the birds seemed to vie with each other in singing their sweetest songs for our special benefit, and the gentle puffs of fragrant atmosphere from over the waters of the inland river fanned our brow. Heaven seemed let down to earth as we journeyed amid such charming surroundings.

While thus traveling, I mused. I thought of life with all its solemn realities and weighty responsibilities, of the struggles and the moral conflicts through which the child of grace must pass. Look at earth in its most pleasing aspect; it has dark and frowning clouds, its disappointments, and heart-breaking dispensations. There is not a rose, be it ever so fair, but that has its thorn. Often, in the most lovely and innocent flower, we find a worm gnawing away at its life. So sin mars and defaces God's universe. And yet, how true it is, notwithstanding the adverse circumstances which meet us at every turn in life, for how many things do the children of men long and toil, as if there were no higher aspirations, or a land more beautiful than earth, and why do they? What is there in or about these cherished objects, which makes them so desirable, and prompts to such continued action for them? It is because it is imagined they have in them the elements of good, because they promise happiness. But how far can they do this? How far is it pretended that they can? Can they remove tears, the pangs of sorrow, the bitterness of afflictions? Can even the gratifications of luxury do it? Can wealth do it? Can honor do it? Can amusement do it? No indeed. They have no such potency. Miserable comforters are they all. Lull to rest the aching head they cannot; soothe the anguish of the mind they cannot; close the fountains of grief they cannot. Tears are wept by the possessor of millions, by the votaries of pleasure, by the laureled hero, by the monarch on his throne.

When despair would brood in midnight darkness over the human family, oh, blessed Hope, sweet messenger of the skies, thou dost point us to him who alone exists pure! the Being who made angels honored and lovely, refulgent with the beauties of holiness; the Mighty One who brooded upon chaos when darkness covered it, and educed from that rude and shapeless mass harmony and life; the Sovereign God, who made man in his own image, after his own likeness; the Saviour who, by his truth and grace, is recovering the earth from the blighting effects of the apostasy; the King eternal, immortal, invisible, the only wise, who dwelleth in light inaccessible and full of glory, whose will is sovereign, whose smile is life, and whose frown is death. He it is, this blessed, supreme, glorious God-man, who was touched with our infirmities, who groaned within himself at human misery, who wept at the grave and on Olivet, this ever-blessed Jesus will welcome us to the summer hills of paradise and show to us the kingdoms of eternity, and lead us to the pure, sparkling fountains of living water. In the glory land, amid the summer hills of paradise, "God shall wipe away all tears from their eyes:" eyes that are to be moistened no more with grief, but are to sparkle forth with happiness forever! And this removal of tears will be complete. Not those caused by sickness and pain merely; not those caused by losses merely; not those caused by bereavements merely, or by scenes of evil, or by indwelling corruption, or by Satanic assaults; but all tears, however caused, he wipes away. No mental darkness, no mental depression, no shattered nerves, no physical suffering, no calamity, no foul enemy, no disturbing sight, sound or sensation, generates a tear! They are wiped away by a Heavenly Father's hand, all wiped away. These tears are removed forever. "God shall wipe away all tears from their eyes; and there shall be no more death, neither sorrow nor crying, neither shall there be any more pain; for the former things are passed away." We might expect that when tears are wiped by a Heavenly Father's hand they would be wiped effectually, and not come again. And they will not. Tears that are gone are among the things which have been and are not again to be. "The redeemed of the Lord shall return, and shall come with singing unto Zion, and everlasting joy shall be upon their heads; they shall obtain the gladness and joy, and sorrow and sighing shall flee away."

> No chilling winds nor poisonous breath
> Shall reach that healthful shore;
> Sickness and sorrow, pain and death,
> Are felt and feared no more.

What can be more blessed than a full realization of what is comprehended in the wiping away of all tears? If God would have the minds of his people rest with delight on anticipations of future joys, how could he better effect this than by giving them a vision of the summer hills of paradise, the New Jerusalem as their promised home, and tell them that in that pure and beautiful land there will be no more death, or sorrow, or tears? Tears we have seen come from sin, as streams from their fountain. To say, then, that in that blessed abode all tears will be wiped away, is to say that all the effects of the apostasy will there cease, paradise be regained, the blessings of the first Eden be restored, and all the struggles, conflicts and sorrows of the Christian terminate in victory and bliss. And this bright prospect Israel's hosts have. To this they are authorized and encouraged to look forward. A city compared to a richly attired bride adorned for her husband, is made ready for their residence. With an eye of faith we can even now behold it "coming down from God out of heaven;" and a comforting, animating prospect it is for us in the present world of funeral processions, disappointments, griefs and tears. On the summer hills of paradise there is health instead of sickness, pleasure instead of pain, songs instead of groans, anthems instead of anguish.

What a contrast, then, does not this world afford when compared with the home of the redeemed. And is it not infinite gain to leave a place like this sin-smitten earth for a place like that? Here the children of God are "born unto trouble;" here pains, infirmities, and diseases invade them; here mental and manual labor and fatigue are theirs; here "their souls are sick with every day's report of wrong and outrage;" here, the world and the flesh try them, and Satan buffets them; here, "they groan, being burdened," their eyes often filled with tears, and their hearts wrung with sorrow. How much better to lay aside all these, to pass from them, go whither they shall never suffer, or sigh, or weep any more, ascend into heaven, pass into glory. Happy exchange! Who can wonder that those having a well-grounded hope of such an inheritance, a lively view of these blessed realities, are ready to leave this "vale of tears," consider it "gain" so to do, say that "it is better, far better," than to linger longer here below? Who can wonder that dying in full prospect of this Jerusalem above, as Moses died on Pisgah's top in prospect of the earthly Canaan, they should be ready to be offered, depart in peace, nay, with joy and triumph?

Oh, the beautiful Eden land! may the contemplation of thy everlasting joys engage all our ransomed souls. May the beautiful prospect of those vernal hills, bathed in the sunlight of eternity, fill our hearts with longings which heaven alone can satisfy. Oh, may it be our happy lot to enter upon the triumphant and rapturous state of God's ransomed, renewed, and glorified people.

> There shall you bathe your weary soul
> In seas of heavenly rest;
> And not a wave of trouble roll
> Across your peaceful breast.

While these thoughts were passing through my mind, turning a bend in the road the spires of Byron appeared to full view, the village itself being half hid from me by the rich foliage intervening. Upon my arrival I delivered God's message. Thence I went to Westfield, and again preached the gospel to an attentive and intelligent congregation; and thence home, feeling that the day had been spent in glorifying my Heavenly Father upon the earth.

But, as before observed, the paper was fast sinking. The gloomy prospect nearly destroyed my peace of mind and discouraged and disheartened me. The circulation ran down to a mere handful, and I had expended all my resources—save my home—upon its continuance. Every issue increased my accumulating debts. No one but myself knew the terrible state of things existing in the office. I asked for credit everywhere I had occasion to make a purchase, for money I had none. Even the employes in the office were asked to wait for their wages. By the first of November I was $2,000 in debt, and every week plunged me $100 deeper, and no prospect of getting out. Driven by desperation. I spent nearly a day in the vain attempt to borrow $100. But it was useless. No one would trust me. My paper-maker refused to furnish me longer with print paper. What could I do? I went here and there among my few personal friends and borrowed $17—all I could obtain, and with this I went to my paper-maker and pleaded for paper.

I confess it took nerve to stand up under all this and to look men in the face without feeling degraded. Only the religion of Jesus Christ saved me from losing confidence in men. Oh, it was so dark!

However, in my distress, I did not mistrust the goodness of God, or lose faith in the work the CENSER was doing. Perhaps it was expedient that I should have this trial of faith. It seemed I had come to that crisis in the paper that help must come, or the paper sink for the want of support. I had deprived myself of even the necessary clothing. My wife had hardly a change. She even thought she would take in washing to help me out. Oh, it could not be possible that, after four and a half years of struggle I must now yield in the conflict. God sometimes deals in a wonderful manner with his people. I cannot tell why he called patient Job to his humiliation or faithful Abraham to his trial of faith. But he suffered it, not to assure himself that these servants would stand the test, but to display through them the power of God. Joseph suffers in Egypt in prison; Daniel goes down into the lion's den; the Hebrews into the furnace of fire, John the Baptist is beheaded and the apostles became martyrs, not to test themselves or to assure God of their fidelity, but to show to the generations of men that the true servants trust their God. Thus we all have our trials. And happy are we if we grow noble, strong and brave under them.

The great and successful men of history are commonly made by the great occasions they fill. They are the men who had faith to meet such occasions, and therefore the occasions marked them, called them to come and be what the successes of their faith would make them. The boy is

but a shepherd; but he hears from his panic-stricken countrymen of the giant champion of their enemies. A fire
seizes him, and he goes down, with nothing but his sling
and his heart of faith, to lay the champion in the dust.
Next he is a great military leader, next the king of his
country. As with David, so with Nehemiah; as with him
so with Paul; as with him, so with Luther. A Socrates, a
Tully, a Cromwell, a Washington—all the great master-
spirits, the founders and law-givers of empires, and the
defenders of the rights of man—are made by the same law.
These did not shrink despairingly within the compass of
their poor abilities, but in their hearts of faith, they embraced each one his cause, and went forth, under the inspiring force of their call, to apprehend that for which they
were apprehended.

But could I still cling to a work so discouraging? Truly
it was a trial of faith. In this dark hour of distress I
bowed my head in the very dust, and in the bitterness of
the ordeal pleaded for heavenly wisdom and divine guidance. Days and nights I pressed my suit—would not let
go the Divine arm until an assurance of some kind was
received. It was a struggle long to be remembered. I had
bitten the dust. The severest trial of all was the opening
of the paper to advertisements. Yet, if I yielded to that
then all my reliance in God and faith in his protection of
his church would be at an end. God only knows how I
was tempted. It is in human weakness I pen these words,
when I say, that like patient Job of old, though forsaken,
apparently, of God and man, yet I *knew* that my Redeemer lived, and I would trust his goodness to the death. The
last issue possible for me to publish was in the press. I
dared not disclose to my readers the terrible condition of
things, lest my enemies, who had done all they could to
ruin me, would crush me financially, before help could
reach me. Doubtless I looked distressed, but I swallowed

my grief, and held up my head as best I could, while those who were secretly hoping I would fail, tauntingly asked, "How are you prospering?"

It is also a true saying that trouble never comes single. I thought my cup was full and running over, but to add discouragement to misfortune, another unaccountable and sore perplexity was the return of the CENSERS—after they had been in the mails a week—by the armful, in a torn, mutilated, and often drenched condition—a thing that never before or since happened. And thus even those who were faithful to the paper in its crisis wrote to me, saying that if they could not get the paper, they would cease to subscribe. Others wanted their money refunded or else have the paper reach them, while still others thought me careless or dishonest. Well, good reader, what could I do? I cried like a child. I could not tell why it was thus. Oh, how discouraged I was. I worked so hard, so patiently, and so carefully in preparing the paper for the mails. And then to have all my efforts thus frustrated, was enough to drive me to distraction. Why my papers were returned thus in a very damaged condition, I have good reason to think was the work of the man who carried the CENSER from the postoffice to the train in this city. He was a Roman Catholic in religion. I had often heard him curse the paper, and he was opposed to the editorials which were being published, and, I am inclined to think, he exposed the mail sacks to the night rains, as the paper usually was taken down in the evening while the train did not arrive until past midnight. But I did not know this until a year later when the same thing was tried, and being informed by the postoffice department through its Chicago agency, I investigated, and found that the above procedure was acted upon. It was the last time I had trouble from that quarter.

All these things combined had exhausted my resources.

I was human. As much as I regretted—and after doing all I could—even contracting debts which would take me years to liquidate—having lost all credit, and being mistrusted on every hand—the last paper, so far as I could see, was going through the press. Was it God's will that the CENSER should go down under such a pressure? If so, I would cling to it as long as human energy could. I feared not to suffer with it. Gladly would I have gone from my office to the stake or the cross, or to meet death in any other way, if by so doing truth would be vindicated. Indeed the mental torture and apprehensions of the approaching failure when my office would be shut by my creditors, was to me more painful than death itself.

As the reader must already have observed, an unforeseen and remarkable combination of circumstances led to the commencement of the CENSER, and by equally unforeseen and remarkable providences has it been sustained. Had it been known beforehand that one-tenth part of the faith, patience and means would have been required for this enterprise, it would, humanly speaking, never have been begun, but Providence only requires us to take one step at a time. The foundations of any great edifice require a heavy investment before anything appears above ground, and Rome took longer to reach her thirteenth mile-stone than she did afterward to conquer the world. Nor are the dark days of any Christian enterprise its worst days. They draw those concerned in it nearer to the throne of God in prayer and watchfulness. The soul that would be great must become so through the school of suffering and of discipline. If you have studied the lives of good, brave men who have walked the path of duty fearfully and faithfully, and have suffered as they traveled, their feet bleeding as they go; if you have taken the book of martyrs and observed how calmly they have bowed their heads to the axe, or how joyously they embraced the stake, if they must go up to glory in flames, or—what is harder to be endured than fagot or scaffold—if you have seen simple-hearted, humble, patient, good men, leading lives of self-denial and reproach, and submitting to loss of place and distinction and comfort, taking joyfully the spoiling of their goods, or preferring the service of God to the pleasures of the world, you have found in them the men whose lives are hid with Christ in God through discipline—for God will have a tried people.

As the night is always the darkest before break of day, as it rains the hardest before the cloud is lifted, so it was with me. The balance turned in my favor. The CENSER was not yet to go to an untimely grave. While the press was rumbling, and the last thousand sheets were being printed, then, humanly speaking, it would never again print the CENSER, but stand idle and silent, and as the day was wearing away, the last mail laid on my desk, and perhaps the last day I would sit at that desk, having about become reconciled to my disgraceful failure, and, as I opened one and another of the letters before me, half hoping some relief might come, and yet having not even a reasonable hope for relief, for I was almost at the last of the letters before me, as I pulled out the contents of the envelope of the letter next to the last one, behold a check for $20 fell upon my desk! Could it be possible! or was it a dream? The surprise and astonishment was so great that my poor aching body and brain almost fainted at the sight of this miraculous "draft of money" and I buried my face in my hands upon my desk and gave God thanks from a heart whose fountains were all broken up. It could not be that so much money was intended for me! The Lord had answered my prayers many times before, but never in a more signal manner. But this was not all, while bowing in humble gratitude, the expressman rushed in at the door with a money letter. I signed the book, and as soon as he had departed, I opened the letter, and behold $12 stared me in the face!. Saved! Saved! I audibly repeated to myself, and my faithful employes, who had overheard me, wanted to know what was saved. I replied, "The CENSER is saved." But I refrain. Dear reader, my feeble pen refuses to write down the scene of rejoicing which then and there ensued. Oh, who can count the mercies of God or tell of his goodness? Oh, why should I ever doubt or mistrust him again. Yet I could not glory in anything I had done, for I had, in mind, at least, given up the conflict, though I had not disclosed it to even my most tried friends. To God belonged all the glory.

More than ever before did I realize that none of us "liveth to himself." The best of us sometimes in the way of life need a little help. I would write this thought upon every heart and stamp it on every memory. " Let us help one another," should be an observance practiced not only in every household, but throughout the world. By helping one another we not only remove thorns from the pathway, and anxiety from the mind, but we feel a sense of pleasure in our own hearts, knowing we are doing a duty to a fellow creature. A helping hand or an encouraging word is no loss to us, yet it is a benefit to others. Who has not felt the power of this little sentence? Who has not needed the encouragement and aid of a kind friend? How soothing, when perplexed with some task that is mysterious and burthensome, to feel a gentle hand on the shoulder and to hear a kind voice whispering: "Do not feel discouraged; I see your trouble: let me help you." What strength is inspired, what hope created, what sweet gratitude is felt, and the great difficulty is dissolved as dew beneath the sunshine. Yes, let us help one another by endeavoring to strengthen and encourage the weak and lifting the burden of care from the weary and oppressed, that life may glide smoothly on and the fount of bitterness yield sweet waters; and he, whose willing hand is ever ready to aid us, will reward our humble endeavors, and every good deed will be as " bread cast upon the waters to return after many days," if not to us, to those we love.

But I took heart once more, and put forth my best effort upon the paper. Nor were my labors in vain, for the receipts on the paper surely and steadily continued to increase, until its income equaled its outgo. Then there was a. balance in my favor at the end of each week. As fast as the means came into my hands I judiciously disbursed them among my creditors. As the sun comes out after a storm, bringing gladness to all, so gleams of returning prosperity cheered my aching heart. The storm-cloud looked black, but the mutterings of the thunder were overpast—it was a receding storm. Occasionally I received a letter speaking in a commendatory manner of the CENSER —then of its being good—then of its comforting and cheering words—then of its excellence and of its being indispensable. I carefully noted all these things, and while I did not fawn to public patronage and popular favor, and never expected to, yet I gratefully thanked the good people, and earnestly prayed that I might merit their approbations.

More than ever did I direct my editorials at the heart. For I greatly desired to do good unto my fellowmen. For it is a Bible truth that if we get the heart right, the head and actions will be right. Let every Christian have a heart that yearns over the spiritual and temporal well-being of his fellowman, be he rich or poor, high or low, then human appointed instruments will cease. This is what the CENSER endeavored to do and shall continue to do. If I fail, it is because I have not the wisdom, and not because I have not the desire or disposition. I have carefully studied Christ's method, how he reached the hearts of the people; and I have also marked the characteristics of the most successful preachers, and find that those who have followed Christ in these respects have been the most successful in winning the hearts of the people to a higher and better life.

If all of us followed the words of Jesus more than we do, we would have greater spiritual power. It is said of him: "Never man spake like this man," and in this respect we never can be equal to the Saviour; but we can all aspire after him. But how true it is that from no human tongue had ever been heard such words of wisdom and power as fell from the lips of the humble Nazarene. His language filled his faithful followers with rapture, but confounded and dismayed his subtle enemies. No wonder that the proud Pharisees were dismayed, and wondered whence he had all this wisdom. No wonder that they were astonished at his doctrine. No wonder that great multitudes followed him, to hear the gracious words that flowed from his lips. Where in all the literature of the world is anything more sublime, more beautiful, more precious to the heart, than the words spoken by Christ? Where is anything that can compare with the sermon on the mount in sublimity and moral beauty?

The sublimity and beauty of the language of Christ rises above everything else that has ever been spoken or written. But more precious to mankind are his expressions of love, his glorious promises, and the words of hope that cheer his faithful followers. "I am with you alway, even unto the end," are the promises which he holds out to his disciples, to encourage them in the darkest hours and most trying scenes of life's conflict. These words are still a balm to the troubled soul, giving assurance of the Saviour's continual presence. From the language of Christ we may ever draw the richest treasures. Here the one who thirsts for true wisdom may obtain the desire of his heart. Here those that hunger and thirst after righteousness may ob-

22

tain living bread and drink freely of the water of life. Here the mourners are comforted and the weary strengthened; those in darkness may obtain light, and the spiritual wants of all may be supplied.

While the whole manner of Jesus was mild and his language full of love, yet his words of reproof were sometimes terrible, causing his opponents to quail before him. How keenly his treacherous enemies must have felt such rebukes as the following: "Woe unto you, Scribes and Pharisees, hypocrites!" "Ye serpents, ye generation of vipers, how can ye escape the damnation of hell?" Though his rebukes are sometimes clothed in such startling language, yet he weeps over the hardness of heart and the unbelief of the people, and prays for his blood-thirsty murderers.

Jesus speaks to the palsied and lame, and they leap for joy, restored to perfect health. At his word the blind receive their sight, the deaf hear, the lepers are cleansed, and the dead hear his voice and arise to life. He says to the afflicted leper, "Be clean," and the leprous scales fall from him, and the life-tide thrills through his parched veins, and again he feels the dew of health cooling his burning brow. To the sin-burdened one he says, "Thy sins are forgiven thee," and the burden of guilt is rolled away and the heavenly light breaks upon the benighted soul.

While in these respects he ever stands above us, yet words, kindly spoken—spoken from the heart—will have a wonderful power and influence over those for whom they were intended. As the breath of the dew to the tender plants, they gently fall upon the drooping heart, refreshing its withered tendrils, and soothing its burning woes. Bright roses they are in life's great desert. Who can estimate the pangs they have alleviated, or the good work they have accomplished? Long after they are uttered do they reverberate in the soul's inner chamber, and sing low, sweet, sounds, that quell the raging storms that may have before existed. And oh! when the heart is sad, and like a broken harp and the sweetest chords of pleasure cease to vibrate, who can tell the power of one kind word? One little word of tenderness, gushing in upon the soul, will sweep the long-neglected chords, and awaken the most pleasant strains. When borne down with the trials and troubles of life, and we are about ready to faint by the way, how like the cheering rays of sunshine, do the kind words come! They drive sorrow away. Kind words are like jewels in the heart, never to be forgotten, but, perhaps, to cheer by their memory a long life, while words of cruelty are like darts in the bosom wounding and leaving scars that will be borne to the grave by their victims.

By the first of January the CENSER had met most of its obligations, and I could work much more cheerfully, though I practiced the closest economy, and persevered in the strictest self-denial.

This, it will be remembered, was a very cold winter, the mercury often ranging from ten to twenty degrees below zero, and continuing there for three or four days in succession. The office was a poorly constructed concern, with only an eight-inch wall and plastered on the bricks. Besides, it was all exposed and open to the bitter cold, and on the days that the wind was in the southwest there was no draft to the chimney. As a result, both myself and my employes suffered very much from the cold. I purchased the best coal stoves to be obtained, and yet I could not warm the office to make it comfortable to work in. Several times we had to adjourn on account of the cold. At times it was almost impossible to make the ink flow so as to print the paper. I was running the office at a great expense in fuel, and the employes suffered beyond endurance. While thus suffering I looked about to see if I could not obtain better quarters.   But there was no building or suitable rooms within my means to be obtained in the city.   It was at this time, I for the first mooted the thought of building an office.   But it was only chimerical, for where would I ever obtain money enough to even purchase the ground, let alone building an office?

But it was a matter of observation of both friend and foe that the CENSER fearlessly stood up for the truth, though by so doing it was unpopular in many quarters.   I could not compromise the gospel, though single handed, and alone I stood against the multitute.   And it is strange with what reckless infatuation people will follow in the way of the multitude, without even pausing to question whether it is in the broad way that leadeth down to death or in the narrow which leadeth to life everlasting.   It grieves my heart to see it thus, how difficult it is to reach this class of people.   However, deceived as they are, they certainly are very enthusiastic, a trait commendable and worthy a better cause, and one which the lukewarm in the church would do well to copy.   In very many localities, by far the largest congregation or audience could be gathered, to listen to smooth-spoken things of man's philosophy, but which has very little of the gospel of Jesus Christ in it.   It seems to be the tendency of the age to either hear or see some new thing.   If you want a throng at your church, get a popular preacher—one who can preach without a Christ in his sermon, and the multitude will come and go like a door upon its hinges.

But that is no evidence of loyalty to the truth.   " The multitude is always on the side of error," was the reply of Luther, when his enemies taunted him with the fact that the Protestants were few compared with the Papists, and from generation to generation there has been a sad verification of his words.

Who was saved when heaven's vast fountains
Did their flood of death begin?
And all flesh on plains and mountains
Perished in its awful sin?
Only Noah,
In the ark of God shut in.

Who was saved from direst horror
At the unexpected hour,
When both Sodom and Gomorrah
Sunk o'erwhelmed to rise no more?
Lot, the faithful,
Was alone removed to Zoar.

Elijah, confronting "four hundred and fifty prophets of Baal" backed by a wicked king and court,—Micaiah opposed by "four hundred men" and a ruler who hated him, —Jeremiah in tears, borne to the dungeon because he would not join the false prophets in the cry of "peace;"— Ezekiel hindered in laying a good foundation by multitudes "daubing with untempered mortar,"—and the Christ of God led away to Pilate's hall amidst the cry of the crowd, "Crucify him, crucify him!"—are but samples of the opposition which truth has experienced in its onward march through the centuries.

Paul, moved by the Spirit of God, forewarned the church, that as it had been in the past so it would be in his dispensation—teachers of error would be numerous; "heaps of them" is the figure he uses. Hear him: "Preach the word; be earnest, in season, out of season; refute error, rebuke, exhort with the greatest forbearance, with teaching; for the season will come when they will not endure wholesome teaching; but having itching ears," i. e., "seeking to hear for their own pleasure; wanting their vices and infirmities to be tickled," "they will heap up teachers for themselves, suited to their own desires; and will turn away their ears from the truth, and turn themselves to fables." It is manifest from this that there was no lack of man-made teachers. God-made teachers, earnest preachers of "the Word," were in the minority. Thus it has been, thus it is, and thus it will be till the appearing of our Lord Jesus Christ as the Judge of quick and dead.

How important is this subject for the consideration of all! Are we in the ministry—called of God to preach the gospel? Our duty is plain; it is with the Word we have to do—not with fables, however pleasing they may be. The revelation of God ought to be more interesting to us than the discoveries of men, the winning of souls than bursts of applause, the favor of heaven than the fellowship of the wicked and worldly. "As the fountains," says Chrysostom, "though none draw from them, still flow on, and the rivers, though none drink of them, still run, so must we do all on our part in speaking, though none give heed to us." Better be saved with the few than lost with the many. Better be a part of God's "remains" than well up in the "heap" of human formation. Better be despised of men for clinging to the Lord's truth than applauded of men for skillfully tickling "itching ears." As the dead frogs of Egypt, when gathered together upon heaps, made the land stink (Exod. vii: 14), so heaps of false teachers make the professed church offensive in the sight of God. Minister of Christ, look to the end. If you would hear the "well done" from the throne, shun not to declare the whole counsel of God as you have opportunity.

I have always firmly believed that the gospel of Christ faithfully preached will be its own vindication. It is of God, and, therefore, will stand the test of honest, faithful investigation. I have somewhere read of a minister, who when he preached wanted to so hold up the cross of Christ that no part of himself could be seen by the congregation. But I fear that many of the namby-pamby, kid-gloved, silver-caned fashionable preachers of to-day want to so hold themselves up to the admiration of the congregation, in their modern butterfly pulpits, that no part of the cross of Christ may be seen. When the great sculptor Phidias was employed by the Athenians to make a statue of Diana, he became so enamored with his work, and so anxious that his name should go down the ages along with it, that he secretly engraved it among the folds of her drapery. When the Athenians discovered it, they indignantly banished the man who had so profaned the sanctity of their goddess. So the spotless robe of Christ's righteousness is profaned by those who would add to it any self-righteous adornings. Christ must be all in all to the soul, or it will be banished forever from his presence.

Well, the seasons do not last always, and the rigors of winter finally passed away, and spring with its sunny hours, balmy air, and lengthening days came in its place. And with the advance of spring came the close of volume fifth. I was thankful to Almighty God for continued health and a sweet disposition. It had been the most trying and distressing year of my editorial life. No consideration could have, persuaded me to go through a similar experience. As I look over the distress of mind, and the depression and the despondency, and constant dread of failing in business I then endured, I wonder that I did not break down in health under it. Yet during this year I was sick but three days, and was but one day confined in bed, and this was in October—in the midst of the depression of mind, and financial embarrassment. The close of the volume found me even with the world so far as debts were concerned. I had paid all my obligations. But so far as I was concerned, I was eight hundred dollars poorer than one year ago. The paper had run eight hundred dollars behind paying its own expenses.

Perhaps it would not be boasting if I should say that very few would have clung to a cause as I did in these dark, discouraging days. Some people think an editor is an enviable person, one I would have exchanged my lot for any occupation whereby an honorable livelihood could be obtained. Only my sense of honor and bound obligation to my subscribers, whose money on unexpired subscriptions I had used, prevented me from retiring from so thankless a task.

But I determined if pluck and energy had anything to do towards making the CENSER a success, it should never go down on my hands. Also I kept to my principles in excluding all advertisements from the paper. I resolved to firmly adhere to this, though by so doing I should be compelled to live on bread and water. I also devoted my best energies to the paper—labored some sixteen hours in each working day of the week to put life and character into it. Nor were my labors unrewarded, for the subscriptions were very liberal, and constantly increasing; in short, the CENSER was prospering.

Volume sixth opened under very flattering prospects; had a good subscription list, and was constantly gaining ground.

Through the clouds and the gloom and the cold, I had again come to the sunshine and the shower and beauty of spring. While my annual labors close amid the alternate snows and rain of April, the GOLDEN CENSER comes fresh and vigorous to the homes of its readers in the loveliest season of the year. Who does not welcome May, the month of flowers and blossoms?

In this latitude and this season, when April is cold and backward—its air filled with snow—we usually have had no realization of spring until about the first of May. As I write, the clouds that hovered over the earth for the past two or three weeks are all passed away. The sky is clear, and the sun shines in all the life-giving power of spring-time, so I am led to exclaim with the poet:

See the young, the rosy spring,
Gives to the breeze her spangled wing!

And May with its gentle zephyrs, and beautiful, golden sun-risings, and balmy air has come, smiling graciously through her floral veil, clothing all nature with her emerald warmth. The light of her eye is reflected on the sparkling waters, her voice in chorus with the feathered songsters re-echoes on the sunlit mountain, in the cool shady dell, and her footprints breathe a fragrant perfume over the mossy carpet. The waters of her newly-refreshed springs and brooklets leap from rock to forest vale, creeping softly —murmuring sweetly the while—into solitude of the sepulchre, and inviting the passing zephyrs to chant a requiem; they adorn the forests and hill with fairy dia-monds—sparkling dewdrops—and ornament the emerald grasses on which the light feet of morning dance as she steps from the golden palaces of Aurora, and slowly de-scends to earth.

The verdure of the meadows enameled with flowers of every hue; the light foliage of the wood, and the luxur-iant, variegated blossoms of the fruit trees, each doubling the charm of the rest—present a lovely, glowing picture. The flocks and herds, roaming freely over pastures and fields, give life and motion to spring's exquisite, quiet beauty, on which the mind of poet or painter can only love to linger.

The great book of nature is turned to its most glowing page, and makes glad the heart of man, as he reads the ever new, ever golden evidences of a kind Providence in the exuberance of beauty fresh before him.

Welcome! thrice welcome, lovely spring! who hath come to chase away hoary winter with his chilling blasts, be-numbing frosts, drifting snows, and driving sleet, giving new life, new hope to all, and reminding us with thy beau-tiful flowers, blossoming trees, and promising crops, of the All-wise Creator, who, in lavishing these abundant pleasures · and delicious fruits upon us, has fulfilled in them the promise that plenty and peace shall be the boon of man from his gracious hand.

With the growth of years comes the growth of strength. First the germ, then the sprout, and finally the sturdy tree. With the blush of early manhood upon my face, in humble prayer, forced in circumstances and distrustful of myself, I had consecrated the pages of the CENSER from its very beginning to the service of God. Those of my readers who have followed me from the first will bear witness that I have redeemed my early pledge to deal plainly and faithfully with the vanities and follies of the present-day religion, which, like a canker, is eating out the spiritual life of Christ's church. I admit I have been radical, but Christ was radical. For a long time it was hard to convince the world that the CENSER was its real friend. I have sailed over rough seas, but the storms and tempests only developed the powers necessary to stem the conflict. There was the world with all its attractions on the one hand, and the cross and bitter cup on the other. To combat with the popular evils of the day, the CENSER, at times, has been like a surgeon's knife that cuts to the quick; but, while I have not spared, it was all for the purpose of properly dressing the wounds. Regardless of praise or blame, I have kept right on in the plain path of duty, taking the Holy Bible as my guide in all things. By that standard I stand or fall. And now, in opening the sixth volume, I desire to say that my convictions in regard to the claims of Christ on his created intelligences for personal holiness and consecration to the work of bringing the world to the knowledge of a merciful and long-suffering Saviour, and of the grand possibilities before every human being, have been deepened.

It is as clear to me as the light at noonday, that in the gospel dispensation "there is neither Jew nor Greek, neither bond nor free, neither male nor female," but all are one in Christ Jesus. And equally clear, that if this world is

brought to the knowledge of the truth, and men and women uplifted from the slums of passion and appetite, where
many now wallow in guilt and shame, the work must be
done by those who claim to be Christ's disciples. And in
this no amount of church-going or Christian giving can
take the place of personal religious work. All these are
proper, and right, and good so far as they go. Whatever
else we may give we must give ourselves in loving obedient
service to the Master.

In this land of plenty where money can be easily obtained by the masses, many are apt to think themselves
excused from earnest and aggressive work in the vineyard
because they give freely of their temporal means. Of
course they would not express this sentiment in so many
words, but it is to be feared that there are not a few who
are quite willing to substitute gold for personal religious
work. When they give of their abundance, they speak of
their offerings as treasures laid up in heaven, and forget
the rebuke of Peter: "Thy money perish with thee, because thou hast thought that the gift of God may be purchased with money," or that God gave them health, means
and prosperity with which to obtain their treasures.
Again, on the other hand, the poor often excuse themselves
from religious work because they are circumscribed and
have not the money of the rich to give. They seem to
overlook the fact that "words fitly spoken are like apples
of gold in pictures of silver," and that even a look of sympathy may be of more value to a tempted, struggling soul
than a mine of gold. God looks at the heart and not at
the purse, and judges by the purpose rather than the deed.
The widow's mite in many a case would outweigh the rich
man's thousands.

Now in all this I do not wish to be understood that
works in and of themselves will save us. It is only the
blood of our Lord Jesus Christ can do that—after we have

done all we could, we are but unprofitable servants at best. Religion means love to God and love to our fellowmen. A love that shows itself in gifts and deeds, but draws its inspiration from Christ, the great fountain head. But whatever else we give, we must give ourselves a whole burnt offering. Not money alone but time and talent and personal service; no part of the price may be kept back. This is the gospel I advocate. My cry has been, is now, and ever will be, Oh, that the house of Israel might lay aside the frivolities, the excessive adornments of the body, worldly amusements, and with heart and hands enter into the glorious privileges of Christ's work, in this age and in these times, when the field is already white for the reaper's sickle, and the laborers are few.

Fully realizing that time is very short, that the golden years of our tabernacling in the flesh are speedily washing up against the shores of eternity, I enter upon the duties and labors which the opening volume imposes upon me.

And ere I lay down the pen, I crave the clemency of my readers the coming year; poor human nature, oh, how frail and liable to err! I make no claims to perfection. God helping me, I can only promise to do the best I know how. In handling the issues of the day, we must "be wise as serpents and harmless as doves," in order to win the hearts of men back to Christ. In your closet while you pray for the heathen, the spread of the gospel, the success of your pastor in his field of labor, do not forget to pray for your patient, toiling editor, who often has heavier burdens and weightier responsibilities to stand up under than the world ever thinks of. And may God bless our dear readers.

With these words I opened volume sixth, hopeful of prosperity, and praying that I might be spared the discomfitures, pains and anxieties of the previous volume.

But, night and day the CENSER office was being built in my mind. I could not get rid of the idea. I dreaded wintering in the old place. I daily made it a subject of prayer. I knew if I had suitable quarters, I could do much better printing. I pressed the matter before my Master. I have faith in answered prayer and a guiding providence. No good thing will our Lord withhold from us if it is for our best interest to have it.

About this time I filled an appointment for a pastor of a neighboring village. While in company with a good brother, after the sermon which treated upon the higher life, he observed that he could not understand why ministers should be so earnest in enforcing the doctrine of holiness. He believed if a man lived as well as he knew how it was all the Bible required of him, and he thought that while many professed holiness, few lived holy lives.

Doubtless this good brother uttered the sentiments of hundreds of people. Very many are slow to believe in the necessity of entire consecration to God, and hence come short of that holiness taught in the Bible. I am of the conviction that consecration must precede holiness of heart and life as much as conviction precedes conversion. And here I think is the stumbling-block in the way of many people. They have not arrived at that point in their Christian profession when they will lay·all upon the altar—self with the rest—and say: " Here, Lord, accept the sacrifice." Let such consecration be made, and holy fire will speedily descend upon the heart thus rendering it. If entire holiness is not taught in the Bible, it is impossible to find words to teach it. Let the words.be selected, and the sentences formed, which, in the clearest and strongest possible manner, may be understood to teach this doctrine,—just such words we would use if we intended to teach it so plainly that no one could possibly misunderstand it,—and turning to the Bible it will be found taught there with equal clearness and force; and, however the words may be varied, a corresponding variety will be found in the Bible.

Holiness of character and life cannot be viewed from any standpoint, or expressed in any words, but what may be found in this holy record; so that every peculiarity of mind growing out of temperament, education, association, custom, or other influences, is fully met; and every one is without excuse. An earnest seeker who objected to the word "sanctification," because of some peculiar ideas then associated in the mind with it, was at the same time deeply convinced of the necessity and privilege of having a pure heart, and that was the leading thought and even burden of the soul; and those precious scriptures, "Blessed are the pure in heart," "Purifying their hearts by faith," suited the case exactly.

The following words and phrases, besides very many others employed by divine inspiration, show the thoroughness, fullness, and variety of the scripture teachings upon this subject:

"Upright," "perfect man," "whiter than snow," "clean," "washed," "cleansed" "from all your filthiness," "from all your idols," "from all filthiness of the flesh and spirit," "from all sin," "from all unrighteousness," "a clean heart," "a right spirit," "pure in heart," "purifying their hearts by faith," "dead indeed to sin," "free indeed," "free from the law of sin and death," "sanctified," "the very God of peace sanctify you wholly," "a glorious church not having spot or wrinkle or any such thing," "perfect and entire, wanting nothing," "perfecting holiness," "filled with righteousness," "with the fruit of the Spirit," "with all the fullness of God," "partakers of the divine nature," "that they also may be one of us," "that they may be made perfect in one," "we have the mind of Christ," "created in righteousness and true holiness," "perfected in love," "thou shalt love the Lord thy God with all thy heart, and with all thy soul, and with all thy mind," "thou shalt love thy neighbor as thyself."

And, to put the matter beyond all question as to what is meant by the holiness taught and required, God declares, "Be ye holy for I am holy" And Jesus says, "Be ye therefore perfect as your Father which is in heaven is perfect," showing that it is the same kind of holiness which God himself possesses. And why not? Does not the child possess the same nature as the parent? It may be comparatively very small and weak, but the very same in nature. And no one thinks of blaming the child for claiming relationship with the parent. Is not the holiness of angels, and was not the holiness of man when created, like the holiness of God? The record tells us that man was made in the image of God. And the apostle writes of those who had "put off the old man," "and have put on the new man, which is renewed in knowledge after the image of him that created him." What a sublime and glorious thought, that we may be not only like angels, but like God himself! And why should it be thought that holiness is too much to claim for the soul redeemed, pardoned, and washed in the precious blood of the Son of God, and created anew by the Divine Spirit? And it may be, this undervaluing ourselves, why we are not more useful. Let the soul once feel that it is purchased with a price, and there will be such a pressure of duty brought to bear upon it, that it must do or die. There is no such thing in reality, though we fear there may be in the name, as an idle Christian.

Why, holiness is the grand central truth of the Christian system; it flashes in every consecrated life, it is written on every revelation from God, it breathes in the prophecy, thunders in the law, murmurs in the narrative, whispers in the premises, supplicates in the prayers, resounds in the songs, sparkles in the poetry, shines in the types, glows in the imagery, and burns in the spirit of the whole scheme from its alpha to its omega—its beginning to its end.

Holiness! Holiness needed! Holiness required! Holiness offered. Holiness attainable. Holiness a present duty, a present privilege, a present enjoyment, is the progress and completeness of its wonderful theme. It is the truth glowing all over and rejoicing all through revelation; singing and shouting in all its history, biography, poetry, prophecy, precept, promise, and prayer; the great central truth of the system, the truth to elucidate which the system exists. If God has spoken at all, it is to aid men to be holy. The wonder is that all do not see, that any rise up to question a truth so conspicuous, so full of comfort.

Let my good reader grasp this grand cardinal doctrine of the Bible and appropriate it, as it is his privilege and duty, as his own. Indeed, so positive and explicit is the Word of God upon this subject, that it has plainly declared that "without holiness no one shall see the Lord." To all who are of the mind of the brother referred to, and who are trying to do as well as they know how, who are content to grope in the valley amid miasmas and malarias, I would say: Come up to the highlands; climb the Lord's holy mountains, and from thence breathe the pure air wafted from the heavenly shores, and look upon the glowing fields flowing with milk and honey of divine goodness. Then will your face shine with heavenly radiance, as did the face of Moses; then will you exclaim with delighted Peter: "Lord, it is good to be here;" then will you move among men, as did Paul, desiring to know nothing save Jesus and him crucified.

As I was returning I happened to pass a beautiful field of grain, when I observed to the husbandman that it was a pleasant day.

"Yes," he replied, "but it is dry."

"A promising field you have," I continued.

"Yes," he replied, "but it will be ruined if we do not have some rain soon."

"A fine lot of cattle you have in yonder pasture."

"Yes," came again, in the same modulation of voice, "but they ain't doing very well just now, as the grass is drying up."

I continued my conversation farther with him, but I could not get him out of the ruts of his gloomy thoughts. And doubtless he is only a representative of a class who never can be satisfied. Unhappy souls! Public torments! The sun shines on them in vain; they only see clouds and feel cold winds. Blessings are poured into their laps to no purpose; they only think of desired things they lack. Virtues shine in their neighbors unseen; faults are discovered in every feature; a virtue seldom mentioned without a depreciating "but." Greet them on a glorious spring morning with congratulations over its brightness, and they will growl back, "We shall get our pay for it;" speak of the noble conduct of Mr. D., and—"Y-e-s, but he had no good purpose in the act," will be flung in your face. Is anyone charged with evil, they believe before they fairly hear; suspicion is taken for certainty; scandal accepted for fact; virtue subjected to discount; a stain presumed on every character; evil motives insinuated where none are apparent. A cloud hangs over their spirits, bitterness drops from their tongue; there is discord within, and chafing without. They absorb no comfort from others, but emit perpetual discomfort most burdensome to companionship. The good recoil from their society, are annoyed by their bitterness, disturbed by their grumblings, offended by their injustice, grieved by their miseries, and discouraged over perpetual failures to infuse sunshine into their experience.

And much of the unhappiness in this world is borrowed trouble. Thus we fret at the weather. Either it is too hot or too cold; too wet or too dry. The crops will be a failure, or something else we cannot help is out of its regular

23

course. All this is wrong—it is more—it is wicked; because we mistrust the goodness and wisdom of God. Why fret at all? If we can remedy that which disturbs our nerves, why not do it, and thereby remove the occasion for fretting? If we cannot remedy it, what good will fretting do?

But all this time I brooded over the thought how I could build an office for the CENSER. It worked so much upon my mind that I in fact went through the city prospecting where would be a good location for my business, and I actually, on the fourth of July, went to a man who had a lot for sale with a view to purchase. But the lowest sum for which the ground could be obtained was twenty-five hundred dollars, and I had just four hundred dollars to my credit in the bank. Not much of a prospect for placing the CENSER building on that lot. But then I did not give up my purpose. I had fully determined to build an office. And when a man determines to do anything, if he has the real metal in him, he will go through fire and water but that he will accomplish his object.

There is a saying, I do not know its author, which is as follows: "Trust in God and keep your powder dry." When I heard it the first time I thought it almost profane. But the more I reflect upon it, the more real common sense I find in it. God meant that we use all our own resources and energies first, and then we may reasonably expect his aid. Acting upon this principle, I applied myself very closely to my business, and I verily believe that God was daily answering my prayer, for my business prospered, subscriptions were coming in and every few days I was able to deposit in the bank. In the meantime I took good care of my credit. I promptly paid cash, and asked no one to trust me. I also denied myself every luxury and even many of the necessaries of life. But while I was thus saving, I did not act the miser. I believe in liberality. Every truly prosperous man is a liberal man.

The first thing I sought to accomplish was to make sure of the ground on which to build. I found men quite willing to wait on me, if I would give them everything I had for security, and pay ten per cent. interest. But I could not be persuaded to enter into such engagements.

While I was prospecting, one day, in the month of August, I found the lot on the corner of Main and Walnut streets, for sale; but the lowest figure was fifteen hundred dollars. At this time I had one thousand dollars in the bank. I offered it to him right in hand if the deed would be transferred to me; but the lot could not be obtained for that amount. After some four weeks I again met Mr. Crawford, who had the sale of it, and asked him about the lot. He said that twelve hundred and fifty dollars was the best figure at which he could make it to me. I asked him if he would give me the refusal of it until the following day. He said he would. The next morning, I went to his office and told him I would give him his price, if he would take one thousand dollars down and wait on me thirty days for the remaining two hundred and fifty dollars.

The reader will understand that I could have purchased the lot on time, but I did not want to do that; I wanted a clear title.

He accepted my proposition, and gave me a trust deed. In twenty-seven days, three days before my time expired, I came with the remaining two hundred and fifty dollars, and the title was duly transferred to me.

This was the first great step towards the new office, and it was successfully taken without distressing my finances. All this was accomplished before the first of December, 1873, and before the CENSER readers knew anything about what was coming.

With such a beginning I felt warranted in unfolding **my**

purposes to my patrons. I set forth the disadvantages under which I was laboring, and the great need of suitable quarters in which I could print the CENSER, and asked for a general renewal, and for a list of three thousand new subscribers, assuring them if I could secure their co-operation to that extent the object would be realized.

There were a few who misconstrued my motives as selfish and grasping, but the great majority believed me sincere and felt I was doing a good work, and hence worthy of the patronage asked. However, weighed down with anxiety as I was, I was very careful not to press the matter publicly, but I did press it at the throne of Grace.

About this time, in addition to my office labors, I preached twice every Sabbath at appointments, one twenty and the other twenty-six miles from Rockford, and which could not be reached by railroad. I usually set out for these appointments on Saturday evening, and often arriving quite late. While riding over the prairies in the fall and winter, I suffered very much from the piercing prairie winds. But I was about my Master's work and was willing to suffer.

While thus facing the storms in reaching my congregations I kept myself mentally warm by meditations, and as I reflect on the vast multitudes destitute of the gospel—spending their Sabbaths in dances and many other sinful diversions, the words of the Lord often came into my mind, "And I sought for a man among them that should make up the hedge, and stand in the gap before me for the land, that I should not destroy it; but I found none." Perhaps not a more graphic picture of general degeneracy can be found in the annals of the Israelites than in the words just quoted. It can not be otherwise than that there was a general corruption of prophets, priests, princes and people. The Lord was in great anger with them, and yet his loving kindness was so great that he sought for a man among them, "that should make up the hedge, and stand in the gap" before him in the land, that he should not destroy it; but he found *none*. How fearful this picture, how widespread the degeneracy of the people, yea, of the whole people, when neither the prophets, priests, princes nor people were true to their allegiance to God! When they had all betrayed their trusts, and not one was found to "make up the hedge." When we witness the frauds and dishonest means employed at the present day to overreach and extort the unsuspecting, and this in an age of advanced intelligence, we may form some idea as to what the people must have been when there was not one found faithful to God. The prophets must have been anything but inspired, the priests profane and unscrupulous, the princes corrupt and disloyal, the people oppressive and cruel. It could hardly have been otherwise. So they were a nation of transgressors—utterly regardless of the claim of God upon them.

Amid such universal ungratefulness and rebellion, it is a wonder that the hot breath of God's slighted mercy did not sweep them from the face of the earth. This would have been man's way. However, God was kind and long-suffering, and instead of sending swift judgment to destroy them, he looked all through their ranks to find one man who would make up the hedge, and stand in the gap. For one man that would stand up for the truth and vindicate justice, and plead the right of God and man. But sad, indeed, it was, there was not even one found.

From these words we may learn two things. First: Men, amid universal prosperity, are prone to forget God, the author of every good. Instead of rendering unto the Creator grateful thanks, they turn their hearts towards the good which he so bountifully gives, and worship it. Second, God is patient, long suffering, and stays merited punishment for a season. Yea, more, he even looks around to see if he can find a man who will have the boldness to

" make up the hedge, and stand in the gap." This is very forcibly illustrated in the words quoted.

Now I am fully persuaded that God is just the same in all ages, and that whoever will stand in the gap, and make up the hedge—*i. e.*, will stand firmly for God, execute vengeance by pleading the cause of God, and vindicating his justice, and denouncing sin in the clearest manner, shall aid in turning away wrath, and in securing the divine favor for others and for himself. Hence it is, that some ministers will preach the thunders of Sinai, and of the terrors of hell, just as they are laid down in the Bible, and show that God is infinitely just in all those fearful threatenings, and that men deserve to be damned who will not accept of blood-bought mercy, and God is pleased with their fidelity, and pours out his Spirit, and saves the very persons who hear the denunciations, and honors himself and his servants.

I know the stale and worn-out apologies used by those who have more refinement than religion, that the age is a cultured one; that men do not wish to be disturbed by the terrors of the law; that God is love. Granted. But do we not find wickedness rearing its scarlet front to the very sky? Take up a daily paper and note its contents. The catalogue of crime is enough to make the blood run cold in one's veins. Now we must have men who will hurl the thunderbolts of the Almighty right at the hearts of evil-doers. It may not be wisdom to take a sinner and hold him over the flames of hell until he cries out for help, yet we must preach of hell, and its awful terrors as freely and as forcibly as we preach of heaven and its glories, and multitudes will be brought to God. The pentecostal sermon, under which three thousand were converted, was of this type.

And am I uncharitable when I opine that one of the rea-

sons why so many ministers are powerless in their preaching is, they do not take sides squarely with God, but for
fear of feeble man, the Spirit's course in them is restrained, and they preach a kind of compromise gospel, which is
an abomination in the sight of God. The modern idea of
culture and refinement has, in some localities, advanced so
far that some of the namby-pamby sort cannot even talk
good plain English—cannot even avail themselves of in-
telligible expressions. Thus, one minister describes a tear
as "that small particle of aqueous fluid trickling from the
visual organ over the lineaments of the countenance, be-
tokening grief." I have heard of one talking in the pulpit of "the deep, intuitive glance of the soul, penetrating
beyond the surface of the superficial phenomenal, to the
remote recesses of absolute entity or beings; thus adum-
brating its immortality in its precognative perceptions;"
while another—and a highly eminent man, head of a college for ministers—when he read a well-known passage of
Scripture, shrank from the plain vernacular, "He that be-
lieveth on me, as the Scripture hath said, out of his—" he
took refuge in the classics—"his ventriculum shall flow
rivers of living waters." Yes, our preachers ought to
know how to use words or else calamities will happen.

No wonder that not a soul is saved from year to year;
and no wonder that the churches backslide under their
preaching. This is a fearful calamity, and this so called
"emasculated gospel" is robbed of its strength and power,
and it is rather a human invention than the "power of
God unto salvation." And it is to be feared that this
very fault is the reason of the "decay of the public conscience," and why such open, barefaced frauds, murders,
adulteries, fornications, suicides, fratricides, and all manner of abominations are committed among us with such
daring effrontery. We need more Boanerges, or sons of
thunder in the pulpit; we need men that flash forth the

law of God like livid lightning, and arouse the consciences of men. We need more Puritanism in the pulpit. Under their teaching there was a different state of the individual and the public conscience from what exits in these days.

Is it possible that the offense of the cross has ceased, or is the cross kept out of view? Is it possible that the holy law of God, with its stringent precepts and its awful penalties, has become popular with the worldling and the sinner? or is it ignored in the pulpit and the press, and the preacher and editor praised for neglect of duty for which their lips and pens should be inspired? I conscientiously believe the only possible way to arrest this downward tendency in private and public morals, is the holding up from the pulpits and the religious press of the land, with unsparing faithfulness, the whole gospel of God, including as the rule of life the perfect and holy law of God. The holding up of this law will reveal the moral depravity of the heart, and the holding forth of the cleansing blood of Christ to cleanse the heart from sin. That ministers everywhere might have glorious results of their labors is as certain as the gospel promises are sure and steadfast if they would stand in the gap, and fill up the hedge, and fully take sides with God, and denounce all manner of sin in the church or out of it, and declare that everlasting destruction awaits the finally impenitent, and that the smoke of their torments will ascend forever and ever. Such plain, faithful, earnest testimonies against the soulless essays *about* religion — the husks on which too many popular churches are fed—would produce a moral revolution. O Lord, pour out thy Spirit upon the ministry of the land, and grant that they may arouse themselves to fill up the full measure of their responsibility, and warn the people of the danger that may beset their feet! And let the people pray for the ministers. Moses pervailed so long as the.

people held up his hands, so shall *your* pastor, prevail if *you* hold up his hands.

Perhaps, in justice to myself, and to correct false impressions, I should here state that excepting this brief ministry of three months, and though I had preached at many places, I never accepted anything for my services, but have often paid my own traveling expenses besides giving my labors. My object was not to make money, but to labor for the good of souls, and if one redeemed soul shall be saved through these humble efforts I shall be amply repaid for all my labors.

But I toiled on faithfully for the accomplishment of what I had undertaken, and I was very much cheered by the substantial evidence, for the people were so united with me in carrying out my contemplated plans, by which I could secure an office building, that by the first of February over 1,500 of the 3,000 new subscribers were secured, and most of the old subscribers renewed. So confident was I that the greatly-needed office would be built, that I secured the services of Geo. Bradley, of this city, at an expense of fifty dollars, to draft the plan of building and to make out the specifications for the same, and on the ninth of March, 1874, the contract for the building was given to Thos. Ennit, and Alvord & Kelly. The building was to be 63 feet deep, 28 feet front on Main street, with two projections so constructed that they would give 20 feet front on Walnut street and a depth of 34 feet. The structure was to be three stories, the first of stone, and the second and third of brick, the stone wall to be 20 inches and the brick wall 12 inches, and the whole to be built of the best material and in the most substantial manner.

Perhaps one of the greatest thrills of satisfaction and of hopes about to be realized was when I beheld the first load of stones going up Main street to the spot where the CEN-SER building *now* is. It then seemed as if one of the greatest undertakings in my life was being accomplished, and, as a friend afterward said to me, that he trembled for me as he saw the walls of such a goodly proportioned building going up, knowing that such a building would cost many thousands of dollars, and he did not know where the money was all coming from, and he expressed my feelings, only he spoke from observation, but in my mind lived the reality. But a year before this, I was praying with that simple trust in God, that if it was for his glory he would open the way for a home for the CENSER, and thereby increase its usefulness. And now the prayer was being answered.

CHAPTER XX.

The Building Gradually Advancing to its Completion—
The Astonishment of those who Despised the Censer—
Unparalleled Success—The Wonderful Circulation of
The Paper—Its New Dress and Enlargement—Conclu-
sion.

In this world time is measured by years. Partings and
separations take place, and friends weep because we shall
see them no more. The Censer had run the circuit of
another year. In more respects than one it had been a
year of unparalleled prosperity. We cast up another stone
in the journey of life and wrote upon it, "Hitherto the
Lord hath helpt us." And what a moment for reflection!
Near the close of the year there is what astronomers call
the *solstice*—the sun, as the word imports, seems to stand
still for a while, as if looking back on the past, and looking
forward to the future, before he makes a new departure in
his annual course. It is eminently fitting that we pause
now and then in the journey of life, and take a glance
backward over the path of our pilgrimage, and note the
way by which God hath led us, and how far, and in what
direction the noiseless foot of time has carried us.

It is true we have toiled through another year. God
only knows. the result of our labor. According to the
measure of ability given us, we have done the best we
could, and yet, after all this, we are but an unprofitable
servant at best. We have tried to faithfully and honestly
hold up to our readers a pure gospel standard, in the kind-
est spirit possible. That we have erred is only human.
As we write, our heart is pressed down with the weight

of responsibility resting upon us, and with the simplicity of a child, we humbly ask for patience, for wisdom, for a tender heart, for an abiding love to labor and toil for the Master. We want to daily breathe the atmosphere of heaven. With these words we closed volume sixth of the GOLDEN CENSER.

The prospects for volume seventh were very flattering. I had print paper enough in store—and all paid for—to take me to the 15th of August, at which time I expected the new building to be completed.

Also by the 1st of May the first story of the new office was completed when the first payment was made. This called for $1,150, leaving me only $150 with which to complete a building on which over $5,000 more must be paid if I met my contract. The contract called for something less than $6,000, and I found before the building was completed that I was out $1,200 more than the original contract. The reader may form some idea of my unbounded faith in God, when I here tell him that when I gave the contract to the parties named at the close of the last chapter I had but $1,300 at my command, and had no reasonable ground of hope where the needed $6,000 was coming from, except that where there was a *will* there was a *way*, and if there was no way God would make one. The contract stipulated seven payments, which were to be made as the building progressed, with ten days' notice before each payment.

With these foundations, and with my head full of doubts and fears, steeped in anxieties, and my heart full of hope and expectant trust, volume seventh opened with considerable improvements over former volumes. While I was anxious as to the issue of my gigantic undertaking, I was also greatly comforted, strengthened and encouraged by the universal satisfaction the CENSER was giving its readers, and the united voice of the people coming up to me from all parts of our goodly land bidding me to be of good cheer.

But I was almost overwhelmed with gratitude when I learned the full returns of my spring receipts. They went beyond all expectation, reaching the unprecedented sum of $1,700. Truly God was in this. On former years my receipts for the same period reached only $500 or $600. If there is an infidel who may read these pages who can explain these evidences on rationalistic grounds, he can do more than I could. As 'the Almighty spoke to Israel's hosts, on the banks of the Red Sea to go forward, so it seemed to me God was commanding me to advance.

I now had $3,000 of the $6,000 needed, and I could see my way somewhat more clearly. It will be remembered I owned a residence which cost me $3,000 and it was worth all it cost. Thus I had enough to make sure of not being bankrupt in my undertaking. This I offered for sale, I was willing to sacrifice all to secure the needed building.

It will be remembered that when I unfolded my purposes of building an office to my patrons, in the last chapter, I asked for three thousand new subscribers; but the CENSER readers and supporters were so enthusiastic and determined that I should succeed that not only the three thousand new subscribers asked for were secured, but several hundred more. Besides these and the prompt renewals, some of my patrons contributed—unasked—$174.-53. Why it seemed like a dream. I could not tell why it was thus, only God was answering prayers. My patrons may often have wondered why I selected for a motto of the paper these words: "In God we trust." Here, good friends, is the explanation. Truly it is all the Lord's doing, and it is marvelous in our eyes.

As the building was gradually rising, and as the payments became due, I promptly met my obligations. Indeed, my builders had to wait on me only long enough for me to write out a check for the amount due. So prompt was I that they declared that they never worked on a job where they had less cause for complaint, and they naturally enough, not knowing the circumstances, imagined me the possessor of some gold mine.

Up to the 20th of June, when my heaviest—and next to the last—payment was to be made, I had not succeeded in selling my house and lot. This necessitated me to secure the loan of $1,000, which I readily obtained, without even mortgaging the CENSER building. With this loan, the general consent of my employes to withhold their wages until I had met my other obligations, and the continued pouring in of receipts on the CENSER, I was fully provided to meet all contracts by the 29th of June.

Had I been an infidel, in contrasting one year ago with this, I should have been compelled to believe that there is a God. As it was, firmly believing in answered prayers, and implicitly trusting in Almighty God, I could very clearly trace the Guiding Hand. It is when we commit all our ways unto the Lord that he provides for us. This is one of the hardest lessons for us to learn. It is so natural and human to fret, mistrust, and apprehend untoward circumstances. I verily believe that if all the churches in the land and all the Christians would live lives of simple trust, peace like rivers would flow down our very streets. There would be no need of resorting to all the expediencies of the world to meet our religious obligations. I do not think God accepts the money filched from the pockets by oyster suppers, church fairs, strawberry festivals, and church auctions. In all these expediencies we copy after the world, without either consulting the Lord or trusting or confiding in his love and goodness. And so long as we take it upon ourselves to meet our church obligations by these unsanctified and questionable means, the Lord will let us, just as he permits the ungodly person to sin. There

are many instances by which I could illustrate and establish the principles above set forth. The Bible is full of
them. God's honor is pledged to be with his people, and
he is good for all he has ever promised us if we will only
meet the conditions of the promise. The path of the just
is a shining way. The righteous are as the sun. Why,
you know the path of the sun to be a radiant path; it is
not only glorious—that expresses but half the truth. It is
glorious because it is radiant. The sun is not like the
moon, a mere reflector, glittering with borrowed light. If
the mountains could be lifted up until they should enclose
it like a wall, and the clouds ascending from the mountains
should concentrate their masses and overarch it like a
roof, it would shine still. Nay, made the more intense by
the confinement, it would turn the mountains into diamonds, and the clouds into crystal, and dash through them
all and fill the world with new splendors.

So with the path of the just. His glory is from within;
it is a radiation. Put him where you will, he shines.
For instance, imprison Joseph, and he will shine out on all
Egypt, cloudless as the sky where the rain never falls.
Imprison Daniel, and the dazzled lions will return to their
lairs, and the king come forth at his rising, and all Babylon bless the beauty of the brighter and better day. Imprison Peter, and with an angel for his harbinger star, he
will spread his aurora from the fountains of the Jordan to
the wells of Beersheba, and break like the morning, over
mountain and sea. Imprison Paul, and there will be high
noon over all the Roman empire. Banish John, and the
isles of the Ægean, and all the coasts around, will kindle
with sunset visions too gorgeous to be described, but
never to be forgotten—a boundless panorama of prophecy,
gilding from sky to sky, and enchanting the nations with
openings of heaven, transits of saints and angels, and the
ultimate glory of the city and kingdom of God. Not only

so, for modern times have similar examples in church and the state. For instance, bury Luther in the depths of the Black Forest, and "the angel that dwelt in the bush" will honor him there; the trees around him will burn like shafts of ruby, and his glowing orb loom up again, round and clear, as the light of Europe. Thrust Bunyan into the gloom of Bedford jail, and, as he leans his head on his hand, the murky horizon of Britain will flame with fiery symbols—"delectable mountains" and celestial mansions, with holy pilgrims grouped on the golden hills, and bands of bliss from the gates of pearl, hastening to welcome them home. These are only a few of the thousands of instances that might be brought forward. Nor are proofs wanting in this remote day. For instance, Muller's great work in Bristol, England; the Home for Fallen Women in New York; the asylum for the afflicted in Boston, and many more humanitarian and benevolent institutions in the land which are raven-fed and provided for by a heavenly Father who knows all our wants. Besides, it does not seem god-like to thrust a religion upon us without giving us the means to support and maintain it, without resorting to the devil's troops for aid. If we would only let God do for us, the world would be taken for Christ in less than ten years. But until people will learn this lesson, the world will groan under its burden, sinners will go down to hell, and only eternity will disclose to us how much of the guilt will be attached to our faithlessness. When people applauded me for my unprecedental success in an undertaking so forbidding, I have always rebuked such by telling them that the glory all belongs to the Lord, I am only the poor worm with which he is threshing a mountain, and just so long as I am passive under the flail of the Almighty, so long will the CENSER be a living wonder and surprise to those who do not recognize the doctrine that God provides. Oh, if I only had the power to impress these grand truths upon the hearts of my readers.

But, as might be expected, I had many letters coming to me warning me of the dangers of flattery and the vanities following success. Well, these good people did not fully know the furnace of affliction through which I had come, and I kindly thanked them for their timely monitions. If there is one thing above another that grieves me, it is to see a poor miserable worm of the dust trying to be proud. I do believe vain people are among the most discontented on the face of the globe. Observe how self-importance makes a man moody and unhappy. He who is always thinking of his own excellences renders himself thereby unfit to enjoy the good of others, and is prone to imagine that every token of affection given to another is an insult offered to himself. Hence he is touchy, sensitive, irritable, and envious. He takes offense when none is meant, and even when those around him are not thinking of him at all he interprets their conduct as if it were studiously discourteous, and goes through the world smarting from wounds that have sprung not so much from neglect of others as from his own over-weening self-conceit.

There is no surer way to make ourselves miserable than to think of ourselves more highly than we ought to think. It isolates us from all about us. It cuts us off alike from human sympathy and divine assistance. It makes us very Ishmaels, with our hands against every man and every man's hands apparently against us. It gives a jaundiced hue to the behavior of those who, so far from meaning to do evil to us, have our best interests at heart, and love us with self-sacrificing affection. The man who has a wound about him, no matter where it may be, feels it to be always in his way. Let him do what he will, or go where he may, he cannot move himself but he is conscious of its pain. In like manner he who has this feeling of self-importance is continually smarting. Somebody has been slighting him. He is constantly complaining of having

24

been insulted, and when honor is given to another he feels nothing but that he has been overlooked. Thus he shuts himself out from every festival, and mopes most of all when others are merry. May God deliver me from this idolatry of self, on whose altar all true nobleness and real happiness are completely immolated.

As the CENSER building progressed towards its completion, the builders were inspired with such confidence towards me that they several times urged me to let them finish the entire structure. The contract only specified the enclosing of the building and the finishing of actually needed rooms. I did not expect, when I let the job, that more than this could be accomplished—and not even this without incurring heavy debts. But my prompt payments inspired my contractors to make their proposals for completing the edifice. I frankly told them I had only money enough to meet my obligations to them. "Well," they said, "we won't crowd you. It will be better for the building and a saving to you to complete the work now. We will give you any reasonable time to pay us in, and will charge you but six per cent. interest." But I supposed that to let them do the work would involve the necessity of mortgaging the building, and, hence, I farther told them that I had a pride about me to keep the CENSER building clear from all mortgages. To this they replied, "We will finish this building as the specifications indicate, and take your note without security or an endorser." I was greatly surprised at the confidence of these men, and said to myself, such confidence shall never be betrayed. So I was persuaded to let them finish the building; which they did.

About this time the circulation of the CENSER had so increased that it was absolutely necessary to use steam power. I had hoped I could defer this necessity until I had strengthened myself a little, for I had invested my last dollar in the building, and ran seven hundred and ten dollars in debt besides. But one of the employes in the office had such faith in the CENSER and confidence in the editor's honesty, and, though he had given me the use of his wages since March, yet he offered to advance the money to purchase the engine; and the engine was duly ordered.

On the last Wednesday in August, 1874, rooms in the new office were sufficiently finished to move, and, accordingly, the employes, as well as myself, were glad to "pull up stakes" and move. Hence the CENSER was removed from Shaw's block to the new office. This made the third move, and, so far as I know, Providence permitting, the CENSER has changed its location for the last time. I am very much opposed to changes. Said a preacher to me when the first number of the CENSER made its appearance, "So you have finally decided to make a trial of it here, have you? You will find it an up-hill business." I calmly replied, though a righteous indignation filled my heart, that "I had set the stake, and I would hang on to it though I should stand shoulder deep in difficulties and oppositions." Well, I have stood to my stake, and now under God's blessing was moving into an eight thousand dollar office, and out from under the clutches of landlords; and the reader may rest assured that I greatly appreciated the change.

We had scarcely located our fixtures in the new office when the new engine arrived, and the second number issued from the new quarters was printed by steam! This was another great triumph. The CENSER in an office of its own and printed by steam! Surely this was climbing the hill of prosperity faster than I had ever anticipated.

However, there were the steam fixtures, the connections, pumps, water and steam pipes, plumbing and many incidental expenses which took several hundred dollars more. By the time the office was in good working condition, I was pretty hard pressed for funds, but I kept up a good heart and trusted in God. He knew where the money was, and, if I deserved it, it would be forthcoming. Still my credit was good, yet I was careful not to assume any more obligations than I could possibly avoid.

While thus struggling along to get square onto my feet again, I found a purchaser for my house and lot; and sold it.

The reader will of course understand that in the economy of things, I combined in the new CENSER building both an office and a dwelling, and hence by selling my house and lot, I was disposing of property I did not need, and upon which I had counted in the building of the office

The sale of this enabled me to take up the note of one thousand dollars which I had given in affecting the loan spoken of above, and also my note given the builders for completing the building. By this stroke of good fortune the new building was all completed, and not a cent of indebtedness upon it!

But the days were shortening and winter was approaching, and by December and January the office was flooded with renewals and new subscribers as never before. I was astonished out of measure! Could it be possible? The CENSER was a child of faith. All along I recognized God in my labors; but now it seemed that the measure of prosperity was filled, heaped up, pressed down, and running over. And to give the reader an idea of the wonderful increase, I present the following table, showing the number of subscribers received, new and renewals, on each day in the last week of the year, for the last four years:

FOR THE YEAR 1871.

Days.		Subscribers.
Monday.	Dec. 25,	41
Tuesday,	„ 26,	31
Wednesday	„ 27,	12

Thursday,	„	28,	89
Friday,	„	29,	45
Saturday,	„	30,	71

Total for the week.......................289

FOR THE YEAR 1872.

Days.			Subscribers.
Wednesday, Dec.		25,	34
Thursday,	„	26,	53
Friday	„	27,	56
Saturday,	„	28,	57
Monday,	„	30,	85
Tuesday,	„	31,	70

Total for the week.......................355

FOR THE YEAR 1873.

Days.			Subscribers.
Thursday,	Dec.	25,	 45
Friday,	„	26,	206
Saturday,	„	27,	 33
Monday,	„	29,	 54
Tuesday,	„	30,	222
Wednesday,	„	31,	 85

Total for the week.......................645

FOR THE YEAR 1874.

Days.			Subscribers.
Friday,	Dec.	25,	238
Saturday,	„	26,	232
Monday,	„	28,	262
Tuesday,	„	29,	137
Wednesday,„„		30,	170
Thursday,	„	31,	173

Total for the week... ⸗ 1,212

Thus it will be seen that for three years prior to 1874, the total number of subscribers received in the last week for three years is 1,289. While for the week ending December 31, 1874, I have 1,212, or nearly as many as in the three preceding years. This certainly is a showing which is very cheering to me, and it is a fair index to the future. Thus the Lord leads us on step by step, and when he sees, or rather when he discovers to ourselves that we can endure prosperity, he sends it us.

When I was bringing the first issue from the press, a gentleman asked me what was to be the object of the paper. I simply told him I did not know—God would open a way. As I advanced, I found that object in the want of a purely religious paper free from secular affairs and advertisements, and one so cheap that it was within the range of all. There are thousands of homes in our land in which there is no religious reading, in which the children are growing up not only ignorant of God and of the principles of Christianity, but who are supplying themselves with hurtful reading. The object, then, of the CENSER was, to reach the masses with a paper at once free from all restraints, and brimful of love and good will, and though that object has only been very partially attained, faith in the importance and practicability of the plan is not diminished. Though the obstacles are strong as the walls of Jericho, yet, like those walls, they may suddenly crumble and leave us free access to the people. It is at all events an object worth devoting one's life to. To reach every street, lane, alley and highway, with selections of the best literature of the day as well as the news, is an object of transcendent importance.

It is said by an experienced observer that there are three stages in the career of every newspaper: "First, noboby will notice it; Second, everybody offers all kinds of advice. Third, from North, South, East and West, people say their advice made the paper." . I do not know about the third proposition, but I do know about the first and something about the second. But in my darkest hours, I simply place my trembling hand in the Father's and trust his leadings, and to-day, I am a living witness that he has always led me by a way I knew not out to victory.

It is a surprise even to me how the CENSER has spread out all over this vast county—from Maine to California, from Duluth to Florida. At this writing, the paper has a circulation of 11,650. I presume that five readers to each copy is not an exaggerated estimate, for in the sparcely set-tled regions—especially in the West—the same copy goes through the whole neighborhood, and I have even found it so in other places. If so, the CENSER weekly has 58,250 readers, or a congregation equal to that of 58 churches containing 1,000 hearers each. Who shall estimate the importance of such an engine, and who is sufficient for the responsibility of conducting it? I can certainly affirm no one. It is only the Spirit of God vouchsafed in answer to prayer who is competent to guide aright such a power. Whilst rightly attributing all that has been accomplished to God, it is proper, gratefully to recognize the means by which he has worked. Many have befriended the CENSER in its struggles, without whose aid there would, humanly speaking, be no GOLDEN CENSER. If the circulation of 11,-650 copies of this paper reaches really, as above estimated, 58,250 every week, what human imagination can take in the audience that is thus addressed. It is an audience enough to overwhelm me when I think of the responsibil-ity. And it is this thought that often makes me tremble when I weigh, and prayerfully decide what shall, and what shall not, appear in the CENSER. Truly, if there is any class of men in all the earth who need the sympathy of the community, and above all the blessing of the Lord Al-mighty, they are the men who stand in the position of ed-itors and publishers of newspapers.

But what has the CENSER accomplished? Its readers can best answer that question, but the paper has been bold, fearless and uncompromising in battling with intemperance and the fashionable sins of the day, in church and out of it. It has earnestly contended for a pure literature. There can be no way to arrest the bad literature of this day but by a firm and unflinching purpose to show the people the sin and folly of undermining reason and sound judgment. There is no way to battle with a bad newspaper but by supplying a good one; no way to fight a bad book but by extending the influence of a Christian book; and I have no doubt that in this struggle God will be stronger than the devil. Now this wave—this tidal wave of bad literature—is covering the land. When Anthony Comstock recently was throttled by a literary villain in Newark, New Jersey, it was only a contest between the bad newspapers of this country and evil incitement and that which is good, and when Anthony Comstock throttled the villain and thrust him in jail, by the strength of God and his own right arm, he did what I hope will be done with all who have anything to do with an evil and corrupt literature. It is high time that Christian men should rise up, and as far as possible organize for the overthrow of this corrupt literature—a literature destroying its thousands and tens of thousands and entering many of the homes of the country to bring nothing but ruin.

Again, the CENSER aims to keep the thought before the people that religion is needed every day in the week. We often only read distinctively secular papers during the week, and when Sunday comes we get in our arm-chair and put on our slippers, and read our distinctively religious papers, when we should live religion every day. Upon this subject Mr. Talmage forcibly says, "How often it is that we see men sitting in church on Sunday night, singing 'Rock of Ages,' rolling up their eyes, and looking pious. They leave their religion in the pew, and say to it, 'Good bye, religion; I will be back next Sunday.' It seems to me a great many Christian men keep their memorandum books in this style: *Monday*—Pay the insurance. *Tuesday*—Settle that note. *Wednesday*—Go to Boston. *Thursday*—Come back from Boston. *Friday*—Settle up some odds and ends. *Saturday*—Pay off the hands. *Sunday*—(After a long pause) Religion. They make it out after a great deal of hard study, when it ought to have been religion from the top of the page to the bottom, and all the way through."

So liberal were my receipts that I was enabled promptly to meet all my obligations, and, on the 15th of January, 1875, I was entirely out of debt, and had seven hundred dollars over and above all liabilities, and all the above named facilities for executing my work. Added to this, I had some five hundred dollars worth of print paper, all paid for, in store.

Well, my cup of joy was full. People from far and near came to look upon the wonderful work, and to satisfy themselves of the truthfulness of the reports that had obtained abroad respecting my work of faith. One lady, who has relatives near this city, heard of the CENSER way down at London, Ont., and when she came to visit her friends, she came to Rockford to look upon that marvelous work. She rode up and down the street several times, admiring the office, and audibly repeating to herself, "The Lord bless the dear boy," and then she called on me, and in the warmest words possible assured me the CENSER was doing a great work in Canada. People have called on me from Connecticut, New York, Massachusetts, Ohio, Michigan, Indiana, Pennsylvania, New Jersey, Maryland, Minnesota, Wisconsin, Kansas, Florida, California, in short, almost every State in the Union, wondering how I could build up such a work without money or even advertisements in the paper, and at a nominal subscription price. I could only reply it was not my work—it was not done by my strength or wisdom—the Lord was in it all—to him be all the glory.

But this was not all. There is no stand-still in this work—no resting on laurels. All my friends told me I must now rest for one year. The strain upon my energies for the past eight months had been quite enough, and I must now take my ease. I had an office, a home, and a library, and all the appliances and facilities for doing a great work, and I ought to be satisfied. But this restless, energetic spirit could not thus idle away the golden moments of life—"better to wear out than to rust out." Idleness is a sin, and I have no right to thus commit sin. Therefore, I told my readers if they would make the subscription list ten thousand, I would enlarge the paper three-eighths over its size as then published. The ten thousand have been secured, and over, as above given. Accordingly the paper was again enlarged at the opening of volume eighth.

Looking into the future with the light of the past, the CENSER must soon become one of the greatest agencies in the country in carrying forward the cause of the world's Redeemer.

I have often heard it repeated that the CENSER is altogether too sober-minded—it never indulged in levity—always talked right to the hearts of men—it was so earnest. Well, I admit it. God forbid that I should be otherwise than sober, faithful and earnest. We are to be pure in heart, pure in speech, and pure in life. The Lord of life and glory has pronounced a blessing on each. "Blessed are the pure in heart, for they shall see God." These words were spoken by him from whose lips there never fell a word in jest. He likewise said, "By their fruits ye shall know them," for "out of the abundance of the heart the mouth speaketh." If then we see persons from whose tongues flow the corrupting streams of trivial language, we are safe in inferring that the fountain—the heart—is not pure. The scriptures tell us that "the tongue is a fire, a world of iniquity and unruly evil, full of deadly poison." And Jesus, knowing frivolity in conversation to be the leprosy of society, adds, "But I say unto you, for every idle word that men shall speak, they shall give an account thereof in the day of judgment." All vain talk—empty, unprofitable, or which does not intend to instruct or edify, is idle. And look at its tendency: It destroys our peace, unfits us for spiritual devotion, lowers us in the estimation of others. How much soever persons may praise one for witticisms or buffoonery, or seem pleased at the time, yet, in their sober moments, they heartily despise such folly. Again, by indulging in lightness and frivolity, we measurably destroy our influence for good. "Familiarity breeds contempt." How exceedingly incongruous to warn sinners to "flee the wrath to come," while in their presence we indulge in levity, or trifling conversation! Who would be likely, on a sick or dying bed, to send for a punning minister or Christian to talk or pray with them? The cry, "Let us be social," is sounded in our ears on every street corner, but let us be very careful, lest, in an ungarded moment, we let the devil enter the heart, corrupt the fountain of our spiritual life, and thus poison the speech of our mouth. The pure in heart shall see God. Can we look down into the well-spring of our being and see "holiness to the Lord," inscribed on every thought? If we must give an account at the last day, let us guard our words, "having our conversation as becometh the gospel of Christ," "speaking the truth in love," "that we may grow up into him in all things." If ever the arch-deceiver is transformed into an angel of light, it is when professing Christians talk and laugh at nonsense. Nothing is so contrary to godliness as levity. Every word we utter influences, for good or evil, some precious, immortal soul. Like as the pebble dropt into the ocean agitates the mighty deep from shore to shore, so our words, though spoken only in jest, sink into some human heart, and often disturb the whole life.

Words spring from thoughts, and tend to acts. Vile words lead to vile deeds. They familiarize the mind with vice, and break down the barriers of purity. Modesty is a safeguard against sin; evil words effectually destroy it. Many a man has talked himself into sensuality, crime, and ruin. Intimacy with evil in thoughts and words blinds us to the vileness of iniquity, and prepares us for sinful indulgence.

There is no habit more ruinous to the mind and heart than that of continually turning into a jest every occurrence of life. The mirth-loving and pleasure-seeking may welcome such a companion in their hours of gayety, but when the clouds of sorrow lower, they turn with loathing from such comforters. They are as useless in society as the idle butterfly. One has well compared such triflers to a sower who scatters only flowers as he passes along. "His course will soon be marked with only withered beauty; while he who sows good grain in the furrows of life will leave behind him a living growth of abiding usefulness."

A great deal of so-called wit in public addresses, even before religious assemblies, as in our Institutes and Conventions, do not glorify God. It is not of a kind we should remember with pleasure with eternity face to face. All irreverence is most displeasing to him.

If "foolish jesting" was something the apostle warned us against, wicked jesting would certainly come still more under condemnation. It is the earnest speaker, who with forcible illustrations, comes down close to our hearts, and makes us feel, what we remember longest and with feelings of deeper interest.

The lesson is obvious:—avoid the dialect of sin. Keep the mouth as with a bridle. " Let no corrupt communication proceed out of your mouth, but that which is good to the use of edifying, that it may minister grace to the hearers."

Let it be our aim rather to do good than merely to amuse. Let us scatter the golden grains as we pass along, rather than the dying flowers. Then may we look down with joy from the sunlit hills of life, on the waving harvest-fields, which angel hands shall gather for the heavenly granaries.

We have influence. Some poor, lost sinner may be watching our actions—our words—if happily they may see something in our Christian deportment that can heal an aching, sin-sick heart. Oh, the solemn responsibility of life! Our Saviour, as if pointing directly at the jester, says it were better for such an one to have a mill-stone about the neck and drown in the depths of the sea, than to offend one of these "little ones." Oh, let us, my dear reader, be pure in HEART, for if the heart is pure our words will also be pure, and the "BLESSED" will be ours, as JESUS hath said, and we shall see GOD!

But the most eventful year of my life was drawing to a close. Prosperity had been poured out upon me like water, and with a cheerful, grateful heart I closed volume seventh of the GOLDEN CENSER.

The eighth volume was opened with the paper enlarged as above stated, and an entire new outfit of type and materials at a great expense. I give a brief extract from the editorial in the first issue of volume eighth, which is as follows:

" With this issue the GOLDEN CENSER enters upon its eighth year. As we look over the history of this paper—first a small semi-monthly, then a weekly, then enlarged, and now enlarged again with an entire new outfit, it is a matter of wonder as we reflect on the unparalleled prosperity, steady progress, and increased usefulness, and it is a cause of lasting gratitude to Almighty God in permitting so humble and unpretending an agency as your unworthy, but ever faithful editor to demonstrate to the religious world that a *religious* paper *can*, and ought to be published without *advertisements* at half the subscription price usually asked for the religious periodicals. Now, while we have proved the above with a seven years' actual trial and increased prosperity, we do not wish to be understood as reflecting on our worthy cotemporaries who disagree with us upon this vital point. God bless them, and may we all work for the glory of God and the salvation of souls. As you look over the enlarged CENSER with its clear beautiful print, doubtless its first readers can see a great advance in its march *onward* in seven years of its existence.

"As the years come and go—and they come and go, oh! so rapidly—we feel more and more our own weakness, and helplessness, and ignorance, and this drives us to the source of all wisdom. As we write we can sincerely say, it is not the consideration of wealth that prompts us to labor and toil for the good of our fellows. We are willing at any time to exchange the *cross* for the *crown*, but until it shall please God to close up our brief span, feeble efforts and misgiving life, we shall bend our energies to the task before us. We have consecrated all to our heavenly Master, and whether prosperity or adversity shall come upon us in the future, we shall glory only in the *cross*.

"Hitherto we have been open and honest with the reader —it is always best to be honest—and have stoutly refused to trick them into subscribing for the CENSER by offering them worthless daubs under the name "chromo," or by giving them sewing machines or dictionaries as premiums, —these things are all well and proper in their place,—but come to the reader with a paper whose subscription price is placed within the reach of all, and which leaves but a small profit, and say to the reader, if you believe in honest toil and self-sacrificing efforts on the part of the publisher, subscribe and encourage the editor; if not, then subscribe for your chromo, sewing-machine and dictionary paper, and pay your two prices for about half as much reading as is contained in the CENSER. We know it pays to be faithful to the public in these particulars. The people have been humbugged enough for some one to show up this villainous business.

"In our efforts to combat with the various forms of evil, we shall be very mild but firm. Some want us to "pitch in and clean out" whatever may be offensive to them. This is not the spirit which will win in the end. The gospel of Christ is a gospel of love and peace. By kindness we are to win the erring from the paths of sin. If we fail in this we defeat the end we wish to accomplish. More than ever are we persuaded that if a man is in trouble we can best make him admire the "mind that is in us" by giving to him, and with a heart of real desire to do him good, help him onto his feet and towards the cross and the Redeemer and heaven. We hate sin, but pity the victim. We can not admire the evil actions of men, but love their souls. If we say pretty severe things against sin, do not blame us. We try to be your friend. At best we can but provoke you to examine whereof we speak and see if the things spoken of are right or wrong. This is fair. As a friend we shall never flatter sin, or think any one the more virtuous because indulging in it."

But this brings the narrative of my life down as far as contemplated in this sketch. Of course my life work is given to the cause so dear to my heart, and which God has placed upon me. As already given, the present circulation of the paper is eleven thousand six hundred and fifty. Now the thought that suggests itself to my mind is, Has the CENSER reached its highest point of usefulness? Shall it stand at a dead water level? To this the answer comes as the sound of many waters, "No." There are yet grander possibilities before it. Time will disclose its history, and unfold its destiny.

What I have accomplished, and how I have accomplished it, has been faithfully set forth in these pages. I am yet in my early manhood. Humanly speaking, there are yet twenty, possibly thirty, years of usefulness before me. That they will be marked with as many struggles, can hardly be expected, and I most sincerely hope that I may be spared similar struggles.

In a financial point of view—estimated by dollars and cents—the building, the ground on which it stands, and the type and material requisite to facilitate the publishing of the Censer, I consider worth about twelve thousand dollars. It cost me more than that, but I prefer to fix the figure below rather than above cost. I do not speak of this to boast how much I am worth or that I earned it with my hands, for it is only lent to me of the Lord, and he could take it from me much quicker than he has given it to me. But I give this information to the reader because I have nothing to conceal, and to inspire the young with noble courage and brave actions in a right cause, and also to publish to the world that the Golden Censer, though started by a poor unpretending and unassuming college boy seven years ago, and without money, credit, friends or even encouragement, and despite the hatred and bitter opposition, and mountains of discouragements, succeeded in carrying forward the paper from nothing to a circulation of nearly twelve thousand and from poverty has accumulated a competency, has acquired surroundings valued at from $12,000 to $15,000. And all this has been accomplished without a single advertisement in the paper, and with a subscription price which even my enemies admit as unprecedentedly low.

While the CENSER is the only paper in the City of Rockford which owns the building in which it is published, it has earned it by honest toil. Within the time since the CENSER has had an existence I have seen the rise and fall of many papers, both religious and secular, papers started with $30,000 and $50,000 capital and three or four pages of advertisements, and a subscription double and treble that of the CENSER. One large metropolitan religious paper not far from Rockford, *its* readers will remember, called the CENSER the *mushroom* of the West, and, though this same great paper has for seven years tried to crush the mushroom, yet it has not succeeded, and God being my helper it will never succeed. And what is a singular fact, that paper, seven years ago had 17,000 subscribers; now it has 13,000. At that time the CENSER had none; now it has nearly 12,000. By the same ratio, where will the *mushroom* stand seven years hence? If God honors let men despise.

Other papers I know which do not pay publishing expenses, and are year by year running deeper into debt, while the CENSER, without making any metropolitan pretentions, has paid its way.

But I take no glory to myself. I am just as dependent upon God in this day of prosperity as I was in the dark days of adversity and disaster.

Aside from the material evidences of God's goodness, the CENSER has accomplished a work which eternity only can disclose. And this, more than anything else, has cheered me in my hours of depression and discouragement.

But why have I written all this? Simply to set before my readers the fact that God cares for us, and hears and answers our prayer, and that nothing can be more pleasing in his sight than a life of simple faith and trust.

From this standpoint, though I know not the future, my prospect for increased usefulness is very promising.

25

But I will trust in the Lord, though I should be called to deeper afflictions than I have recorded in this narrative, for it is good always to trust in God.

To every young man and woman I would say, seek none other employment but what you can ask the blessing of God upon. And with faithful toil, continued perseverance in untoward circumstances, earnest devotion to God and your calling, honest and open hearted to all men, and with form erect and face set toward heaven, you will, yea, you must, succeed. God bless the young people! I have a lively sympathy for them, for I have been down in the dark stream, and have struggled with adversity, as I can but hope and pray none of my readers may ever be called upon to undergo. But in it all, I bless God for the furnace of affliction.

I find, as I come in contact with young people that many care little for the solid works, such as philosophy, astronomy, history and chemistry, and that class of books which is likely to call out their mental faculties. Said a gentleman of culture in my hearing recently, "A friend of mine is the owner of a large telescope, and being benevolent, he invited all the young people to his observatory to study the siderial heavens. But, strange to say, very few cared to come, as they had no taste for such study—preferring their evening parties and their trashy novels." Ah, my young friends in the neglect of mind culture, you lose much in time, and more in eternity. For in the study of the works indicated above, you are not only enabled to understand the operations and the causes which produce certain effects in the mechanic arts, but it will make you more intelligent and skillful in whatever occupation you may choose for life. Even the wayside flower has added charms to the botanist. Notice with what pleasure do intelligent and cultivated minds contemplate the works of nature, the arts and sciences found in the outer world. We search with eagerness into all the mysteries of botany and zoology, chemistry and geology, physiology and astronomy, and many other useful sciences. We number and name the different species of plants, analyze the vegetation of flowers and trees, watch the tender grass starting in the spring, gaze through the microscope at the full-blown flowers, noting their varied, beautiful, artistic tints and hues. We name the leaves and mark their perfect formations, and wonder how such varied, charming beauties can spring forth from the earth through the combined influence and action of hydrogen and soil, the atmosphere and rays of the sun, day and night, heat and cold, rest and action, nature and nature's God. We wonder that plants and flowers can subsist on that which is a deadly poison to man, and that we can breathe and thrive on that which is poison to them. They die, and we flourish by their death. We die, and they in turn feast, grow and thrive by our death.

By the aid of geology we search for the hidden wonders and treasures of the earth, and find that two-thirds of its surface is composed of fossilified rocks, the remains of plants and animals in a petrified state; that shells not larger than a grain of sand form entire mountains; that there are deep beds composed of shells so small that forty millions are required to make a cubic inch! We then analyze the sixty-one distinct elements of which the earth is composed, noting the changes produced by time, the atmosphere, storms and fluids; penetrate the interior of the earth, and see of what it is composed; and name and classify each soil, mineral or strata of rocks. We then traverse the universe, noting the variableness of the earth's surface—springs and brooks, creeks and rivers, ponds and lakes, plains and valleys, hills and mountains, seas and oceans. We climb to the top of Etna, and pause upon its summit, and wonder if we can not penetrate its depth and discover the causes of its tremulous voice, nervousness, sleepless nights, and its overwhelming fury, when it speaks in thunder tones, darkening the heavens with smoke and ashes, sending forth rivers of boiling lava, submerging thousands of people, towns and cities, and building up vast mountains as lasting monuments of its power.

We next examine the water with the microscope and find it teeming with life and action; philosophize upon the mists and tides, calms and currents of the ocean; go down into its depths, bridle the whale, traverse the chambers of the deep, name and classify the shells and fishes, gaze upon the treasures of gold and silver, diamonds and jewels, ships, mighty armaments, and the millions of men and women who have gone there to sleep until the resurrection morn.

We then harness steam, hitch it to the engine and drive it with fury over continents and oceans, opening all the inhabitable portions of the universe to commerce, missionaries and education. Talk to the world through the medium of the telegraph, almost annihilating time and space. We compute the seconds of time and estimate the millions who have lived since the morning of creation. Name the insects and animals, and admire the infinite variety of birds. We develop the size and strength of the bones and muscles, tissues and tendons, nerves and brain of man. We try our artistic skill, and write the Declaration of Independence and the Lord's prayer within the circumference of half a dime; build the telescope with which we penetrate the boundless regions of the solar system, count the stars, name the satellites, worlds and suns whirling in their orbits with a speed greater than that of sound or the flight of a cannon ball; estimate their dimensions, their velocity, their daily and annual revolutions, their inclination to and distance from the sun. We ascertain the speed of light and sound, the weight and density of water and the atmosphere, and search for inhabitants in the planets. Our minds long to discover heaven and the angels, God and all his mighty works.

But why specify the many objects which are replete with interest, and more startling and astonishing than the contents of worthless books piled mountain high. If our young people were to turn their minds to such studies, there would be no telling what the next generation might not accomplish.

A man came into my office one day full of bitterness against his neighbors, saying they had overreached and cheated him, and had slandered his character. I listened to his story patiently for an hour or more. I was crowded with work and pressing duties called me elsewhere. So I intimated to him several times that time was precious. But he had his Bible with him with leaves turned down at texts which indicated, as he thought, the characters and doom of his neighbors unless they repented. Upon my positive refusal to longer listen to him, he abruptly arose from his chair, muttering that I was in league with his enemies, and that all the world was against him. Poor fellow, I felt sorry for him, for I knew his heart was not right nor was he the possessor of that crowning virtue which the apostle places at the head—or rather the end—of a long list. With extended observation of men and things, and with considerable experience, I am compelled to say that there is no grace in the Christian character that shines more highly than charity. There is so much of harshness and cruelty in the world that when a man exercises this grace he is immediately set down as weak and compromising. We demand absolute perfection in others, while our own lives are full of imperfections. We are ever on the judgment-seat, judging everybody but ourselves. We pass sentence against a man not only for what he says and does, but we presume to understand his motives. Now if the Master were here he would say, "Judge not, that ye be not judged; for with what judgment ye judge, ye shall be judged: and with what measure ye mete, it shall be measured to you again." But men are rash and hasty; instead of trying to help the erring, or those whom they regard as erring, they hasten to pass sentence against them. Instead of trying to shield them from the storm, they seek to take away whatever shelter they may have. If Peter were here he would say to all Christians, "Above all things have frequent charity among yourselves; for charity shall cover the multitude of sins." Dr. Clark, in commenting upon this passage, says, "A loving disposition leads us to pass by the faults of others, to forgive offenses against ourselves, and to excuse and lessen, as far as consistent with truth, the transgressions of men."

Christian charity will prompt the soul to put the most favorable construction on the acts of others. Because others cannot see, and do not act as we act, we are not to condemn them for unintentional wrong. When a brother commits an impropriety, or even an immorality, we are not at once to raise the cry of hypocrite. If Paul were here he would say, "Let him that thinketh he standeth take heed, lest he fall." "For my own part," says John Newton, " if my pockets were full of stones I have no right to throw one at the greatest backslider upon earth. I have either done as bad or worse than he, or I certainly should if the Lord had left me a little to myself." As a religious duty, we ought to search our pockets to see how many stones we have there; and after we have searched our pockets then we should search our hearts and see if the spirit of fervent charity dwell there.

An incident is recorded in the history of the Macedonian emperor, that might be studied with profit by many a Christian. A painter was employed to furnish a sketch of the monarch. The emperor, in one of his battles, had been struck with a sword upon his forehead, which left a very large scar. The painter, who wished to make the monarch appear to the best advantage, drew the sketch so as to represent him leaning on his elbow, with his finger crossing the scar. "Let us put the finger of charity upon the scar of the Christian as we look at him, whatever it may be,—the finger of a tender and forbearing charity,—and see, in spite of it, the image of Christ notwithstanding." But how many there are who, in sketching Christian character, will not only expose every scar they can, but make them deeper and longer! We are constantly in need of charity, and desire others to extend it to us; but how slow we are in extending it to others!

The spirit of Christian charity is so poorly understood that when a man is found sympathizing with the erring, he is at once suspected of being in league with them. The world is full of men who would make stern judges, but not many who would make good mediators. Lord Bacon says that the ancient councils and synods, when they deprived a minister of his office, never recorded the offense, but buried it in perpetual silence. Call you that Christian charity? If it is, then where shall we find it in this day? Christian charity, while it does not wink at sin nor strike hands with the sinner, makes allowances for the weakness of human nature, and stands ready to put the most favorable construction on the acts of those who are tempted to do wrong.

There is evidently too much difference made between a living man and a man when he is dead. While living, he is made the subject of severe criticism; but as soon as he is dead, almost everybody is ready to go and cover his grave with the mantle of charity. Why is this? Is a dead man better than a living one? Will the exercise of charity now that he is dead do him more good than if he were living? The difference, I opine, is this: It is a solemn thing to talk about the dead. But is it, in reality, any more solemn than to talk about the living? What we say and think of men while living we ought to be willing to say about them when they are dead; for death has not made them better or worse. I have known men against whom many hard things were said while living. They were suspected of many evil things. But the moment they died, every lip was sealed, except to speak of their good qualities. If Peter were among the disciples to-day he would stand but a poor chance; for he committed a most terrible blunder. But the Master had not yet ascended on high, and Peter was saved from utter ruin. If he had been left wholly to his brethren they might have cast him entirely away; but Jesus showed them that although Peter had acted badly, he was still a better man than his acts would seem to indicate. He had not lost all confidence in him, else he would not have committed to him such important trust—"Peter, feed my sheep."

One of Mr. Whitefield's admirers, who was bitterly opposed to Mr. Wesley, met him one day and said, "Mr. Whitefield, do you think we shall see John Wesley in heaven?" Mr. Whitefield replied, "You ask me whether we—that is, you and I—shall see Mr. Wesley in heaven.' Certainly not." "I thought you would say so," said his admirer; "thank you sir." "But stop, my friend," said Mr. Whitefield, " and hear all I have to say about it. John Wesley will be so near the throne, and you and I so far off, that we cannot expect to see him." The difference between these two men was simply this: Mr. Whitefield had Christian charity, and his friend had not. The want of Christian charity among those who profess to be the disciples of Christ has no doubt driven some into skepticism. Lord Byron says: " I date my first impressions against religion from having witnessed how little its votaries were actuated by true Christian charity."

But we are all passing along life's journey, and we go over the road but once: how important that we go right. This being so, if therefore, there be any kindness I can show, or anything I can do for my fellowmen, let me do it now. Let me not neglect or defer it, for I shall not pass this way again.

And why not let the whole celestial way be lighted up with that same light which shone so brightly there when first we felt the peace of heaven in our souls? You know how it may be with you. The lamented Dr. James Hamilton once gave utterance to this beautiful thought: Suppose that every one were to mark in golden letters the text which has been the means of saving his soul. The apostle Paul would mark the words, "Saul, Saul, why persecutest thou me?" for it was these words, spoken by Jesus from the dazzling light, that made him a new creature. In the Bible of the Macedonian jailor, the letters would be found at Acts xvi: 31: "Believe on the Lord Jesus Christ, and thou shalt be saved;" for embracing this simple offer he rejoiced, believing in God, with all his house. Martin Luther would print the text, "The just shall live by faith," in gold: for that text, spoken by the gentle lips of the vicar general, guided him to peace; and the young monk of Erfurth, reduced by fasts and tears and struggles to the verge of the grave, found rest in the wounds of Jesus. In the Bible of Bunyan, the mark would be found at "Yet there is room." It was through the lattice of these words that he first saw the cross, and he thought God had put them into the Bible to meet his special case.. Thus the words of life have unfolded to us the mighty power of God to speak peace to the troubled soul. But, by and by, it will be granted to the pure in heart to see God. Even now they see his beauty reflected in the sea and sky. They see his majesty in the firmament. They see his power in the measureless forces ever at work around them, in the winds, the waves, the flowers and trees, in things animate and inanimate,.which hide God from the carnal mind, but disclose his presence to those that love him. They see

God in his providence. He stands revealed to'them in the joys which brighten their pathway, and in the sorrows by which they are chastened. They see God in all the ordinances of his house. In the hymns of praise, the public prayers, the preached word, the sacraments. He manifests himself unto them as he does not unto the world.

In this world, the veil of the flesh shuts out the brightest beams of his glory—in the heavenly world, with unveiled faces, they shall stand in his presence and behold the King in his beauty. They shall look upon him, and mind and heart shall feed upon the grace, and the grandeur and the glory of his countenance, and the soul shall drink in the rapturous delight of the vision, and be transformed into the image of the glory it beholds.

It may not be out of place, before I lay down my pen, to answer, by anticipation, objections that may arise in the mind of the young reader who may read these pages. I have received many letters of which the following is only a sample:

TOLEDO, Ohio, July 2,.1875.

ED. GOLDEN CENSER:—I hardly know whether I am doing right in taking the liberty of addressing this letter to you, but if I am taking too much liberty I hope you will be so kind as to excuse me. I have read with interest the closing chapters of your sketch, giving an account of the trials and difficulties which you passed through. Judging from the conclusion which you gave in your last chapter, I should think you attributed all your success to God in answer to your many prayers, or in other words, you have prayed that God would give you success in business, and you have had success and declare that God has answered your prayer. Now, I do not deny the virtue of prayer, yea, I believe in the power of prayer, but I want to ask, does God answer all such prayers? S. W. McN.

The editor's heart beats warmly for the struggling every-where. It is with deepest sympathy for the young that I pen these few lines. I have, before now, gone five blocks out of my way to make a purchase of some young man just starting in business. Oh, ye fathers and mothers, if you want to cheer, strengthen, and ennoble the young men and young women, show to them by precept and example that you have a " God bless you " for them. I have seen the time when those three words have removed mountains of doubts, fears, and despondencies. God bless our young men and women, and if a kindly word from me shall encourage, cheer, or strengthen them to nobly dare and do, to stand up under dark clouds, they shall have it.

I firmly believe all I have written in regard to answered prayer. It is impossible to exhaust, or even do justice to this subject in the brief space left me. The Bible is full of recorded answers to prayer. I have already treated upon the subject, and hence will not recur to it here. But let me say this: Expect to suffer, expect disappointments. It is only then you put yourself in the condition to receive help from God. One of the hardest lessons I had to learn when I commenced going to school was that I was a grown up fool. When I had mastered that lesson, then I was prepared to learn from any event in life, from the prattling child to the sober, thinking philosopher. I also discover one great misapprehension in many good people, as in the case of the young man above, namely: the too-anxious looking for results. The youth read the editor's exper-ience, and at once desired the *results*—not the *experience* —of a thirty-three years' life of suffering, forgetting that the editor endured privations for fifteen years, studied hard for seven years, and then toiled amid mountains of dis-couragements for seven years more before success followed. The question I put to every young man is: Are you will-ing to pay the price of success? If so, you shall have it.

Nothing but hard toil, close application, patience under discouragements, and an unwavering trust in God, will ever bring the golden crown of answered prayer. The men whose fame or goodness you may covet have literally worn themselves out in hard work. Indeed, there is no merit without the closest application. As a general rule, the world very poorly appreciates true goodness, or suitably rewards noble efforts. But what is that to us? God sees his workmen, and will take care of them.

True, it is glorious to see immediate results and continuous blessing upon our labor in the gospel field, or in any department of labor in which we may be placed, when the plowman overtakes the reaper, and the treader of grapes him that soweth the seed. In the language of another: Success in a good cause is grand and inspiring. And the question sometimes arises, is not our lack of success mainly our own fault, the result of our faithlessness, coldness, disobedience and sin?

This question is one of solemn import. Does God see in us such uncleanness as unfits us to bear the vessel of our Lord? Does he see in us such a savoring of "the things that be of men" that he is forced to say, "Get thee behind me Satan"? Does he see in us such vanity and boastfulness that he cannot allow us to succeed, lest vainglory prove our ruin? Does he see in us such intermeddling inquisitiveness as to "What shall this man do? that he must silence us with his solemn question, "What is that to thee?" Has he seen our yet unfelt weakness, and said to us as to the apostles, "Tarry ye till ye be endued with power from on high," and is he waiting until we know our need and come to seek his help?

Many of these questions should come to us with solemn force, and we should learn that, until the heart is right in the sight of God, no blessing, no success, no real, enduring spiritual prosperity, can attend our labor.

And yet we must not be discouraged, or unduly depressed; nor must the faithful child of God estimate his standing by his apparent prosperity in his work. All are not great; all are not destined to be alike prominent. The body has many members; the tongue may make the most noise, and possibly do the most mischief of any, and yet it is not the whole body, for other members which have never caused a sound are still important and indispensable.

Our great concern should be, not for visible results, for God does not always see fit to grant them. Noah preached faithfully, but how few believed. Abraham followed the Lord, but how few were his companions. Lot feared the Lord, but little did the Sodomites care for that. Elijah was a mighty prophet, yet he thought himself alone, and desired to die. Paul found all Asia turned against him, and stood alone for God in the presence of Rome's imperial tyrant; and One greater than all could marvel at the unbelief which hindered his own beneficent work.

From such instances we may learn that God has a gauge for success of which we have no idea; and that the day of small things is often the day of power and glory to the saints of God. It was through the despised Mordecai that deliverance came to Israel. It was the three Hebrew captives that held at bay the whole idolatrous empire of Babylon, and sent the scoffing throng of idol worshipers home to adore Almighty God. It was in exile on the lone Isle of Patmos, that John saw visions of eternal beauty such as mortals never had seen; and it was in Bedford jail, shut out from labor, and hindered from usefulness, his life a seeming failure, that John Bunyan, kept from the exercise of his tinker's calling, wrote that book which has been unmatched in circulation, and perhaps in usefulness, by any human production.

It is blessed to see the fruits, but if the tears in which we sow shall hide fair visions, if when walking in our integrity in the path of obedience we see no results, let us not too soon declare, "I have labored in vain, and spent my strength for naught;" let us leave our case with God, and rest upon his word in patient hope.

How much that has been reported as fruit in this world shall prove to be like the apples of Sodom in the judgment day! How many lofty piles of wood, hay and stubble shall pass away in one brief hour! There are many glittering crystals that are useless and destitute of value, and there are priceless gems that look like dingy pebbles until the great lapidary shall polish them as the stones of a crown. And how much that now seems weak, and mean, and feeble, and dim, and of no account, shall shine in magnificent beauty when the Lord shall reveal all things in his kingdom. Then shall the withered seed that was sown in faith and tears expand as a glorious and immortal flower. Then shall the wayside word that fell upon the sinner's heavy ear find its echo in the music of eternal gladness, in the rapture of unending song.

Young man, young woman, be brave, estimate, if it be possible, the value of your soul, grasp the grand possibilities before you. They that would be great, must first be the least. We must learn to suffer the will of God as well as to do it. Never despise work—hard hands, sunburnt face or sweating brow. He is the true king who possesses soiled hands and a pure heart! Toil on then, and heaven will bless you. Your labor is not in vain in the Lord. There may be sadness and sorrow, and discouragements here, but the ages to come shall make amends for all. And in the ever-brightening, ever-broadening glory of the perfect state, the estimates of human judgment shall be reversed, the conclusions of human wisdom modified, and many that are last shall be first, and many that are first shall be last.

There is a beautiful passage in Habakkuk which is very appropriate to this subject of faith and simple trust in

God. The prophet says, "Although the fig tree shall not blossom, neither shall fruit be in the vines; the labor of the olive shall fail, and the fields shall yield no meat; the flock shall be cut off from the fold, and there shall be no herd in the stalls; yet I will rejoice in the Lord, I will joy in the God of my salvation." A sublimer exhibition of simple trust in God is not to be found in all the annals of history. . Think of the land desolated as the prophet pictures it before us, and yet amid famine, pestilence and disease, he exclaims, "I will rejoice in the Lord." Dear reader, write these thoughts upon your heart, claim the promises of scripture, and choose God, who is too wise to err, and too kind to be forgetful, as your portion, and then will you be prepared to meet all the vicissitudes of life?

CONCLUSION.

Dear reader, you have now followed your unassuming editor's life, in narrative, from his childhood home of affluence upon the Rhine, Germany, through the devious paths of fortune; you have seen him in his happy home over the great water, on the ocean-rocked vessel, in the sudden revelation of the stern reality that poverty had taken the place of plenty, suffering the bitter gnawings of hunger, his mother's tears, driven out a poor beggar boy and buffeted from door to door amid summer's heat and winter's cold; you have witnessed the ruin which rum made in the breaking up and scattering of the family; you have followed him from his mountain home in West Stephentown, New York, to his new home in Albany, Wisconsin; traced the changes that came over him, the calamities, misfortunes, abuse, his being driven out help-less and abandoned; saw him pass a terrible night in the wild woods utterly helpless and nigh unto death; have traced him in his weary travels bathed in tears until his

heart would break because there was none to pity; you
again saw him flee from the comforts of another home
impelled by fear, and then shamefully wronged by human
monsters; saw his mind turned from the channels of right
knowledge, until in his infidelity he attempted to burn the
Bible; then fleeing for life, struggling against poverty,
resisting temptation; then again gathering up the golden
moments and improving his opportunities; you saw him
at the age of sixteen learning his letters in a Sabbath-
school, and the oppositions through which he passed to
obtain a knowledge of the rudiments of the language; the
repeated failures and disappointments in his pursuit of an
education; you saw him as an apprentice, as a school boy,
as a student at the University, as a generous brother fleeing to the aid and protection of one who appealed to him;
of the deep distress and unsuccessful efforts to provide a
livelihood; you saw the influence brought to bear upon him
which gave birth to the GOLDEN CENSER, the bitter opposition and derisive laugh by knowing ones; you saw him
hang on, surmounting every difficulty in establishing a
paper which already has blessed thousands; and lastly, you
see him the victor in the conflict. You have seen him led
through dark waters, and drink the cup of adversity to its
very dregs, yet, in all this, you have observed his simple
confiding trust in God. That these things have worked together for good, is evident from the sympathy for the
suffering, the sorrowing, and the unfortunate which everywhere is manifest on every page of the GOLDEN CENSER.

Finally, dear reader, trusting that these light afflictions,
which are but for a moment, will work out a far more exceeding and eternal weight of glory in the better land, he
thanks you for your kindness and waits to meet you in
heaven where tears are unknown.

www.ingramcontent.com/pod-product-compliance
Lightning Source LLC
Chambersburg PA
CBHW051518100726
47898CB00005B/1501